DON'T SAY A WORD

By

Barbara Freethy

PRAISE FOR THE NOVELS
OF BARBARA FREETHY

"Freethy has a gift for creating complex, appealing characters and emotionally involving, often suspenseful, sometimes magical stories." -- Library Journal

"Barbara Freethy delivers strong and compelling prose." – Publishers Weekly

"Fans of Nora Roberts will find a similar tone here, framed in Freethy's own spare, elegant style." – Contra Costa Times

"A fresh and exciting voice in women's romantic fiction." – Susan Elizabeth Phillips

"Freethy skillfully keeps readers on the hook." – Booklist

"Superlative." – Debbie Macomber

"If there is one author who knows how to deliver vivid stories that tug on your emotions, it's Barbara Freethy." – Romantic Times

DON'T SAY A WORD

By

Barbara Freethy

Prologue

25 years earlier

She took her bow with the other dancers, tears pressing against her lids, but she couldn't let those tears slip down her cheeks. No one could know that this night was different from any other. Too many people were watching her.

As the curtain came down one last time, she ran off the stage into the arms of her husband, her lover, the man with whom she would take the greatest risk of her life.

He met the question in her eyes with a reassuring smile.

She wanted to ask if it was all arranged, if the plan was in motion, but she knew it would be unwise to speak. She would end this evening as she had ended all those before it. She went into her dressing room and changed out of her costume. When she was dressed, she said good night to some of the other dancers as she walked toward the exit, careful to keep her voice casual, as if she had not a care in the world. When she and her husband got into their automobile, they remained silent, knowing that the car might be bugged.

It was a short drive to their home. She would miss her house, the garden in the back, the bedroom where she'd made love to her husband, and the nursery, where she'd rocked...

No. She couldn't think of that. It was too painful. She had to concentrate on the future when they could finally be free. Her house, her life, everything that she possessed came with strings that were tightening around her neck like a noose, suffocating her with each passing day. It wasn't herself she feared for the most, but her family, her husband, who even now was being forced to do unconscionable things. They could no longer live a life of secrets.

Her husband took her hand as they walked up to the front door. He slipped his key into the lock and the door swung open. She heard a small click, and horror registered in her mind. She saw the shocked recognition in her husband's eyes, but it was too late. They were about to die, and they both knew it. Someone had betrayed them.

She prayed for the safety of those she had left behind as an explosion of fire lit up the night, consuming all their dreams with one powerful roar.

Chapter One

Present Day...

Julia DeMarco felt a shiver run down her spine as she stood high on a bluff overlooking the Golden Gate Bridge. It was a beautiful, sunny day in early September, and with the Pacific Ocean on one side of the bridge and the San Francisco Bay on the other, the view was breathtaking. She felt like she was on the verge of something exciting and wonderful, just the way every bride should feel. But as she took a deep breath of the fresh, somewhat salty air, her eyes began to water. She told herself the tears had more to do with the afternoon wind than the sadness she'd been wrestling with since her mother had passed away six months ago. This was supposed to be a happy time, a day for looking ahead, not behind. She just wished she felt confident instead of... uncertain.

A pair of arms came around her waist, and she leaned back against the solid chest of her fiancé, Michael Graffino. It seemed as if she'd done nothing but lean on Michael the past year. Most men wouldn't have stuck around, but he had. Now it was time to give him what he wanted, a wedding date. She didn't know why she was hesitating, except that so many things were changing in her life. Since Michael had proposed to her a year ago, her mother had died, her stepfather had put the family home up for sale, and her younger sister had moved in with her. A part of her just wanted to stop, take a few breaths, and think for a while instead of rushing headlong into another life-changing event. But Michael was pushing for a date, and she was grateful to him for sticking by her, so how could she say no? And why would she want to?

Michael was a good man. Her mother had adored him. Julia could still remember the night she'd told her mom about the engagement. Sarah DeMarco hadn't been out of bed in days, and she hadn't smiled in many weeks, but that night she'd beamed from ear to ear. The knowledge that her oldest daughter was settling down with the son of one of her best friends had made her last days so much easier.

"We should go, Julia. It's time to meet the event coordinator."

She turned to face him, thinking again what a nice-looking man he was with his light brown hair, brown eyes, and a warm, ready smile. The olive skin of his Italian heritage and the fact that he spent most of his days out on the water, running a charter boat service off Fisherman's Wharf, kept his skin a dark, sunburned red.

"What's wrong?" he asked, a curious glint in his eye. "You're staring at me."

"Was I? I'm sorry."

"Don't be." He paused, then said, "It's been a while since you've really looked at me."

"I don't think that's true. I look at you all the time. So do half the women in San Francisco," she added.

"Yeah, right," he muttered. "Let's go."

Julia cast one last look at the view, then followed Michael to the museum. The Palace of the Legion of Honor had been built as a replica of the Palais de la Legion d'Honneur in Paris. In the front courtyard, known as the Court of Honor, was one of Rodin's most famous sculptures, *The Thinker*. Julia would have liked to stop and ponder the statue as well as the rest of her life, but Michael was a man on a mission, and he urged her toward the front doors.

As they entered the museum, her step faltered. In a few moments, they would sit down with Monica Harvey, the museum's event coordinator, and Julia would have to pick her wedding date. She shouldn't be nervous. It wasn't as if she were a young girl; she was twenty-eight years old. It was time to get married, have a family.

"Liz was right. This place is cool," Michael said.

Julia nodded in agreement. Her younger sister, Liz, had been the one to suggest the museum. It was a pricey location, but Julia had inherited some money from her mother that would pay for most of the wedding.

"The offices are downstairs," Michael added. "Let's go."

Julia drew in a deep breath as the moment of truth came rushing toward her. "I need to stop in the rest-room. Why don't you go ahead? I'll be right there."

When Michael left, Julia walked over to get a drink of water from a nearby fountain. She was sweating and her heart was practically jumping out of her chest. What on earth was the matter with her? She'd never felt so panicky in her life.

It was all the changes, she told herself again. Her emotions were too close to the surface. But she could do this. They were only picking a date. She wasn't going to say "I do" this afternoon. That would be months from now, when she was ready, really ready.

Feeling better, she headed downstairs, passing by several intriguing exhibits along the way. Maybe they could stop and take a look on the way out.

"Mrs. Harvey is finishing up another appointment," Michael told her as she joined him. "She'll be about ten minutes. I need to make a call. Can you hold down the fort?"

"Sure." Julia sat down on the couch, wishing Michael hadn't left. She really needed a distraction from her nerves. As the minutes passed, she became aware of the faint sound of music coming from down the hall. The melody was lovely but sad, filled with unanswered dreams, regrets. It reminded her of a piece played on the balalaika in one of her music classes in college, and it called to her in a way she couldn't resist. Music had always been her passion. Just a quick peek, she told herself, as she got to her feet and moved into the corridor.

The sounds of the strings grew louder as she entered the room at the end of the hall. It was a tape, she realized, playing in the background, intended no doubt to complement the equally haunting histo.ic photographs on display. Within seconds she was caught up in a journey through time. She couldn't look away. And she didn't want to look away—especially when she came to the picture of the little girl.

Captioned "*The Coldest War of All*," the black-and-white photograph showed a girl of no more than three or four years old, standing behind the gate of an orphanage in Moscow. The photo had been taken by someone named Charles Manning, the same man who appeared to have taken many of the pictures in the exhibit.

Julia studied the picture in detail. She wasn't as interested in the Russian scene as she was in the girl. The child wore a heavy dark coat, pale thick stockings, and a black woolen cap over her curly blond hair. The expression in her eyes begged for someone—whoever was taking the picture, perhaps—to let her out, to set her free, to help her.

An uneasy feeling crept down Julia's spine. The girl's features, the oval shape of her face, the tiny freckle at the corner of her eyebrow, the slope of her small, upturned nose, seemed familiar. She noticed how the child's pudgy fingers clung to the bars of the gate. It was odd, but she could almost feel that cold steel beneath her own fingers. Her breath quickened. She'd seen this picture before, but where? A vague memory danced just out of reach.

Her gaze moved to the silver chain hanging around the girl's neck and the small charm dangling from it. It looked like a swan, a white swan, just like the one her mother had given to her when she was a little girl. Her heart thudded in her chest, and the panicky feeling she'd experienced earlier returned.

"Julia?"

She jumped at the sound of Michael's booming voice. She'd forgotten about him.

"Mrs. Harvey is waiting for us," he said as he crossed the room. "What are you doing in here?"

"Looking at the photos."

"We don't have time for that. Come on."

"Just a second." She pointed at the photograph. "Does this girl seem familiar to you?"

Michael gave the photo a quick glance. "I don't think so. Why?"

"I have a necklace just like the one that little girl is wearing," she added. "Isn't that odd?"

"Why would it be odd? It doesn't look unusual to me.

Of course it didn't. There were probably a million girls who had that same necklace. "You're right. Let's go." But as she turned to follow Michael out of the room, she couldn't help taking one last look at the picture. The girl's eyes called out to her—eyes that looked so much like her own. But that little girl in the photograph didn't have anything to do with her—did she?

* * *

"It cost me a fortune to get you out of jail," Joe Carmichael said.

Alex Manning leaned back in his chair and kicked his booted feet up onto the edge of Joe's desk. Joe, a balding man in his late thirties, was one of his best friends, not to mention the West Coast editor of *World News Magazine,* a publication that bought eighty percent of Alex's photographs. They'd been working together for over ten years now. Some days Alex couldn't believe it had been more than a decade since he'd begun his work as a photojournalist right after graduating from Northwestern University. Other days—like today—it felt more like a hundred years.

"You told me to get those pictures at any cost, and I did," Alex replied.

"I didn't tell you to upset the local police while you were doing it. You look like shit, by the way. Who beat you up?"

"They didn't give me their business cards. And it comes with the territory. You know that."

"What I know is that the magazine wants me to rein you in."

"If you don't want my photographs, I'll sell them somewhere else."

Joe hastily put up his hands. "I didn't say that. But you're taking too many chances, Alex. You're going to end up dead or in some prison I can't get you out of."

"You worry too much."

"And you don't worry enough—which is what makes you good. It also makes you dangerous and expensive. Although I have to admit that this is some of your best work," Joe added somewhat reluctantly as he studied the pile of photographs on his desk.

"Damn right it is."

"Then it's a good time for a vacation. Why don't you take a break? You've been on the road the past six months. Slow down."

Slowing down was not part of Alex's nature. Venturing into unknown territory, taking the photograph no one else could get, that was what he lived for. But Alex had to admit he was bone tired, exhausted from shooting photographs across South America for the past six weeks, and his little stint in jail had left him with a cracked rib and a black eye. It probably wouldn't hurt to take a few days off.

"You know what your weakness is?" Joe continued.

"I'm sure you're going to tell me."

"You're reckless. You forget that a good photographer stays on the right side of the lens." Joe reached behind his desk and grabbed a newspaper. "This was on the front page of the *Examiner* last week."

Alex winced at the picture of himself being hustled into a police car in Colombia. "Damn that Cameron. He's the one who took that photo. I thought I saw that slimy weasel slinking in the shadows."

"He might be a weasel, but he was smart enough to stay out of jail. Seriously, what are you thinking these days? It's as if you're tempting fate."

"I'm just doing my job. A job that sells a lot of your magazines."

"Take a vacation, Alex, have some beer, watch a football game, get yourself a woman—think about something besides getting the next shot. By the way, the magazine is sponsoring a photography exhibit at the Legion of Honor. Your mother gave us permission to use the photographs taken by your father. You might want to stop by, take a look."

Alex wasn't surprised to hear his mother had given permission. Despite the fact that she'd hated everything about his father's job while they were married, she had no problem living off his reputation now. In fact, she seemed to enjoy being the widow of the famous photojournalist who had died far too young. Alex was only surprised she hadn't pressed him to attend. That might have something to do with the fact that he hadn't returned any of her calls in the past month.

"Why don't you check out the exhibit tonight?" Joe suggested. "The magazine is hosting a party with all the movers and shakers. I'm sure your mother will be there."

"I'll pass," Alex said, getting to his feet. He needed to pick up his mail, air out his apartment, which was probably covered in six inches of dust, and take a long, hot shower. The last person he wanted to talk to tonight was his mother. He turned toward the door, then paused. "Is the photo of the Russian orphan girl part of the exhibit?"

"It was one of your father's most famous shots. Of course it's there." Joe gave him a curious look. "Why?"

Alex didn't answer. His father's words rang through Alex's head after twenty-five years of silence: *Don't ever talk to anyone about that picture. It's important. Promise me.*

A day later Charles Manning was dead.

* * *

It didn't take Julia long to find the necklace tucked away in her jewelry box. As she held it in her hand, the white enamel swan sparkled in the sunlight coming through her bedroom window. The chain was short, made for a child. It would no longer fit around her neck. As she thought about how quickly time had passed, another wave of sadness ran through her, not just because of the fact that she'd grown up and couldn't wear the necklace, but because her mother, the one who had given it to her, was gone.

"Julia?"

She looked up at the sound of her younger sister's voice. Liz appeared in the doorway of the bedroom a moment later, the smell of fish clinging to her low-rise blue jeans and bright red tank top. A short, attractive brunette with dark hair and dark eyes, Liz spent most of her days working at the family restaurant, DeMarco's, a seafood cafe on Fisherman's Wharf. She'd dropped out of college a year ago to help take care of their mother and had yet to go back. She seemed content to waitress in the cafe and flirt with the good-looking male customers. Julia couldn't really blame Liz for her lack of ambition. The past year had been tough on both of them, and Liz found comfort working at the cafe, which was owned and run by numerous DeMarcos, including their father. Besides that, she was only twenty-two years old. She had plenty of time to figure out the rest of her life.

"Did you set the date?" Liz asked, an eager light in her eyes.

"Yes. They had a cancellation for December twenty-first."

"Of this year? That's only a little over three months from now."

Julia's stomach clenched at the reminder. "I know. It's really fast, but it was this December or a year from next March. Michael wanted December." And she hadn't been able to talk him out of it. Not that she'd tried. In fact, she'd been so distracted by the photograph she'd barely heard a word the wedding coordinator said.

"A holiday wedding sounds romantic." Liz moved a pile of CDs so she could sit down on the bed. "More music, Julia? Your CD collection is taking on mammoth proportions."

"I need them for work. I have to stay on top of the world music market. That's my job."

"And your vice," Liz said with a knowing grin. "You can't walk by a music store without stopping in. You should have bought some wedding music. Have you thought about what song you want to use for your first dance?"

"Not yet."

"Well, start thinking. You have a lot to do in the next few months." She paused. "What's that in your hand?"

Julia glanced down at the necklace. "I found this in my jewelry box. Mom gave it to me when I was a little girl."

Liz got up from the bed to take a closer look. "I haven't seen this in years. What made you pull it out now?"

Julia considered the question for a moment, wondering if she should confide in her sister.

Before she could speak, Liz said, "You could wear that for your wedding—something old. Which reminds me..."

"What?" Julia asked.

"Wait here." Liz ran from the room, then returned a second later with three thick magazines in her hands. "I bought up all the bridal magazines. As soon as we get back from Aunt Lucia's birthday party, we can go through them. Doesn't that sound like fun?"

It sounded like a nightmare, especially with Liz overseeing the procedure. Unlike Julia, Liz was a big believer in organization. She loved making files, labeling things, buying storage containers and baskets to keep their lives neat as a pin. Since taking up residence on the living room futon after their parents' house had sold, Liz had been driving Julia crazy. She always wanted to clean, decorate, paint, and pick out new curtains. What Liz really needed was a place of her own, but Julia hadn't had the heart to tell Liz to move out. Besides, it would be only a few more months; then Julia would be living with Michael.

"Unless you want to start now," Liz said, as she checked her watch. "We don't have to leave for about an hour. Is Michael coming to the party?"

"He'll be a little late. He had a sunset charter to run."

"I bet he's excited that you finally set the date," Liz said with a smile. "He'd been dying to do that for months." Liz tossed two of the magazines on the desk, then began to leaf through the one in her hand. "Oh, look at this dress, the satin, the lace. It's heavenly."

Julia couldn't bear to look. She didn't want to plan her wedding right this second. Wasn't it enough that she'd booked the date? Couldn't she have twenty-four hours to think about it? Julia didn't suppose that sounded very bridal-like, but it was the way she felt, and she needed to get away from Liz before her sister noticed she was not as enthusiastic as she should be. "I have to run an errand before the party," she said, giving in to a reckless impulse.

"When will you be back?"

"I'm not sure how long it will take. I'll meet you at the restaurant."

"All right. I'll pick out the perfect dress for you while you're gone."

"Great." When Liz left the room, Julia walked over to her bed and picked up the catalogue from the photography exhibit. On page thirty-two was the photograph of the orphan girl. She'd already looked at it a half-dozen times since she'd come home, unable to shake the idea that the photo, the child, the necklace were important to her in some way.

She wanted to talk to someone about the picture, and it occurred to her that maybe she should try to find the photographer. After researching Charles Manning on the Internet earlier that day, she'd discovered that he was deceased, but his son, Alex Manning, was also a photojournalist and had a San Francisco number and address listed in the phone book. She'd tried the number but gotten a message machine. There was really nothing more to do at the moment, unless...

Tapping her fingers against the top of her desk, she debated for another thirty seconds. She should be planning her wedding, not searching out the origin of an old photo, but as she straightened, she caught a glimpse of herself in the mirror. Instead of seeing her own reflection, she saw the face of that little girl begging her to help.

Julia picked up her purse and headed out the door. Maybe Alex Manning could tell her what she needed to know about the girl in the photograph. Then Julia could forget about her.

* * *

Twenty minutes later, Julia pulled up in front of a three-story apartment building in the Haight, a neighborhood that had been the centerpiece of San Francisco's infamous "Summer of Love" in the sixties. The area was now an interesting mix of funky shops, clothing boutiques, tattoo parlors, restaurants, and coffeehouses. The streets were busy. It was Friday night, and everyone wanted to get started on the weekend. Julia hoped Alex Manning would be home, although since he hadn't answered his phone, it was probably a long shot. But she had to do something.

She climbed the stairs to his apartment, took a deep breath, and rang the bell, all the while wondering what on earth she would say to him if he were home. A moment later, the door opened to a string of curses. A tall, dark-haired man appeared in the doorway, bare chested and wearing a pair of faded blue jeans that rode low on his hips. His dark brown hair was a mess, his cheeks unshaven. His right eye was swollen, the skin around it purple and black. There were bruises all over his muscled chest, and a long, thin scar not far from his heart. She instinctively took a step back, feeling as if she'd just woken the beast.

"Who are you and what are you selling?" he asked harshly.

"I'm not selling anything. I'm looking for Alex Manning. Are you him?"

"That depends on what you want."

"No, that depends on who you are," she stated, holding her ground.

"Is this conversation going to end if I tell you I'm not Alex Manning?"

"Not if you're lying."

He stared at her, squinting through his one good eye. His expression changed. His green eyes sharpened, as if he were trying to place her face. "Who are you?"

"My name is Julia DeMarco. And if you're Alex Manning, I

want to ask you about a photograph I saw at the Legion of Honor today. It was taken by your father—a little girl standing behind the gates of an orphanage. Do you know the one I'm talking about?"

He didn't reply, but she saw the pulse jump in his throat and a light flicker in his eyes.

"I want to know who the little girl is—her name—what happened to her," she continued.

"Why?" he bit out sharply.

It was a simple question. She wished she had a simple answer. How could she tell him that she couldn't stop thinking about that girl, that she felt compelled to learn more about her? She settled for, "The child in the picture is wearing a necklace just like this one." She pulled the chain out of her purse and showed it to him. "I thought it was odd that I had the same one."

He stared at the swan, then gazed back into her eyes. "No," he muttered with a confused shake of his head. "It's not possible."

"What's not possible?"

"You. You can't be her."

"I didn't say I was her." Julia's heart began to race. "I just said I have the same necklace."

"This is a dream, isn't it? I'm so tired I'm hallucinating. If I close the door, you'll go away."

Julia opened her mouth to tell him she wasn't going anywhere, but the door slammed in her face. "I'm not her," she said loudly. "I was born and raised in San Francisco. I've never been out of the country. I'm not her," she repeated, feeling suddenly desperate. "Am I?"

Chapter Two

Alex could hear the woman talking on the other side of the door, which didn't bode well for his theory that he was dreaming. That blond hair, those blue eyes, the upturned nose—he'd seen her features a million times in his mind. And now she was here, and she wanted to know about the girl in the photo. What the hell was he supposed to say to her?

Don't ever talk to anyone about the photo or the girl.

His father's words returned to his head. Words that were twenty-five years old. What would it matter now if he broke his promise? Who would care? For that matter, why would anyone have cared?

He'd never understood the frantic fear in his father's eyes the day the photo had been published in the magazine. All Alex knew for sure was that he'd made a promise in the last conversation he'd had with his father, and up until this moment he'd never considered breaking it.

His doorbell rang again. She was definitely persistent.

Alex opened the door just as she was about to knock. Her hand dropped to her side.

"Why did you say I was her?" she demanded.

"Take a look in the mirror."

"She's a little girl. I'm an adult. I don't think we look at all alike."

He studied her for a moment, his photographer's eye seeing the details, the slight widow's peak on her forehead, the tiny freckle by one eyebrow, the oval shape of her face, the thick, blond hair that curled around her shoulders. She was a beautiful woman, and dressed in a short tan linen skirt that showed off her long, slender legs, and a sleeveless cream-colored top, she looked like a typical California girl. He felt a restless surge of attraction that he immediately tried to squash. Blondes had always been his downfall, especially blue-eyed blondes.

"Did your father know the little girl's name or anything about her?" she persisted.

"He never said," Alex replied. "Can I see that necklace again?"

She opened her hand. He stared down at the white swan. It was exactly the same as the one in the photograph. Still, what did it mean? It wasn't a rare diamond, just a simple charm. Although the fact that this woman looked like the orphan girl and had the necklace in her possession seemed like a strong coincidence. "What did you say your name was?"

"Julia DeMarco."

"DeMarco? A blond Italian, huh?"

"I'm not Italian. I was adopted by my stepfather. My mother said my biological father was Irish. And she is—was—Irish as well. She died a few months ago." Julia slipped the necklace back into her large brown handbag.

Adopted. The word stuck in his head after all the rest. "You didn't know your biological father?"

"He left before I was born."

"And where were you born?"

"In Berkeley." Her lips tightened. "I've never been out of the country. I don't even have a passport. So that girl in the photo is not me."

"Just out of curiosity, how old were you when you were adopted?"

"I was four," she replied.

And the girl in the photograph couldn't have been more than three.

He gazed into her eyes and knew she was thinking the same thing.

"I was adopted by my stepfather when he married my mom," she explained. "And she wasn't Russian. She never traveled. She was a stay-at-home PTA mom. She did snacks for soccer games. Very all-American. There is no way I'm that girl. I know exactly who I am."

She seemed to be trying damn hard to convince herself of that fact. But the more she talked, the more Alex wondered.

"You know, this isn't your problem," she said with a wave of her hand. "And I obviously woke you up." Her cheeks flushed as she cleared her throat and looked away from him.

Alex crossed his arms in front of his bare chest, not bothering to find himself a shirt. "I just got off a plane from South America."

"Were you taking photographs down there?"

"Yes."

"How did you get hurt? Not that it's any of my business."

"You're right. It's none of your business."

She stiffened at his harsh tone. "Well, you don't have to be rude about it."

Maybe he did, because he didn't like the way his body was reacting to her. The sooner she left the better. He was smart enough to avoid women who wanted more than sex, and this woman had "more than sex" written all over her.

"Are you sure there's nothing else you can tell me about the photo?" she asked.

He sighed. Obviously, he hadn't been rude enough. "Look, you're not the first person to wonder who that girl was. There was quite a hunt for her when the photograph was first published. Everyone wanted to adopt her."

"Really? What happened?"

"She couldn't be found. Our governments weren't cooperating at that time. International adoptions were not happening. It was the Cold War. In fact, no one was willing to admit there even were orphans in Moscow." It wasn't the whole story, but as much as he was willing to tell her. "Besides the fact that you have blond hair and blue eyes, and you have the same necklace, what makes you wonder about that photo? Don't you have family you can ask about where you were born? Don't you have pictures of yourself in Berkeley when you were two or three years old? What makes you doubt who you are?" Once the questions started, they kept coming.

"I don't have family I can ask," Julia replied. "My mother was estranged from her parents. They washed their hands of her when she got pregnant with me. And there aren't any photos, not of her or of me, until she married my stepfather. She said they got lost in the move from Berkeley to San Francisco."

"That's not much of a move. Just over the Bay Bridge."

Her lips tightened. "I never had any reason to believe otherwise."

"Until now," he pointed out.

She frowned. "Damn. I can't believe I'm doubting my own mother just because of a photograph in a museum. I must be losing my mind."

If she was, then he was losing his mind right along with her, because everything she said raised his suspicions another notch. A familiar jolt of adrenaline rushed through his bloodstream. Was it possible this woman was that girl? And if she was, what did that mean? How had she gotten from Moscow to the U.S.? And why didn't she know who she was? Was she the reason his father had told him to never speak about that photo? Was she part of something bigger, something secret? Had his father found himself in the middle of a conspiracy all those years ago? Alex knew better than anyone that photographers could get into places no one else could.

"I wish I could talk to my mother about this," Julia continued. "Now that she's gone, I have no one to ask."

"What about your stepfather?"

"I suppose," she murmured, "but he's had a rough year. My mom was sick for a long time, and he doesn't like to talk about her."

"There must be someone."

"Obviously there isn't, or I wouldn't have come looking for you," she snapped.

"What was your mother's name before she became a DeMarco?"

"It was Sarah Gregory. Why?"

"Just wondered." He filed that fact away for future use.

She suddenly started, glancing at the clock on the wall. "I have to go. I have a family birthday party at DeMarco's."

"DeMarco's on the Wharf?" he asked, putting her name together with the seafood cafe on Fisherman's Wharf.

"That's the one. Gino DeMarco is my stepfather. It's my aunt Lucia's birthday. Everyone in the immediate family, all thirty-seven of us, will be there."

"Big family," he commented.

"It's a lot of fun."

"Then why go looking for trouble?"

Her jaw dropped at his question. "I'm not doing that," she said defensively.

"Aren't you? You think you're the girl in the picture."

"You're the one who thinks that. I just want more information about her."

"Same thing."

"It's not the same thing. It's completely different. And I'm done with it. Forget I was ever here."

Julia left with a toss of her head. Alex smiled to himself. She wasn't the first blonde to walk out on him, but she was probably one of the few he wouldn't forget. She might be done with the matter, but he was just getting started. Unlike Julia, he did have someone else he could talk to—his mother. Maybe it was time to return her calls.

* * *

Kate Manning loved parties, and she especially enjoyed being the center of attention as she was tonight. Actually, the party was in honor of her late husband, Charles Manning, whose photographs were on display, but that was beside the point. She was here, and he wasn't. She'd had twenty-five years to come to terms with that fact, and there was nothing to do but keep moving on. Maybe that seemed cold to some, but she was a practical woman, and as far as she was concerned, the love she'd had for her husband had been buried right along with him.

She was now sixty-two years old, and after two failed marriages in the last twenty years, she'd resumed using the Manning name. This exhibit in honor of Charles's work had put her back on the society A-list, and she was determined to stay there. She'd been dropped from most invitation lists three years ago when her then husband, a popular city councilman, had slept with an underage girl, causing a huge scandal. He'd been booted out of office, and she had been shunned by her supposed friends. But now she was back, and if she had to play the tragic widow of a brilliant photographer, then that's exactly what she would do.

It had also occurred to her in recent weeks that she might be able to augment her income by selling Charles's photographs to a book publisher. While she wasn't poor by any standards, she was acutely aware that her lifestyle required a steady income, and if there was still interest in Charles's work, then who was she to deny the public the opportunity to buy a book of his photographs? She just needed to convince Alex to go along with it. But he was a lot like his father—stubborn, secretive, and always leaving to go somewhere. It was no wonder he wasn't married. He couldn't commit, couldn't settle, couldn't put a woman before his work— just like Charles.

"Kate, there you are."

She put the bitter thoughts out of her mind as Stan Harding came up to her. Stan had been one of Charles's closest friends and the best man at their wedding. He was also one of the many photo editors Charles had worked with over the years. Stan was semiretired from World News Magazine as of last year, working only on special projects, like putting together the photographs for this exhibit.

A handsome man, just a few years older than herself, with stark white hair, a long, lean frame, and a strong, square jaw, Stan was one of the most intelligent and interesting men she'd ever known. He'd been married briefly years ago, but his wife had died of cancer the year she and Charles had split up. For a brief moment back then, she'd toyed with the idea of getting together with Stan. But his loyalty to Charles, even after Charles had passed away, had always been too high a hurdle to clear. She'd had to settle for his friendship.

"Hello," she said, accepting his kiss on the cheek with a pleased smile.

"Are you having a good time, Kate?"

"Better now that you're here."

"You always say the right thing," he said with a smile.

She certainly tried. "We've gotten a wonderful response to the exhibit. I can't believe how many people have come tonight." The room was literally overflowing with men in formal suits and women in beautiful cocktail dresses. Waiters moved through the crowd offering champagne and gourmet appetizers prepared by one of San Francisco's best chefs. She felt a little thrill run through her as she complimented herself on her efforts. She hadn't thrown the party by herself, but she'd done a lion's share of the work, and it was turning out perfectly.

"You did a fine job," Stan said, as he gazed around the room. "Charles would be proud."

She wasn't so sure about that. Charles had hated her need to socialize and host parties, and he'd never been one to brag about his work or take the credit he deserved. He'd even asked the magazine to print his pictures without a byline on occasion. She'd never understood his reasoning.

"I thought Alex might be here," Stan continued. "Joe said he got back into town today."

And he hadn't called her. She didn't know why she felt hurt. It wasn't as if they were close, even though he was her only child. The rift had started years ago. Alex had blamed her for the breakup of his family. Then Charles had died, and Alex had hated her ever since. He didn't act that way on the surface, and they certainly never spoke about anything as personal as Alex's feelings, but she knew the truth.

"The photos Alex took in South America were amazing," Stan added. "You must be very proud of your boy."

"I am, of course." She grabbed a glass of champagne from a passing waiter and took a sip. "I spoke to Joe earlier about doing an article on Alex and Charles, a side-by-side look at the father and son," she added. "It would sell a lot of magazines."

Stan nodded, a twinkle in his eye. "I'm sure it would. I understand Alex is quite popular with the ladies."

Kate didn't doubt that. Alex had his father's roguish good looks, thick dark brown hair, light green eyes, and strong, muscular build, with not an ounce of fat on him, probably because he kept too busy to eat. He was always on the run, always looking for the next great shot. She sometimes wondered if he bothered to sleep. She certainly couldn't see herself in him anywhere—he was the spitting image of his father. She suddenly realized that spitting image was walking straight toward her. She threw back her shoulders, feeling a sudden pang of nervousness.

"Mother," he said with a cool smile.

"Alex. What on earth are you wearing?" She couldn't believe he'd come to the party in blue jeans and a black leather jacket. He frowned at her question, and she mentally chided herself for getting his back up so fast. But, dammit, couldn't he think about propriety once in a while?

"It's nice to see you, too, Mother." His smile warmed as he nodded to Stan. "What's up?"

"Not much. Glad to see you made it safely back," Stan said. He stepped forward and gave Alex a brief hug, much as a father would a son. Over the years Stan had tried to fill the gaps in Alex's life by showing up at his ball games or school graduations. It made Kate feel a bit sad and a little angry to realize that Alex could hug Stan but not give her even a light pat on the shoulder.

"You should have called me, Alex," she said abruptly. "I was worried sick after I saw that photograph in the newspaper of you being dragged off to jail." She pursed her lips as she studied the purple swelling around his eye, and some latent maternal instinct made her say, "That must hurt. Did you see a doctor?"

"I'll live. Don't worry about it."

"You have to stop taking so many chances. You're not superhuman. I don't understand why you're willing to risk your life on perfect strangers."

"I'm just doing my job. But I didn't come here to talk about my job."

"Why did you come?" she asked sharply. She didn't like the intense look in her son's eyes. When he wanted something, he tended to go after it with all that he had. Maybe that was the one trait he got from her.

Alex motioned them toward a quiet corner. "It's about one of Dad's photographs—the orphan girl at the gates. Did Dad ever talk to either one of you about that picture or the girl?"

"He didn't talk to me about any of his photos," Kate replied, still feeling the pain of Charles's distance even after all these years. "Especially the ones he took on that last trip to Moscow. Now if you'll excuse me, I have some people to greet. Stop by the house tomorrow, Alex, and we can talk more." By tomorrow, she'd have her wits about her. She'd be ready to deal with Alex's questions then. Tonight she just wanted to enjoy the party.

Alex watched his mother walk away, not surprised that she'd given him such a sharp answer. After twenty-five years she was still pissed off at his father. That would probably never change. She looked good, though. Her hair was a dark copper red, and she had the face and the figure of a woman at least ten years younger. He knew she cared about her appearance. He didn't know what else she cared about. He never had.

Alex glanced over at Stan, seeing a thoughtful look on the older man's face. "What about you?" he asked.

"What do you really want to know? Cut to the chase, Alex."

Alex hesitated, then said, "I want to know if there's a chance that the Russian orphan girl is alive and well and living in the United States."

Stan's eyes narrowed. "Why would you ask that question?"

"Because I think she came to my apartment today." Alex was a pro at reading people's expressions; he'd had plenty of practice behind his camera. Even though Stan tried to cover his reaction with a bland smile, Alex could tell that he was surprised, maybe even shocked. His face paled and his eyes glittered with an odd light. Stan knew something, but what?

"That's impossible," Stan replied.

"Why is it impossible? Do you know what happened to that girl?"

"What I know is that the photo was not supposed to be published. I can't tell you any more."

"Can't or won't? My father has been dead for twenty-five years. Surely there are no secrets left to protect."

Stan stared at him for a long moment, then drew him farther into the corner of the room so that there was no chance they could be overheard. "Like you, your father sometimes got involved in things he should have left alone."

"What does that mean?"

"It means butt out, Alex. Do what your father asked. Don't talk about any of it. If the woman comes back, tell her she's crazy. Tell her that girl in the photograph died a few weeks after that picture was taken. End of story."

"But she's not dead, is she?"

"In all the ways that matter, she is. Forget about her, Alex. Trust me. You do not want to reopen the past."

Alex suddenly wanted nothing more.

* * *

DeMarco family birthday parties were always big, loud

affairs. Tonight the cafe was filled to the brim with Italians of all ages, shapes, and sizes. The small tables were dressed in red-checkered tablecloths, candles gleaming in each floral centerpiece. The food was plentiful, the wine flowed, and laughter filled the room like music. This was her family, Julia reminded herself. It didn't matter that she was the only blonde in a sea of brunettes. It didn't matter that she wasn't a DeMarco by blood. They loved her. They treated her as if she were one of their own. She just wished she had more in common with her family, that she didn't feel so out of step with her father and her sister. Not that they ever tried to make her feel that way. She just did.

"Julia, you're not eating." Her aunt Lucia, a short, plump woman with pepper gray hair, paused by the table, her face disapproving. She pointed to Julia's untouched lobster ravioli. "Is it too spicy? Shall I get you another plate?"

"It's perfect. I'm just full."

"How could you be full? You ate nothing."

"Hey, she has to fit into a wedding dress in a couple of months. Don't fatten her up yet," Liz interrupted, joining Julia at the table. "But since I hate to see food go to waste..." She pulled Julia's plate across the table and picked up her fork. She took a bite and nodded approvingly. "Excellent."

Lucia beamed her approval. "You I don't worry about. But Julia..." She gazed at Julia again. "Since your sweet mother died, you just don't seem yourself."

"I'm all right," Julia said. "I'm just not hungry."

Lucia sighed, but held her tongue as Michael joined them at the table.

Michael kissed her aunt on the cheek, then smiled at Julia. "Have you told them?"

"Liz did. She got here before me. You know what a big mouth she has."

"I couldn't keep it to myself," Liz said with a laugh. "I'm so excited. It seems like I've been waiting forever for this wedding."

"I feel the same way," Michael said with a laugh.

"We're very happy for you," Lucia said. "Now, you must be starving. I'll fix you a plate of food."

"That would be great."

"And I'll get you a beer," Liz added, following Lucia over to the bar.

Michael sat down at the table. "Big party."

"Like always," Julia replied. "How did your charter go?"

"Fine. Sorry I'm late. I got hung up talking to my father about our advertising. I want to make changes. He doesn't. Same old argument. What did you do this afternoon?" he asked, reaching across the table to take her hand in his, his thumb playing with the engagement ring on her finger. "Did you go shopping for a wedding dress?"

She shook her head. "No. I'm sure Liz wants to do that with me."

"Just make sure you get something sexy and low cut."

She smiled as she knew she was meant to, but it must have looked halfhearted to Michael, because the light disappeared from his eyes. "What's wrong, Julia? You've been acting strange since we left the museum."

"You'll think I'm crazy if I tell you."

"I could never think that. If something is bothering you, I want you to share it with me. I'm going to be your husband."

She gazed down at their intertwined hands and knew she had to be honest with him. "I'm feeling rushed."

"Because of the December wedding date?"

She glanced back up at him and nodded. "It's fast, Michael. Only a little over three months."

"We've been engaged for a year."

"But not a normal year. Not a year of just being together without my mom being sick and endless trips to the hospital."

"I understand that you're still sad, Julia, but it will get better. And it will get better faster if we're together. I can't wait to get on with the rest of our lives. I have so many plans for us. I promise to do everything I can to make you happy. And I honestly believe that once you get into the wedding planning, you'll feel more confident that this marriage is absolutely right. She thought about his words. He might be right. Maybe she just needed to be settled. But how could she settle down when there were so many questions running through her mind? "There's more," she said slowly. "I've been thinking about my past, about my real father and who my mother was before she married Gino."

Michael looked at her in confusion. "Why would you be

thinking about all that now?"

"That girl in the photograph at the museum. She looked just like me, and she was wearing the same necklace that my mother gave me when I was a little girl."

"I don't understand. You're saying you're... Russian?"

She winced at the incredulous note in his voice. It did sound ridiculous coming from his mouth. "I'm saying I don't know who I am," she amended. "I don't have anything from before my mom married Gino. Nothing—no pictures of anything or anyone. It's like I didn't exist before I became a DeMarco."

"Didn't you ever ask your mother about your real father?"

"Of course I did, hundreds of times. She wouldn't talk about him. She said he left us and what did it matter?"

"It doesn't matter, Julia," he said, squeezing her hand. "You don't need him. You don't need anyone but me, and I don't care about your bloodline."

But she did need something besides him—she needed the truth. "I have to find out who I am, where I come from. It's important to me."

"Before the wedding?"

She nodded, seeing a flicker of annoyance cross his face. "Yes."

"And this is all because of some photograph?"

"That was the trigger, but to be honest, if it wasn't that, it would have been something else."

His eyes narrowed at that comment. "Because you want to postpone the wedding? Is that what you're trying to tell me?"

She wasn't quite sure how to answer that question. "It's just so fast."

"Yeah, that's what you said." He sat back, releasing her hand. "Look, Julia, just let things ride for a few days, see if you feel the same way in a week or two, before we change the date. If we don't take December, we'll have to wait another year. I know how much you love history, and I think the museum would be the perfect setting for you."

"I know." God, she felt so guilty. Michael had been so happy earlier. Now his face was pinched and tight, his eyes filled with disappointment.

"Here's your beer." Liz set the bottle down on the table,

glancing from Michael to Julia, then back at Michael again. "Who just died?"

"Julia wants to postpone the wedding," Michael said glumly.

Julia sighed, wishing Michael had not shared that piece of information just yet.

"Are you out of your mind?" Liz asked in astonishment. "Why would you want to wait? You have the best place in the world to get married and the perfect guy. What's wrong with you, Julia?"

"Good question," Michael said, standing up. "Maybe you can talk some sense into your sister, Lizzie. I'm going to find some food."

Liz quickly took his seat. "Tell me what the problem is," she said as Michael left.

"I just need more time. I don't want to rush into marriage."

"Rush? If you go any slower, you'll be moving backwards."

Julia looked away from her sister's determined face, wondering if she could make a quick exit through the front door. But a tall, dark-haired man with light green eyes blocked that door. Her breath caught in her chest. Alex Manning? He'd cleaned up, shaved, showered, and put on more clothes, but it was definitely him. What did he want? Did he know something? Did she want to know what he knew?

Oh, God! She suddenly felt terrified that she was about to go down a path from which there would be no turning back.

"Who's that?" Liz asked, following her gaze.

Julia looked at her sister. "What?"

"Is that man the reason you want to postpone your wedding?"

"Maybe."

"Julia! How could you?"

"It's not what you think, but I do have to talk to him." She jumped to her feet and crossed the room, intercepting Alex before one of her aunts could shower him in cheek kisses, plates of ravioli, and cake. "What are you doing here?" she asked.

"I wanted to see your face again."

Julia fidgeted under his sharp, piercing gaze. "And?"

"I talked to someone about the photograph."

Julia pulled him out the front door of the cafe and onto the deserted pier, where darkness and shadows surrounded them. "What did you find out?"

"I was told to tell you that the girl died a few weeks after the photograph was taken. I was also told to butt out and mind my own business. That's not my style."

She wasn't sure how to read the gleam in his eyes. "What is your style?"

"To find the truth. Are you up for it?" he challenged.

Goose bumps raced down her arms. She should be focusing on her relationship with Michael and her wedding—she had a million things to worry about, things that were far more important than that old photograph. But something inside of her wouldn't let it go. All the questions about herself that she'd never had answered suddenly demanded attention. Maybe once she knew those answers, she'd feel more confident about moving on with the rest of her life.

"Yes," she said. "I want to find out who that girl is."

"Whatever it takes? Because there's no turning back once we get started."

She bristled at his controlling tone. "Look, I'll turn back whenever I want. So—"

"Then I won't help you."

He started to leave. He was actually going to walk away from her? In fact, he was six feet away before she said, "Wait. Why are you acting like this?"

He hesitated for so long she wasn't sure he would answer. Then he said, "The only reason I'm here is because you bear a striking resemblance to that girl. The necklace and the fact that you have no concrete evidence of where you lived before the age of four are also intriguing. But I promised not to talk to anyone about that photo. I won't break that promise with you unless I know you're committed to finding out the truth about that child."

"Who would have asked you to promise such a thing?"

"Are you in or are you out? Because I tell you nothing unless we have a deal."

She could see the resolve in his eyes. If she said she was out, she'd never see him again, and she'd never know if that picture had anything to do with her. She could research it on her own, but she wouldn't know where to start. Alex would have more contacts, more information. Oh, what the hell. It wasn't like she was selling her soul. She drew in a breath, praying she wouldn't regret her decision. "I'm in. Tell me what you know."

He met her gaze head-on. "My father didn't take that picture. I did."

Chapter Three

"What do you mean, you took that photograph?" Julia asked, shocked by his statement.

"Just what I said. I was with my father on that trip to Moscow."

"But you're young. You must have been a little boy then."

"I was nine."

"I don't understand." Julia sat down on one of the wooden benches outside the cafe. She could hear the laughter and the music from inside the restaurant, but they sounded like a million miles away.

Alex sat down next to her. "I went to Moscow with my father," he explained. "It was the first and only time he took me with him on one of his assignments. My father was photographing a cultural exchange—an American theater group performing in Moscow. It was 1980. The Cold War was beginning to thaw, and both sides were eager to show that East and West could come together. My father got me a small part in the play so that I could go with him. It's a long story, but bottom line—my parents had separated that year, and this was the only opportunity my dad and I had to spend together. A few days after we arrived, he had a meeting one afternoon in Red Square. I got bored, and I picked up his camera. I wandered away, pretended I was shooting pictures the way I'd seen my father do. That's when I saw the girl at the gates." He paused, his eyes distant, as if he were recalling that moment. "She looked like she was in prison. I moved closer and said something to her, but she answered too softly for me to hear.

She was... terrified. So I took her picture."

"I can't believe it. You were actually there? You saw her? You talked to her?" Julia searched his face, wondering if there was any possible way she'd ever seen him before. But she had no memories of her early childhood. She never had. Other people said they could remember events when they were two or three. Why couldn't she?

"After I took her picture," Alex continued, "I heard my father call my name and I ran back to him. I never told him I took the shot. My dad sent his film back to the magazine to be published. It wasn't until the magazine came out a few weeks later with that photo in print that he realized what I'd done. I'd never seen him so furious."

"Why? What did it matter? It turned out to be a famous shot."

Alex's lips tightened and a hard light came into his eyes. "I don't know why he was so upset about it. He wouldn't say, but he made me promise never to tell anyone I took the photo or that I saw the girl. He told me to forget she ever existed. There was fear in his eyes. I don't know if I realized that at the time, but in retrospect I believe he knew something I didn't."

"Like what?" she asked with a bewildered shake of her head. "How could a photo make someone afraid? I don't understand."

"All I can think is that the girl or the background of the picture revealed something that no one was supposed to see."

Julia thought about that for a moment. "Didn't you say there was a public reaction after the publication, that people were searching for that girl, but no one could find her?"

Alex nodded. "Yes. I have to admit I wasn't paying much attention at the time. My father died the day after that picture was published. That conversation we had about it was the last one we ever had, which is why it stuck in my mind."

"What?" Julia stared at him in shock. His voice was matter-of-fact, but his words were horrifying. "Your father died the day after the photo was published in the magazine? What happened to him?"

"Car accident," Alex said shortly, as if he couldn't bear to go into more detail. "My dad managed to travel all over the world without a scratch, but he lost his life a few miles from here on the Pacific Coast Highway." He looked off into the darkness, his profile hard and unforgiving.

Julia wanted to ask more questions, but there was so much pain in his voice, she couldn't bring herself to break the silence.

Finally, Alex turned back to her. "At any rate," he said, "I want to take another look at the photo. I think there's a good possibility the negative might still be in my mother's possession. The magazine gave her all of my father's work after he died. In the meantime, you should try to find some concrete evidence of your life before the age of four, especially when you lived in Berkeley. Your mother must have had friends, neighbors, someone who would remember seeing you as a baby. If you find them, your questions will be answered."

"But yours won't be." She realized his interest had more to do with the promise he'd made to his father than with her. She had just been the catalyst. Her quest had suddenly become his quest. He was taking over, and she didn't like it. What if he found out something about the photo that reflected poorly on his father? Would he share it with her? What if she was that girl and his father had covered something up about her? "I want to look at the photo with you," she said. "Especially if you have the original negative."

"I'll let you know what I find," he said as he stood up.

"That's not good enough. I told you I was in for the long haul. Commitment works both ways. Together means together, Alex."

"You don't sound like you trust me, Julia," he said with a little smile that made her trust him even less.

"I don't. I'm sorry if that hurts your feelings."

He laughed at that. "Don't worry about it. I don't have feelings to hurt. By the way, there's some guy staring out the window at us, and he looks pissed off. Do you know him?"

Julia turned her head to see Michael standing by the cafe window. "Yes, I know him," she said with a sigh. "He's my fiancé."

"You're engaged?"

She nodded, wondering how she would explain Alex to Michael.

"He's going to be a problem, isn't he?" Alex asked.

"I think he might be."

* * *

"Why don't you just go out there?" Liz asked, wishing Julia

would return to the cafe sooner rather than later. Michael had been staring out the window for a good five minutes, and while Liz would have liked to take a look herself, she'd managed to refrain. She thought if she sat at a nearby table, sipping her red wine and acting unconcerned, Michael would feel the same way, too. So far it wasn't working.

"Who is he?" Michael bit out. "I've never seen him before."

"I'm sure he's no one important."

"Then why is she talking to him out there?" Michael asked, turning to face her. "Why not invite him inside? Why all the secrecy?"

Liz shrugged. "It's quieter outside. Why don't you sit down and have a drink with me?"

"Julia has been acting funny all day—at the museum and here tonight. I don't know what's going on with her. I thought we were finally moving on. I thought I'd given her enough time. I know I can make her happy if she'll give me a chance. Don't you think so?"

"Of course, Michael."

He let out a heavy breath and turned back toward the window. Julia *was* acting oddly, Liz thought, booking a wedding date today, and then telling Michael tonight that she wanted to postpone the ceremony. It didn't make sense. Michael was such a great guy. He had his own business. He was successful, good-looking, kind, and a family man. He'd been supportive during their mom's illness and the funeral. She didn't think they could have made it through their mother's death without him. She couldn't understand why Julia was hesitating for even a second.

If she had been the one Michael wanted, she'd have married him the day after he asked. Not that he'd ever noticed her in that way. She was just the kid sister, the short brunette, the flaky one, who served up shrimp cocktails and clam chowder in bread bowls all day long. Julia was prettier and far more interesting with her passion for music and her job at the radio station. There was no way Liz could compete with her. Although she did have bigger breasts. It was a small distinction, but one she was happy to make.

A loud clatter made her turn her head just in time to see her father, a tall, normally nimble man, stumble into a table and chairs. Her aunt Rita pushed him down into the chair and told him she'd bring him some coffee. Liz frowned. He was drinking so much lately. He'd always loved his red wine, but now it was vodka and scotch and lots of it.

Gino rested his head in his hands. He'd developed prominent streaks of gray in his black hair in the past year. His cheeks were pale and he was far too thin. Liz got up and walked over to him. "Daddy, are you okay?'

"I'm fine," he said, lifting his head. He offered her a dazed, drunken smile. "You're a good girl, Lizzie."

"You should eat something. Have you had any food?"

"I'm not hungry. I think we need another toast. To my daughter and her fiancé." He looked around. "Where's Julia?"

"She's outside talking to a friend. You can toast her later."

"Lucia, we must have champagne," Gino yelled across the room. "We must drink to Michael and Julia."

"Dad, please. Just have some coffee." Liz sent Aunt Rita a grateful look when she brought over a mug of hot coffee. "Here you go."

He waved a hand in disgust. "I don't want coffee. I want champagne. This is a party."

"You're embarrassing your daughter," Rita said sharply. "Drink the coffee, Gino."

He pushed it away, got to his feet, and staggered across the room to the bar. Liz knew she should probably go after him, but dammit, she was tired of chasing him. It was Julia's turn. She glanced across the room and saw that Michael was still staring out the window.

Maybe she couldn't set her father straight, but she could do something about Michael and Julia. She walked over to him and said, "If you're not going to get her, I will."

Michael grabbed her arm as she moved toward the door. "Stay out of it, Lizzie."

"Excuse me?"

"I want her to come in on her own."

"I don't care how she comes in. My dad is drinking himself to death over at the bar, and she needs to help me get him out of here."

"Your uncle is taking care of Gino," Michael said, tipping his head toward the far side of the room. Gino was now sitting down in a booth with her uncle and a pot of coffee.

She felt marginally better seeing them together. "He's really got me worried," she confessed. "He's like a lost soul right now, completely adrift. My mom took care of him. She did everything, the cooking, the cleaning, the housework. She paid the bills. She even did the books here at the restaurant. I don't know how he gets through the days without her. Actually, he's barely getting through the days." She shook her head, feeling helpless.

"You worry too much about your family," Michael said, putting a reassuring hand on her shoulder. "But I understand. I'm the same way."

Liz nodded. It was nice to have someone who understood. "Let's sit down. Yesterday you said you had something to tell me, and I still haven't heard what that something is."

"That's right," Michael muttered, as he pulled out a chair, joining her at the table. "Now I think I may have jumped the gun."

"About what?" she asked.

He hesitated for a long moment, then offered her a sheepish smile. "I bought a house."

"You did what?" She couldn't have heard him right. He hadn't just said he'd bought a house, had he?

"I bought a house. It's down the street from Carol's home," he added, referring to his younger sister. "She knew the seller. I was able to make an offer before the owner put it on the market. It's small and needs a lot of work, but it's perfect. It's near the Marina, on Waterside. It has a small garden in the yard, and it's close to the rec center where I play basketball."

"Has Julia seen it?"

"No, I want to surprise her. What do you think?"

What did she think? She thought he was crazy. But it was certainly a romantic gesture. She had to give him that.

"Say something, Lizzie. You're making me nervous."

"It's just that a house is such a big thing to do on your own, Michael." Liz had a feeling Julia would not be happy to have been left out of the decision making. "Why didn't you show it to Julia before you bought it?"

"Because she would have put me off, told me to wait until we got married, and this was too good a deal to pass up. I want us to have our own home, Liz. No more apartment living. I want to own something, put down roots, start a family. I want to give Julia back some of what she lost when your mother died." He gave her an earnest smile. "It's a two bedroom, so we'll have plenty of room for a baby. With my sister down the street, we'll have family nearby. I was so afraid we wouldn't be able to afford a place in the city that I knew I had to grab this one."

"That makes sense," she said slowly. "When are you going to tell Julia?"

"I want to fix it up first. It needs a lot of paint, some landscaping. I'm going to start work on it tomorrow. The escrow doesn't close for another two weeks, but the owner has already moved out and said I could do whatever I wanted."

"Wow." She didn't know what else to say.

"You can't tell Julia about it until I'm ready. Promise me, Lizzie."

"I promise. This is your secret to tell."

"I will make her happy," he said with determination. "I just want her to give me a chance to do it. I thought I'd pinned her down today; then tonight she got the jitters again." He paused. "Did she tell you about a photograph she saw at the museum that she thinks is her?"

"No. What are you talking about?"

"She saw some picture of a little girl standing in front of an orphanage in Russia twenty-something years ago, and for some bizarre reason, she thinks it could be her."

"What?" Liz's jaw dropped in amazement. "That's crazy. She's not Russian, and she was never an orphan."

"Yeah, well, she suddenly doesn't know who she is."

"She's a DeMarco. She's my big sister, that's who she is," Liz said, with a burst of anger. It was one thing for Julia to question getting married, but why on earth would she start thinking she was someone she wasn't?

"You should remind her of that."

As Michael finished speaking, the door opened, and Julia entered the restaurant alone. She sat down next to Liz, her cheeks flushed, a guilty look in her eyes. Liz felt a shiver of uncertainty race down her spine. What was Julia feeling guilty about? That man? Or was it something else? Something that would throw their lives into chaos again? The past year had been horrible. They were finally getting back to an almost normal state where she didn't feel like crying every day. She didn't want to deal with any more problems. Which meant she didn't want to ask Julia what she'd been up to outside the restaurant.

Apparently Michael didn't feel the same way. "Who was that?" he asked, an edge to his voice.

Julia hesitated for a moment, then said, "A photographer."

Liz felt a wave of relief. "Of course, a wedding photographer. I told you it was nothing," she said to Michael.

The tension on his face eased as well. "You were talking to a wedding photographer? I thought you weren't sure about planning the wedding yet?"

"I'm not, but—"

Before Julia could finish, they were interrupted by Lucia, who held a digital camera in her hand. "Come, come," Lucia said. "We're going to take a family picture for my birthday present. Now, before your father falls down."

"Dad is drinking again?" Julia asked Liz.

"I don't think he's stopped in the past six months," Liz replied, wondering why Julia hadn't noticed. "We're going to have to do something."

"He'll be all right," Lucia interrupted with a wave of her hand. "He's grieving. It's understandable. Now, it's picture time. And smiles all around. You, too," she said to Michael. "You're practically family."

"Am I?" Michael asked, looking at Julia. "Am I practically family?"

"Of course you are," Liz said when her sister couldn't seem to get the words out. She grabbed both their hands and pulled them to their feet. A moment later they were swept up in the DeMarco crowd, and Liz breathed a sigh of relief. Maybe if they could just survive this night, Julia would get over whatever was bothering her and return to being her reliable older sister who was about to marry the man of her dreams. But as Liz took her place in the group portrait, she couldn't help glancing toward the door, wondering if the man in the black leather jacket and blue jeans had really been a wedding photographer. He'd had a doozy of a black eye. She hadn't met many wedding photographers who looked like they'd just gotten out of a bar fight. But if he wasn't a wedding photographer, who was he?

* * *

Julia spent most of Saturday morning going through the storage unit that was filled with the remnants of her mother's life. After the funeral, her father had made a sudden decision to sell their home, saying he couldn't bear to live in it without his beloved wife.

Julia had suggested he wait, but he would have none of it, and within three months the house was gone, Gino now lived in a two-bedroom apartment a few blocks from the wharf, Liz had moved in with Julia, and what they hadn't had time to go through had been put in this storage locker.

Looking through her mother's things was unbelievably depressing. Julia wished she didn't have to do it alone, but she couldn't ask Liz to help. She couldn't talk to anyone about the picture—except Alex Manning. In the cold light of day she'd had to question why she'd agreed to work with a man who'd been beaten up, thrown in jail, and kicked out of Colombia. And that was just last week. She'd found that information in a recent article in the Examiner. Further research on the Internet had unveiled the fact that his reputation for being a brilliant photographer was only surpassed by his reputation for getting into trouble. The last thing she needed was more trouble.

But she'd made her deal with him and she'd stick to it—at least as long as it made sense. Or until she had proof that she was not that girl.

So far she had no proof of anything. As her mother had told her, there were absolutely no photos of either of them before the wedding pictures taken when her mother had married Gino. It was as if they'd come into existence at that moment. But her mother had had a life before Gino, thirty-three years of life. She'd had parents and grandparents, and she'd grown up somewhere. But where?

Her mother had told her she was from Buffalo, New York. That was the only information she'd ever shared. She said if her parents didn't want her, she didn't want them. Julia had often wondered about her grandparents, but loyalty to her mother had kept her from asking questions or requesting to see anyone. After all, they hadn't wanted her, either. Now she had a feeling she would have to find them if only to prove the truth about her birth.

Sitting back on her heels, she considered again how best to do that. How did one find a needle in a haystack? For that matter she couldn't even find the haystack. She had nothing to trace, not one little clue.

"Julia?"

She looked up as her sister appeared in the doorway. Liz was dressed in running shorts and a tank top, her brown hair swept up in a ponytail. She looked like she'd just come from a jog. Liz was one of those people who liked to run and work out. Julia's favorite form of exercise was a long walk to Starbucks followed by a latte. "What are you doing here?" she asked.

"Looking for you. I stopped by Dad's place. He told me he gave you the key. What are you looking for?"

"I'm not sure."

"Michael told me that you think there's some mystery about who you are," she said with a quizzical look in her eyes.

"I have some questions," Julia admitted.

"How can you have questions now?" Liz demanded, her expression filled with hurt. "Our mother just died. Our father is drinking himself into oblivion every night, in case you haven't noticed. And your fiancé is upset that you want to postpone your wedding. Don't you have enough on your plate? Do you really need to find your birth father now? After all these years?"

Liz made some good points. The timing wasn't right. Then again, it had never been right. Which was how Julia had reached the age of twenty-eight without knowing who her biological father was. But he wasn't really the issue. "I'm not trying to find my father," she said. "I just want to know who I am, where I was born. I saw a picture at the museum. It was the spitting image of me. And the little girl had on a necklace just like mine."

"The one with the swan? That's why you were looking at it?"

"Yes."

"Michael said the girl in the picture lived in Russia. How can you think it's you? You were never in Russia."

It sounded worse coming from Liz's mouth. "I know it seems crazy. But that photo started me thinking about how I don't have any pictures of me or Mom before she married Gino. Isn't that odd? I thought if I came here, I might be able to find something that would prove I was living in the United States when I was three years old."

Liz stared at her like she was out of her mind. "Are you having some sort of breakdown, Julia? You're acting like a mad person."

"No, I'm acting like a person who doesn't know where she came from. It's different for you, Lizzie. You know who both your parents are. I only know about my mother. I don't know about my real father or my grandparents on my mother's side. And I can't remember anything from when I was little, which is also driving me crazy. Why don't I have any memories from that time in my life?"

"A lot of people don't remember when they're really young. I don't remember much."

"You don't have to remember, because I can tell you everything," Julia replied. "I was there from the minute you were born. No one that I know besides my mother was there from the minute I was born. And she's gone."

"All right, fine." Liz perched on the edge of an old trunk. "Did you ask Dad about it?"

"Not yet. He had a big headache and a hangover. I didn't want to bring it up if I could find something some other way."

"And that man you were with last night? Is he involved in this search?"

"He's the son of the photographer who took the picture." Julia didn't explain that Alex was the one who had taken the picture.

"And he thinks it's you, too?"

"He thinks it's worth looking into."

"You're both nuts," Liz said flatly.

Julia sighed. Liz tended to have a closed mind and could be very judgmental. She was always the last one to try anything new, and she often refused to look at problems in her life. She hadn't been able to accept their mother was going to die until she'd actually died. Up until then, Liz had insisted that their mother would get well, that life would return to normal. Maybe it was her age. She was six years younger than Julia, and she still wanted and needed to be protected. Julia usually tried to do just that, but not this time.

"Don't you have to work this afternoon?" Julia asked, deciding to change the subject.

"Not for a while yet. I think you're taking a risk, Julia. You could lose Michael over this ridiculous search that will probably turn up nothing in the long run. Do you want to take that chance?"

A few months ago, make that a week ago, Julia would have said no, that she was happy with the way things were, but the photograph in the museum had opened up her eyes to the fact that the status quo had changed when her mother died. There was nothing to hold her back now. She could finally ask the questions and find the answers that she needed to fill out the missing part of her life. Michael should be able to understand that and so should Liz. "I'd rather look now than later," she said. "When I get married, I want to do it knowing everything I need to know about myself. If Michael can't give me a few days to figure that out, then he should be the one you're talking to, not me."

"Are you sure it will take only a few days?"

"I'm not sure about anything. I'm taking it one step at a time. And while I know you hate it when people don't do exactly what you want, you're going to have to let me do this, Liz, because I'm not willing to stop until I get some answers."

"Have you considered the fact that you might be better off not knowing, that maybe Mom had a good reason for never telling you about your past?"

She had considered that, more than once. "That might be true, but I think the not knowing is worse."

"I hope you're right about that."

"So do I."

"Have you found anything yet?" Liz looked around at the mess Julia had made. "You've certainly been thorough. I still can't believe this is all we have left of Mom's life. It doesn't seem like much."

"I know. I keep thinking there must be more. Although I haven't come across any paperwork, birth certificates, that kind of thing, so maybe there is more. I remember putting a lot of boxes in Dad's spare bedroom when he moved."

Liz frowned. "I can't believe he's happier living in an apartment. He should have stayed in the house. Mom loved that house. And I'm still pissed off at him for selling it."

"The house had too many memories. He couldn't stand it."

"It's going to be strange this Christmas. No tree in the corner of the living room, no Christmas dinner around the big table. It won't be the same at Aunt Lucia's house."

"No, it won't." Julia could see how much Liz hated that thought. "But we'll still make it a good holiday. We have each other. That's what matters."

"I guess. Are you done here?"

"Almost. I have one more box to go through."

Liz kneeled down next to Julia as she opened the last large box. Instead of their mother's clothes, they found children's clothes.

"I remember this outfit," Liz said, pulling out a pink jumper. "I used to love it."

"And I used to wear this sweater all the time," Julia added, pulling out a blue sweater with embroidered flowers on the front. "I wonder why Mom kept these clothes. She was always doing spring-cleaning. I rescued a few things from the garbage on more than one occasion."

"That's true, but these were our favorites." Liz dug farther into the pile. "I guess she had a sentimental soft spot after all. Who knew?"

"There's a lot we don't know about her, Liz. I spent all night thinking about what I don't know about her, like where she grew up and where she spent her summer vacations. Where she went to school, who her friends were, her first boyfriend. She never talked about herself, and we never asked. Why didn't we ask?"

"I guess I wasn't that interested," Liz admitted, the smile quickly disappearing from her face. "I thought we'd have more time."

"Me, too." Julia touched her sister's hand to comfort. She was still the big sister, and she'd promised her mother she'd always watch out for Liz. "Even though we knew the diagnosis, we couldn't stop hoping. And Mom never wanted to say good-bye. She never wanted to talk about the end, even though we all knew it was coming."

"You're right. She asked me two days before she died to take her out into the garden so she could decide what to plant in the fall." Liz blinked back a tear, then reached back into the box. "I see something. Hey, what's this?"

She pulled out a hand-painted wooden doll about ten inches tall. The artwork on the doll was intricate and detailed. A woman's face was painted on the round head, a wreath of white flowers on her dark hair. The larger, cylinder-like body of the doll showed the woman's costume, a white dress with three feathered tiers and a floral pattern that mixed red flowers and green leaves. Along the base of the doll was a circle of swans that glistened in the lacquer finish. Julia's heart skipped a beat. The swans matched the one on her necklace. And she knew this doll. She'd held it in her hands before. "It's stunning," she murmured.

"I don't remember seeing it before," Liz said.

Julia took it out of Liz's hand. She opened the top and found another doll inside, then another one, and another. "It's a nesting doll," she said. "It's called a matryoshka doll."

"What? How do you know that?"

"I don't know how I know that." Julia looked from the doll to her sister, feeling like she was about to fall over the edge of a cliff. "But I know what it is. It's a Russian doll. And it's mine."

Chapter Four

"I need to look through Dad's negatives," Alex said to his mother as she ushered him into the living room of her two-story house in Presidio Heights.

"And good morning to you, too," Kate Manning said sharply. She sat down on a spotlessly clean white couch that took up one wall of the large room, and crossed her arms in front of her. Dressed in a light blue silky pants outfit with a pair of impractical spike heels, she looked very sophisticated. Alex couldn't remember ever seeing her in sweats or tennis shoes, and certainly never without her makeup. She had always been very conscious of her appearance.

Alex sat down in the antique chair across from her, sensing this would not be the easy visit he'd hoped for. Time had not mellowed his mother's attitude, and he was reminded of why he rarely chose to visit her. If he wanted to get anywhere with her, he better backtrack and start over. "Sorry, Mother. How are you?"

"I'm fine, not that you care. It's been months since we've spoken."

"We saw each other last night."

"Before that. Don't get cute with me, Alex. You don't return my calls. You don't answer my e-mail, and you couldn't be bothered to remember my birthday."

"I sent you a card."

"Three weeks late."

"I was in a remote jungle in Africa. The mail service wasn't good."

"You always have an answer to everything," she said with a wave of her well-manicured hand. "Just like your father."

Alex sighed. How many times had he heard that phrase? Just like your father. Well, he was proud to be just like his father. But that wasn't an issue he intended to discuss with her. "Do you still have Dad's negatives?"

Her mouth drew into a tight frown. "I might. Why would you want them after all these years?"

"I'd like to take a look at something."

"At what? Are you here about that photo taken in Moscow? The one you were asking about last night?"

"Maybe." He saw something flicker in her eyes, and he couldn't help wondering what it was.

"Your father was very upset after that trip," she murmured. "Or maybe it was later—when the photo was published in the magazine. I overheard him yelling at Stan about it. He never told me what the problem was." She paused, a question in her eyes, a question he still couldn't answer. When he didn't speak, she added, "Then it was too late to ask. Your father was gone, and you were so angry with me, you wouldn't look at me—not even at the funeral." Her voice caught, and he saw an expression of pain in her eyes. "When you did speak to me, you told me I'd broken up the family. But that wasn't completely true, Alex. I didn't do it alone."

"I don't want to get into our family history," he said quickly.

"Then you shouldn't be digging up the past. Your father had a lot of secrets. That last year of his life—he was different. I didn't know what caused the change. Maybe it was his job. Maybe it was me. Maybe it was another woman," she said with a bitter edge to her voice.

"You don't have any proof there was ever another woman." He couldn't refrain from defending his father. He'd heard her make the comment a number of times, and it irritated the hell out of him.

"I may not have proof, but I know something was off. Charles used to get calls from a woman late at night. I heard her voice more than once. He said she was a business associate, but he was a freelancer, and there were no female editors working at any of the magazines."

"You can't be sure of that."

"Oh, I am. I checked." She paused, her mouth tightening in a hard line. "I'm not sure I ever told you this, but I spent most of my childhood watching my mother turn a blind eye to my father's cheating. I swore that I would never do the same. I wouldn't allow your father to turn me into a pathetic, hopeless, helpless woman like my mother, who was suddenly shocked to realize the whole town knew her husband was cheating on her."

Alex had known his mother wasn't close to her parents, but he'd always thought it was because she was ashamed of their blue-collar roots. Her father had been a plumber, her mother a waitress. Apparently there had been more to the story.

Kate drew in a deep breath, a frown on her face now, as if she were sorry she'd said so much. "I just want you to leave the past alone, Alex."

"It's funny that you would say that. You're the one who is throwing a spotlight on Dad's work every chance you get. You hated his job, and you probably hated him, too, yet here you are acting like the tragic widow, and it's been twenty-five years and two marriages since you were with him."

"I'm not acting like a widow. That's what I am. You'll never understand the relationship I had with your father or how I felt about his work," she said hotly. "But I know what it was, and I have every right to make sure his photographs continue to be recognized. I'm even negotiating a possible book contract."

"Really." He studied her thoughtfully, not liking the way she avoided his gaze. "Why? Do you need the money?" Her home was beautifully decorated, her clothes expensive and well made. She didn't look like she was short of cash, but he had no idea where she stood with her personal finances. Her last two husbands had not been rich, but very comfortable. And if he knew his mother, she'd gotten her fair share in the divorces.

"I'm surprised you would ask, Alex. You've never shown any interest in my personal well-being."

"That's not an answer. But it's your business." He got to his feet. "Where do you have the negatives?"

"They're in a box in the hall closet. I want them back, though, Alex. I may need them for the book."

"Fine."

"Wait. Don't go like this," she said, holding up her hand in a plea for him to stay. "I don't want to fight with you."

"We've never done anything else," he said with a shrug.

"Because you've always seen your father as the hero and me as the villain. That's not the way it was."

"Mother, it's over. It was over a lifetime ago. I've moved on."

She shook her head. "If you've truly moved on, leave the negatives here."

"I can't do that."

She gave him a searching look. "Why do you care about that photo?"

He debated for a second, not wanting to confide in his mother, but he had to give her some explanation, so he said, "I want to know more about that girl."

"After all these years? Why now? Has something happened?"

"No, nothing has happened," he lied, preferring not to get into the subject of Julia. "I've always wondered whether that photo was cropped, if something important was left out of it when it was published in the magazine."

Her eyes narrowed. "Why on earth would you wonder that?"

"I'm curious, and I have some time before my next assignment."

"I don't believe you, Alex." Her eyes turned reflective. "You know something you're not telling me. Your father knew something about that picture, too. He was so upset when it was published. The night before he died, he stopped by here to give me a check, and I could see that he was afraid of something." She took a breath. "I've never said this to you, Alex, but I'm not sure that car crash was really an accident."

Her words hit him like a punch to the gut. He had to force some air into his chest so he could breathe. "What? What are you saying?"

She gazed straight into his eyes and said, "I think someone deliberately ran your father's car off that road."

* * *

His mother's words were still ringing through Alex's mind when he entered his apartment an hour later. His father's car hadn't been deliberately run off the road. The car crash was an accident. It had been raining. The roads were slick. The other car was simply going too fast when it sideswiped his father's car. His father lost control and drove off the edge of a cliff into the Pacific Ocean. That's what everyone had said and what he'd reminded his mother of a short while ago. But as he stared at the box now resting on his coffee table, he saw his father's face the day before his death, the fear in his eyes when he'd made Alex promise never to tell anyone about that photo or that girl. Were the two events somehow tied together?

They'd never recovered his father's body. The currents were too strong. He'd been swept out to sea.

Was that true... or a convenient explanation to cover up something more sinister?

His mother had no proof of her suspicions. She said she'd mentioned her doubts to Stan, and Stan had told her that the police report was clear that it was an accident.

They'd never found the other driver. There had been no witnesses.

Dammit. He hated all the doubts suddenly racing through his mind. Why had she brought it up now, after all these years? Just to throw him off? To create a mystery where there wasn't one? To make her widowhood even more dramatic? To get a bigger book deal?

His phone rang, and he reached for it, hoping it wasn't his mother calling him back with another bombshell. "Hello?"

"Alex, it's Julia. I found something in my mother's belongings. I want to show it to you."

"Where are you?"

"I'm at work right now. Can you meet me at my apartment in a half hour? It's in North Beach, 271 Lexington, apartment 2C."

"What did you find?"

"I don't want to get into it over the phone, and I just have a minute before I have to go back on the air."

"On the air?" he echoed.

"I host a radio show on KCLM 86.5. I've got to run. I'll see you soon."

Julia was a disc jockey, Alex thought as he hung up the phone. That surprised him. He walked over to his stereo and turned on the radio, just in time to hear her beautiful, sexy voice.

* * *

"You're listening to '*World Journeys with Julia*,' " Julia said into the microphone. "Next up is Paolo Menendez, who brings us a delicious blend of reggae, calypso, and Caribbean rhythms from Cartagena on the Caribbean Coast." Julia flipped off the microphone and pushed the button on the computer to start the next set of songs.

She sat back in her chair, staring at the matryoshka doll. Since she'd discovered it in her mother's belongings, she'd been racking her brain trying to remember where it had come from. She remembered holding on to it really tightly, and for some odd reason she had the vague feeling that someone had tried to take it away from her and she'd started crying. She hadn't stopped until the person had given it back. Unfortunately, that person was just a dark shadow in her mind. It must have been her mother. It couldn't have been anyone else.

As she was putting the doll into her large brown leather handbag, the door to the control room opened, and Tracy Evanston walked into the room. A twenty-six-year-old African-American woman with dreadlocks and a nose ring, Tracy hosted the three-to-five show featuring the best of jazz music.

"Hey," Tracy said. "I love this guy you have on now. Any chance we could get him to perform at the concert?"

"He wasn't available," Julia replied. "Believe me, I tried." It had been her job to book musicians for a special charity concert the station was sponsoring in the fall, and she'd been fortunate enough to get a good list of talent. They were hoping to raise enough money to fund music programs in the local schools, one of her pet projects.

"Too bad," Tracy replied. She tossed her keys down on the desk and picked up the schedule. "You are working too many hours, Julia. How are you going to do all this work and plan a wedding?"

Julia inwardly sighed at the mention of her wedding. "I don't know yet. I'll work it out."

"Why don't you take some time off? I'll happily take over some of your work. My little sis is off to college next year, and I want to help her if I can. So keep that in mind if you need to take off a few days. I can use the extra money."

"I will."

Tracy suddenly straightened, glancing out the glass window that led into the production room. "Oh, my. Who is that nice piece of work?" she asked.

"His name is Alex Manning," Julia replied, feeling unsettled by Alex's sudden appearance. She'd told him to meet her at her apartment, not here where she worked. She didn't want to bring up her past in front of Tracy, who wouldn't be shy about asking a lot of questions that Julia didn't want to answer.

"And how do you know him?" Tracy asked with a mischievous smile. "Is he the reason you've been stalling Michael on setting a wedding date?"

"Don't be ridiculous. I just met him yesterday."

"Well, he is fine. Don't tell me you haven't noticed."

Of course she'd noticed. But she wasn't interested in him on any sort of personal level, which meant her palms should not be sweating and there shouldn't be a shiver running down her spine, but there was, especially when Alex tapped on the window and smiled at her. She was definitely attracted. A normal response, she told herself. As Tracy had said, Alex was a good-looking man. Maybe she was just noticing because she was engaged, and she wasn't supposed to want anyone else.

What was she thinking? She did not want him. He was just the means to an end, a person to help in her search. That was it.

"Julia, ten seconds," Tracy said, motioning toward the microphone.

"Oh, right." She flicked on the microphone, watching the computer screen in front of her count down the seconds. "You've been listening to 'World Journeys with Julia.' Join me again tomorrow from one to three, when we'll take a musical tour through the Congo. Next up is jazz specialist Kenny Johnson." She punched the button to play the string of commercials that separated their segments. "Have a good show," she said to Tracy as she stood up.

"You have a good—whatever," Tracy said with a sly smile. "Don't do anything I wouldn't do."

"That leaves me a lot of options."

"Just remember you're not married yet. You can still change your mind."

"That won't happen." Julia picked up her bag and walked into the production room where Alex was waiting. "You were supposed to meet me at my apartment."

"I thought I'd check out where you work. I didn't picture you as a DJ," he added with a smile, "but you sound good on the radio. You have a great voice."

"Thanks." She wasn't surprised he didn't see her as a disc jockey. Most people thought DJs were wacky people, which might be true for some, but not all, especially not at KCLM, which played a wide variety of music. "I'm also a producer for some of our other shows. We're a small station. Everyone wears more than one hat." She waved her hand toward the massive collection of CDs in the room. "I'm a music fanatic, in case you were wondering."

"Then it sounds like you have the right job."

"It's perfect for me. Do you like music?"

"I play a little guitar," he admitted. "When I'm home, which isn't often. What about you?"

"I play the piano, the drums, and a little saxophone. I'm pretty much mediocre at them all," she said candidly. "I would have been a musician if I'd had any talent. Instead I play other people's masterpieces."

He grinned. "The next best thing."

"Exactly."

"I enjoyed hearing Paolo Menendez," Alex added. "I saw him perform in Cartagena. He played an acoustic guitar solo that was out of this world."

"You saw him play?" she echoed, feeling extremely envious. "It must have been amazing. I would kill to hear him in person, but he never travels to America."

"Maybe you should go to Cartagena."

"That's a thought," she replied, but she knew it was impossible. There was no way she'd ever get Michael to Cartagena.

"Does your fiancé share your passion for music?" Alex asked curiously.

She shook her head. "Not really. Michael likes pop and rock, but he listens mostly to sports radio. Anyway, I wanted to show you this." She reached into her handbag and pulled out the matryoshka doll.

"It's a Russian nesting doll. I found it in my mother's things.

It's my doll. I remembered that as soon as I saw it."

She watched for his reaction, but Alex didn't give anything away. Instead he took the doll from her hand and studied the design.

"There are smaller dolls inside," she added.

He set the doll on the desk and took it apart, one piece after the other.

"What do you think?" she asked.

"I don't know. It's just a doll."

"It's a Russian doll."

"I bet they sell them here in the United States."

His pragmatic answer disappointed her. "Don't you think it's rather telling that I would have a Russian doll?" she persisted.

"Maybe, but it doesn't prove anything. The doll isn't in the photo. And there aren't any marks that identify this doll as being made in Russia."

"Look at the swans. They're just like the swan on the necklace."

"I saw that. Did you notice that there are dolls missing?" he asked her.

She sent him a blank look. "What do you mean?"

"The first two fit together perfectly, but there are gaps between the others. You have five dolls. I'm guessing that there were more."

"I can't imagine where they would be. I went through everything that belonged to my mother. This is all I came up with." She perched on the edge of the desk. "Damn, I thought I was on to something."

"You still might be," he conceded. "We can research this doll, see what we can find out. There might be some way to trace where it came from."

"That sounds like a good idea."

"I've been known to have a few."

"Where do we start? The Internet? I have a computer at home. We can go there."

"Why don't we get something to eat first?" he suggested. "I haven't had time to shop for food. Besides, we can kill two birds with one stone. There's a Russian deli near my apartment. The owner came over from Russia about ten years ago. Maybe she can tell us something about your doll."

"Another good idea," she said with a grin. "I'm impressed."

"I'm just getting started, Julia."

The smile on his face and the sparkle in his light green eyes took her breath away. Her body tingled and her heart began to race. She forced herself to look away, focusing on putting the doll back together and regaining her composure. She didn't know why Alex was having such an effect on her, but whatever the reason she had to get over it—and fast. She was engaged. She was committed. She was supposed to be in love.

"Ready?" Alex asked.

She nodded, still avoiding his gaze. As he headed for the door, she looked through the glass, catching Tracy's eye. The other woman gave her a thumbs-up sign. Julia wanted to tell Tracy it wasn't like that, that she wasn't interested in Alex, but she was afraid that would be a lie.

* * *

Dasha's Deli was located in the heart of the Haight, where parking was scarce, so they decided to leave their cars at Alex's apartment. The short walk to the deli took them past tattoo parlors, funky art galleries, jewelry stores and shops touting sixties souvenirs, flower children T-shirts, black lights, and beads. "This is a great neighborhood," she said to Alex as they stopped at a traffic light. "Have you lived here long?"

"About six years."

She sent him a sideways glance. Even though he'd cleaned up his act from the day before, his face was still bruised, his dark hair a little too long, his jeans faded, and his T-shirt a bit wrinkled. He was definitely not a nine-to-five business executive or a corporate worker bee. He was a photojournalist who roamed the world, a free spirit. No wonder he'd chosen to live here when he was in town. "This neighborhood fits you," she said.

He nodded in agreement. "It does. Freedom to be different is a luxury in many corners of the world. It's nice to be reminded that it still exists here in San Francisco."

The somber note in his voice reminded her that he'd probably seen some horrific sights in his travels. "Is it hard? Photographing how the rest of the world lives?"

"Sometimes."

"But you love it?"

"Most days I do. Lately, I don't know..." His voice dropped away. "Hey, we're here."

Julia was disappointed to see the deli sign. She wanted to hear what Alex had been about to say. "What do you mean, lately?" she prodded.

"It's a long story, and I'm hungry."

"Will you tell me the story while we eat?"

"Probably not," he said candidly. "It would kill your appetite."

"Alex. You can't start something and not finish it."

"We're here to solve the story of your life, not mine," he reminded her. "Let's keep our focus." He opened the door and waved her inside. "After you."

As Julia entered the restaurant, the delicious smells of fresh breads and cakes assailed her. The bakery counter was immediately to her left, the deli counter on the other side of the room, a crush of small tables in the middle. It was a little late for lunch, but there was still a good crowd, so they took a number and waited. As they did so, Julia searched her brain for some sense of familiarity with the Russian smells. They warmed her heart, made her mouth water, but was that just because they were so tantalizing or because she remembered them?

A short, round woman in her fifties with dark brown hair, black eyes, and a nurturing smile called their number, then greeted Alex by name when they stepped up to the counter.

"You have been a stranger," she said with a heavy accent. "Where have you been?"

"All over the world," he replied. "I brought a friend with me today. Julia, this is Dasha." Julia smiled and said hello as Alex went on to explain. "Julia has a Russian doll that she found in her mother's things. We're hoping, if you have a few minutes, you might talk to us about it."

"Of course," Dasha said. "I would be happy to look at your doll. But first you will eat. What do you like?"

"I'm not really sure," Julia said. "It all looks wonderful."

"Then we will give you a sampling. When you come back, you will order your favorites."

"That sounds perfect."

Dasha filled several plates with a variety of foods.

Julia couldn't imagine how they would get through it all. They sat down at a small table against the wall and unloaded their trays. "This is too much," Julia complained. "I'll never eat it all."

"That's what I said the first time, but I was wrong." Alex tipped his head toward the bowl of soup by her elbow. "Try the borscht first," he suggested. "It's the best."

Julia looked down in fascination at the deep purple soup, topped with a dollop of sour cream. "What's in it?" she asked.

"Cabbage, leeks, potatoes, and beets. That's what gives it the purple color."

She took a heaping spoonful, murmuring with appreciation at the delicious taste. "It's good. Hot and hearty."

"You're not a picky eater, are you, Julia?"

"Not at all. I love to try new food. You?"

"I'd starve otherwise. Where I go the food choices can be very exotic."

"What's the worst thing you've ever eaten?"

Alex thought for a moment. "A wormlike bug in the Amazon. They fry 'em up like french fries, but they still taste like worms."

"Why did you eat it?"

"I was hungry," he said with a laugh. "And I didn't want to offend my host. I was hoping to get his permission to take some photographs, so I ate what he ate."

She admired his determination. "Are there some lines you won't cross to get your shot?"

"Not that I can think of. It's my job to get the picture no one else can get. If that means eating worms, I eat worms." He pointed toward her plate. "Try the cabbage rolls next. They're stuffed with beef. Delicious. No worms, I promise," he added with a grin that was incredibly appealing—irresistible in fact.

She found herself smiling back and thinking what an interesting man he was and how different from Michael. Alex was worldly, adventurous, and probably a little reckless, or a lot reckless. But she wasn't here to analyze him; she was here to get answers about her doll. Since Dasha still had a line of customers, Julia dug into her cabbage rolls, then a tomato and cucumber salad followed by piroshki, pastry puffs filled with chicken. When she pushed her plate away, she was completely stuffed. "I'm never eating again," she said.

"You haven't tried any of the desserts yet."

"Stop. You are a bad influence." As she finished speaking, Dasha came over to their table.

"Did you enjoy?" she asked, smiling at their empty plates.

"Very much," Julia replied. "It was all wonderful."

"Good. Now, you wanted to ask me something." She took a seat next to Alex and offered Julia an inquiring look.

Julia took the doll from her bag and set it on the table between them. "I found this doll among my mother's belongings and wondered if you could tell me anything about it."

"Oh, my, this is lovely," Dasha said. She slowly turned the doll around with an admiring gaze. "Beautiful. And very unique. The matryoshka doll is meant to be a symbol of motherhood and fertility. The smaller dolls inside are the babies." She paused for a moment. "The woman's face reminds me of someone. I can't think who. Oh, look at that." Dasha pointed to a tiny mark on the bottom corner of the doll. "There was a famous artist named Sergei Horkin, who used to sign his paintings with this S slash mark. I believe he did paint a few dolls. I can't remember whether it was the subject that was a famous person or if the famous person was the one who commissioned the doll. Either way, this doll could be very valuable if he was indeed the artist."

"Really?" Alex asked. "Is this Sergei still alive?"

"No, no, he died many, many years ago in the 1930s."

"The 1930s? Do you think the doll is that old?" Julia asked in surprise.

"I'm not an expert, but it might be."

"Do the swans or the art have any significance?" Alex inquired.

"Swans are often used in Russian stories," Dasha replied. "Swan Lake, for example:"

"A beautiful ballet," Julia said, glancing at Alex. "Have you seen it?"

"No, but I take it that the ballet has something to do with a swan."

"A sorcerer casts a spell that forces young women to live as swans unless they secure a man's undying devotion," Julia explained. "Siegfried, a prince, falls in love with the swan queen,

Odette, but the sorcerer makes his evil daughter, Odile, pretend to be Odette and tricks the prince into promising his love to her. In the end, Siegfried and Odette realize they can only consummate their love by dying together."

"Very romantic," Alex said dryly. "You must die to get love. Hell of a choice."

"But their love was worth dying for," Julia reminded him. She could see that Alex was not at all touched by the story. She wondered if he'd ever been in love. He certainly had a cynical side to him. Was that because of a love gone wrong or no experience with the real thing?

Alex turned to Dasha. "Is there anything more you can tell us?"

"You should talk to my cousin, Svetlana. She runs a shop on Geary called Russian Treasures. She knows everything there is to know about these dolls."

"We'll go there now," Julia said, excited to have a lead.

Dasha quickly dashed her eagerness with a shake of her head. "Unfortunately, Svetlana is out of town until tomorrow night. The girl who runs the shop when she is gone doesn't know anything. She's an American teenager. If you go on Monday, Svetlana will be back then." Dasha stood up. "Now, I must return to work. Don't be a stranger, Alex. And you come back, too, Julia. You look good together."

"Oh, we're not together," Julia replied quickly. "I'm engaged to someone else. Alex and I are... We're practically strangers."

"Sometimes strangers end up lovers," Dasha said. "It happened to me when a stranger asked to share my umbrella in the rain." A soft look came into her eyes. "We were both supposed to be with other people. We'd made promises, but love doesn't always go as one plans, and sometimes promises have to be broken. We've been together forty-two years now, and we've been through many rough storms, but they're easier to bear when there's an umbrella to share and a stranger who has become a good friend." Dasha smiled and returned to the deli counter.

Julia felt a little awkward after that pointed story. She didn't want Alex to get any ideas.

"Relax, Julia," he said abruptly. "I'm not offering to share my umbrella with you."

"That's good. Because I'm engaged."

"You've mentioned that."

"You probably don't even carry an umbrella, do you?"

"It would only slow me down," he replied.

"And a woman would slow you down even more."

He met her gaze head-on. "I've never met one yet who could keep up with me. Are you ready to go?" he asked, getting to his feet.

She hesitated, battling the impulse to continue their personal conversation. Whether or not Alex had a woman in his life or wanted one was not her concern or her business. She was simply curious, but she could see by the determined look in his eyes that he was eager to move on. "Yes, I'm ready." She put the doll back into her bag. "I wish we could talk to Svetlana today. Do you think we should go by her shop anyway?"

"Why don't we look up Sergei Horkin on the Internet? Maybe we can find something about his paintings there. I'd like to get back to my apartment. I picked up a box of my father's photos at my mother's house earlier today. I still want to find that negative."

"Can I help you look?" she asked impulsively.

Alex hesitated. "Don't you have other things to do?"

"Nothing as important as this."

"Really?" he asked curiously. "Does your fiancé feel the same way?"

"Michael wants what's best for me. He'll understand." At least she hoped he would.

Chapter Five

Liz found Michael halfway up a ladder in front of the small two-bedroom house he'd bought near the Marina as a surprise for Julia. She smiled as he tried to keep his balance while dipping the roller into the paint tray on top of the ladder. He really was a good-looking guy, she thought, with his wind-tossed light brown hair, ruddy cheeks, and strong build. Even dressed in paint-spattered jeans and a T-shirt, he was handsome and sexy. Julia was crazy to think she could put this man on the back burner and not risk losing him. Or maybe Julia wasn't crazy; maybe she was just sure of their love. Michael had certainly been devoted to her the past year.

"You missed a spot," she said, pointing to the area above his right shoulder.

"Hey, Lizzie," he said with a wave. "Just in time. I could use a hand."

"You look like you could use more than a hand. Don't you need a crew to do this?"

"I can do it myself." He climbed down the ladder, wiping his hands on his jeans. "Or with a little help. What are you doing right now?"

"I wasn't planning on painting," she said, her hand itching to wipe the splash of paint from his face. She forced herself to put her hands in her pockets.

"My brother bailed out on me, and I want to get the front done today. I have charters to run tomorrow. I could really use your help."

"I don't have anything to wear."

He unbuttoned his shirt and shrugged his arms out, tossing it over to her. She caught her breath at the sight of his muscular chest covered with a nice spattering of black hair.

"You can wear mine over yours," he said.

"Are you sure?"

"Absolutely. I can work on my tan."

She didn't think he needed to do that. His body was already nicely browned. She put his shirt on over her tank top. It smelled like sweat and Michael, a heady scent. She was losing it. Michael was a friend, almost a brother, and soon to be her brother-in-law. She needed to get out more, have some dates, find herself another guy to get all hot and bothered about.

"Have you spoken to Julia today?" he asked.

She was glad he'd brought up Julia. It put a nice solid wall between them. "I saw her earlier."

"Is she still thinking about looking for her real father?"

"Yes. I tried to talk her out of it, Michael, but she's stuck on it. You know how she is when she gets curious about something. She can't stop until she figures it out. Remember that puzzle she worked on for three weeks straight until she finally put all the pieces together?"

"This isn't a puzzle. It's her life. And mine, too. I want her to focus on getting married."

"I understand."

"You don't think there's any possibility she's connected to that photo, do you?" he asked.

"No," Liz said. "That's a crazy thought. Julia is not Russian. She's just... Julia." She frowned, realizing that she didn't know Julia's ethnic background. But what did it matter? Julia had been happy with herself for twenty-eight years. Why did she have to suddenly change now?

"Maybe it's an excuse," Michael said, his lips tightening, a hurt look entering his eyes. "So she doesn't have to think about the wedding or move forward with our plans. She's stalling."

"I'm sure that's not true. It's probably the wedding that has brought it all to her mind. She's thinking about family, about changing her name, about having kids with you, and she wants to know about her past, so that there won't be any surprises later."

"There's nothing she could find out about her past that would change the way I feel about her. I wish she could understand that."

Once again Michael impressed her with his complete and total devotion to her sister. "You're an amazing man," she couldn't help saying. "Julia is lucky."

"You should tell her that."

"Believe me, I have."

Michael glanced back at the house. "Why don't I give you a tour before we start painting? You can tell me what you think of my surprise."

* * *

"Damn," Alex muttered, as they neared his apartment building. His mother was getting out of a silver gray Mercedes parked at the curb. This couldn't possibly be good. He didn't want to talk to her again. And he especially didn't want to talk to her in front of Julia. But his mother had already seen them. She was waiting on the sidewalk for them.

"Who's that?" Julia asked.

"My mother," he said with a sigh.

"You don't sound happy to see her."

"I'm not," he muttered. "She's the devil."

"She can't be that bad."

"You don't know her. Why don't we keep it that way?" He paused in mid stride. "I'll catch up to you later."

"You want me to leave?" she asked in surprise. "I thought we were going to look for the negative."

"I'll call you when I find it." He cast a quick glance at his mother, who was now frowning and tapping her foot impatiently on the sidewalk.

"Does your mother know something about the picture?" Julia asked, a suspicious note in her voice. "You seem awfully eager to get rid of me."

"Alex," his mother called. "I need to speak to you." She began walking toward them, and Alex had no choice but to meet her halfway.

"What's up?" he asked tersely.

"Aren't you going to introduce me to your friend?"

"Julia, this is my mother, Kate Manning."

"It's nice to meet you," Julia said.

"And lovely to meet you, too," Kate replied. "I rarely get a chance to even say hello to Alex's friends. He keeps them far away from me."

"What are you doing here, Mother?" Alex interrupted.

"I told you. I need to speak to you. Why don't we go upstairs into your apartment? You can offer me a drink while I get better acquainted with your friend."

"She's not my friend," Alex growled.

"Well, thanks a lot," Julia murmured.

"My mother's version of friend is not the same as yours. She thinks I'm dating every woman I'm seen with."

"Well, you must admit you do date a lot of them," Kate interjected.

Since it was quickly becoming apparent that he wouldn't be getting rid of either woman any time soon, Alex opened the door to his building, and the three of them walked up the stairs to his third-story apartment.

"You really should get a bigger place in a nicer building," his mother said, breathing a bit heavily from the climb. "One with an elevator. It's not like you can't afford it. Alex is very successful," she added to Julia. "One of the most sought-after photographers in the world today. Just like his father was."

"That's what I understand," Julia said, sending Alex an amused smile.

"*Celeb Magazine* wants to list him as one of their ten most eligible bachelors," his mother continued.

"Really?" Julia said. "That's very impressive."

"How long have you known each other?" Kate asked.

"About twenty-four hours."

Kate seemed taken aback by Julia's response. "Oh, I thought--"

"You didn't think. That's the problem," Alex interrupted. He opened the door to his apartment and ushered them inside. Tossing his keys down on the table, he put his hands on his hips and said, "Now, what do you want?"

His mother wasn't at all intimidated by his abruptness. She simply squared her shoulders and looked him straight in the eye. "I want your cooperation," she said. "I'm meeting with a reporter at the Tribune this afternoon. She does the People Watch section. Her name is Christine Delaney. You've probably heard of her."

"I don't read the gossip column."

"She wants to interview both of us in connection with the exhibit. I'd like you to come with me. It would be great publicity for your father's work and for you."

"I'm busy, and I'm sure you can handle it on your own."

"It's important that she speak to you as well as me," his mother persisted. "In fact, I'm not sure there will be a story if you don't come."

He saw the steel in her smile and heard the determination in her voice, but he did not intend to give in. "Like I said, I have things to do."

"Your father—"

"Don't play that card," he warned her. "You're the one who wants publicity, so go for it. I'm sure you can find some other angle to the story. I'm not interested."

His words created a long, tense silence between them. He could see the anger in his mother's eyes, but she obviously didn't want to create a scene in front of Julia. Maybe it was a good thing she'd stayed.

"Fine," his mother said finally. "If that's the way you want it." She turned to Julia and offered her a gracious smile. "I'm sorry if I interrupted. My apologies."

"It's no problem," Julia said, sending Alex a questioning look.

Julia obviously didn't understand why there was so much tension between him and his mother, but he didn't intend to explain it to her. He was relieved when his mother started to leave without further comment. His relief was short-lived, however, when she paused, then turned, giving Julia a thoughtful look.

"Have we met before?" his mother asked.

"I don't think so," Julia replied.

"You look very familiar. Your eyes... I feel as if I've seen you somewhere. I'm very good with faces, and yours..."

Alex moved quickly across the room, opening the door to his apartment, hoping to get his mother out of the room before she developed the picture in her mind. He was too late.

She snapped her fingers. "The photograph. The orphan girl behind the gates." She looked at Alex, a question in her eyes. "The one you wanted the negative for. Is she the reason you came looking for it?"

"Don't be silly."

"I don't think I'm being silly," his mother said, her sharp mind adding up the facts. She studied Julia for a thoughtful minute, then said, "What are you up to, Alex? Is it possible that Julia is the girl in the photo?"

"Don't you have an interview to get to?" he countered.

She hesitated, glancing down at her watch. "You're right. I have to go. But we definitely need to talk. We'll finish this later."

"There's nothing to finish."

"Oh, I think there is. It was nice to meet you, Julia—whoever you are," she added with a troublemaking smile.

Alex shut the door quickly behind his mother. "Great, just great," he muttered.

"Why didn't you tell your mother you think I'm that girl?" Julia asked.

"I don't want her involved. She's very manipulative, and she always has an agenda. You don't want to become an item on her agenda, trust me."

"You don't make her sound very nice."

Alex knew he was probably painting her more black than he needed to, but his feelings about his mother were complicated and prejudiced by past experience. "She's not important," he said. "Let's look for that negative."

"Of course she's important. She's your mother," Julia said, obviously not willing to drop the subject.

"I'm a little old to need a mother." He saw a shadow pass through her eyes, and he was reminded that she'd recently lost her mother, someone she'd obviously loved very much. "Let's stick to your life and your family."

"She's a beautiful woman," Julia said, ignoring his comment. "Is she married?"

Alex sighed, knowing he could give Julia some information now or spend the next hour dodging her questions. "Okay, I'll give you this much and that's it. My mother uses people to get what she wants, mostly men. She's never worked a day in her life, but she lives well, because she marries well, and she does it over and over again. She married my father because he was an up-and-coming photojournalist. She thought she'd get famous along with him. Unfortunately, he left her behind most of the time and preferred to have his photos printed anonymously. Two years after my father died, she married a doctor—he had money, a big house, and a really nice Porsche. He also liked to gamble. Eight years later, he lost thirty grand in Las Vegas, and she kicked him out. Three years later she married a successful lawyer, a city councilman. He was a great guy, until he had an affair with a high school girl and ruined his life and my mother's life in the process. That was three years ago. I'm not sure when husband number four will make his appearance, but I don't really care. She lives her life. I live mine. End of story. All right?"

"All right," Julia replied, without making further comment.

He was surprised by her restraint. He was also surprised that he'd told her as much as he had. But it was too late to take it back now. "The negatives are in that box," he said abruptly, moving toward the coffee table.

Julia followed him across the room and sat down on the couch. For some reason her silence really annoyed him. He told himself to forget about it, forget about her, and get down to business. Then he made the mistake of looking into her eyes, of seeing warmth, compassion, understanding, and the ice around his heart cracked just a little. Damn her.

"Just say it," he ordered.

"Say what?"

"Whatever you're thinking, so we can get past it."

"I think we should look for that negative," she said.

"You don't want to talk about my mother or what I just told you?" He still couldn't quite believe it. Most women he knew were insanely curious when it came to his personal life.

"What's important is that you don't want to talk about it," she replied. "I can respect that."

"Good." He sat down on the edge of a chair and pulled the box over to him. His breath caught in his chest as he saw the photo lying on top of a pile of papers. It wasn't one of his father's famous historical pictures. It was a family portrait taken when they were still a family. At six years old he'd sat between his parents with a happy smile, believing that his life would always be wonderful. Why the hell was he doing this? He didn't want to go back into the past. There was nothing there for him. "I don't need this," he muttered, setting the photo on the table.

"What is it?" Julia asked, as she picked up the picture. She paused, then said, "You all look so happy."

"Sometimes pictures do lie, especially when the subjects know they're being photographed. That's why I always try to take candid shots where I can capture the real feelings, the real emotions. None of that phony smile crap."

"Maybe it wasn't phony at the time," she suggested.

"Two years after that photo was taken, my parents separated. They would have officially divorced if my father hadn't died in the meantime."

"I'm sorry, Alex."

"Yeah, well, it's not a big deal," he replied.

"I'm surprised you didn't grow closer to your mother after your father died," Julia said. "It was just the two of you."

"She's the one who split up the family. I was extremely pissed off at her. By the time I wasn't angry anymore, she was dating and planning her second wedding." Alex tossed her a pile of photos and negatives. "Start looking through those."

For the next hour there was nothing but blessed silence as they both went through the photos, prints, press clippings, negatives, and other assorted papers in the box. "It's not here," Alex said with annoyance. He'd been so sure they would find the negative. "I don't understand it. Everything else is here, including the other negatives from that trip."

"I guess it was a long shot. In twenty-five years anything could have happened to it." Julia picked up an envelope and her eyes narrowed. "This is weird. It's addressed to Sarah. That was my mother's name."

A chill ran through him as her gaze met his. Another coincidence? Or a clue?

"There's nothing in it, though. It's empty," Julia said, shaking out the envelope. "It couldn't have been addressed to my mother, could it?"

"Of course not."

"There are probably a million Sarahs in the world. Just like there are millions of matryoshka dolls and swan necklaces." The pitch of Julia's voice grew higher with each word. Finally, she threw the envelope down and stood up. "This is crazy. I have to go," she said shortly.

"Just like that?"

"I have things to do. I have a wedding to plan and a fiancé who needs me. And this is just ridiculous," she added, waving her hand in the air in frustration. "We can't find the negative. We can't find anything. And I know who I am. I don't need to do this."

"I thought you did. I thought you wanted the truth," he reminded her. But he could see the wheels spinning in her head and knew she was talking herself out of the whole idea.

"No, I don't. I'm just going to forget about it. I'm sorry I dragged you back into the past, Alex. Thanks for your help. But I'm done."

She grabbed her purse and was at the door before he could get to his feet. He thought about stopping her, but in the end he let her go, because she was running scared, and he couldn't blame her. Looking down at the envelope, he wondered if there was any possible way that his father and Julia's mother were somehow connected. If they were, it wasn't that far of a stretch to link Julia to the photograph. As he stared at the envelope, memories of a dark-haired woman meeting with his father in the square all those years ago flashed into his mind.

Had that woman been Sarah?

* * *

The next day Julia attended Sunday morning Mass surrounded by DeMarcos. They took up almost three rows at St. Mark's Catholic Church. This was her family. This was her place in the world, she thought, as the priest spoke about community. It was almost as if he were speaking directly to her, telling her that the most important thing in the world was to cherish the people around her. The sermon only reinforced her decision to let the matter of the photograph go.

Seeing her mother's name written on that blank envelope in Alex's apartment had terrified her. She didn't even know if it was the same Sarah, but she had suddenly realized exactly what she was about to do—dismantle everything she knew about herself, her mother, and her past. She couldn't do it, so she'd run. Alex must have thought she was completely nuts. She wondered if he'd continue to look into the photo. He seemed to have his own reasons for wanting to know if the girl was her.

Well, it didn't matter. She was done. And that was that.

So why couldn't she stop thinking about it all?

It wasn't just the picture that kept returning to her mind; it was Alex. She was intrigued by him, more than she should be. He'd told her only the beginning of his story, and she wanted to know the rest of it. She wanted to know more about his relationship with his mother and also with his father. She wanted to know what drove him now to roam the world in search of the perfect photograph, sometimes risking his life in the process.

But she wouldn't hear the rest of his story, because they had no reason to speak again.

Maybe it was better this way. She was engaged. Her attention was supposed to be solely on Michael. Even now, he was reaching for her hand, giving it a squeeze, as if he sensed she was drifting away from him and he wanted to pull her back. He was such a good man. She loved him. There was just a tiny, tiny part of her that wasn't sure she was in love with him the way she should be.

She stood up with the rest of the congregation as the Mass ended, waiting for the priest to walk down the aisle so they could file out of their pews. The solemn, reverent atmosphere immediately became more festive when the DeMarcos hit the sidewalk outside the church and began chatting about anything and everything as they walked the few blocks to her aunt Lucia's house, where they would share their traditional Sunday brunch.

Julia was happy not to have time for quiet or personal conversation. She knew she should tell Michael that she was giving up the search, but she wasn't quite ready to bring it all up, not with so many people around.

By the time they entered the house, Lucia's two-story home was already crowded with cousins, aunts, and uncles. A large buffet was set up on the dining room table. The men tended to gather in the living room, usually watching one of the televised football games, while the women put the food out and gossiped about their lives, and the kids played out in the yard or upstairs in the attic, where Lucia's grandchildren had set up a fort.

Liz grabbed her hand as they paused inside the front door. "Come help me in the kitchen," she said.

"I'll be back," Julia told Michael. He nodded, already drifting over to the big-screen television set.

"I haven't had a chance to talk to you since yesterday," Liz said as they walked down the hall to the kitchen. "You were asleep when I got home last night. What have you been doing? Did you find out anything about that doll?"

"Not really," Julia said evasively.

"Did you talk to that man again—the photographer's son? What's his name?"

"Alex Manning. I did speak to him, but—"

"There you are," Gino said, coming through the kitchen door. "My two girls."

Julia received a kiss on both cheeks from her father, watching with a smile as he did the same to Lizzie. Gino DeMarco had always been an affectionate and passionate man with a big personality. When he walked into a room, you knew he was there. Her mother had been much more restrained, quieter, sometimes overshadowed by Gino's light.

"I want to talk to you, Julia, about this wedding of yours," Gino said. "Lucia tells me that I have not been paying enough attention, so now I am paying mention," he declared. "What can I do to help? Besides a write a check, which of course I am happy to do."

"Thanks for offering, but at the moment it's all under control."

"Under control?" Liz echoed. "You haven't done anything yet. And didn't you tell Michael you were postponing the wedding?"

Gino looked disturbed by that piece of information. "Is something wrong?"

"No, everything is fine. Can we talk about this later?" Julia asked. She stepped aside as another one of her aunts came out of the kitchen with a large tray of lasagne.

"I just want it to be the happiest day of your life, as my wedding to your mother was for me," Gino said, his eyes watering, his mouth trembling with emotion.

Julia blinked back her own tears. At least she knew one thing for sure. The marriage between her mother and this man had been one of love and passion. Whatever else was up in the air, she could hold on to that certainty. Lizzie was called away by their aunt Lucia to take some appetizers out to the living room, which she did reluctantly. Gino surprised Julia by pulling her into one of the bedrooms off the hall.

"Is something wrong?" she asked him.

"I know you went to the storage locker yesterday," Gino said, concern drawing lines around his eyes and mouth. "I didn't get a chance to ask you why."

Julia didn't want to tell him that he'd had the chance; he'd just been too hung over to take it. But she didn't have the energy to deal with his drinking today. For the moment he was sober, and he was waiting for an answer. She wasn't sure what to say. Her decision to leave the past alone began to waver. Maybe if she asked just one question or two...

"I was hoping to find something in Mom's belongings about the first couple years of my life," she said, not wanting Gino to think she was looking for her real father. That wasn't the case, and she didn't want to hurt him. He'd been the only father she'd ever known, and he'd been a good one. Even without the words, though, she saw shadows fill his eyes.

"Your mother wondered if the day would come when you would ask questions she didn't want to answer."

"You talked about it?" Julia asked in surprise.

"Yes, of course."

"What did she tell you?"

"Very little, I'm afraid. She said it was too painful to discuss."

"That's what she told me, too. But I feel a bit lost without any..." She searched for the right words -- "any photos of myself as a baby, or knowledge of not only who my biological father was, but who my grandparents were. I don't know where my mother grew up or anything about her life before you and me. I don't know what she looked like when she was a young girl. And I find myself really wanting to know."

"Because she's gone, and it's too late to ask her," Gino said with a touch of insight that she thought he'd lost in the past few months when he'd dulled his brain with alcohol.

"Maybe that's true," she said, deciding not to tell him about the photo for now. "Do you know anything about her life before she met you, or before she had me?"

He thought for a moment. "Let's see. I must know something."

"That's what I thought, too, but then I realized I didn't know much."

Gino frowned, his eyes reflective. "I know Sarah went to

college at Northwestern near Chicago. She said she lived over a coffee shop on University Avenue. That's when she picked up her caffeine habit, she mentioned something about a roommate named..." He pursed his lips as he thought. "What was her name? Jackie. Yes, I think it was Jackie."

"I thought she went to college in New York," Julia laid in surprise. "The only thing she ever told me about her past was that she was born in Buffalo and lived in upstate New York most of her life. She said she came to California after college to visit a friend and never went home."

"I don't believe it was after college but much later, Sarah mentioned that she came here for a friend's wedding when you were three years old. She loved it so much she never left. And she said you did much better in the California climate. Something about allergies."

"I don't have allergies."

"I guess they improved when you got here."

"I thought I was born in Berkeley. She said we lived in Berkeley." Julia shook her head in confusion. Why were such simple facts so convoluted?

"You were living in Berkeley when I met you," Gino said. "That's true."

But how long had they been in Berkeley? Her mother had married Gino when Julia was four and a half years old. "Tell me again about your first meeting," she said, knowing the story, but wondering if she'd missed something in the details.

"Sarah brought you into the restaurant. She had met Lucia at a fabric store, in some workshop on draperies or something. They both loved to sew. Lucia told her about the restaurant, so Sarah brought you over one day to see the lobsters. You were a pretty little girl. I think I fell in love with both of you at the same time," he said with a warm, loving smile. "Lucia suggested that I let Sarah make up some new curtains and tablecloths for the cafe. I agreed. Three months later we were married. I thank God Lucia met Sarah and brought her to me. She was my angel." His voice caught, and he wiped his hand across his eyes. "I'd never met a woman who wanted to give up her whole life for me."

"What do you mean?" Julia asked, struck by his words. "What did she give up?"

"Well..." He thought for a moment. "She gave up her friends in Berkeley, and when I told her I wanted to have another child and have her stay home, she readily agreed. I don't know if I can explain it, Julia. Sarah just became an integral part of my life. And selfishly I never questioned her devotion or her lack of friends and family away from me. I was happy that we never had any conflicts about where to spend the holidays." He paused, letting out a small sigh. "I know you want to ask me about your biological father."

"Not because I don't have a terrific father," she assured him. "And it's really not about him—whoever he is. It's about my mother, and my grandparents. I don't even know their names. I don't know if they're still alive or what they did for a living or if they ever wanted to see me. I feel like I should know that much."

"Henry and Susan Davis," he said abruptly. "Those are your grandparents' names."

Her heart skipped a beat. "How do you know that?"

"Sarah told me. I don't really remember why or what we were discussing at the time."

"But Mom went by the last name of Gregory before she married you. How did she get from Davis to Gregory?"

Gino stared back at her, puzzlement in his eyes. "I don't know. I suppose I could be wrong. Maybe your grandparents' last name was Gregory and not Davis. I'm not sure, Julia. The important thing is that Sarah's parents disowned her when she got pregnant. That was the end of their relationship, and Sarah was adamant about not having any contact with them. I didn't feel it was my place to press her for more information, and frankly I didn't care who had come before me. As I said, I liked the fact that I had the two of you to myself, that you became DeMarcos in every sense of the word. But I guess that wasn't fair to you."

Julia didn't know what was fair anymore. But she did know that none of her questions had anything to do with Gino. "You don't have to apologize. I've had a great life. No complaints."

"Just questions," he said.

"Yes. Do you remember anything about where Mom and I lived in Berkeley? An address maybe? Or the name of one of her friends?"

"You lived in a little apartment over a garage. Sarah said she'd only lived there for a month or two. I went there once or twice. I think the street was Fremont or Fairmont. Does that help at all?"

"It might. At least I know the names of my grandparents. That's something. One last question: I found a Russian doll in the storage locker among Mom's things. Did she ever tell you if she'd traveled to Russia?"

His eyes widened and he laughed. "Russia? Are you kidding? Your mother hated to travel. I'm sure she never left the country."

"If she had left the country before she met you, she would have had a passport, right? Did you ever see a passport? I didn't find any of Mom's personal papers in the storage locker."

"I haven't gone through the office things, which are in boxes in my apartment. I don't remember seeing a passport. But your mother paid all the bills and kept track of the paperwork. I left all that to her, so I don't have any idea what's there."

"Could I take a look sometime?"

"Sure, whatever you want, Julia. Is that it?"

He hadn't told her much, but the few details he had shared with her teased at her mind, making her reconsider her plan to stop researching her past.

"I think we should have some wine, some food, and some good conversation," Gino said when she didn't reply. "Shall we join the others?"

"Sure."

As they left the bedroom, they went in opposite directions. Her father headed toward the makeshift bar in the kitchen while Julia joined Michael at the end of the buffet line in the dining room.

"Everything okay?" Michael asked, putting his arm around her shoulders. "You disappeared for a while."

"I was talking to Dad."

"About his drinking?"

Julia felt a spark of guilt at the question. She probably should have been talking to him about his drinking, but she'd been too caught up in her own problems. "We didn't get to that," she muttered.

"He's still grieving over your mother. I'm sure he'll slow down soon."

"I hope so."

"I have an idea. How about a sail this afternoon?" Michael

asked, an inviting smile on his face. "It's a beautiful day."

"I have to work. You know that. One to three every Sunday," she reminded him.

Irritation flashed through his eyes. "I wish you'd get rid of that shift. It would be nice to spend more time on the weekends together."

She'd heard him make that comment before. While she appreciated the fact that he wanted to spend time with her, he didn't seem to understand how important her job was to her. "I'm lucky I can host my own show on the weekends, Michael. I get bigger audience numbers than when I host the ten-to-midnight weekday shows. Besides, I thought you were running a charter today."

"Not until sunset. You could join me for that. You'll be done with your show by then."

"It's a possibility," she said tentatively. She didn't mind sailing, but it wasn't her first choice of things to do, especially when Michael was running a charter. She usually felt like the odd man out and spent most of her time wishing she'd stayed home and gotten caught up on her bills, her laundry, and the other details of her life.

"Julia," Liz interrupted, holding out Julia's cell phone. "I heard it ringing in your purse. He said it was important."

Julia took the phone from Liz, noting the frown on her sister's face. "Hello," she said, moving away from Michael as she did so.

"Julia, it's Alex. Something's come up. We need to talk."

"I told you I was done." She walked into the living room, casting a quick look behind her to make sure no one was close enough to overhear. Fortunately, Liz was talking to Michael, diverting his attention from her.

"I just got a call from a newspaper reporter," Alex continued. "Apparently my mother told her that I'd found the world's most famous orphan. And she gave her your name."

"What?" Julia asked in shock. "Are you kidding me? Why would she do that?"

"Obviously to generate publicity for the exhibit. The reporter just called me. I tried to persuade her that my mother was wrong, but this woman is very persistent. I'm sure she's going to track you down. And I wanted you to be ready."

"Great. What am I supposed to tell her?"

"That's up to you."

"Dammit, Alex, how could your mother do this to me?"

"It wasn't about you. It was about what she wanted. It's always about that. I told you she's manipulative."

Julia heard the bitter note in his voice, but at the moment she was too wound up to respond to it, too focused on what this meant for her and her family. "I'm not going to talk to a reporter about that photo."

"You may not have a choice."

Julia saw Michael waving at her from the dining room. "I can't talk right now. I'll call you later." She ended the call, forced a smile on her face and went back to join him.

"Who was that?"

She licked her lips, not wanting to lie to him, but liking the idea of telling him the truth even less. "Just a friend," she said evasively. "It wasn't important."

"Liz seemed to think it was." His eyes narrowed. "Was it the guy you were talking to Friday night outside the restaurant? The photographer?"

"Yes," she said.

A hard glint entered Michael's brown eyes. "He's not a wedding photographer, is he?"

She had no choice but to answer honestly. "No, he's the son of the man who took the photo that I saw at the museum."

"Julia." His voice was filled with disappointment. "I can't believe you're still thinking about that."

"I'm sorry. I was going to stop, Michael. I was planning to tell you that today, but Alex said that a reporter has gotten wind of it and wants to talk to me."

"A reporter? Are you out of your mind?" he asked in amazement. "You're taking this to the press? You're going to kill your sister and the rest of your family. Do you know that?"

"It was never my plan to take it to the press, but I have to figure out what to do now that it's already there. This reporter thinks I'm that girl in the picture."

Michael shook his head, a tense line to his lips. "You tell them you're not that girl and that's the end of the story."

"Do you think they'll believe me?"

"Why wouldn't they? It's as crazy an idea as I've ever heard. Do you honestly think you and your mother were living in Russia when you were a baby? Don't you think she would have told you about that? I know you have a big imagination, but even you must admit that this is absurd. You're grasping at straws, Julia, and I know why."

"Why?" she asked, almost scared to hear his answer.

"You want a reason to postpone the wedding. That's it, isn't it?"

Chapter Six

"Why did you do it?" Alex asked as he faced his mother late Sunday afternoon. Unable to get her on the phone, he'd come to her house. He'd found her sitting calmly in her living room, sipping a glass of red wine and addressing invitations for a party she was hosting in a few weeks. "Why did you tell the reporter that Julia was the girl in the photograph?"

"You told me to find an angle, and I did," she said, no apology in her voice.

"You used an innocent woman to generate publicity for yourself."

"For the exhibit," she corrected. "For your father's work and for yours. If you'd come with me to the interview, I wouldn't have had to bring up Julia's name." She settled back against the white cushions of her couch. "Now, why don't you tell me where Julia DeMarco came from?"

"I'm not going to tell you anything. You obviously can't be trusted."

"Oh, please," she said with a careless wave of her hand. "I didn't do anything wrong. Maybe I jumped the gun a bit, but it's obvious you think Julia is that girl, or you wouldn't have come here looking for the negative to that picture."

Alex stared at his mother, amazed at her brash confidence, her belief that she could do no wrong. She was so focused on her own life, her own goals, that she couldn't see anyone else. Nor apparently could she see the potential consequences of her actions.

"You told me to drop this," he reminded her. "Just yesterday morning we had a discussion about whether or not I should be looking into anything connected with the Moscow trip. You even suggested the possibility that Dad's accident was not an accident." He paused, giving his words a moment to sink in. "So how do you explain why you suddenly decided to publicize a picture taken during that last trip? Did you consider the possibility that Dad's accident and that trip, maybe even that picture, were somehow connected?"

His mother's expression faltered at his question, and her hand was noticeably shaky as she set down her glass of wine on the coffee table. "I—I didn't think about your father's accident being tied to that photo. Why would I?"

"Because you suggested it yesterday," he said in angry frustration. "You're the one who put the idea in my head."

She stared at him for a long moment. "I don't know what I think about your father's accident. And I didn't plan on telling the reporter about Julia. It's just that Christine appeared so bored when you didn't show up. She kept checking her watch and didn't seem to be paying any attention to me. I wasn't sure she'd write even one line about the exhibit. I knew I needed to catch her interest, and Julia's face was fresh in my mind. It just came out."

"That's the problem, Mother. You never think before you speak."

"How would you know, Alex? You barely spend any time with me," she snapped. "And you act like I was trying to hurt you. I just wanted to get the most publicity I could get for the exhibit. It's not only for me, Alex. It's for you, too. Don't you want the world to know about your father's work?"

"You should have gone into politics. You always know how to spin things. But you shouldn't have done this," he said, seeing a flash of guilt in her eyes. "And you know it."

"I'm sorry if I spoke out of turn. But I'm sure you can fix it. Just set up a meeting with Christine Delaney. Convince her I was wrong and give her something else to write about. She was really interested in you, and she's a single, attractive woman. I'm sure you can charm her into another story."

"You don't have any moral boundaries, do you?"

"I didn't say sleep with her; I said charm her. Honestly, Alex, you make such a big deal out of nothing. You're so self-righteous and judgmental, just like your father. The rest of us aren't good enough for you." She picked up her wine and took another sip. "It's not as if you haven't broken the rules before. When it's what you want, like the perfect photograph, it's a different story. Then you'll do whatever it takes. When I ask you to bend a little, you act like I just told you to kill someone."

It bothered him that there was some truth in what she said. It wasn't as if he hadn't played fast and loose with the rules before. But this was different.

"What happened with the negative?" she asked, changing the subject. "Did you find it? Were you able to see the full picture?"

"I didn't find the negative. It must have been destroyed."

"What are you going to do next?"

"I'm going to check with Joe and Stan to see if the negative could still be at the magazine."

She nodded. "If there's anything I can do to make this better, I will. And I promise not to speak out of turn again. If you'd like me to call Christine, I will. I'll tell her I was wrong."

"No, I'll do it," he said. He didn't want his mother to get any more involved in the matter.

"Fine. Whatever you want."

He stood up, then paused, thinking about the envelope with the name Sarah on it. His instincts told him not to share any further information with his mother; then again, who else did he have to ask? "You mentioned something about another woman in Dad's life," he said slowly. "Did you ever have anything more concrete than a suspicion? Like a name?"

"Sarah," she said immediately, her mouth drawing into a tight line. "He used to talk to someone named Sarah on the phone late at night. Whenever I came in the room, he'd hang up. But sometimes I'd listen outside the door, and I'd hear him laughing or whispering."

A wave of uneasiness swept through him at that piece of information. "Do you know Sarah's last name?"

She gave a quick shake of her head. "I asked Charles, but he never answered me. He said she was an old friend, and I was paranoid. He always said I was paranoid, but I wasn't, Alex. I knew something was off with him before we separated. I knew he was lying to me. He was too evasive, too distracted, too secretive.

When I asked him to trust me enough to tell me the truth, he couldn't. That's when I told him I wanted a divorce. It wasn't because I didn't love him. It was because I loved him too much."

Alex didn't want to get into a discussion of his parents' marriage. His own memory was not one of love, but of bitter discord about everything and anything. They'd fought, yelled, screamed at each other. Then his father would slink into the shadows, and his mother would slam her bedroom door. He had often wondered how they'd ever gotten together in the first place. But he had to admit he'd put the blame on his mother more than his father. He'd heard her yelling, but he'd never seen evidence of his father's secrecy.

"There are always two sides, Alex," she said softly now. "To every story."

He looked into her eyes, searching for truth and honesty, but deep down inside he still didn't trust her not to be exaggerating or even lying about the past. "I've got to run," he said. "Just don't talk to anyone else about Julia or that photo, all right?"

"Does this mean you won't be leaving town anytime soon?"

"Not until I get to the bottom of this mystery."

"Are you personally interested in Julia?"

"I barely know her," he prevaricated.

"She's a beautiful woman."

She was beautiful, and he hadn't been able to stop thinking about her since she'd showed up at his door on Friday. But he didn't intend to share that with his mother.

"You always loved that photo," Kate said with a speculative glint in her eye. "I caught you staring at it more than once after your father died. That little girl—she called out to you in some way."

"Because I didn't know why she was so important. And I still don't. But I'm going to find out."

The violin solo playing through her headphones was hauntingly beautiful, meant to soothe and relax. The tension in Julia's neck and shoulders had just begun to ease when the phone on her desk rang yet again. Since she'd returned home from her afternoon radio show, the phone had been ringing every fifteen minutes. It was always the same person, Christine Delaney, a reporter with the *Tribune*, who asked her to call back as soon as possible. She had no intention of calling her back. What would she say?

Julia slipped off her headphones in time to hear Christine's voice on the answering machine. She glanced away from the offending phone to meet Liz's annoyed glare. Her sister, wearing yoga pants and a sweatshirt, sat with her bare feet propped up on the coffee table, a bowl of ice cream on her lap, the television blaring reruns of Seinfeld.

"She's not going to stop calling until you call her back," Liz said, as she muted the television. "This is really annoying."

"And I should tell her what?"

"That you're not that girl."

"I need proof."

"Is that what you're looking for on the Internet?"

Julia stared at the computer screen in front of her. That's exactly what she was doing. She'd put in the few small clues her father had given her, hoping that somewhere there might be some information she could tie back to her mother.

Liz set her bowl down on the table, got up, and crossed the room to peer over Julia's shoulder. "You're looking at obituaries?" she asked with surprise. "Who do you think died?"

"My grandparents, maybe. I know they lived in Buffalo. And their last name was Davis. Henry and Susan Davis."

"Have you found anything?"

"I think so. Maybe." Julia pointed to the screen, to the name Henry Davidson. "It's not Davis, but it's close, and the first names are the same."

"Mom's maiden name was Gregory."

"I know that's what she told us, but Dad said he believed her parents' names were Henry and Susan Davis. He never asked why the names were different."

"What does the paper say?"

" 'Henry Davidson, age eighty-one, native of Buffalo, died after a long illness. He is survived by his wife, Susan.' It goes on to talk about his work as an engineer, his marriage of fifty-nine years, and his charity endeavors. There's nothing about a daughter."

"Then it can't be the same family."

Julia looked at Liz and saw nothing but skepticism in her brown eyes. "You think I'm making too big of a leap?"

"Yes. Susan and Henry aren't unusual names. Their last name was Davidson, not Davis, and there's no mention of a daughter named Sarah."

As Julia listened to Liz compute the facts, she was acutely aware of how different they were. Liz saw the negatives. Julia saw the possibilities. Even now, she had butterflies racing through her stomach at the thought of having located her grandparents. Maybe the facts didn't add up exactly right, but her instincts told her she was on to something. "You're overlooking some important points," she argued. "They live in Buffalo, same city, same names. The ages are right. I think it's worth looking into."

"What else did Dad tell you today?" Liz asked. She cleared a corner of the desk and sat down on it.

"He said Mom went to Northwestern University. He mentioned a roommate named Jackie. They lived on University Avenue, over a coffeehouse."

"Mom always did love her coffee," Liz said with a wistful note in her voice. "I never had to set my alarm. I woke up to the sound of the coffeemaker beeping every morning at seven a.m. She said she couldn't talk until she had her morning coffee." She let out a sigh, then said, "But I don't see how any of that information is going to help you."

"At least I know where she went to college. For some reason, I always thought she went to Berkeley—I guess because we were living there when she met Dad. He said he only went to our apartment twice. He couldn't remember the address, just the street name, Fairmont or Fremont. I found both streets in the city, but they're long, seven to ten blocks each. If I went house to house, it could take me months to find anyone who remembers a tenant from twenty-five years ago. I have nothing but crumbs to go on." As she finished speaking, Julia felt depressed. Liz was right. She had no useful information to go on, except maybe the obituary. If she tracked down Susan Davidson, she could at least close that door or find a new way into her mother's past. "I wonder if I could get Susan Davidson's address on the Internet," she muttered, her fingers flying across the keyboard.

"And if you find her, what will you say?" Liz asked.

"I'll deal with that moment when I get to it."

"Look, Julia, what's really going to change if you find your grandmother?" Liz asked. "Nothing, that's what. You'll still be you, and she'll still be the woman who turned her back on our mother. What on earth would you want to say to her?"

Julia stopped typing to look at her sister. "I don't know what I'd say to her. But she's not just my grandmother, Liz. She's yours, too."

Liz appeared taken aback, as if that thought had never occurred to her. "I—I guess you're right," she said slowly. "I think of Nonna as my grandma."

"Well, you may have another grandmother. Aren't you at all curious about Mom's background?"

A moment passed before Liz shook her head. "No, I'm not curious. I don't need another grandmother. We have a huge family, Julia, with more occasions and dinners and lunches than I even want to attend. I don't feel like I'm missing anything, and I don't understand why you do." She put up a hand as Julia started to answer. "I know, I know. You have a bigger hole to fill than I do, because you weren't raised by your biological father. But even if our positions were reversed, I don't think I'd feel the same way. We had a great life. And it seems wrong to do this now that Mom's gone and Dad's upset. It's like a slap in the face to him. Mom dies and you have to find your real father."

But that wasn't what she was doing. She wasn't looking for her father at all. She was looking for her mother, for their past, the one they'd shared in the four years before Sarah had married Gino. She wasn't trying to slap her father in the face or make him feel like he'd done a bad job, but she could certainly understand why Liz or even her father might see things differently.

"I spoke to Michael after you left for work today," Liz said, breaking the lengthening silence between them. "He's trying to be patient, but he waited through Mom's illness, the funeral, giving you time to grieve, and now this. How can you ask him to put your relationship on hold again?"

Julia didn't know how to answer. Everything Liz said was true. Michael had been patient. He had waited for her. But was it so unfair to take a couple of days to look into a picture that was bothering her? "Michael and I have the rest of our lives to be together. I'm only asking for a little time," she said. "I haven't even canceled our wedding date yet. It's been two days since I saw that photograph. Can I just have a few minutes to figure out if it should be important to me?"

Liz frowned. "I suppose that's not completely unreasonable. I just don't want you to lose Michael. And I don't want you to create any more problems for our family."

Before Julia could reassure Liz that that was not her intent, the doorbell rang. She got up to answer it, thinking it was Michael. It wasn't.

The flash went off in her face, the light momentarily blinding her.

"Miss DeMarco? I'm Christine Delaney."

Julia blinked as the tall, brunette woman standing in the hall came into focus.

"I must say, I can see the resemblance," Christine added, lowering the camera in her hand. "I've spent most of the day studying your photograph." She slipped the camera back in her bag and pulled out the catalogue from the photography exhibit. It was opened to the page featuring the orphan girl.

Julia swallowed hard, trying to get her wits about her.

"How did you get to this country?" Christine asked.

"I can't talk to you right now." Julia moved to shut the door, but Christine stuck her foot out.

"Wait, don't go. I promise not to bite. I just want to be the one to share your story with the world."

"There is no story."

"There must be. I did some research and found out there was quite a buzz when that photo was first published. A lot of people wanted to adopt you. I'm sure everyone will be interested in knowing what happened to you." Christine offered a warm, inviting smile that was meant to encourage Julia to confess.

"I'm sorry, I can't," she said abruptly. "Please just go away."

"Is that it?" Liz interrupted, grabbing the catalogue from Christine's hands. "Is this the famous picture?" She paused. "Oh, my God." Liz looked from Julia to the photo and back again. Her face turned white, her eyes wide in disbelief.

Very aware that the reporter was watching them with extreme interest, Julia grabbed Liz's arm and pulled her back into the apartment. She managed to shut the door in Christine's face, throwing the dead bolt into place to make sure she couldn't get back in.

"Call me when you want to talk," the reporter yelled. "I'm slipping my card under the door. I promise to tell your side of the story."

Julia put a hand to her racing heart as quiet returned to the apartment. Christine was gone for the moment, anyway.

"I get it now," Liz said as she met Julia's gaze. "This little girl..." She shook the catalogue in her hand. "She looks just like you when you were a kid."

Julia felt an immense relief that Liz finally understood why she was so unsettled. "Michael didn't see the resemblance."

"Maybe because he didn't know you back then. But I did." She glanced back down at the photograph. "I still don't understand how this child could be you, though. How could you have been in Moscow? And in an orphanage? Unless you're thinking that Mom adopted you?"

"I don't see how she could have," Julia replied. "It was the Cold War. No one was adopting babies from Russia back then." She took the catalogue out of Liz's hand and looked at the photograph once more. "This girl is at least three years old."

"I agree," Liz said. "It's completely impossible that you're that girl."

"And I can't let myself think even for one second that I wasn't Mom's child," Julia continued. "Mom used to say how we had the same nose and the same long legs. I can't bear to think it's not true." She closed the catalogue, wishing she could put away her doubts just as easily.

"It is true," Liz said forcefully. "You're my sister and our mother's daughter. Maybe this girl is your double. They say everyone has one in the world. This is yours. It's just a coincidence."

"I agree, but I have to know for sure. If I can find something to prove I was here in the United States when this photo was taken and that girl was in Moscow, then I'll be able to let it go. Will you help me, Liz?" She saw the conflict run through her sister's eyes.

"I don't know, Julia. I'm afraid." Liz paused for a long second. "Maybe you want to know the truth, but I'm not sure I do. I don't want to lose you."

"That won't happen. We'll always be sisters, no matter what."

"You say that now, but—"

"But what? You can't think that our relationship would ever change. It won't. You have to believe me," she said, determined to convince Liz of that fact.

"I don't know what to believe. I hate that this is happening. It's too much. Mom died just a few months ago. Why can't things be normal for a while?"

Julia had always tried to give Liz what she needed. That was her job as the big sister. And right now her sister needed her to back off from searching for her past. But she couldn't do it. She'd taken care of Liz all her life, and she'd spent the past two years watching over her mother. This time she needed to put herself first.

Liz picked up her sandals and slipped them on. "I'm going for a walk."

"I'll go with you."

"No, I need to think. I'll take my phone. Don't worry about me. You have enough to worry about."

The apartment was quiet after Liz left, too quiet. Julia paced around the room, too restless to return to the computer. Liz, who certainly hadn't wanted to see any resemblance between the girl in the photo and Julia, hadn't been able to look away from the picture. That simple fact made Julia even more determined to find the truth. But she couldn't do it alone. She needed help. And there was only one person she could ask.

* * *

"Thanks for coming by," Alex said as he opened the door to Joe Carmichael. Joe was dressed in faded blue jeans and a bright orange T-shirt. A San Francisco Giants cap covered his balding head.

"Don't thank me yet. I've come empty-handed," Joe replied, holding up his hands in evidence. "I spoke to Ellie, who keeps track of everything at the magazine. She couldn't find any negatives belonging to your father. She said she looked everywhere."

Alex hadn't really expected a different answer, but it was still disappointing. "Thanks for checking."

"Want to tell me what this is about?"

"Not right now."

Joe gave him a speculative look. "Am I going to have to bail you out of jail again?"

"I never say never."

"Does this mean you're temporarily out of commission? Or should I give you your next assignment?"

Alex felt a familiar rush of adrenaline that came with the thought of a new assignment. He loved the anticipation of a new challenge, and he very much wanted to say yes, he was ready for his next job. Why shouldn't he leave? Julia had already bailed on him. Maybe it would be better to turn his back on the past and move on. But he hated leaving loose ends, unanswered questions.

"I think I have my answer," Joe said. "It never takes you this long to say yes."

"I'm in the middle of something," Alex admitted. "I need a few days to clear it up. Then I'll be back in business."

"Just let me know when you're ready or if you need my help."

"I will." Alex opened the door to his apartment, surprised to find Julia in the hall, her hand poised to knock.

"You're home," she said, her hand dropping to her side. "And I'm interrupting."

"No, you're not. I was just leaving," Joe said, giving Alex a grin. "No wonder you're not ready to leave. It's about time you thought of something other than work."

Alex didn't bother to explain Julia's presence. And she didn't seem inclined to explain it, either. He supposed he could have introduced them, but after an awkward minute, Joe cleared his throat and said, "I'll see you around."

"Who was that?" Julia asked as Alex ushered her into his apartment.

"An editor I work with. What's up? I thought you were done with me, done with the photo, done with everything—despite the fact that we had a deal."

His harsh words brought a flush of red to her cheeks, and he saw guilt in her gaze. "I got scared when I saw my mother's name on the envelope. That's why I ran. I came back because that reporter you told me about has been calling me, and a short while ago, she showed up my door and took my picture before I could stop her. She wants to tell my story, but I don't know what my story is." She paused. "I know I blew you off yesterday. I was wondering if I could have another chance."

Alex wanted to say no, to send her on her way, because his life would be much easier without her in it. But she was part of his unfinished business, at least until he knew for sure that she wasn't the girl in the photograph. He shut the door to his apartment. "Come in." He walked over to the couch and moved a stack of newspapers so she could sit down.

"You have a lot of papers," she commented.

"I like to keep up with what's going on in the world. And check out my competition."

"You take photos for newspapers, too?"

He nodded, taking a seat on the armchair across from her. He winced a bit as he moved. His rib was almost healed, but now and then he still got a twinge.

"Are you all right?" Julia asked, her sharp eyes not missing a thing.

"Fine."

"I couldn't help noticing the black eye and the bruises the other day. I looked you up on the Internet. I guess you got into some trouble in Colombia."

"The local police didn't care for some of my photographic choices. They threw me in jail for a few hours, and for fun a couple of guys beat the living crap out of me," he replied, leaning back in the chair. He put his feet on the coffee table between them, and added, "It wasn't a day in the park, but I lived."

"It sounds awful." She tilted her head thoughtfully. "Why do you do it? After experiences like that, why do you go back for more?"

"I haven't gone back yet."

"But you will."

It wasn't a question but a statement, and he had no choice but to agree. "I will. I like what I do. It's challenging, and I run my own life. As a freelancer, I go where the stories are and sell my photos to the highest bidder."

"Do you ever get tired of the traveling, the conditions that you have to live in?'

"Sometimes—when I haven't seen a shower in a few days or had a decent meal. But I've always had itchy feet. I can't stay too long in one place. I get restless." He paused, more than a little curious about her, although his instincts told him that getting to know her better wasn't in his best interest. Still, he couldn't stop the questions from coming out. "What about you? Are you a traveler?"

"I'd like to be, but I haven't been anywhere yet." She played with her hands, twisting the diamond engagement ring on her third finger.

He wondered again where her fiancé was and why he wasn't getting involved in her search for the truth. Not that Alex wanted him involved, but it seemed odd.

"I'm an armchair traveler," Julia continued. "I let the music sweep me around the world. But one day I'd like to go in person."

"What's stopping you from going right now?"

She shrugged. "I have responsibilities. Or I did, anyway. Every time I thought about going somewhere, there was always a reason why I couldn't. Especially during the last two years," she added. "My mom was sick for a long time. I didn't want to go far."

"And now?" he pressed her. "Do you have big honeymoon plans?"

"We haven't gotten that far, but Michael doesn't really like to travel. He's a homebody."

"He doesn't know what he's missing. There are places on this earth that you should definitely see."

"Like where?" she asked eagerly, leaning forward, her blue eyes lighting up with interest. "Tell me about some incredible place that you've been."

He thought for a moment. "The Iguazu Falls in South America are spectacular. They border Argentina, Brazil, and Paraguay. The power and the roar of the water thunders through your body. It feels like the earth is opening up." He saw the falls in his mind, but his memory didn't do them justice. His camera hadn't been able to capture their beauty, either. Maybe some things couldn't be frozen in time.

"They sound amazing," Julia said. "Where do you go next, Alex? Do you know?"

"Not yet. I just got back from a six-week trip through South America. It was long and hot, not to mention painfully sickening in..." His voice trailed away as he realized how much he was sharing with her. The more involved they got, the more complicated everything would become. And he preferred to keep his relationships simple.

"What do you mean, painfully sickening?" she asked, obviously not willing to let the conversation go.

"I don't want to talk about it."

"You can't just stop in the middle of a sentence."

"Sure I can. It's not pretty, Julia. It's not something a woman like you needs to hear about."

She stiffened at that. "What do you mean, a woman like me?"

"Beautiful, innocent, untouched by the grim reality of life."

"You're wrong, Alex. I just faced a very grim reality. I watched my mother die. Don't talk to me about being untouched by terrible pain."

"I'm sorry." He paused. "It's just that the poverty and violence some people in the world endure are beyond inhumane. Lately, I've begun to wonder what the hell good I'm doing taking someone's picture right before their head gets blown off."

He saw her shock and was glad. Maybe now she'd let the subject drop.

She didn't. "Did that really happen to you?" she asked quietly.

"Yes."

"When?"

"Last year."

"How did you deal with it?" she asked.

He had a hard time resisting the compassion in her eyes, and for the first time ever he found himself wanting to tell someone about one of the worst hours of his life. "I tell myself that at least I got the picture. At least her story will be told. Her death won't be hidden away like so many others, because I was there. Hell of a rationalization, but it keeps me sane."

She stared at him for a long moment, and he sensed she was reading his mind or maybe his heart. "But it doesn't make the pain go away, does it? Who was she?"

"Just a woman who wanted my help." He drew in a long, shaky breath as memories of that night filled his head. "Her eyes were black as midnight and absolutely terrified. She knew her husband was coming after her. He'd accused her of committing adultery. But she'd been raped by a man in the village." Alex shook his head, wanting to rid himself of the image that was printed indelibly on his brain. "I should have done something. I should have seen him coming, but I was looking at her, aiming my camera, and the next thing I knew, she'd been shot through the head. It was so clean, one small hole in her forehead, almost like a beauty mark. Her eyes were still open when she hit the ground. She was still looking at me, begging for my help, but it was too late." His stomach churned, and he battled back a wave of nausea. "But at least I got the picture, right?"

"That photo was important," Julia said slowly and deliberately. "You made her life and her death matter. Your work throws a spotlight on injustice in the world. That's a noble calling."

"Don't try to make me into some hero," he said harshly. "I was thinking only of myself. I should have helped her, not photographed her. I'll never forgive myself for making that choice. It made me realize how often I don't see the person, only the shot, only the award-winning photographic record."

"So she changed the way you think."

"Yeah, and I wish she hadn't. It was easier the other way." He rose. "I need a beer. Do you want one?"

"Sure," she said.

He used his time in the kitchen to regain his control. He was pissed off at himself for telling Julia so much, but in an odd way, it was a relief to share it with someone. He pulled two beers out of the refrigerator, popped the tops, and took the bottles back to the living room. Julia was on her feet, gazing at some of the framed photographs on his walls.

"This is your work, too?" she asked, taking a beer from his hand.

"Yes. Why do you sound surprised?"

She waved her hand toward the colorful garden landscape. "I didn't take you for a flower guy."

"I have my moments," he said with a smile. "I took those shots when I was in college. I was just figuring out how to use my cameras. When I moved in here, I needed to put something on the walls, and I figured the women I brought home would like 'em."

She smiled back at him, and the somber mood between them lightened. "So you ask women if they want to come home with you and see your pretty pictures?"

"I don't phrase it quite like that."

"I'll bet."

He took a swig of his beer. "Why don't we get back to you, Julia? Tell me again what happened with the reporter who came to your door."

"She wants to interview me. She's very persistent. I told her I have nothing to say, but I think I'm going to have to tell her something. The question is what?"

"What do you want to say?"

"I'm not sure. But I'm even more concerned about what I want to do next. I don't suppose you have any brilliant ideas?"

"Find out who you are. Before someone else does." He looked her straight in the eye. "I told you when we first met that you couldn't back out until this was over, and you can't. Not because I say so, but because when you came to me you set things in motion, and with a little help from my mother they're still in motion."

"You're right. I spoke to my father earlier. He gave me a few tips that I took to the Internet. It's a long shot, but I may have a lead on my grandmother."

"Really?"

She nodded. "The names are slightly different, but she may live in Buffalo, New York, where my mother said she was born. My father also told me my mother went to Northwestern, but I don't know—"

"Your mother went to Northwestern," he cut in. "My dad also went to Northwestern." Alex's nerves began to tingle the way they always did when his instincts told him he was on to something.

Her gaze filled with uncertainty. "It's a big school. Do you think there's a connection between them?"

"We did find that envelope with the name Sarah on it. How old was your mother?"

"She turned fifty-eight right before she died."

"And my father would be fifty-nine if he'd lived, so they would have been in college at the same time. My mother told me that a woman named Sarah used to call my dad late at night. He said she was an old friend." Alex thought for a moment, wondering where they could take this lead. "Old friends," he repeated. "That's it. I need to talk to Stan."

"Who's Stan?"

"He used to work at World News Magazine. He was my father's editor, but more importantly, he was one of his best friends. And I know that friendship dated back before my parents got married. Maybe he can tell us more about Sarah."

"Can you call him now?"

"Absolutely." He reached for the phone. A few minutes later he had an invitation from Stan to come by the house. "We can go now."

"We're really going to do this, aren't we?" Julia asked, her expression tense and uncertain.

"Second thoughts again?"

"I'm a little afraid of what we'll find out," she said, her beautiful blue eyes reflecting her every emotion. She would never be difficult to read. Everything she felt could be seen on her face.

"I'm more afraid of living the rest of my life not knowing why that photo was important to my father," he countered. "But I can go on my own."

"No, I said we were in this together, and that's the way it's going to be." She slipped her hand into his, and his entire body stiffened.

He had the irresistible urge to seal her promise with a kiss. How crazy was that?

Julia slipped into the passenger seat of Alex's car, her heart pounding and her stomach doing flip-flops. There had been a moment back there in Alex's apartment when she'd actually thought he was going to kiss her. The look in his eyes... She could see it now, that glitter of desire, want, need. Something inside of her had responded to that look. She'd started to lean forward; then Alex had stepped away, grabbing his keys, calling out orders to go into the hall while he turned out the lights and locked his apartment. He'd obviously thought better of whatever impulse had made him look at her like that. It was just as well. She was engaged. And they were just... She didn't know what their relationship was, but it certainly wasn't close enough to involve kissing.

She cast him a sideways glance. He seemed tense. She didn't know if he was thinking about what had passed between them or worrying about what would come next. And she certainly didn't feel brave enough to ask the question.

A few minutes later Alex drove into Presidio Heights, where stately homes and high-rent apartment buildings lined the ridge above Cow Hollow and bordered the historic Presidio Park. "Your father's friend certainly lives well," Julia commented. "These homes are beautiful."

"Stan moved here a couple of years after my father died. His wife had also passed on. I don't know if he inherited some money or what, but this house is quite a step up from the condo he used to live in. He's the kind of man who enjoys being surrounded by beauty, whether it be art, antique furniture, the perfect gold cuff link, or a woman."

"He didn't remarry?"

Alex shook his head. "He said he never would. I'm sure he has his reasons. Here we are."

Stan's home was located at the top of a very steep hill, a renovated Victorian at least three stories tall. It was impressive and a bit off-putting, Julia thought. She couldn't imagine why a single man, who had to be nearing sixty, would want to live alone in such a large house. Then again, she didn't understand why her own father had sold their spacious, comfortable family home and moved into a small apartment. To each his own, she supposed.

They were halfway down the walk when the front door opened. Stan must have been watching for them. He greeted them with a warm smile. "Hello, Alex."

"Thanks for agreeing to see us," Alex replied.

"No problem. You know you're always welcome."

"This is Julia DeMarco."

"Hello," Julia said, comforted by Stan's friendly handshake. He seemed like a nice man and hopefully was someone who could help them. She paused inside the house, struck by the spotless, sparkling beauty of the hardwood floor in the entry, the ornately carved staircase that led to the second floor, and the tall arched doorways leading into the living room and dining room. "Your home is stunning," she murmured.

"Thank you. Why don't we go into my study? It's more comfortable there. I've got a fire going. It's a bit chilly out tonight, and my old bones get colder these days."

Stan didn't appear old. He was very tall and thin, and dressed in well-tailored slacks and a charcoal gray cashmere sweater. He was obviously a man who liked to dress well as much as he liked to live well. His study was just as impressive as the rest of the house, with dark red leather couches, a thick throw rug in front of the stone fireplace, and an antique desk and chair by a large bay window. She imagined he had an incredible view in the daytime. She sat down on the couch next to Stan while Alex took a chair across from them.

"Now, what can I do for you?" Stan asked.

Alex leaned forward, resting his arms on his knees. "I need some information about someone my father used to know. Her name was Sarah. I don't know her last name, but I'm hoping you do."

Surprise flashed through Stan's eyes. "I thought you wanted to talk to me about the photo of the Russian girl." As he finished speaking, his gaze moved to Julia's face.

She wondered what he saw when he looked at her, but his expression was difficult to read. "We'll get to that," Alex replied. "Right now, I'm more interested in Sarah. Do you know who I'm talking about?"

Stan sat back against the couch. "Your father had a friend named Sarah. Someone he went to school with at Northwestern. Is that who you mean?"

"What was her last name?" Julia asked sharply.

"It was Davis, I believe," Stan replied. "Sarah Davis. Why do you ask?"

"My mother's name was Sarah," Julia answered, the words spilling out in excitement. "But her maiden name was Gregory, or it might have been Davidson. Are you sure it was Davis, not Davidson?"

"I think so. Why?"

"Julia's mother also went to Northwestern," Alex interrupted. "We wondered if our parents knew each other."

"Why don't you ask your mother?" Stan inquired, directing his gaze toward Julia.

"She passed away six months ago."

Stan swallowed hard and a pulse jumped in his throat. "I'm sorry to hear that."

"Can you tell me about the Sarah you knew? What did she look like? Did she and Alex's father have some sort of romantic relationship? Did you know both of them?" Julia asked.

"Whoa, slow down," he said, putting up a hand in defense.

"I'm not sure I have the right to discuss Charles's personal business."

"He's not here to protest," Alex said. "And I can't see why he'd care, unless you know something about him and Sarah that we don't?"

Stan thought for a moment, then said, "I met Sarah twice. She was a brunette, average height, dark brown eyes, very pretty, and quiet. She let Charles do the talking. Their friendship lasted after they graduated from college. He once told me that they had a lot in common."

"Like what?" Julia asked.

"He didn't say."

"Mom thinks he was having an affair with Sarah," Alex interjected. He saw Julia start and knew he'd taken her by surprise as well.

"You never told me that," she said.

"I didn't know the person my mother was referring to was your mother—although we still don't know that for sure since the last names are confusing." A sudden thought occurred to Alex. He was surprised it hadn't occurred to him before. "You don't happen to have a picture of Sarah, do you, Julia?"

"Actually, I think I do." She reached into her purse and pulled out her wallet. She flipped past the pictures of Liz and some other girlfriends. "This was taken at my college graduation." She handed Stan the photo. "Is she the woman you knew?"

"Yes, that's her," Stan said. "That's Sarah Davis."

"Damn," Alex swore.

"What?" Julia asked. She saw a new light in his eyes. "What did you just remember?"

Chapter Seven

Alex took the photograph from Stan and gave it a long, careful look. He finally had the proof they were looking for. But Julia wasn't going to like it.

"What is it?" Julia asked again, her eyes worried. "Tell me."

Alex pointed to the woman in the photograph. "I think I saw this woman talking to my father in Red Square that day in Moscow."

Julia started shaking her head even before he finished speaking. "My mother never went to Moscow. She didn't travel. She was afraid to fly. We never went anywhere that we couldn't get to by car. You're wrong. You have to be wrong."

"I don't think I am," he said gently.

She stared at him with pain and confusion. "But you don't know for sure, do you? You were just a little boy."

"That's true. It's possible that I'm mistaken." He didn't think he was wrong, but something inside of him wanted to get that look of betrayal out of her eyes.

Julia turned to Stan. "Do you know if my mother—if Sarah— was in Moscow when that photograph was taken?"

"I don't know," Stan replied. "Alex was there. I wasn't."

"What do you know about that trip?" Alex asked. "Was there some hidden agenda that I was unaware of?"

"You need to let this go, Alex," Stan said abruptly.

"Give me a reason to let it go."

"It could be dangerous to you, to your mother, maybe even to Julia."

"Be more specific."

Stan's gaze darted away in an evasive manner. Alex was surprised and disappointed. He'd always counted on Stan to be up front with him, tell him the truth no matter what it was. Now he had the distinct feeling that Stan was about to lie to him.

"Your father made several trips to Russia in the two years before he died," Stan said finally. "He was fascinated with the country and the people. He took any opportunity he could to get an assignment over there. He even got you into that theater group, so he could take you with him. He wanted you to see that part of the world, and he wanted you with him. I told him it was a mistake. I believed that Charles was sticking his camera into places where it didn't belong. He had a few run-ins with the government, but we were usually able to smooth things over. I wasn't sure that would always be the case. So I told him to be careful, to follow the rules and not take photographs of anything he wasn't cleared to shoot."

"Like the photo of the girl in the orphanage," Alex said. "What was in that picture that no one was supposed to see?"

"I don't know. Charles wouldn't tell me, but he was upset that the photo had been published. He hadn't realized it was on the roll he sent to the magazine."

Alex knew why, because he'd taken the photo. "What else did Dad say?"

"He asked me to look out for you and your mother if anything happened to him."

Alex felt the hairs on the back of his neck stand up at those strangely prophetic words. "My mother doesn't think Dad's death was an accident. Is that what you're saying, too?"

Stan's eyes filled with regret and guilt. "There were a lot of unexplained details. They couldn't find another car or your father's body. And—"

"They didn't find your father's body?" Julia interrupted, her blue eyes wide with shock. "You never told me that, Alex."

He swallowed hard. "I don't like to think about it." He paused, knowing that he had to explain, even though it made him sick to his stomach to go back to those memories. "They found his car, but everything inside of the car was ripped and washed away, the seat cushions, the steering wheel, the spare tire... It was a twisted shell of metal. I saw it when they pulled it up the side of the cliff. They were still trying to find my dad..." He drew in a much-needed breath. "They searched all the next day. Mom and I waited at the edge of the bluff. I thought I'd see him again. I thought they'd find him swimming or floating the way he'd taught me to float on my back when I got tired."

"Oh, Alex, I'm so sorry," she whispered.

Her words brought him back from the past, and he was grateful. Clearing his throat, he said, "Yeah, well, it's over. Or at least I thought it was over." He shot Stan an angry look. "I didn't know at the time there were so many unanswered questions. Why didn't you get those answers, Stan? You were one of my father's best friends. You should have raised hell if you had doubts. You should have made those detectives work overtime to get to the truth."

Stan's mouth drew into a hard line. "I was going to do just that, but I got a call from a man named Daniel Brady. He was a close friend of your father's, too. He worked for some government agency; I was never sure which one. He was very cagey about who he was and what he did. After your father's accident, Brady told me to back off. He said you and your mother would be in danger if there was further investigation."

"That's bullshit," Alex said, jumping to his feet. He couldn't believe what he was hearing. Stan had suspected that his father had been killed and hadn't done anything about it? That was completely out of character.

"Alex, calm down," Stan said, putting out a placating hand.

"The hell I will. You turned a blind eye because someone told you to? I don't buy it. And you shouldn't have bought it, either. What aren't you telling me, Stan? Because there has to be more."

Stan slowly stood up, so they were looking directly into each other's eyes. "I don't know any more. Frankly, I never wanted to know more. I wasn't like your father. I didn't care about people trapped by a government half a world away. He wanted to help them, but he couldn't, because he was only supposed to photograph them. He was frustrated. I think he decided to take some action that he shouldn't have taken. When Brady told me to mind my own business, I didn't see any point in going against him. I couldn't bring your father back, but I could do what he asked—I could look after you and your mother. And that's what I did."

"My father didn't take that picture. It was me. I took it." Alex paused, seeing surprise in Stan's eyes. "He never told you that?"

"No, he didn't."

Alex paced back and forth in front of the fireplace. Stan's comments raised so many questions in his mind. Even if his father had wanted to take action, he wouldn't have gotten involved in another country's politics... Or maybe he would have. Alex had certainly had similar thoughts in the past year—that taking a picture wasn't enough. There were times when he'd been able to get into places and see things he wasn't supposed to see because he had a press pass and a camera. Had the same thing happened to his dad? Had he seen an opportunity to help and taken it? Had he died because of it?

Or had he died because Alex had taken that picture?

God, how could he live with himself if that were the case? Knowing that he might be responsible for his father's death made his chest tighten and his breath come short and quick. He felt dizzy and had to sit down. Julia was suddenly beside him, her hand on his thigh.

"It's not your fault," she said urgently.

He looked into her blue eyes and saw that little girl again. Maybe it wasn't his fault. Maybe it was hers. He'd been drawn to her then, and he was certainly drawn to her now. If he'd walked away before, none of this would have happened.

"She's right," Stan said. "We don't know if your father's death had anything to do with that photograph."

"It's a hell of a coincidence then," Alex replied. "Let's examine the sequence of events. The photograph is published. My dad comes to me in a panic, making me swear not to tell anyone, and the next day he's dead. Some government agent tells you to back off. Even my mother thinks the accident is suspicious. We're developing a pretty clear picture of what went down. Now we need to figure out why. What was in that damn photo that was so disturbing? Do you have the negative? I asked Joe, and he couldn't find it in the magazine files."

"I assume your mother has it."

"She doesn't."

"Then it must have been destroyed." Stan paused. "It's not important, Alex. It all happened a long time ago. There's nothing to be gained by traveling back to the past. You won't be able to change anything that happened. You can't bring your father back. Sometimes you just have to let go."

"Like you did? You let go too damn fast," Alex said, fixing Stan with a hard glare. He saw Stan's face pale and knew he'd struck a nerve, but he didn't care. The man who'd been like a father to him for most of his life now seemed like a stranger. How could he have failed to push for an investigation into his best friend's death? It was unthinkable, inexcusable. "Tell me something, Stan," he continued when the older man remained silent. "Why did you encourage my mother to put my father's photos in the exhibit, especially the picture of the little girl?"

Stan shrugged. "It's been twenty-five years. There was so much publicity at the time of the photo—people searching for the girl, wanting to adopt her—I didn't think there was anything more to come of it now than had come of it before."

"What happened back then?" Julia interrupted. "When people were searching for the girl, what did they find out?"

"There were inquiries to adoption agencies," Stan answered, "about how the child might be adopted. Someone in the government contacted the orphanage and was told it had no record of the girl. We printed that in the magazine a few weeks later. Eventually the interest died down."

"Someone in the government?" Alex echoed. "Let me guess: Daniel Brady?" Stan didn't have to answer. The truth was written across his face. "Where is this Daniel Brady now?"

"I have no idea."

The answer was smooth, but Alex didn't buy it. "That's funny, because I would have thought that you might have called him as soon as I told you that Julia came knocking on my door last Friday."

A nerve twitched in Stan's neck, and his lips tightened. "What will it take to convince you to drop this search, Alex? The last thing your father would want is for you to keep digging into his personal matters. He wanted to protect you."

"I'm not a child. I don't need protection." He looked at Julia. She hadn't said much during their conversation, but he was sure she had taken in every word. "What do you think?"

"I think we should find out what happened," she replied in a firm, determined voice.

"I agree." Alex got to his feet. "I want to talk to Daniel Brady."

"I'll have him get in touch with you," Stan replied.

"Why don't you give me his number?" Alex countered.

"You can trust me, Alex. I'll let him know you want to talk to him." Stan took a breath. "Is there any way I can ask you not to involve your mother?"

Alex uttered a short, harsh laugh. "Believe me, that's not something I'm considering. She already talked to one reporter about Julia being that girl."

"She shouldn't have done that."

"Well, she did. And now this reporter is intent on finding out Julia's story. Why don't you tell Mr. Brady that?"

"I will."

"Good. Ready?" Alex asked Julia.

She nodded, offering Stan a soft good-bye and a thank-you. Alex didn't feel inclined to offer either. He was almost at the door when Stan called him back.

"Alex, don't go there."

"I have to."

Julia waited until they were in the car, seat belts fastened, engine running, before she asked, "So where are we going?"

"You'll see," he said.

* * *

Julia should have guessed where they were headed as soon as they left the city, but it wasn't until she saw the Pacific Ocean and Alex pulled off at a vista point on Highway 1 that she realized his full intention. Without a word, he turned off the car and stepped out onto the gravel-filled parking area. She hesitated for a moment, wondering if he'd rather be alone. But as she thought about exactly what had happened here, she knew he shouldn't be on his own. She got out of the car and walked over to the waist-high wood railing at the edge of the cliff. The air was colder here, with the wind blowing spray off the ocean.

Her pulse sped up as she looked over the railing. It was a clear night, and the stars and moonbeams lit up the scene below. It was at least a two-hundred-yard steep drop to a rugged beach filled with sharp rocks, boulders, and crashing waves that thundered in and roared out. The ocean took what it wanted... when it wanted. There was no escape, not if one got too close to those powerful waves.

Here, at night, in the dark, Julia could imagine all sorts of terrifying monsters in that black sea, waiting to claim another victim. Instinctively, she took a step back from the railing. She'd never particularly liked heights. She always felt that odd sensation of knowing how easy it would be to slip over the edge. Shivering now as her vivid imagination made her even colder, she wrapped her arms around her waist. She wanted to go back to the car. In fact, she wanted to go home, but she couldn't leave Alex here alone to picture the most terrifying night of his life.

She thought back to his earlier words, when he'd told her how he'd waited on this bluff for the search-and-rescue team to bring up the mangled car and, he'd hoped, to bring back his father, still alive, still in his life. How scared and lonely Alex must have felt. She wondered why his mother had brought him here. Why hadn't he been kept protected at home, surrounded by other loving relatives?

"This is where it happened," Alex said finally, his voice deep and husky, filled with emotion.

She glanced at his hard profile. His gaze was on the beach below, his thoughts obviously in the past. She remained silent, willing him to share whatever he needed to get out. Alex wasn't a man to confide his personal problems. She sensed that he carried most burdens alone, especially the heavy ones, the ones that touched his heart. The fact that he'd even brought her here told her that his defenses were weakening, that his need to find the truth about his father's death was overshadowing his need to stand solitary and strong.

"This is where my dad's car went over," he continued. "All these years I thought it was an accident. He was driving too fast. He liked speed. He always had. The roads were slick. It was raining, and he couldn't see. There were so many plausible reasons why he went over the side of this cliff."

"Those reasons could be true," she offered tentatively. "We don't know for sure that they're not."

"I know. I can feel the truth in my gut."

She didn't know what to say. No words could take away the pain he was feeling, especially now that he thought he was responsible for what had happened. He'd taken that photograph. With that one reckless, impulsive act, he'd put something in motion, something neither of them understood.

"Why were you so damn important?" he muttered, shooting a frustrated glance in her direction.

"I don't know. I wish I did."

"We have to find out."

"We will," she said with determination. Her doubts about her mother and her own past were bigger now, but her resolve was also stronger. She would know the truth, whatever it took. Which brought her back to her own part of the story. "Do you really believe you saw my mother in that square? And don't answer quickly," she added, putting up her hand. "Think about it. Because it's important that you get it right."

He turned to gaze at her, his face a mix of shadow and light. "I'm good with faces, Julia. I know that's not what you want to hear."

"How could my mother have been in Moscow that day?" The thought was inconceivable.

"It makes some sense—if she was friends with my father."

Julia considered that for a few moments. She didn't want to believe Alex was right. She preferred to think he was mistaken. He'd only glanced at the photograph of her mother and herself. And her mother was so average in looks—brown hair, brown eyes. There was nothing spectacular about her. She could have resembled a thousand women. But Julia was afraid to take the rationalization too far. If she were going to try to deny everything they discovered, she'd never get anywhere. So she forced herself to open her mind.

"Let's say she was there," Julia said aloud. "Maybe I was there, too. Maybe my mother put me in that orphanage while she was meeting with your father. She might have thought of it as a day-care center, a temporary babysitter."

"I suppose," he said slowly, but she could tell he wasn't buying her theory.

"It is possible," she persisted. "At least give me that."

"You couldn't have just been there on vacation, Julia. It wasn't easy to visit Russia at that time. Your mother would have had to have a good reason."

"What about that theater group? My mom and I could have been part of the group, too. We should look into that." The more she thought about it, the more that seemed like a possibility.

"Don't you think you would have remembered a trip like that?" he asked.

"I don't remember anything," she said in frustration. "The years before my mother's wedding to Gino are a complete blank. So why would I remember that?"

"Sorry." He paused. "It does seem odd that your memories don't begin until you're adopted by your stepfather. I wonder why you can't remember at least bits and pieces of your earlier years."

She could see where he was going, and she didn't like it. "You think I'm blocking something out, don't you?"

"It's just a thought."

"Fine. If you don't agree with my theory, what's yours?"

"About my father or your mother?"

"Both."

Alex rested his elbows on the railing. "It probably wouldn't have been unthinkable for my father to get caught up in some Moscow intrigue. I've been tempted a few times to step out from behind the camera. I just never knew he felt that way. He always told me that a good photographer stays detached, remains an observer. But if he saw something that bothered him, maybe that would have changed his mind."

"So you think he could have been spying for the government? Isn't that what Stan implied was going on?"

"I'm not willing to go that far. My dad loved photography. He was never without his camera. I don't believe it was just a front. It was a part of him. When he was shooting, he was in another world. I wanted to be a part of that world. I knew that from the time I was a little kid." Alex looked back down at the water and sighed heavily. "I thought I knew my father. All these years I thought I knew who he was. And now he seems like a stranger. How did that happen?"

She could hear the pain in his voice, and it touched her deeply. Alex had followed in his father's footsteps. Now those footsteps were taking him down a path he didn't want to go. He'd thought of his father in one way for so long, he couldn't think of him differently. Just as she couldn't think of her mother as anyone but the quiet, suburban mom she'd grown up with. Trying to picture her mother meeting a man in a Moscow square was impossible.

"At least I know one thing," Alex continued. "My dad's accident was no accident. I should have realized that years ago. One minute he was terrified. The next minute he was dead. That wasn't a coincidence. And it was all because of that damn picture."

A cold wind blew Julia's hair across her face. As she peeled the wet strands off her cheeks, she realized that the fog was coming in. The stars had disappeared. The moon was going into hiding, too, and they were being covered by an ice-cold blanket of mist. It was as if the universe were taunting them, telling them they would only see the truth when it was time, and not a second before. She moved closer to Alex, wanting his warmth, needing his strength. She felt suddenly afraid of what was coming.

She put a hand on his arm. She could feel the muscles bunched beneath his sleeve. He was as tense as she was, and angry, too, furious with himself. It wasn't a reasonable anger, but how could she convince him of that?

"You're not responsible," she told him again. "You were a little boy when you went to Moscow. You took a picture. That's all you did. You can't take the rest of it on."

"My dad told me not to play with his camera," he said, his voice rough and filled with contempt for his own actions. "I didn't listen. If I had, my father would still be alive."

"I know I can't make you feel better—"

"You can't," he said, cutting her off. "Don't even try, Julia. Just stop talking."

She stared at his hard profile. He looked so alone, so lost in his misery. She wanted to help him, but he wouldn't let her. He was a proud man who had high expectations for himself. He didn't tolerate failure or incompetence, and right now he was blaming himself for something he couldn't have prevented.

"It's a terrible feeling, isn't it? To suddenly realize that everything you thought you knew about yourself and your parent might be false."

"Hell of a feeling," he muttered.

"But you're not alone. I'm here. And I know what it's like to suddenly wonder if my life has been built on a lie."

He turned to look at her. She could barely see his face. The fog was thicker now. It surrounded them, dampening their clothes and their skin. She felt as if they were the only two people in the world, lost on an island of shifting truth.

She shivered. Alex opened his arms.

She didn't know who moved first, but suddenly her breasts were pressed against his chest and his mouth was on hers, and she wasn't cold anymore. She was warm, deliciously warm. She took in his heat like a dry sponge, letting it soak into every corner of her body from the top of her head to the tips of her toes. She didn't want to think anymore. She didn't want to try to remember. She wanted to forget... everything.

His lips were salty from the ocean air, his mouth hot, demanding, reckless. All the emotions they were feeling—the sadness, the anger, the need, the frustration—played into the dance of their tongues. Alex's hands tangled in her hair, trapping her in a kiss that went on and on. Everything else was vague and shadowy, but this moment was real, and Julia didn't want to let it go. Finally, they broke apart, their hot breath steaming up the cold air.

"Oh, my God," she said, putting a hand to her still-swollen, tender lips. "That wasn't supposed to happen."

Alex's gaze was locked on her face. "I'm not going to apologize."

"We need to go. Right now." She practically ran to the car. Alex moved more slowly. She had her seat belt fastened by the time he slid into the driver's seat. "Don't say anything," she warned. "Just take me back to your apartment, so I can get my car."

"It was just a kiss, Julia."

It was more than a kiss. She knew that deep in her heart, and she suspected he did, too.

Chapter Eight

After muttering a quick good-bye to Alex at his apartment building, Julia drove home, telling herself that everything was fine. So they'd kissed. It had been a brief, energy-charged moment, a simple release of tension, that hadn't meant a thing to Alex, and nothing really to her. It wasn't a big deal, and she had to stop thinking about it. She had more important matters to worry about: her mother, Alex's father, that damn trip to Russia that seemed to inexplicably connect Sarah to Charles. She still didn't want to believe that Alex had seen her mother in the square that day, but she had to be willing to look at the facts. Sarah and Charles had been friends. She'd start there and move forward. She wondered if Gino had ever heard Sarah mention Charles. It was worth asking.

As Julia paused outside her apartment door to locate her key, she heard laughter coming from inside, male and female laughter. Liz and Michael. She drew in a deep breath, fighting the urge to turn and run. She didn't feel up to dealing with either of them tonight. She felt so conflicted, so mixed up. And she knew they'd only tell her she was crazy and that she should drop the whole thing. But it was late, and they'd worry and probably wait up for her if she didn't show up. She might as well face them now.

Putting what she hoped was a casual smile on her face, she unlocked the door and stepped inside. Liz and Michael were sitting on the couch watching television. A bowl of popcorn was on the coffee table, as well as two glasses and a couple of soda cans.

"It's about time," Michael said, jumping to his feet when he saw her. He ambled over and gave her a kiss. She turned her face just slightly, so his lips caught the corner of her mouth. She moved away quickly, feeling guilty that she didn't want to kiss him, that another man's taste still lingered on her lips.

"What have you two been doing?" she asked him, as she put her handbag down on the small oak dining table by the kitchen.

"Watching Comedy Central. Your sister has a very odd sense of humor."

"It's the same as yours," Liz said from the couch where she stuffed a handful of popcorn into her mouth. "You laughed so hard you were crying."

"No, that was you," he retorted.

Julia smiled at their exchange. "I think I'll make some tea. It's cold outside. Winter is coming."

"The slow season," Michael said, following her into the kitchen; it was barely big enough for one, much less two. "I'll be happy if the rain stays away for another month or two," he added. "I can use the cash. I've been thinking about our honeymoon."

"You're not supposed to tell me," she said quickly, cutting him off. "It's traditionally a secret."

"I want to make sure you like the idea."

"I trust you," she replied. And she did trust Michael. It was herself she wasn't so sure about.

"So, where have you been, Julia?" Michael leaned against the kitchen counter, his arms folded across his chest, a speculative look in his eyes.

She filled the kettle with water and turned on the heat. "I've been trying to figure things out," she said vaguely.

"Liz told me about the reporter who showed up here earlier. Has anything else happened?"

"That's probably the worst of it," she lied. The worst of it was that she'd kissed another man. But she couldn't tell him that. He would only be hurt.

"I took another look at the photograph. Liz showed me the catalogue," he said. "I'll admit there's some resemblance between you and that girl, but there are millions of blue-eyed blondes in the world. And that photo was taken twenty-five years ago. I just don't think it's you, Julia. I think you're reading into it more than you should."

She heard the earnest conviction in his voice and knew he

wanted desperately to convince her of that fact. But too much had happened that he didn't know about. "I'm afraid I do think it's me," she said.

"Why?"

"A lot of reasons. The girl's face, the necklace, the fact that my mother very carefully hid the details of my early life." She waved her hand in the air. "My mother was incredibly secretive. I'm only beginning to realize how much care she took to cover up her past. What I don't know yet is why she felt compelled to do that."

Michael let out a sigh that sounded like a mix of disappointment and frustration. She couldn't blame him. How could he understand when she couldn't?

"Are you sure you're not just latching onto some dramatic backstory to replace the emptiness in your own life?" Michael asked.

It was a fairly insightful comment coming from Michael, who was usually more pragmatic and not inclined to analyze anything. Was she doing that? Was she adding drama to a blank space to make it more interesting, more important? It would be better if she were doing that. Then in reality nothing about her life would be a lie, and there would be no mystery to solve.

"Julia, think about it. You got into this the second we set our wedding date. I think you panicked when you realized that we were finally moving ahead with our plans. You jumped onto the first passing ship, and that photograph was it." He moved suddenly, planting himself in front of her, tilting up her face with his finger so that she had to look at him. "It's okay," he said. "It's all right to admit to being nervous. Marriage is a big step. It's forever. You don't have to make up a reason to postpone the wedding. I'll call the Legion of Honor tomorrow and tell them to cancel the December date. We'll find somewhere else after the first of the year, when you're ready. All right?"

"Yes," she agreed, feeling a weight slip off her shoulders. "Because I can't think about getting married until I know who I really am."

His mouth drew into a taut line. "Julia—"

"I'm sorry, Michael, but my mind is made up. You may be right about some of my motivation, but there's something wrong about the background story my mother gave me, and I can't let it go until I know what that something is."

"No matter who you upset in the process?"

She stepped away from him as the kettle began to sing. She turned off the heat and pulled two cups out of the cupboard.

"Liz was upset earlier," Michael continued. "She was almost crying when she came to see me. She said she was afraid of losing you to your past. With your mother gone, it's tough on her to see you being pulled away."

"I understand. I don't want to hurt Liz, but this is something I have to do."

"You're pulling away from me, too," he said, his eyes troubled. "I thought it was because I was pressuring you too much about the wedding, but is there some other reason? Is it that man who's helping you? Were you with him tonight?"

She wished she didn't have to answer that question, but Michael was waiting. "Alex and I went to speak to a friend of his father's."

"Why?"

"Because apparently there's some connection between his father and my mother. They knew each other in college. We're still trying to figure out the rest."

Confusion ran through his eyes. "I don't understand. Now you're tied to this guy, too?"

"I don't know yet. I have only bits and pieces. Nothing makes sense. That's what I'm trying to tell you, Michael. It's not my imagination. There's something wrong with the story my mother told me about our past."

He considered that for a long moment. "Okay, so why don't you let me help you? I can do whatever he's doing. I can look on the Internet. I can go with you to talk to people."

She was surprised by his offer. "You would really help me, feeling as you do about the matter?"

"I want to be the guy you turn to, not this Alex," he said, with irritation.

"He's involved, Michael. He's my key to the past."

"And that's all he is to you?"

She hesitated for a split second too long. "Of course that's all he is," she said, but it was too late. She saw anger flare in his eyes. "Michael—"

He put up his hand, cutting her off. "No. You've said enough for now. It's clear to me we won't have a reasonable discussion about our future until you get the answers you're looking for, which won't be tonight, so I'm going home. I'm running a fishing charter at five o'clock in the morning. We'll talk tomorrow."

She was relieved to postpone the discussion. "All right."

"Come here." He opened his arms, and she moved into his embrace. He held her tight for a long moment, resting his chin on top of her head. "I don't want to lose you, Julia," he murmured. "I wish you could see that the future is more important than the past."

She didn't know what to say to that. Michael knew everything about himself. He could trace his ancestors back to a villa in Tuscany a hundred years ago. He didn't understand that her world kept shifting beneath her feet. That she had to find something solid to stand on.

He leaned in and kissed her long and hard. She kissed him back, because she really wanted to love him. But there must have been something missing, because when he pulled away he looked even more troubled than before. They had to talk. She had to tell him. They had to be honest with each other.

"Michael," she began again.

He shook his head. "No, not now. I don't want you to say anything until you're sure. I'll see you tomorrow."

Julia blew out a breath as he left. She had a feeling she was sure—sure that she couldn't marry him. But she was so confused. She didn't want to hurt Michael. She didn't want to make a mistake in either direction. She needed time to think. But tonight her mind was too full to concentrate. Maybe tomorrow, in the cold light of day, everything would make more sense.

* * *

"I'd like to thank Guillermo Sandoval for being our guest today," Julia said, smiling at the slim, classically trained Brazilian musician whose group would be playing popular Latin American rhythms later that night at a San Francisco nightclub. "There are still tickets available for tonight's performance. Don't miss Guillermo's intriguing blend of samba, choro, and bossa nova, the music of his homeland. We'll be giving away two free tickets after this message from our sponsor." Julia hit the button to go to commercial and took off her headphones. "Thank you so much for coming," she said as Guillermo got to his feet. "I know eight o'clock in the morning is early for a musician."

He smiled. "I didn't mind. It was my pleasure. Your station has wonderful programs, important music that should be shared with the world."

"I completely agree." Julia escorted him out of the control room as the next on-air host arrived to take over at the microphone. In the lobby, the receptionist offered Guillermo coffee and pastries. Julia stopped by her cubicle to check her messages and found Tracy in her chair, reading the newspaper and eating a doughnut. With only four full-time employees at the station, they were very casual about sharing office space. "What's up?" she asked.

"Not much. Good interview." Tracy popped the rest of the doughnut into her mouth.

"Thanks. Anyone call while you were sitting at my desk?"

"Only about half a dozen people. How did you suddenly get so popular?" Tracy tossed a yellow pad in front of Julia, on which she had scribbled several messages. "Your sister called twice. Michael, your father, and some guy named Alex, who I'm betting is the hunk who came by to see you the other day, also called."

Julia stared down at the list of names. It was early in the morning. What on earth could have happened?

"That guy, Alex, said to call him before you call anyone else," Tracy continued.

That definitely didn't sound good.

"Is this all part of the wedding mania? Or is something else happening?" Tracy asked.

"It's a long story."

"If you need to talk, I'm here. Now I'll get out of your way. Let me clean this stuff up."

As Tracy picked up the newspaper, one of the sections slipped to the desk. Julia picked it up, her heart stopping at the headline and the photograph. "Oh, my God," she murmured. "I can't believe they printed this."

"Printed what?" Tracy grabbed the paper from Julia's hand, then whistled under her breath. "You're a celebrity, girl. Not the best picture of you I've ever seen, but... Wow." She looked at Julia with a question in her eyes. "Is this why everyone is calling?"

"I think so." Julia glanced back at the newspaper, reading the headline again: *FOUND! World's Most Famous Orphan.* How could they print such a thing without any proof? She took the paper back from Tracy, flipping to the page with the article, where there was another photo of Julia as well as one of Alex. The story focused on the exhibit and the fact that one of Charles Manning's most famous subjects was now living in San Francisco. They gave her name, spoke of DeMarco's Seafood Cafe, and finally admitted that, while the photographer's widow, Kate Manning, said they were almost convinced that Julia was the orphan girl, proof had not been clearly established.

"Is it true, Julia? Are you her?" Tracy asked.

"I don't know. What I do know that is no one should have printed this article without concrete evidence."

"They always print gossip in this section. It's what sells the newspaper."

"Well, they shouldn't print anything that isn't a fact. This story could hurt a lot of people—my father, my sister, Michael." She shook her head in frustration. She should have realized that once the reporter had a photo of her, she would probably print it. "Dammit, what am I going to do?"

Tracy offered her a compassionate smile. "I have no idea, but I think you're about to be rescued by the cavalry."

Julia looked up to see Alex stride through the front doors of the office, a grim, determined expression on his face.

She ran out to the lobby to meet him, the paper still in her hand. "I just saw this. I had no idea they would run a story based on nothing."

"I know. Are you all right?"

She shook her head, feeling completely overwhelmed. Her head was spinning so fast she was dizzy. She didn't know what to do first, where to turn. When Alex held out his arms, she moved into his embrace without a second thought. He pressed her head to his chest, and she closed her eyes, feeling for the moment that she was in exactly the right place.

Unfortunately, the moment ended far too soon. "I did some research this morning on your grandparents," Alex said, stepping away from her. "I found Susan Davidson, the surviving spouse of Henry Davidson. I called her on the phone and asked her if she had a daughter named Sarah."

Julia's eyes widened. She'd been thinking about contacting Susan Davidson, but hadn't quite found the nerve to take that step. "What did she say?"

"She said Sarah died twenty-five years ago in a fire."

"No!"

"She also said that Sarah attended Northwestern and not a day went by but that she didn't miss her daughter."

Her nerves began to tingle. "Did she know about me?"

He shook his head. "No. She said Sarah died single and alone. Then she started crying and had to hang up."

"That doesn't make sense," Julia murmured. "Twenty-five years ago I was three years old. And my mother said that her parents disowned her when she had me, so why would they have thought she was all alone? Wouldn't they have wondered what happened to the baby? To me? It must be a mistake. This Susan Davidson is not my grandmother."

"I think she is," Alex said, refusing to go along with her.

She met his gaze and saw nothing but confidence. "Why? We don't have any evidence."

"Sure we do. Don't start running scared again, Julia."

She bristled at his brisk tone. "I'm not doing that. I'm examining the facts."

"No, you're trying to twist the facts, undo the connections, but you can't. Your father gave you the names of your grandparents, Henry and Susan. They had a daughter named Sarah, and she went to Northwestern. It all matches."

Maybe it did. Maybe she was just scared to connect the dots. Thinking about vague, nebulous grandparents was different than actually speaking to them.

"But you're right," Alex continued. "We shouldn't jump to conclusions without further investigation. That's why I bought two plane tickets for Buffalo, New York. We're on the ten-forty-five flight, and if we're going to make that flight, we need to leave now."

Her jaw dropped in amazement. "Are you out of your mind? I can't go to Buffalo."

"Of course you can. Even with the time difference and a short layover in Chicago, we can be there by eight o'clock tonight."

"What about my family? I can't leave them to fend for themselves, especially with this article in the newspaper." She dreaded having to return calls to Liz and Michael, who would probably not be happy about this latest development.

"Without you the story will die down faster," Alex argued. "Tell them to say, 'No comment,' until you get back. This is the best lead we have, Julia. We have to take it."

"What about Daniel Brady?"

"Haven't heard from him. I left Stan another message. They both have my cell phone number. We'll be back tomorrow."

Julia hesitated for a long moment. It was one thing to move along in her daily life and do a little research, but flying across the country was a big step. Still, the sooner she got some answers, the better. And she was curious about whether or not this woman was her grandmother. "Did you tell her about me?" she asked. "Did you tell her we were coming?"

"I didn't get a chance. She hung up too fast. I can go on my own if you'd rather stay here. I thought you might—"

"Want to meet her," Julia finished. "I do. If she is my grandmother, she's probably the only person who can tell me about my mother. I need to stop by my apartment and pick up some clothes. And I'll bring the necklace and the matryoshka doll. Maybe she'll know where they came from."

"And some photographs of your mother," Alex said. "I want to make sure we have the right woman."

* * *

It was just after eight o'clock in the evening when they landed in Buffalo. Julia was glad she'd grabbed a coat before leaving San Francisco. The northeastern air was much colder, and the clouds were threatening rain, maybe even snow, and it was only September. She couldn't imagine her mother, who had shivered in sixty-degree weather, living on the East Coast with its long and brutal winters. Maybe that was one of the reasons why she'd never gone back. But deep down Julia suspected her mother's reasons had nothing to do with the weather.

Alex rented a car and put Julia in charge of the map as they made their way out of the airport. They'd decided against calling Mrs. Davidson in advance. Since Alex had spoken to her that morning, at least they knew she was in town, and hopefully she would be at home. Julia still couldn't quite believe that she'd jumped on a plane and flown across the country with barely an hour's notice. But she was already glad that she'd come. No matter what they learned, at least she could see the city where her mother had spent the early part of her life.

It turned out that her grandmother didn't live in Buffalo proper but in the nearby suburb of Amherst, an upscale neighborhood with gracious old homes set back from the street, lots of trees, and beautiful yards. Alex parked in front of a white two-story house with light blue shutters and colorful floral window boxes. Julia wondered if this idyllic place was where her mother had grown up. It was hard to believe she would have turned her back on such a home, or on her parents, for that matter.

Before they could get out of the car, a woman came through the front door. The light went on as she crossed the porch to pick up the newspaper. She was a small woman, barely five feet, with short, dark brown hair. She wore a burgundy velour warm-up suit, her feet in tennis shoes. Was this her grandmother?

Julia bit down on her bottom lip, feeling suddenly terrified to talk to the woman.

"Showtime," Alex said.

"Don't say it like that," she snapped at him. "This isn't funny. This is my life."

She could tell by his expression that he thought she was overreacting, but he was wise enough not to say so. "Are you ready?' he asked instead.

"No, but I don't think that will change in the next few minutes." Julia glanced out the window and saw the woman giving them a curious look. She probably wondered why they were parked in front of her house. Julia stepped out of the car and moved up the walkway. "Mrs. Davidson?" she said in what she hoped was a friendly voice.

"Yes. Who are you?" the woman asked warily. "I won't be buying anything."

"And we won't be selling anything," Alex said, flashing her a reassuring smile.

Julia saw Mrs. Davidson relax under that smile. The man could certainly put on the charm when he wanted to. "We'd just like to speak to you for a few moments," Julia told her.

"About what?"

Julia hesitated, not sure how to begin. "About your daughter," she said finally. "Sarah."

Mrs. Davidson gasped and put a shaky hand to her heart. "Sarah?" she echoed. "Why would you want to talk about Sarah?" She turned to Alex. "You're the man who called this morning, aren't you? I told you my daughter is dead, and I really don't care to talk about her with strangers. If you'll excuse me—"

"Wait." Julia drew in a deep breath, knowing there was no easy way to deliver the news. "I'm not a stranger. Sarah was my mother."

"No." The woman began to shake her head, her eyes wide in disbelief. "No, that's not possible. Sarah was killed in a fire. She didn't have any children. You're thinking of another Sarah."

"Show her the photo," Alex advised.

Julia reached into her purse and pulled out the photo of her mother and herself taken at her college graduation. She handed it to the older woman. Mrs. Davidson moved so she could look at it under the light. Alex and Julia followed, waiting for her reaction. It wasn't long in coming.

As she studied the photo, her breathing came short and fast. "That's her. That's Sarah, my baby girl." She lifted her head to stare at Julia in bewilderment. "She's older in this picture. I don't understand. She died twenty-five years ago."

Julia swallowed hard. "No, she didn't. That picture was taken seven years ago. I have others, some from last year and the year before."

"She's alive? Where is she? I want to see her."

Damn. She hadn't phrased that right. "I'm sorry, but I should have started by saying that my mother died six months ago."

A flood of emotions ran through the older woman's eyes. She opened her mouth to speak but no words came out. Then she began to sway. "I—can't—breathe."

Alex grabbed the elderly woman just before she hit the ground. He swung her up into his arms and carried her into the house.

"Oh, my God!" Julia felt incredibly guilty. Had she caused her grandmother to have a heart attack or a stroke? She wasn't a young woman. She was thin and frail, and she'd lost her husband only a short time ago. Julia immediately regretted blurting out the news about her mother without any warning. "I shouldn't have said it like that," Julia murmured. "I should have softened the blow."

"There was no way to do that." Alex set Mrs. Davidson down on a floral-print sofa in the living room, pulling a pillow under her head. He put his finger against her pulse and bent his head to check her breathing. "I think she just fainted."

"Maybe I should get some water or a cold towel."

"Good idea."

"I hate to walk around her house, though. It's not like she invited us in."

"Well, we're in now," Alex said. "And since she identified Sarah as her daughter and your mother, then you're family."

"I can't believe it." Julia stared down at her grandmother. Her skin was pale, her face lined and wrinkled, especially around her eyes and mouth. Judging by her reaction, she'd obviously loved Sarah very much. But why on earth did she think Sarah had died in a fire? And why had Sarah said her parents disowned her because of her pregnancy? Julia had so many questions. She wanted her grandmother to wake up, to give them some answers. But they would have to go slow. The woman was probably in her early eighties. Who knew how strong she was? "Do you think we should call 911? What if something is really wrong with her?"

"She's coming around," Alex said.

Sure enough, her grandmother was moving her arms and legs. She blinked a few times, then opened her eyes, her expression more dazed than before. "What—what happened?"

"You fainted," Alex said gently, as he knelt beside the couch. "Right after we told you about Sarah."

Susan stared at them both, then struggled to sit up. "I don't understand any of this. Who are you people? Why are you here? Is this some kind of a cruel joke?" Anger entered her voice.

"It's not a joke." Julia sat down on the other end of the couch while Alex stood up and backed away, giving her grandmother some space. "My name is Julia DeMarco. My mother, Sarah, told me years ago that her parents disowned her when she got pregnant with me. I always believed that to be the truth until Alex called you this morning and you said that Sarah died twenty-five years ago."

"She died in a fire," Susan began, then stopped. "But that picture you showed me... Can I see it again?"

Julia handed her the photo and watched the myriad emotions cross Susan's face as she studied the picture. She traced Sarah's figure with a shaky finger.

"This is her, my baby, but she's so much older than when I last saw her."

"She was fifty-one then, fifty-eight when she died this year."

Susan started shaking her head again. "She was thirty-three when she died. I know, because it was right after her birthday. We got a call from Chicago," she said haltingly. "A woman we didn't know. She said she was Sarah's next-door neighbor and that she had horrible news. There had been a fire in their apartment building. Sarah didn't get out. There was nothing but ash when it was over." Her voice caught and she struggled for control. "I couldn't believe Sarah was dead. I thought it was a nightmare, and I would wake up, but I didn't." She turned to Julia, her brown eyes big, pleading, filled with pain. "Why? Why would anyone tell me that she was dead if she wasn't?"

Julia swallowed hard, her heart breaking at the agony on her grandmother's face as she relived the moment when she'd heard her daughter was dead. Only now she had to grapple with the fact that Sarah hadn't died then. She'd lived for another twenty-five years, but she'd never gotten in touch. Why not?

"My mother said that you turned her away when she got pregnant," Julia said again. "Do you know why she would have told me that?"

Susan's face was a portrait of confusion. "I don't know. Sarah was pregnant once, when she was twenty-seven years old. She had an ectopic pregnancy, in the tubes, you know. She had a lot of complications. The doctor said she'd never have children after that. She was devastated by the news. Her boyfriend left her. He couldn't bear the thought of marrying her and not having kids. It was a very sad time."

Julia couldn't believe what she was hearing. "But she had me, and she had another child, too, my little sister, Elizabeth. She had two pregnancies after that one."

"How old are you?" Susan asked.

"I'm twenty-eight. My mother was thirty when she had me.

How could you have not known about me? That would have been three years before she supposedly died in that fire."

Susan started to speak, then began to cough, choking on the emotion, Julia thought, as her grandmother's cough turned to sobs. Susan struggled to get up. "I have to..." She didn't finish her sentence, but they could hear her crying all the way to the bathroom.

"This is awful. We're killing her," Julia whispered. "I don't know what to do."

"You can't stop now," Alex said. "You're in the middle of it, and she deserves to know the truth, too, don't you think?"

"Maybe she would have been happier not knowing. I'm ruining her life. Her daughter lied to her and never visited her or spoke to her in twenty-five years." Julia shook her head, not understanding how her mother could have done such a thing. The woman who had raised her had been kind, gentle, and compassionate. How could she have turned her back on her family? Unless there was some misunderstanding... That had to be the reason. Sarah had obviously believed the Davidsons didn't want her. Why?

"I wish my grandfather was still alive," she said to Alex. "Maybe he knew more than he shared with his wife."

"Somebody knew something," Alex said. "If we ask enough questions, maybe we'll get to the truth."

"This is hard."

"Just stay focused on what we're trying to accomplish."

She eyed Alex thoughtfully. "Is that what you do when you're in a difficult situation—you simply put your heart on hold?"

"It's how I survive."

"I don't know if I'm made that way. I hate hurting people."

"In the long run you might be helping her. She may have lost her daughter again, but she's gained two granddaughters. That should be worth something."

She smiled at his attempt to make her feel better.

"That didn't work, but I appreciate the effort." She rose as Susan walked back into the room with a box of Kleenex. Her eyes were red and swollen now, and she appeared to have aged ten years since they'd arrived, but she wasn't crying anymore. That was something. "Are you all right?" Julia asked.

"I don't think so. But I want to hear the rest of your story."

"I'm glad," Julia said, offering her a thankful smile. "It means a lot to me."

"You're really my granddaughter?" There was a note of wonder in her voice, but no sign of anger or disappointment.

"I think so. Why don't we sit down? We can start at the beginning, wherever that is."

"Why don't we start with Sarah and her years at Northwestern," Alex suggested as Susan and Julia took seats on the couch.

Susan twisted a Kleenex between her fingers as she considered Alex's question. "Sarah was in Chicago a long time. After she got her bachelor's degree, she went to graduate school to get a master's degree. She wanted to work at the United Nations, something important like that. She always had big dreams of changing the world. She used to sit with my mother for hours, listening to her stories of life in the old country. I think that's where her passion for the language began. She would often call my mother on the phone just to practice her accent."

Julia's heart skipped a beat. She had the terrible feeling she knew what accent Sarah had been practicing. She looked to Alex and saw the same gleam in his eyes.

"What language did Sarah speak?" Alex asked.

"Didn't I say? I'm sorry. My mother was Russian. Sarah spoke fluent Russian."

Chapter Nine

Julia couldn't stop the gasp that slipped through her lips. "Your mother was Russian?"

"Yes, my mother came over to this country right before the revolution. She never lost her accent or her desire to speak her native language. I'm afraid I didn't share that desire. It embarrassed me that my mother spoke a foreign language, but Sarah was different. My mother came to live with us when Sarah was a teenager. They loved each other very much. They had a special bond." Another tear drifted down her cheek. "My mother died when Sarah was twenty-four. It was a very difficult time for her. They were so close." She wiped her face with her tissue.

It was too much to take in, Julia thought. She had so many questions, she didn't know which one to ask first. She got up and paced around the living room, too restless to sit. She walked over to the mantel and picked up a photograph of Susan and a man who was obviously her husband.

"That's Henry," Susan said. "He died last year."

Julia picked up another photograph, one of Sarah as a little girl, sitting at a piano—the same piano that was in the corner of the living room. "She told me she didn't know how to play the piano," Julia murmured.

"Really? Sarah was very good at it," Susan said.

"It's strange. I've seen the picture, but I don't feel as if we're talking about the same person."

"I don't, either," Julia replied.

"Tell us what happened after Sarah got her master's degree,"

Alex interrupted. "What kind of work did she get?"

"She got a job teaching Russian at a university," Susan replied. "She fell in love with a professor there. He was the father of the baby she lost. After he broke up with her, she quit her job, and I'm not sure what she did next. She told me she was traveling, taking time for herself. We didn't see her much, a handful of visits in three years. Then she was—gone."

"You never had a fight or disagreement that harmed your relationship?" Julia asked.

Susan shook her head. "Nothing. The last time we spoke she said she loved me very much."

"When was that conversation?" Alex asked.

"About two weeks before they told me she died."

Alex frowned at her answer. "Didn't you ask questions? Didn't you inquire into the circumstances of her death?"

"Alex, give her a chance to explain," Julia said quickly. Alex wasn't nearly as emotionally involved with Susan as Julia was, and she wanted him to take it easy on her grandmother.

"I'm sorry. I don't mean to push you. I just wonder how you came to believe Sarah was dead."

"Henry asked all the questions. He went to Chicago, and spoke to the police. They said the fire was due to a spark near a gas can. There was an explosion. By the time the fire department got there, the town house was engulfed in flames. Sarah was the only one at home. Her roommate was actually out of the country at the time. So she escaped..." Her voice broke, and tears began to stream down her face once again.

"It's okay. You don't have to say any more," Julia told her.

"When Henry asked to see her... they said there was nothing left to see." Susan drew in a deep, painful breath. "We buried her ashes in the cemetery down the road. I've gone there every year on her birthday. I pray for her and I talk to her and tell her about our family, our life." She sniffed as her mouth crumpled once again. "How could she have been alive and not let me know?"

Julia had no idea how Sarah could have let her mother suffer the way she had. For twenty-five years she'd kept her silence, allowing her mother to believe she was dead. Unless... was there another explanation? Had there been a third party involved in the deception? Had Sarah been told her parents didn't want her at the same time her parents were being told she was dead? Was that even remotely possible? There was a time discrepancy. And that time was what bothered her the most. Sarah had supposedly died when Julia was three years old, about the time that photograph was taken. But Sarah had always told Julia that her parents had disowned her when she became pregnant.

"I just can't understand why Sarah would have hurt me that way," Susan added, dabbing at her eyes. "I thought I'd cried out all my tears, but they just keep coming."

"I'm so sorry," Julia said, feeling helpless in the face of such terrible grief. "I shouldn't have come here and dropped these revelations on you."

"You said I have another granddaughter, too?"

Julia nodded. "Elizabeth. I call her Lizzie. She and I have different fathers. I don't actually know who my father is, but my mother married Gino DeMarco when I was five years old, and nine months later Lizzie came into the world. She's twenty-two now. And she's beautiful. She looks a lot like our mother."

"You don't look anything like Sarah," Susan said.

Julia knew Susan didn't mean anything by her somewhat harsh words, but they still stung. "She used to say I had her nose and her long legs, but you're right. We really didn't look much alike."

"And she told you that we disowned her?"

"That's what she said."

Susan shook her head in disbelief once again. After a moment, she asked, "Where do you all live?"

"San Francisco."

"That's so far. How did Sarah end up in San Francisco?"

Julia could only shrug. "She never spoke of her past. She said it was too painful. And she kept her silence up until the day she died."

"How did she pass?"

"She had breast cancer. She fought hard for two years before she lost the battle."

Susan's eyes teared once again. "My mother had breast cancer. They shared that, too." She paused for a long moment. "I'm glad Sarah got to be a mother, that she found love." Her voice was heavy with sadness. "I'm sorry she didn't want her father and me to be a part of her life. That I'll never understand."

Julia looked to Alex for help. She didn't want to say any more. It seemed as if every word that came out of her mouth only brought her grandmother more pain.

"Maybe we should go," he suggested.

"No, don't go," Susan said suddenly. "Not yet. I have so many questions to ask. Do you have any other photos of your mother?"

Julia nodded. "Yes, I brought several with me. I was wondering if you had any pictures of her when she was a little girl."

"Upstairs." Susan stood up. "I'll show you everything I have, and you'll tell me about your life together. And maybe somewhere we'll find some answers."

* * *

It was after midnight by the time they left Susan's house and checked into the hotel near the airport. Julia was exhausted but also wired. She'd seen her mother's bedroom as well as dozens of photographs of Sarah as a little girl. She'd learned about her grandfather, grandmother, and assorted relatives. They'd shared stories and tears. Alex had been as patient as a saint through it all. She glanced at him now as they took the elevator to the third floor and walked down the hall to their adjoining rooms, wondering what he was thinking.

"Are you going to go to sleep right away?" she asked. "I feel like talking."

"That's all you've been doing for the last four hours." He unlocked his door and opened it. "Aren't you talked out yet?"

"Not really. We probably bored you to death, didn't we?"

He shrugged. "It wasn't too bad."

"I guess I'll see you in the morning." She checked her watch. "Which is in about five hours. Good night."

"Good night."

She walked into her room and set her purse and a small overnight bag on the table. Sitting down on the edge of the bed, she flipped on the television, but it was late and there was nothing on but infomercials. She turned off the set, knowing she should just go to bed, but her head was spinning with everything she'd learned. She smiled when she heard a knock on the connecting door. Opening it, she said, "Did you change your mind?"

"I can't sleep either." Alex walked past her and sat down on her bed. He stretched out his legs, resting his back against the headboard and patted the mattress next to him. "Why don't you sit down?"

She hesitated, her instincts telling her that that could be a dangerous move. They'd been so caught up in the search, she'd been able to ignore her attraction to Alex. But now they were alone in a hotel room, and the kiss they'd shared the night before was back in her mind.

Had that been only last night? So much had happened since then.

"What's the matter, Julia? You look worried."

"I'm engaged."

"Yeah, you've mentioned that a few times."

She sat down on the side of the bed, deliberately putting some space between them. "I should call Michael and Liz, too. They're both probably wondering where I am. And I have so much to tell Liz."

"I thought you left messages for them."

"I didn't say where I was, just that I'd be home tomorrow."

"Sounds like a good message to me. Do you really want to tell them over the phone?"

She thought about her options. With the time difference, it would be only nine o'clock in San Francisco. Still, what would she say? That she was in New York with Alex, that she was at this moment sharing a bed with him? That didn't sound like a good idea. They would be back tomorrow. It would be easier to explain everything then.

"You're right. This information should be delivered in person. I'll talk to them both tomorrow." She didn't like his knowing smile. "What? Why are you grinning at me like that? Did I say something funny?"

"You keep making excuses not to talk to your fiancé. Don't you ever ask yourself why that is?"

"I've been a little busy lately. And what do you know about it anyway? Have you ever been in love? Ever been engaged, married, or shacked up with someone?"

"Do they still call it 'shacked up'?"

"You know what I mean. Don't be evasive."

"Have you heard the phrase 'it's none of your business'?"

"That doesn't apply to us. We're friends, and friends share."

"You don't have many male friends, do you?"

"What? Is your love life a secret?" She pulled her legs up beneath her, sitting cross-legged on the bed, so she could face him. "There must have been a serious girl at some point in your life. You're in your thirties, right?"

"Thirty-four," he said. "There have been a few women, one serious. We lived together for about a year when I was in my twenties. She wanted more than I could give her. End of story."

She eyed him with interest, pleased he was finally telling her something. "She wanted marriage?"

"A house, kids, the whole deal. But I was just starting my career. I knew I wasn't ready for any of that. I thought she might wait, but she didn't." His voice was dispassionate, cool, but there was something in the tightness of his expression that told Julia he wasn't as uncaring about the failed relationship as he pretended to be. "After that, I focused on work and put relationships on the back burner."

"It sounds kind of lonely, Alex."

"Believe me, it's not," he said, the grin back on his face.

"I'm not talking about sex. I'm talking about relationships."

"That's the difference between men and women. We want sex. You want a relationship. I realized a long time ago that I'm not cut out for the married life. I like to be free—just like my father."

"But your father married your mother," she pointed out.

"Yeah, and look how well that turned out," he said in a voice filled with sarcasm.

"You're not your father. Maybe things would be different for you now that you're older. You're established in your career. You're successful. Maybe it's time to try another relationship."

"Are you volunteering?"

"No." She immediately squashed that idea. "I'm—"

"Engaged. Yeah, I got that. You're on your way to a permanent address, what every woman wants."

His arrogance put her back up. "How do you know what every woman wants? That's a very generalized statement."

"That's what you want, isn't it?"

She started to answer yes, then stopped. Is that what she

wanted—a permanent address? She'd been raised to want that. But did she? Did she really?

"It's not that difficult a question, Julia," he said dryly.

"I was going to say yes, but the truth is I'm not sure what I want anymore. Every girl grows up thinking about marriage, a home, and babies. I know I want children someday, but not anytime soon. I have things I want to do first."

"Like what?"

"Travel. I want to see some of the world. I'd also like to get my radio show nationally syndicated. And there's this charity that brings music to poor children in other countries. They provide musical instruments to those who can't afford them. I run a concert in San Francisco that helps out the charity, but I'd like to do more. I believe that music brings a peace and a harmony to people, that it inspires and heals and..." She paused at his smile. "Too much information?"

"Not at all. I like it when you get fired up about something. Your eyes sparkle."

"I'll admit I'm a fanatic about music. When I play a piece on the piano or bang out a rhythm on some drums or just listen to a song on the radio, it changes me. It makes me feel better, more powerful and capable, less stressed. It transforms my life for those brief moments. I want everyone to have a chance to feel that way. Is there something wrong with that?"

She didn't know when his opinion had become important to her, but it had, and she seemed to wait forever for him to respond. She licked her lips in nervous impatience and saw his gaze drop from her eyes to her mouth, and just like that the air between them became charged with electricity.

"Alex?" she prodded. "You were going to say?"

"I have no idea. You distracted me."

She swallowed hard at the desire flaring in his eyes. "Maybe you should go back to your room."

"Just when things are getting interesting? Weren't you the one complaining that I always stop in the middle of a conversation?"

"Which you just did. I was telling you about my passion, and you didn't even respond."

"Oh, I responded all right," he said. "Believe me."

She felt a warm flush wash over her cheeks. "That's not what I meant."

"You want to know what I think, Julia?"

She slowly nodded. "Yes."

"I think you're the most fascinating, beautiful woman I've run across in a long time. I like your passion for music. I like that your dreams are big and bold. And I like the way you lick your bottom lip when you feel things you shouldn't feel—the way you're doing now." He held out his hand to her. "Come here."

Her breath caught in her chest. She couldn't. It was tempting, but it was wrong. "I can't."

He swung his legs to the floor and moved so quickly she didn't realize his intention until his arms came around her shoulders and his face moved within inches of her own. "You know what an engagement period is for? To figure out if the person you're going to marry is the one you really want."

"I think it's just supposed to give you time to plan the wedding," she said somewhat desperately.

"I want you, Julia. I think you feel the same way, even though you're fighting it as hard as you can."

"Even if I did want you," she said breathlessly, as his mouth moved closer to hers, "it would be a fling for you, a one-night stand. You said yourself that's not what I'm about." But wasn't that exactly what she wanted right now? His hands were stroking her back, his breath hot on her face, his mouth so temptingly within reach. Every instinct she had was telling her to go for it.

Her cell phone rang, the sound hitting her like a splash of cold water in the face. She jumped back. Alex's hands fell to his sides.

"Saved by the bell," he mocked. "Are you going to answer it?"

She grabbed the phone out of her purse and saw it was Liz. "There's no way I can tell her where I am right now. She wouldn't understand. I don't understand." She stared at him, feeling as angry with him as she was with herself, because he was confusing her even more. "I'm supposed to be in love with Michael. I don't know why I want you so much," she said honestly, "but I think you need to go back to your room."

"What I need is you. One kiss."

"It won't stop there."

"It will—unless you don't want it to."

"You're the devil, you know that?"

"I've been called worse. Don't you want to be sure, Julia? If you're really supposed to marry your Michael, then this won't bother you at all."

Before she could answer, his mouth covered hers with a purpose and determination that cut through her defenses. She might have been able to fight him, but she couldn't fight herself, too. She wasn't that strong. One kiss, she thought. Then she could get him out of her system.

* * *

"Julia still isn't picking up her phone," Liz complained. Michael didn't answer. He was busy scraping wallpaper off what would be the master bedroom in his new house. His shirt was unbuttoned, and there was a fine layer of perspiration across his chest. She drew in a deep breath and forced herself to look away and focus on the matter at hand. She'd been calling Julia off and on all day, but aside from one brief message from her sister stating that she was on to a new lead, there had been nothing but silence. "I need to talk to her about the newspaper article. And a man called our apartment earlier. He had a heavy accent, and he asked for Julia. His voice made my skin crawl." Which is why she'd come running to Michael's house.

Michael paused, wiping the sweat off his forehead with the back of his hand. "What kind of an accent?"

"He sounded Russian. Just when I start believing that Julia is completely crazy to think she's that girl in the photograph, something happens to change my mind."

"I need a beer," Michael said. "You want one?"

"Absolutely." She followed Michael down the hall, into the family room/kitchen. "Hey, what's with the sleeping bag and pillows?" she asked, pointing to the pile in the corner.

"I've been sleeping here. That way I can work late and start early."

"On the floor?"

"It's not that bad," he said with a laugh. "Did anyone ever tell you you're a spoiled brat?"

"I think Julia has mentioned it a few times."

He opened a beer and handed it to her. "I don't have any glasses."

"This is fine."

Michael leaned against the counter as he sipped his beer. "Tell me more about the phone call. What did the guy say?"

"He asked for Julia. No, wait. He twisted her name. It sounded like 'Julia.' I said she wasn't home. He asked me where she was, when she would come back, if she had a cell phone number he could contact her on. He said he had to speak to her immediately. I tried to put him off. He got agitated, started saying something in Russian, I guess. Then the line went dead. I think he was calling from a pay phone. There was a lot of background noise." She shook her head, feeling edgy and restless. Too much was happening too fast, and she was in the dark about most of it. "I really need to talk to Julia."

Michael nodded. "I'm sure she'll call you back."

"She hasn't so far. This isn't fair, Michael. She stirs up a hornet's nest, then leaves me to fight off the stinging bees."

He smiled at that. "You do love to be dramatic."

"I'm not being dramatic. My life is spinning out of control. So is yours, in case you hadn't noticed."

"I've noticed," he said heavily. "But Julia is worth waiting for."

Liz wasn't so certain of that. The last few days seemed to be pulling Michael and Julia farther and farther apart. Michael was renovating a house and planning for the future. Julia was digging up skeletons and searching for her past with a man who wasn't her fiancé. She wondered why Michael wasn't more bothered by that fact.

"Why don't you help me scrape some wallpaper," Michael suggested. "It will take your mind off your problems, and I could use the help."

The last thing she wanted to do was scrape wallpaper. Then again, she didn't particularly want to go home, where the doorbell and the phone would keep ringing with mysterious strangers laying claim to her sister. "Fine," she said. "On one condition: We work for an hour, then play some cards."

Michael loved blackjack. In fact, he'd been the one to take her on her first casino trip to Lake Tahoe after her twenty-first birthday. Julia had stayed on the beach while Michael had shown Liz how to play craps, blackjack, and poker. She'd been hooked ever since. "I have cards in my purse," she said.

"You carry cards with you?"

"I have to admit I was hoping to talk you into a game. On your break, of course. I know you're obsessed with this house."

"I am obsessed with it," he admitted. "It's the first place that's mine. I've been living with my family my whole life. I've never had a place of my own. This is what I've always wanted."

"It's a great house."

"Julia will like it, don't you think?"

For the first time she heard some doubt in his voice. "Sure, she'll love it."

"You're just saying that, aren't you?"

"I don't think it's the house you have to worry about," she told him.

He frowned. "I know, but the house is the only thing I can control at the moment. Julia is the wild card."

Chapter Ten

"Enough," Alex said, breaking off the kiss. He jumped off the bed, running a hand through his wavy brown hair.

Julia blinked, dazed by the last few minutes of passion and desire. "What?"

"This is..." He waved his hand in the air as if he couldn't come up with the word. "A mistake," he said finally. "I don't poach on another man's turf. What the hell am I doing? And what the hell were you doing—kissing me like that? How can you say you're going to marry a man, then kiss someone else like your heart is up for grabs—or at least your body."

She bristled at his accusatory tone. "You're the one who pushed me into a kiss. This wasn't my idea. You started it."

"You weren't fighting it. You were kissing me back."

"You took me by surprise."

"Yeah, well, the surprise ended more than a few minutes ago."

She stared at him, and then sighed. "You're right. I kissed you back. I couldn't stop myself. I'm a terrible person."

"Why don't you break up with this guy, Julia?"

"Because it's complicated. Michael stood by me through the worst months of my life. He held my hand while I watched my mother die. He comforted me. He did whatever I asked. He was a rock."

"So you say, 'Thank you.' You don't say, 'I do.' "

"My mother loved him. She was so happy the day we got engaged. She told me Michael was everything she'd always wanted for me. It was the first time she seemed proud of me. She didn't encourage my love of music. In fact, she discouraged it. She thought the radio station job was silly. She wanted me to get married, have kids, build a family of my own."

"So you said yes because of your mother?" he asked in amazement. "I still haven't heard a good reason. Do you love the guy at all?"

"Of course I love him. I just said that, didn't I?"

"Actually, you didn't. You said you owed him and it made your mother happy."

"I do love him. Michael is wonderful. He's probably too good for me."

He stared at her for a long minute. "So what's this about? You have a fling with the bad guy, then you marry the good guy, and everything works out great for you? What happens when you get tired of the good guy—are you going to have an affair?"

"I would never do that," she said, jumping to her feet in anger. "What kind of woman do you think I am?"

"I don't know. More importantly, I don't think you know. You are probably the most confused person I have ever met."

"You're the one who confused me because you took my damn picture twenty-five years ago." It felt good to yell at him, to let off some steam.

"And I am sorrier than I can ever say."

She sighed as he began to pace around the room. "What are we doing, Alex? We're both exhausted. We're not thinking rationally. We should call it a night and get some sleep."

"I'm not going to sleep. I'm too wired, even more now than I was before," he said. "You have a way of doing that to me, Julia."

She knew the feeling. She felt edgy and her stomach was churning. "Let's turn on the radio."

"Why?"

"Because there's probably some good music on. It always helps me relax." She knew she was probably about to make another mistake, but it seemed to be a night for mistakes. "I don't really want to be alone. Would you stay? Just hang out with me, no touching, no kissing."

His hesitation was obvious.

"It's a big bed." She sat down on one side of the bed and placed two pillows in the middle, building a little barrier. "I'll stay on my side. You stay on yours."

"You trust me to do that?"

She didn't even hesitate. "Yes."

He debated for another second. "Fine. I'll stay."

"Good." She turned on the radio, running through the stations until she heard a violin and viola playing Mozart's Duo in B-flat Major. "Isn't this beautiful?" she asked, leaning back against the bed. Already she was feeling better.

Alex stretched out on his side, resting his head on his elbow. He listened for a moment, then said, "It's nice."

"Nice? That's a lukewarm word. There's a perfect harmony between the two instruments, a pure, splendid tone. It's so powerful I can feel the music within me."

"It's nice," he said again with a small smile. "I prefer a saxophone or a trumpet, something announcing its entrance into the piece."

"I could find something else."

"No, this is fine. You like it. That's good enough for me."

She stared up at the ceiling, letting the music take the tension out of her shoulders, her neck, her entire body. She tried not to think about everything that had happened that day. There was too much to absorb, too many revelations to analyze.

"Julia?"

She turned her head to look at Alex. "Yes?"

"Beautiful."

"That's a better adjective for the music than nice."

"I wasn't talking about the music," he said, with a dangerous look in his eyes. "I was talking about you."

Oh, God. She had a feeling those pillows between them weren't going to be enough to keep them apart. She drew in a deep breath, then closed her eyes, conflicted over whether she wanted Alex to make a move or not. She heard him shift on the bed. Her body tensed, and then she realized he'd turned away from her. Was he angry? Should she say something?

"Relax, Julia," he said a moment later. "We don't have to figure out everything tonight. There's always tomorrow."

* * *

After an almost six-hour flight, they landed in San Francisco just after eleven o'clock Tuesday morning. Alex was used to traveling and sleeping very little, but he had to admit he was tired. They'd only had a few hours of sleep the night before. And that sleep had been more than a little restless. Lying next to Julia with just a few pillows between them had been quite a test of his self-control. It wasn't the right time—for either of them. He should never have kissed her, never given in to that impulse. But the more he got to know her, the more he liked her, and the more he found her irresistible.

At least their trip had been a success. Julia had found her grandmother. They'd learned quite a bit about Sarah's past. Now they had to concentrate on unraveling the rest of the secrets.

His cell phone rang as they were walking out to the parking lot, and he didn't recognize the number. "Hello?" he asked warily, not sure whom to expect.

"Alex Manning?" a man asked.

"Yes."

"This is Daniel Brady, Alex. I saw the photo in the newspaper, and I spoke to Stan Harding. I think we need to talk."

"We certainly do."

"Can you meet me at the Cliff House in a half hour? I'll buy you a drink."

"All right. I'll be bringing Julia with me."

"I wouldn't have it any other way. See you then."

"Who was that?" Julia asked as he ended the call.

"Daniel Brady. He wants to meet us in thirty minutes."

Her eyes lit up. "That's great news. Finally, everything is clicking into place."

"Let's hope so."

* * *

A layer of fog hung over Ocean Beach, painting the sky a dull gray. Alex parked in the lot next to the Cliff House, a historic three-story restaurant overlooking the Pacific Ocean and Seal Rocks, where the sea lions came to play. Set at the most western edge of San Francisco, the Cliff House also offered a view of the large ships about to sail under the Golden Gate Bridge, into the harbor of San Francisco. Alex had visited the restaurant once before when he was a child. His father had told him stories about the restaurant and its once-famous neighbor, the Sutro Baths, an extravagant public bathhouse built in the 1800s that was later turned into a seaside amusement park. The baths and the amusement park were long gone, but the restaurant remained.

As soon as they got out of the car, an older man stepped from a charcoal gray sedan parked across from them. Dressed in casual tan slacks and a long-sleeve brown shirt, he appeared to be in his sixties. His light brown hair was thin on the top and cut short. His stomach had a bit of a paunch to it. He had a cigarette in his mouth, which he quickly stubbed out as he approached them.

"Alex, you look well."

He didn't know why he was surprised or unsettled by the fact that the other man had recognized him. "Daniel Brady?" he asked.

"That's me." Brady offered Alex a smile and removed the dark glasses that covered his brown eyes. "And you must be Julia. I saw your picture in the paper. It didn't do you justice." He paused. "I know I offered to buy you a drink, but something has come up, and I won't be able to stay. Why don't we take a walk and talk for a few minutes?"

Alex fell into step alongside Brady, with Julia following a step behind. "Why have I never heard of you?" he asked. "Stan said you were a good friend of my father's, but I don't recall your name ever being mentioned. And I know we've never met before."

"Your father and I saw each other when we were both on assignment, usually in another country."

"So you do work for the government?" Alex asked. "Do you happen to have any identification?"

Brady chuckled at that question. "I've got a driver's license. Will that do?" He paused and pulled his wallet out of his back pocket. "You're not as trusting as your father."

"Since he's dead now, I'll take that as a compliment," Alex said sharply. There was something about Brady—maybe his smug smile, or his knowing manner, that irritated him. He took the license from Brady's hand and gave it a quick glance. The face was the same. The address was in Maryland. "You're a long way from home."

"I always am."

"What about a government ID?"

"What I do doesn't require ID. I've been on the job for thirty-seven years now. I can get you a character reference if you feel you need one."

"What exactly do you do for the government?" Julia asked.

Alex watched Daniel closely, wondering how he'd react to such a pointed question.

Daniel simply smiled and said, "That's classified, I'm afraid." He slipped his license back into his wallet, then into his pocket.

"If you can't answer that question, maybe you can answer this one," Julia continued. "Am I that girl in the photograph?"

"I can see why you might think so," Daniel replied. "But even if you believe you're that girl, you must say you're not. You must call the newspaper and tell them they're mistaken. Any other reporters you speak to must get the same comment."

"Why?" Alex asked sharply. "Why should she lie?"

"For her own safety." Daniel's expression turned somber. "The photograph revealed something that was supposed to be hidden, but your father didn't know that. He made a mistake. He paid for it."

Alex felt his heart stop. Stan had implied that his father's accident had been a result of the photograph, but he wanted to hear Daniel Brady say it. "Are you telling me my father was killed because of that picture?"

Daniel hesitated for a long moment, then said, "His accident was highly suspicious. The only reason I'm telling you that is because Charles was my friend, and you're his son, and he wouldn't want the same thing to happen to you."

"That's not good enough. Who killed my father? Who ran him off the road? Tell me, dammit." Alex took a step closer to Daniel. He wanted to grab Brady by the collar and shake him until the truth came out. "I'm tired of vague innuendos. I want the facts. And I want them now."

"I've told you all I can tell you, Alex, without putting you in danger."

"To hell with that. I can take care of myself."

"And Miss DeMarco? Do you want to risk her life as well as your own?"

"I can take care of myself, too," Julia replied. She shot Alex a look that told him to keep going and not back down. He intended to do just that.

"If you won't tell me about my father's death, then tell me about the picture," Alex demanded. "What do you know about it that I don't?"

Daniel glanced around, as if he was worried about being overheard, but they'd moved a hundred yards away from the restaurant, and there was no one in this part of the parking lot. "I want to help you, Alex, but I'm caught between a rock and a hard place. I don't know if you know this, but your father saved my life once. I was a young agent. I got into some trouble in Germany. Your father came to my rescue. I owed him. And the day after that photograph was published in the magazine he contacted me. He said he was calling in my debt. He wanted me to protect you. I promised him I would."

"In case you haven't noticed, I'm a grown man. Whatever promise you made ended a long time ago."

"I don't think so."

"Look, Julia's picture has been printed in the newspaper. This story is coming out whether any of us want it to. If you know something, you need to tell us, so that we're not stumbling around in the dark. I think my father would appreciate the need for you to be honest with me."

Daniel thought for a moment. He looked away from them, gazing out at the ocean. Alex wondered if he was thinking about Charles having met his end in that same ocean, just a few miles away. The sea was waiting for an answer, and so were they.

Finally Daniel looked back at them, his jaw tense, his eyes wary. "All right. I'll tell you this much. I believe Julia is the girl in the photograph."

Alex's heart fell to his stomach. He'd suspected that was the case ever since Julia had knocked on his door, but now someone was actually saying it out loud. He glanced at Julia and saw shock and fear on her face.

"Are you saying my mother was there?" Julia demanded. "Did you know her, Mr. Brady? Did you know my mother?"

"Yes, I knew her a long time ago," he admitted. "Sarah was in Russia with the theater group. She worked behind the scenes as a costumer."

"Oh, my God. She was there." Julia turned to Alex. "My mother was there. You did see her. I didn't want to believe you, but you were right."

Alex was surprised that Brady had told them about Sarah. "So Sarah's identity and the reason why she was in Russia aren't classified?" he challenged.

Brady shrugged. "I barely knew the woman. She was friends with Charles and Stan. Stan helped her get into the theater group."

"She must have taken me with her," Julia said. "I must have gotten a Russian visa or whatever as part of the tour, just like you did, Alex. And she must have put me in the orphanage so someone would watch me while she was meeting with your dad."

Alex still wasn't sure he bought Julia's scenario, but he looked to Brady for the answer. "Is that true? Did Sarah leave Julia at the orphanage for some reason?"

Brady hesitated. "That sounds right."

He was lying. Alex's gut instinct told him the man was lying. "Then why would anyone care that Julia's picture was taken? She was an American girl."

"She wasn't supposed to be there. Certain places were off-limits to foreigners. No one wanted to acknowledge that there were orphans in the Soviet Union, and they certainly didn't want photographs taken of such venues. That's why the government denied all knowledge of the girl." He paused. "Now, will you let this go? There's nothing more to know."

"Of course there is," Alex said harshly. "No one killed my father because there weren't supposed to be orphans in Moscow. What was the real reason? And who did it?"

"I don't know who did it. Whoever took him out was a pro."

"I don't understand," Julia said, interrupting them. "Why would anyone kill Alex's father after the picture was printed? What could they possibly gain from that? The deed was already done. What was revealed was revealed."

"That's an excellent point," Alex said slowly. "Why would anyone have gone after him then?"

"It was punishment. Payback. They'd given him access to their country. He'd abused their trust."

"Who the hell is *they*?"

"I've told you everything I can. Drop this line of inquiry, Alex, before someone else gets hurt."

"What about my mother?" Julia asked. "She was in Moscow,

too, and if I was the girl in that photo, and she was connected to me, then she should have been in danger, too. But no one came after her. Did they?"

A pulse jumped in Brady's throat. "I don't know. She was lucky, I guess."

"Lucky?" Alex echoed. "That's your answer?"

"Sarah went into hiding after that picture was published. Her cover was good."

"Her cover was good?" Julia repeated, as if she couldn't believe what she was hearing. "You're talking about my life, my stepfather, my little sister, the past twenty-five years we lived with my mother, with Sarah. It was a cover?"

"It sounds like you had a good life, Miss DeMarco. Maybe you should leave it at that."

"I can't. Not until I know who my mother really was."

Brady glanced down at his watch. "I'm sorry, but I have to go."

"You can't leave yet," Julia protested. "I have more questions."

"They'll have to wait," he replied.

"What if we need to talk to you again? How do we get ahold of you?" Alex asked.

"Call Stan. He knows where to find me."

"How does he know?" Alex asked suspiciously. "How are you and Stan friends? Was Stan involved in whatever went on in Moscow, too? You said that he got Sarah into the theater group. What exactly was his role?"

"Stan was your father's editor."

"I know that, but what did he have to do with setting up cultural exchanges in Moscow?"

"Stan is a patron of the arts," Brady said with a secretive smile. "He worked behind the scenes of many cultural exchanges in Russia and other countries. Why don't you ask him about it?"

"I think I will," Alex said slowly. He thought back to his conversation with Stan and knew that the other man had definitely not shared any of his own involvement in that Russia trip. Why? Was he hiding something else?

"I do need to go," Brady said. "If you want to reach me, call Stan. I'll get back to you as soon as I can. I want to be of help to you and Julia—whatever you need. The most important thing is that you both back out of this, get rid of the press, and go on with your lives." That said, he turned and walked to the car.

"What do you think?" Julia asked when they were alone.

"He was lying at least some of the time."

"I agree, but which part of the time? The time when he was talking about my mother or your father... or about Stan?"

"Hell if I know." Alex dug his hands into his pockets and stared out at the ocean. "My father was murdered. That's what I know for sure."

"I'm sorry, Alex," she said quietly. "But it still wasn't your fault."

"It was someone's fault."

"Let's take a walk on the beach," Julia said. She kicked off her high-heeled sandals and rolled up the cuffs of her blue jeans.

"I don't want to walk on the beach. It's foggy, it's cold. And we should be doing something." Although he couldn't quite think of what that something was.

"It's not as cold as Buffalo. The sand will feel good between your toes. And we need to think before we act. Come on, Alex."

"Fine." Alex slipped off his tennis shoes and socks and followed her onto the sandy beach. For a while they just walked, absorbing the sounds of the waves crashing on the shore, the seagulls squealing as they dipped in and out of the water, and the low drone of a small airplane cruising along the coast. As the minutes passed, the fog began to lift, rays of sunshine peeking through. By afternoon it would probably be completely sunny, but for now Alex appreciated the fog. It mirrored the way he felt inside. There were sparks of light in his brain, but still a thick curtain wouldn't let him see all the way to the truth.

The cool, moist sand felt good beneath his feet. The sensation brought him back to reality, grounding him in the present, taking him away from the past. He couldn't remember the last time he'd walked on a beach. He'd always been too busy for such simple, time-wasting pleasures.

He paused as Julia bent over to pick up a shell. Her long, thick, wavy blond hair blew loosely about her shoulders, and he itched to put his hands through her hair again, the way he had the night before, trapping her face to his kiss. His gut tightened at the memory. Julia was a beautiful woman. It was no wonder he was attracted to her. Unfortunately, it wasn't just her body he found immensely appealing; it was her personality, her willing-to-try attitude, her determination to know the truth even if it hurt, her curiosity in the outside world, and her kindness, her compassion, her softness—a softness that would probably get her into trouble if she trusted the wrong people. He would have to make sure she didn't do that. He would have to protect her.

But first he had to figure out who the wrong people were. He walked down to the water's edge, thinking once again that the sea held the answers. His father had died in this ocean, his hopes and dreams for the future lost in the waves. All because of a photograph. How could he ever forgive himself? His father's death was all his fault. And there was no way to change any of it.

A sharp wind picked up off the ocean, spraying his face with water. For a split second he wondered if his father was trying to tell him something. Was he wrong? Was he buying into a story that someone was trying to sell him? Why should he believe Daniel Brady or Stan or even his mother? None of them had given him one ounce of proof.

"Help me," he muttered. "Help me figure out what to do next. Should I talk to Brady? Should I talk to Stan? Is there someone I'm not thinking about?"

A large wave took shape, growing in size and power as it rolled toward the beach. It crashed against the sand just a few feet away, the water coming all the way up to him, washing his feet and the bottom of his jeans in water. Was it some sort of answer?

"A little cold for wading, isn't it?" Julia asked, as she came over to him.

"I didn't move fast enough."

"You didn't move at all. What are you thinking, Alex?"

"Nothing."

"I don't believe you. I know you're hurting inside, and you're not the kind of man who admits that. You like to be big and strong and invincible. And you hate it when you're not."

She had that right. He hated feeling weak, powerless, the way he did right now. The hatred had begun a long time ago when his parents had told him that they were separating, that his father wouldn't live with them anymore, that he'd only see him occasionally. And those powerless feelings had grown after his dad died, after the funeral, after he was left alone. So he'd created a life for himself in which he was in control. He worked for himself. He called his own shots. He decided when to go and when to stay. Everything had worked fine... until now.

"It's hard to lose a parent," Julia continued. "When my mom died, I felt as if I'd lost my right arm. I didn't think I would ever feel whole again. I can't imagine what that would have felt like if I'd been a child, as you were when your dad died, especially since your mother isn't the warm and fuzzy type."

"I hated her," Alex admitted. "For a long time I wouldn't even talk to her. I blamed her for keeping me away from my dad, for the year I'd lost while they were battling for a divorce. I even thought she'd driven him out that night, on that wet, rain-slicked road. I believed they'd had a fight and he was driving too fast. I guess I was wrong."

"You don't sound sure."

He turned to her. "I'm not sure. Everyone lied before. Who's to say they're not lying now?"

She shook her head, understanding in her eyes. "I don't know. Do you think Brady was lying about my mother being in Russia?"

He knew she wanted a different answer than the one he could give, but he had to tell the truth, at least the way he saw it. "No, Julia. I'm sorry, but I think your mother was in Russia."

"I don't want to believe it."

"It makes sense that she was there. Think about it. She was friends with my father. Her grandmother was Russian. She was passionate about the country, fluent in the language. Of course she was there."

Julia frowned. "Then I must have been there, too."

"Yes."

She lifted her chin, a light of battle coming into her eyes. "Okay, then. She was there, and I was there. We have to find out why. What next?"

What to do next—that was a hell of a question. "You could do what Brady said—lie, tell everyone you were born and raised in Berkeley, and that you never left the country. Then you'll be free of this mess. You can marry your Michael and live happily ever after."

"With my past buried in a mystery? That's not me, Alex." She paused. "Actually, that was me. I never had the courage to look at myself in the mirror and question who I was. I let my mother die without asking her the questions I wanted to ask. I was too scared. And I'll tell you something: I'm still scared. But I'm not walking away this time. I'm going to follow this trail to the end of the road—even if that road leads me all the way to Russia."

Chapter Eleven

When Julia entered her apartment she found Liz sitting at their kitchen table with the sewing machine out and a pile of fabric all around her.

"Hey," Julia said tentatively as she set her bag on the floor. She wasn't sure what to expect from Liz. She'd received a dozen messages on her cell phone begging her to call, but she'd kept putting it off, wanting to talk to Liz in person. Now she wished she'd done it over the phone. Her sister's attention was focused on the material she was stitching, and Liz gave no indication that she'd even heard Julia come in. She was obviously angry.

"What are you working on?" Julia asked, stalling with trivial conversation. Although she was a bit curious about what Liz was planning to do with the yards of floral fabric spread out in front of her.

"A project," Liz muttered. She stopped sewing and glanced at Julia. "So you finally decided to come home. What's the occasion?"

Julia sighed at the tone of Lizzie's voice. She was tired from her trip, confused about everything she'd learned. She didn't want to fight with Liz, but she had a feeling it was inevitable. "I left you a message that I was staying with a friend," she said.

"Does this friend have a name? Oh, wait, let me guess—Alex Manning."

"We were following a lead. In fact, I have some news to tell you."

"I'm not really interested, Julia. Since it's obvious you don't care what I'm doing, I don't care what you're doing."

Julia pulled out a chair and sat down across from her. "Don't be like that, Liz. Don't make this hard."

"Is that what I'm doing?" Liz asked, hurt in her big brown eyes. "How could I be making your life difficult when I haven't seen you in twenty-four hours? Did you ever consider that my life might have gotten harder when you disappeared and the press had no one to follow but me and Dad?" Liz began to pull the pins out of the fabric, her movements jerky and angry.

"Have they been bothering you?" Julia asked, feeling guilty. "I am sorry, Liz. I thought they'd wait until I surfaced again."

"Where did you go?"

"I went to Buffalo, New York."

Liz's jaw dropped. "You're kidding. You went all the way across the country yesterday and came back today?"

Julia nodded. "I found our grandmother."

Liz stabbed herself with a pin and yelped. She put her finger in her mouth, licking off the drop of blood.

"Are you okay?" Julia asked.

"What did you just say?"

"I found our grandmother, Susan Davidson, the woman I read about in the obituary."

Liz swallowed hard, then sat back in her chair, drawing in a deep breath of air. "I can't believe you went to see her without telling me."

"I wasn't sure you'd support me," Julia replied.

"You're right. I wouldn't have supported you. Dammit, Julia, it's one thing to screw up your own life.

Why do you have to mess up mine, too?" she asked. "I was finally feeling normal after a year of uncertainty, and now you're turning everything upside down."

Julia heard the pain in Liz's voice and wished she could make it better instead of worse. But there didn't seem to be any way to get to the truth about her own life without touching on Liz's life. She had to make Liz understand that there was a positive side. After all, they now had a grandmother they hadn't had before. That was something. She reached for her handbag and pulled out the photos Susan had sent back with her.

Before she showed the photos to Liz, she needed to tell her the rest. "There's something else you have to know. Mrs. Davidson thought that our mother died twenty-five years ago. She was told that Sarah perished in a fire."

Lizzie's face was a picture of confusion. "I don't get it."

"Mom let her parents believe she was dead." Julia didn't know how else to put it. She and Alex had run through a number of scenarios, including the fact that maybe someone else had intervened, making both Sarah and Susan Davidson believe the relationship was over for different reasons. But who that third person would have been was unexplainable. "I don't know exactly what happened," Julia said as Lizzie remained silent, obviously digesting the news. "Mom said that her parents disowned her. Mrs. Davidson told me that Sarah died in a fire. One of them lied, or someone else lied, but the bottom line is that Mrs. Davidson knew nothing about us or our life with Sarah."

"Stop calling her Sarah. She's Mom," Lizzie complained.

Julia nodded, but she knew that she was starting to think of her mother as Sarah more and more, maybe because it helped delineate the person that her mother was before she'd married Gino. "These are photographs of our grandparents and Mom when she was little." She set the stack down on the table in front of Liz. "You look a lot like Mom when she was younger."

Liz hesitated. She stared at the photos as if she were afraid they would jump up and bite her. "I don't think I want to look at them."

"They won't go away just because you don't look."

"Don't push me," Liz snapped. "You're the one who's always whining about feeling rushed. Can't you see you're doing the same thing to me?"

"I'm sorry. You're right. I've had more time to think about this than you have. If it helps at all, Mrs. Davidson is really nice, and it was clear to me that she adored Mom."

"Then why did she disown her?"

"She said she didn't do that," Julia repeated. "She didn't even know about me. The last she knew was that Mom was single and alone. She didn't even believe Mom could have kids because of an ectopic pregnancy she'd suffered a few years before I was born."

"She must be lying. Or maybe this Mrs. Davidson was hiding something. She and her husband could have done something horrible to Mom when she was a child. Maybe she was abused or something..." Liz waved her hand wildly in the air as she tried to come up with reasons for the confusion.

"I honestly don't think Mom was abused by our grandparents," Julia replied. "Mrs. Davidson couldn't stop crying when she found out who I was. She couldn't understand why Sarah would have wanted her to think she was dead. She loved her so much."

"Then why would Mom have lied to us? If you don't think Mrs. Davidson is lying, then you think Mom did."

"I'm afraid I do," Julia admitted, even though it hurt to say the words. "Mom must have had her reasons. She told Gino the same story, that her parents had told her she was dead to them after she got pregnant with me. She never veered from that story."

"So there's something we're missing," Liz said. "I don't think we should take this woman's word over Mom's word. We don't know Mrs. Davidson at all."

"She'd like to know us. She'd like to come out and meet you— when you're ready," Julia amended quickly when Liz began to shake her head.

"That's not going to happen. I don't need another grandmother, especially one I don't trust. Mom didn't want us to know them. That's good enough for me. I don't even care about her reasons. She always wanted to protect us. Whatever she did had to be for that purpose."

Julia wished she could have such blind faith in their mother, but there were too many details blurring the picture of the mother she'd known. "There's more, Liz."

Liz put up her hand. "Please, stop. I don't want to hear more."

"Mom majored in Russian in college," Julia said, ignoring her plea. "Her grandmother, our great-grandmother, was a Russian immigrant. Apparently they spoke fluent Russian together." Liz didn't want to believe her. Julia could see the denial in her eyes. "Don't you think that means something?"

"I don't know what it means. You're driving me crazy. You have so many questions about everything. Why can't you just love the things you have, the people with you, instead of always wanting more? Why can't you be satisfied for once in your life?" She jumped to her feet. "I have to go to work."

"Don't run out, Liz. We need to talk about everything."

"No, we don't. Here's what I think. You do what you want, and leave me out of it."

Liz grabbed her keys and purse and strode from the room. Julia stared after her, wondering how they had gotten so off track with each other. During the past year they'd been closer than close, sharing the work it took to keep their mother comfortable and happy. Now they were as far apart as they had ever been.

Liz would say it was Julia's fault. Maybe it was. Maybe she did want too much.

But unlike Liz, she couldn't turn a blind eye to the lies that had been told. She'd spent her whole life stopping herself from asking the questions that mattered, afraid she would hurt her mother. But her mother was gone now, and it was time she got the truth—the whole truth.

* * *

Stan didn't seem surprised to see Alex when he showed up at his front door. "I thought you might come by," he said, waving Alex into the house. "Did you meet with Brady?"

Alex nodded, following Stan once again into his study. "We did. He basically confirmed what you suggested, that my father was murdered."

"I'm sorry, Alex. Do you want to sit down? Can I get you something to drink?"

"No, thanks." Alex paused. "There's something that's been bothering me since I left Brady."

"What's that?"

"He said you were friends with Sarah, that you got her the job with the theater company, and that you, in fact, were one of the primary players in setting up the whole trip. He also said it wasn't the first time you were involved in a cultural exchange between our countries. Why didn't you mention that when Julia and I were here on Sunday?"

Stan frowned, his lips drawing into a tight, irritated line. "Brady shouldn't have told you that."

"Because it isn't true, or because you didn't want us to know? You told Julia and me that you'd only met Sarah twice. That was a lie."

"There weren't many more meetings than that," Stan said. "My involvement with Sarah was limited. Charles told me she was excellent with a needle and thread. The group needed several costumers, so she was recommended for the trip."

"What about the exchange itself?"

"I made a couple of calls."

Alex suspected it was more than a couple of calls. Stan was being far too evasive. "Were you in Russia with my father?"

Stan walked around the desk by the window and sat down, putting up a barrier between them. He pressed his fingertips together, then said, "No, of course not."

The words were delivered in a firm, steady tone, no hint of a lie. Alex had no reason not to believe Stan, but he couldn't shake the uneasy feeling that he hadn't asked exactly the right question. Still, Stan had been his father's closest friend, and even after his dad's death, he had kept in touch. He'd made the effort to come to Alex's games, his high school graduation. Stan had helped him get his first camera, his first job. Alex had never believed they had anything but a completely honest relationship. Now because of a few small details, he had doubts.

Alex sat down in the chair in front of the desk. He picked up a pen and twisted it between his fingers. "Tell me more about your connection to the theater group."

Stan tilted his head to one side. "I made a few calls with government officials that facilitated the exchange. I did it for Charles. He was the driving force behind the entire effort. He obviously had another agenda besides photographing the event."

"Which you must have known at the time."

"I suspected," Stan admitted, "but I didn't ask questions."

"You should have. What about Sarah?" he continued. "Did she have Julia with her when she went to Russia? Because it's becoming very clear that Julia is that girl in the photo."

Stan shrugged. "I didn't know anything about Julia. I have no idea why she was in that orphanage, if she is in fact that girl. I do know the photo was a problem for Charles. He didn't tell me why, except that he was furious it had been printed without his knowledge. I already told you that, Alex."

"How could you not know if Julia was with Sarah? Brady said you were friends with both of them. And you must have helped the performers acquire papers for their travel."

"That wasn't my job. And Brady is mistaken. I wasn't friends with Sarah. Charles was. Everything that involved her was done through him."

"What about this theater group? Can you put me in touch with anyone who was on that trip with my dad and Sarah?"

Stan's mouth turned down in a displeased frown. "Alex, please, just drop it already."

"That's not going to happen, especially now that I know my father was murdered to keep him silent about something. He might have lost his voice, but I haven't. And I'll speak for him when I know the truth."

"That kind of reckless behavior could get you silenced as well."

"I'll take that chance."

Stan shook his head. "You're just as crazy as your father. He always thought he could beat the odds, too, but look what happened to him."

"You should have found his killer twenty-five years ago, Stan. You should have looked harder."

Anger flared in Stan's eyes. Alex felt a momentary flash of guilt, but he quickly discarded it. He wouldn't take back his words. It was the truth. Stan should have made sure the investigation continued, instead of letting the government shut him up.

"I don't understand why you didn't," Alex added. He waited for Stan to offer an explanation, but he remained silent, so Alex came up with his own answer, an answer he didn't like at all. "Did they threaten you? Was that it?"

"Leave it alone."

"I can't, dammit," Alex said loudly, bringing his fist down on the edge of Stan's desk. "Why can't I get a straight answer from anyone?"

"The night your father died, I received a message on my answering machine. The voice was garbled, but the message was clear. If I asked any questions, my parents would be killed. I'd already lost my wife. And Charles was gone, too. There was nothing to be gained by pursuing the truth. It wouldn't have helped you or your mother. Charles wouldn't have wanted you to grow up thinking he'd been murdered. I know that for sure." He gazed into Alex's eyes. "Would you have made such a different decision?"

"Yes, I would have seen justice done for my friend," Alex said without hesitation. "Is that it—the whole truth?"

Stan hesitated for a split second too long. "That's it," he said. "Now will you let it go?"

"No, because unlike you, I don't have anything to lose."

"What about Julia? Are you willing to risk her life? And the lives of her family, her sister, her stepfather, her friends?"

Alex's eyes narrowed. "How do you know so much about her?"

"Brady filled me in."

"Of course." Alex stood up. "I want to talk to someone in that theater group who was in Moscow. Where do I look?"

A brief pause followed his question; then Stan said, "The Sullivan Theater Group out of Los Angeles. I'm sure you can find their number. A woman named Tanya Hillerman sits on their board now. She was an actress during the Moscow tour."

"You had that information on the tip of your tongue," Alex said, wondering why.

"I figured you'd be asking. You're stubborn as hell." Stan rose from his chair. "As you said, you're a grown man now and capable of making your own decisions, so I'll leave you to it. Just be careful. Don't underestimate the enemy."

"I wish I knew who the enemy was."

* * *

Alex made the call from his car after retrieving the number for the Sullivan Theater Group from Information. After working his way through a receptionist and a secretary, he was given a number for Tanya Hillerman. As he waited at a red light, he punched in her number. The phone rang three times before a woman's voice came over the line.

"Hello," she said.

"Tanya Hillerman?"

"This is she. May I help you?"

"I hope so. I'm interested in speaking to you about a cultural exchange that took place in Moscow twenty-five years ago."

"Who are you?' she asked, an edge to her voice now.

"Alex Manning." He heard her sharp intake of breath.

"The photographer? I thought you died."

"That was my father, Charles," he said. "Is that who you're thinking of?"

"Oh, yes, Charles. You're his son. The little boy who stood at the back of the stage and tried to blend in with the scenery."

"That's me," he said wryly. He had hated that brief stint on the stage. Even though he hadn't had a speaking part, he'd felt very self-conscious. He was much more comfortable behind the lights than under them.

"What did you want to ask me, Mr. Manning?"

"I assume by what you just said that you were there."

"You don't remember me? I was the star, you know. I actually played out a death scene on stage. It was my trademark. No one could die like me. It was very slow and painful to watch, but I enjoyed it."

Alex didn't know how to respond to that. He cleared his throat. "Can you tell me if you remember a costumer named Sarah Davidson or Gregory?"

"Sarah? Let me think. There were a few girls who worked behind the scenes. Was she the dark-haired girl with the big brown eyes?"

"You tell me."

"I do remember a woman like that. She was very quiet, and new to the company, but excellent with a needle and thread. That was the first and only trip she made with us. She didn't continue on with the company after that trip."

"Do you know if she had a child with her, a little girl?"

"There were some children in the company like yourself, Alex. I don't know if one of them belonged to this Sarah." She paused. "I'm surprised you're not asking me more questions about your father."

He stiffened. "What should I be asking?"

"Well, I always thought your father had other reasons for being in Russia—reasons that had nothing to do with our theater exchange. It was even rumored that he might be some sort of a spy. I thought it was very dangerous and sexy. I flirted with him madly, but he never flirted back."

"He wasn't a spy; he was a photographer. And he was married," Alex added pointedly. Defending his father came naturally, but as he did so, he wondered if he had the right. Tanya

Hillerman was the third person to imply his father was a spy. Could they all be wrong?

"I think he said he was separated," Tanya continued. "It didn't matter. He wasn't interested in me. He had more important things to do. I knew it even if he didn't say it." She paused. "It was a different world back then. No one trusted anyone, especially over there. The KGB watched us like hawks, worried we would tempt some of their artists with our American ways. It was terrifying at times. Your father and I spoke about it once. He had such passion for the Russian people. I worried that it would get him into trouble. Up until that trip, I'd never not been free, but that week I felt trapped. I never wanted to go back there. And I never have. When did your father pass away?"

"A few weeks after that trip," Alex said shortly.

"He was so young, so vibrant. How did it happen?"

"A car accident."

"Oh, dear. That's terrible. Such a shame. He was a very talented photographer."

"Yes, he was."

"Are you still involved in the theater, Mr. Manning? If you grew up to look like your father, I imagine you'd make a wonderful leading man."

"No, I'm not in the theater. I'm a photographer, just like my dad." He hung up the phone, wondering if that was true. He'd always thought he'd followed in his father's footsteps. Maybe he hadn't. Because right now those footsteps seemed to be leading him far away from what he'd always believed to be true.

* * *

Christine Delaney, the reporter from the *Tribune*, was waiting in the lobby of the radio station when Julia finished her show Tuesday afternoon. As soon as she saw Julia, Christine put up a hand in apology. "I'm sorry about the hit-and-run photo the other day."

"I don't think you're sorry at all," Julia replied. "And I have nothing further to say to you." Julia tried to sidestep around her, but Christine got in her way.

"I've done some research, Miss DeMarco. I found someone who used to work at the orphanage in Moscow where your picture was taken."

Julia couldn't believe what she was hearing. "You contacted someone in Russia?"

Christine's smile was smug. "Actually, the woman lives in the United States now. She came over about six years ago. She was a cleaning woman at the orphanage. She didn't want to talk to me at first, but I assured her that I would keep her anonymous."

"Why would you do that?" Julia asked suspiciously.

"Because I want your story, not hers." Christine paused, giving her a speculative look. "She told me that everyone in the orphanage was instructed to say that you were never there. They were threatened with death if they spoke about your presence. She said you were there for only one day, and she believed your parents were in serious trouble with the government."

Julia tried hard not to react, not to reveal anything to Christine, but inside she was reeling. She had to say something. She had to buy some time. She fell back on what Alex had suggested earlier. "I'm not that girl. It's a mistake. I was born and raised in Berkeley, California. I have a birth certificate to prove it." She did have a birth certificate, something she hadn't considered before now.

"Birth certificates are not that difficult to obtain, not if you know the right people," Christine said.

"I don't know what you mean," Julia replied, even though she suspected Christine was right about fake birth certificates being easy enough to get. She had to find a way to convince Christine to move on to another story. "I don't think I look like that girl in the picture," she said with as much cool as she could muster. "In fact, I'm considering suing your newspaper for printing that photo and suggesting all kinds of lies." She hadn't been considering any such thing, but Christine didn't have to know that.

"And you just happened to be hanging out with Alex Manning the other day as his mother told me? Please, Miss DeMarco, don't insult my intelligence. You're that girl and I'm going to prove it."

"Why would you want to?"

"Because it's a great story, and the newspaper never lets me write about anything but celebrities. This is my big break. I can help you. I've already found someone who worked at the orphanage. If you really want to know who you are, you need me."

"I know who I am," Julia said flatly. "I don't need you for

anything." She walked out of the station, hoping to leave Christine behind, but the woman followed her onto the sidewalk.

"You say that now, but you'll change your mind," Christine said. "I'm very persistent. I don't give up."

"And you won't change my mind," Julia retorted. She wondered if she could make a fast break for her car, which was parked just down the street. That's when she saw a man watching her. He was built like a linebacker with a square, muscular body. Dirty blond hair showed beneath a baseball cap. A pair of dark sunglasses hid his eyes, and he wore a tan jacket over slacks. She couldn't tell his age, but he was probably in his fifties. As Julia stared at him, she wondered why he didn't look away, why he was searching her face as carefully as she was searching his. Was he another reporter? He certainly didn't look like one, but she hadn't had that much experience with the press.

"Miss DeMarco," Christine said, drawing her attention back to her. "Please, let me tell your story. I really need this break."

Her smile was meant to be disarming, but Julia didn't buy it. "I'm not your break," she said, "and I'm busy."

Christine thrust her card in Julia's face. "Call me anytime, night or day."

Julia took the business card and stuffed it into her pocket. As Christine left, the man came toward her. He said something she didn't understand. It took her a moment to realize he was not speaking English. He repeated his comment in a more agitated, determined voice, his arms gesturing. She backed away, his tone making her nervous.

The door to the radio station opened behind her, and two of her coworkers came out. She latched onto them in relief. "Hey, where are you guys going?" she asked, feeling there was safety in numbers.

"Coffee. Want to come?" Tracy asked.

"Yes, sounds great." She cast a quick look over her shoulder. The man had moved down the street, but he was still watching her. She linked arms with Tracy and walked in the opposite direction. She was probably letting her imagination get the better of her, seeing danger where it didn't exist, but Brady's warning that her questions could get her into trouble was still fresh in her mind. She didn't want to suddenly disappear as Alex's father had. Until she knew which people in her life were telling the truth and which ones were lying, she'd trust no one.

* * *

A half hour later Julia was back in her car, driving across town to her apartment. Her coworkers had walked her to her car after she'd mentioned the strange guy who appeared to be watching her. Much to her relief, he'd disappeared. She pulled into a parking spot in front of her building and got out. As she did so, she saw Liz heading up the steps. When it appeared that Liz was planning to ignore her, Julia called out for her to wait. Liz made a face but did as she was asked, tapping her foot impatiently on the ground. "What?" she asked.

"I want to go up with you."

"Why? You haven't wanted to do anything else with me."

Julia sighed, wondering how long her sister's bad mood would last. "I'm getting really tired of your attitude, Lizzie."

"Likewise, sis," Liz said sarcastically. "By the way, the family, our family, if you still consider them family, wants to throw you an engagement party at DeMarco's in a couple of weeks. Aunt Lucia wants you to call her and pick a date."

"What did you tell her?"

"Nothing. I'm staying out of your so-called wedding plans."

Julia thought that was a good idea since she knew a conversation with Michael was long overdue. To her credit, she had tried to call him from the radio station, but he'd been out on his boat. She'd have to catch up with him later.

Julia and Liz walked up the stairs together. Liz seemed to have nothing to say, and Julia didn't know how to break the silence without drawing another sarcastic remark. "I wish we could be on the same side," she said as they reached their door.

"I'm on the DeMarco side. I don't know what side you're on."

Julia blew out a frustrated breath and opened the door. Her jaw dropped at the sight of their apartment. It looked as if a bomb had gone off. The room was in shambles. "Oh, my God!" She put a hand to her mouth, feeling like she was going to be sick.

"What's wrong now?" Liz demanded, pushing past her, only to stop abruptly and gape in amazement. "Someone broke in," she said, stating the obvious.

"I can't believe this," Julia said, dazed. Their home hadn't been just robbed, but ransacked. The drawers in their desk had been dumped on the floor. The CD cases were open and broken apart. The cushions on the couch and the upholstery on the kitchen chairs had been slashed. Fear swept through Julia at the violence of the burglary. She grabbed Liz by the arm. "They might still be here," she whispered. "We have to get out."

Julia looked toward the hallway and the closed bedroom door. They never closed the bedroom door. They turned and ran.

Chapter Twelve

Julia and Liz didn't stop running until they reached the sidewalk, where they drew in gulping breaths of air.

"We have to call the police." Liz reached for her cell phone with a shaky hand. "Oh, God, Julia, you don't think they're going to come after us, do you?"

"No, of course not." Her chest heaved as she struggled to calm her racing heart. "They're probably gone. I just didn't want to take a chance. Not after I saw what they'd done to the cushions on the couch and the chairs. They must have had knives."

Liz paled. "Let's get farther away," she suggested.

"Good idea."

When they reached the other side of the street, Liz made the call while Julia stared up at her bedroom window, which faced the street. She thought she saw the curtain move. Was someone in there watching them? She heard Liz talking to the police and knew she had to call Alex. She pulled out her cell phone and punched in his number, relieved when he answered right away.

"You have to come over," she told him, her lips trembling so hard it was difficult to get the words out. "Someone broke in to my apartment. They might still be there."

"I'll be right over. Stay out of the apartment, Julia. In fact, you should get yourself to someplace safe."

"Liz and I are across the street. She's talking to the police. It's the middle of the day. Nothing will happen to us here," she said, hoping it was the truth.

"Keep your eyes open," he advised. "I have a feeling this

burglary wasn't random."

"I don't think it was, either, Alex. They didn't steal our stereo or our television, but they slashed the pillows on the couch like they were furiously angry or completely crazy."

"Or looking for something in particular," Alex said. "Do you have any idea what that could be?"

"I don't know. I can't think. I'm shaking."

"All right, relax. We'll figure it out."

"Maybe the swan necklace or the matryoshka doll," she said. "Maybe that's what they were looking for."

"Do you know if they were taken?"

"They're still in my purse from our trip to Buffalo." She put a hand on the strap looped over her shoulder.

"Hang on to that bag. I'll be there in five minutes."

Julia closed the phone and saw that Liz had finished her call. "What did the police say?"

"They're on their way." Liz gave Julia a worried look. "This has something to do with you and that photo, doesn't it?"

"I have the terrible feeling it does."

* * *

The police arrived at the same moment as Alex. They searched the apartment first, then let Julia, Liz, and Alex into the living room. The damage was as bad as Julia remembered. All the tiny pieces of their lives were strewn across the room: magazines, books, knickknacks, the fabric Liz had been working on, and Julia's CD collection. Even the pictures on the wall had been stripped down and thrown onto the floor. It didn't look as if the burglars had missed one inch of the room.

The police asked them to look around and see if anything was taken. It was impossible to tell with the mess, but obviously expensive items and even a twenty-dollar bill on the kitchen counter had been left untouched, which was even more worrisome. After a long discussion about whether they had any enemies or knew of anyone who might have wanted to hurt them, the police said they believed the apartment had been turned by a pro, someone who was looking for something in particular.

Julia glanced to Alex, wondering if she should mention the photo and the Russia connection, but saw by the almost imperceptible shake of his head that he thought it would be better to keep that information to themselves. But she could give the police something. "There was a man watching me when I left work today. He made me so nervous, I didn't go to my car; I went and got coffee with my friends. When I came back a half hour later, he was gone." She gave them the description of the man, although she could tell by their expressions that they believed it was a stretch to connect some man who might have been watching her to the vandalism done in her apartment.

"Are you going to tell them about the picture?" Liz whispered to Julia.

"There's nothing to tell yet," she murmured. "I don't think we want more media attention, do you?"

"No," Liz replied, a scowl on her face.

"We're done for now," one of the officers said. "You should both be careful. If they didn't find whatever they were looking for, they may be back. Stay with friends tonight, and if you think of anything that will help us investigate, give us a call." He handed Julia his card.

Julia slipped it into a pocket, her fingers coming into contact with the card Christine Delaney had given her earlier. She had a feeling she wouldn't be calling either one of them, but she said, "Thank you."

Michael arrived as the officers were leaving. His eyes widened in shock when he saw the state of their apartment. "What happened?" He looked from Julia to Liz, his gaze settling on Alex. "Who are you?"

"This is Alex Manning," Julia said, realizing they'd never actually met. "Michael Graffino."

The two men sized each other up, then connected for a brief, wary handshake.

"So, what's going on?" Michael asked again.

"Isn't it obvious?" Liz asked. "Julia's search has now put us in danger."

"Someone broke into your apartment because of the photograph?" Michael echoed in surprise. "Are you sure?"

"No, we're not sure," Julia replied. "We don't know."

"What we do know," Liz cut in, "is that nothing was taken, but everything was ripped apart by a big, sharp knife."

Michael's attention shifted to the cushions on the couch. His skin turned pale. "God! What if you'd been here when they came? You could have both been killed."

That thought had crossed Julia's mind as well. And she could see that his words had stirred Liz up even more.

"We're lucky that didn't happen," Julia said.

"Lucky? You call this lucky?" Michael asked sharply. He shot Alex a hard look. "What do you think about all this? You don't seem to be saying much."

"I think Julia has it covered."

"And I think Julia needs to stop this craziness before something worse happens."

"She can handle herself," Alex replied.

"And she can speak for herself, too," Julia interrupted, drawing their attention back to her. "We shouldn't jump to conclusions until the police finish their investigation." Actually, she was already jumping to conclusions, but she didn't want to share them with Michael or with Liz. She needed to talk to Alex alone. But Michael would have none of that.

"Why don't you leave?" Michael said to Alex. "I'll take care of Julia and Liz." He put a protective and proprietary arm around Julia's shoulders.

She could hardly knock it off, but she didn't like the way Michael was staking his claim, or the way Alex was looking at her, as if he couldn't believe she was standing there letting Michael take control. She sensed the situation was on the verge of exploding into something even worse.

"Maybe you should go, Alex," she said quietly, silently pleading with him to understand.

Alex hesitated, an unreadable look in his eyes. Then he shrugged. "Sure. Call me later."

Julia had to fight the urge to run after him. She was far more interested in talking to him about what this break-in might mean than in dealing with Michael and Liz, who were both annoyed with her. But she knew she couldn't leave. She had to talk to them first. She owed them that much.

Liz walked over and shut the door behind Alex, then put her hands in the pockets of her jeans as she stared at Julia and the destruction surrounding them. "This is scary," Liz said. "What kind of people are you mixed up with?"

"I don't know," Julia muttered.

Michael pulled her around so he could gaze into her eyes. "Julia. Please. I'm asking you. Let this search of yours go. Call the newspaper. Tell them they were wrong. You're not that girl. And your family needs to be left alone."

"Don't you understand, Michael? It's too late. Everything is in motion. I told the reporter I wasn't that girl. She didn't believe me. And it's obvious that someone who saw my picture in the newspaper thinks I'm that girl. And it looks like that someone believes I have something that I'm not supposed to have."

"What? What do you have?" he asked impatiently. "Is there more you haven't told me?"

She couldn't even remember what she had told him. Her head was spinning with bits and pieces of information. "I don't know what I have that they want. Maybe it's the swan necklace. Maybe it's the matryoshka doll. It's possible that it's old and valuable. Your guess is as good as mine. I'm just glad they were in my bag, not the apartment."

"So they might come back looking for them, looking for you," Michael said.

"I hope not. And I'm just guessing that that's what they're looking for. I really don't know." She still needed to go to the Russian shop and talk to Dasha's cousin, Svetlana, about the doll. She'd forgotten all about that part of the story. Maybe that's what she would do next.

"Julia, this is too dangerous," Michael said. "If you come forward, if you make a public statement that you're turning over these items to the police, whoever did this might back away."

"Or they might not." She could see the disappointment in his eyes. "I'm sorry, Michael, but I don't want to turn over my necklace and that doll to the police. They're the only clues I have to my past. I have to finish my search."

"At what cost? You and Liz could have been killed. If you aren't thinking about yourself, what about your sister?"

"Yeah, what about your sister?" Liz echoed. "Listen to him, Julia. He's making good sense. Yesterday some man called here. He had a Russian accent. He kept calling you Yulia. And he seemed agitated when I couldn't put you on the phone. He scared me. There was something in his voice." She paused. "I wonder if he was the one who did this."

Julia wondered if he was the same man who'd been outside the radio station. Maybe she shouldn't have run from that man. Maybe she should have stayed and confronted him, instead of taking off like a scared child.

"You need to back off," Michael urged. "If you show complete disinterest in the story, perhaps the press will move on to something else."

"I think Michael has a point. Without you, the story has no teeth," Liz added.

How could she fight both of them? Julia wished Alex hadn't left. She could have used another person on her side. "I'm sorry," she repeated, with a helpless wave of her hand, "but I can't stop. The reporter told me today that she spoke to someone who worked at the orphanage in Russia. She's digging deep and digging fast. She's determined to solve the mystery of that little girl with or without me. Even if I do nothing, she's moving forward. I need to stay ahead of her, just in case..."

"In case what?" Liz asked.

She drew in a breath. "In case I have to protect Mom's reputation."

"What does that mean?"

"I'm not sure yet, but there's a good chance that Mom and I were in Russia when that picture was taken."

Liz's gaze darkened with some emotion. "How do you know that? Do you have proof?"

"I'm working on it."

"What did the person at the orphanage tell the reporter?" Liz asked. "Could she identify you?"

"No, apparently she just said that the employees were threatened with death if they spoke of the girl at the gates."

"Oh, come on. That's a little dramatic, isn't it?" Michael scoffed.

Julia tipped her head at the mess surrounding them.

"And this isn't dramatic? I think someone made a very powerful statement here today."

He couldn't argue with that. "All right. What are you going to do next?"

"Start cleaning, I suppose," Julia replied.

"You can't stay here. You'll have to come to my apartment. We'll go from there."

"There's no room at your place. You're living with your brother. And what about Liz?"

"Yeah, what about Liz?" her sister echoed again.

"You can stay with your father," Michael told Liz. He glanced back at Julia and shook his head. "And you—I guess I might as well tell you this now. I was going to wait until it was ready—until you were ready—but since you need a safe place to stay..."

"What are you talking about?" Julia asked, confused again.

"I'm going to start cleaning up the bedroom," Liz said, interrupting them. "I'll be in the other room if anyone needs me."

Her sister certainly seemed eager to be gone all of a sudden. "You don't have to leave," Julia said.

"Yes, I do," Liz said with a nod. "Believe me, I do." She hustled out of the room, making a point of closing the bedroom door behind her.

Julia turned back to Michael. "What is it? What do you want to tell me?"

He took a moment, then said, "I bought us a house, Julia— near the Marina. It has two bedrooms and a garden. You're going to love it."

His words came out in a rush. She blinked, sure she hadn't heard him correctly. "Excuse me? What did you just say?"

"I think you heard me."

"I don't think I could have," she said with a definite shake of her head. "You better say it again."

"All right." His chin lifted and his shoulders went back as he said, "I bought us a house, Julia, a place for us to raise our children and grow old together. It's what you've always wanted. It's your wedding present."

Stunned by his words, she didn't know what to say, how to react. It was all too much. The day had been one bad surprise after another.

"Say something," Michael instructed.

"What should I say? I can't believe it. You bought us a house?"

Michael's brown eyes lit up with eagerness as he grabbed her shoulders. "It's great, Julia. It's a fixer-upper, which is the only way I could afford to buy in that neighborhood. There's a school nearby, about three blocks away. You'll be able to walk with the kids. And the recreation center is close by. You can take your yoga classes there, and I can play in the basketball leagues. It's the perfect place for us to start our life together."

"I already go somewhere for yoga," she said, not sure why it seemed important to tell him that in the face of everything else he'd said.

"So maybe you'll change your mind, and switch to the rec center. I can't wait to show you the house. I wanted it to be completely done before I did. But this is better. You can help me fix it up the way you want it."

"Does it matter what I want?" she asked.

"Of course it does," he replied, the light dimming in his eyes. "I love you. I want you to be happy."

"Then why didn't you tell me about the house? Why didn't you show it to me before you bought it? Don't you think we should be making these decisions together? A house is a huge purchase."

"I'm the man. I want to provide for you and our children. It's the way I was raised."

"First of all, we don't have children yet. You make it sound like they're already here." And that little fact had drawn goose bumps down her arms. "Second of all, I want kids, but not yet, not really soon."

"You're almost thirty. How long do you want to wait?"

"I don't know—until I'm ready. My God, Michael! You bought us a house without telling me. Don't you think that's crazy? How did you even afford it?"

"I've been saving for years. I've always wanted a place of my own, real estate, my land, my house, something I can put my mark on. And no, I don't think that's crazy. I think it's smart. I think that kind of foresight makes me a good man."

"Except you just said 'my,' like, three times. What happened to 'our'? What happened to us making decisions together as partners?"

"And how the hell would I get you to make such a decision? You can't even focus on our wedding, much less the rest of our life," he snapped back.

"That's not an excuse for leaving me out of the loop. Not on something this big."

"I thought you'd be happy that I took care of it for you."

"Happy? How could I be happy? You didn't consider my feelings."

"And you've been considering mine? I've asked you to give up this search a half dozen times now, and your answer has been hell, no. You don't care what I think at all. And you're not even giving this house a chance. You might love it."

"It's not the house. It's the fact that you bought it without telling me, that you're planning our lives without my input. That's not right, Michael." She knew the moment of truth had finally come. She had to face their relationship head-on. "We're not right."

"Just stop there—"

"No." She shrugged out of his hold. "I can't stop. I have to tell you how I feel."

"It's that guy, Alex, isn't it?" he demanded furiously. "He's the reason you're pulling away from me. You're attracted to him, aren't you?"

"This isn't about him," she said, sidestepping the issue of attraction. "It's about you and me. Us. It's my fault, Michael. I let things go on for too long. And I'm sorry about that."

He shook his head. "Don't."

"You're one of the best men I've ever known. The way you took care of me and Liz during Mom's illness was unbelievably kind and generous. But I've known for a while now that you and me... that we're not right for each other."

"We're perfect for each other," he said desperately. "How can you say that?"

"Because it's true. Because you don't see me the way I am. I never said I wanted a house. I never said I wanted kids in the next five years. You just assumed I did. And I should have corrected you a long time ago."

"I know you want kids."

"But I want other things first," she said passionately. "I'm beginning to realize how narrow my life has been. Mom was so strict about things I could do or not do, who I could see, where I could go, and I let her control me. And I started letting you do the same thing."

"I love you," he said with genuine, heartbreaking sincerity.

"I love you, too," she whispered, "but not the way a woman loves a man she's going to marry." She knew she was hurting him, and she felt horrible. She'd never wanted to bring him pain.

"You're just confused because of your past and this mystery you're chasing," he said, not willing to let go of his dream. "You'll feel differently when it's over, when that guy is out of your life."

"I won't. It's true I'm confused. But the one thing I've come to realize in the past few days is that I want to live my life to the fullest. I don't want to have regrets. I don't want to stop myself from asking questions or stating my opinion because I'm afraid the person I'm talking to will get hurt. I want to be free, Michael. I want to travel. I want to work on my music, on my goals. And I don't want to cheat myself or you. That's what I'd be doing if I married you."

"You're making a mistake," he said flatly. "A big one this time. Has he offered to travel with you? To help you with your music? To show you the world?"

She shook her head. "Alex hasn't done any of those things."

"But if he asked you to go with him, you'd go."

"It's not about him," she said, refusing to let herself even consider that question.

"You can protest all you want, but I think you're lying." He paused, his jaw tight, his mouth set in a hard line. "I guess it's over then."

She glanced down at her left hand and slowly pulled off the engagement ring he'd given her almost a year ago. She handed it to him. "You're a great guy, Michael. I hope you find someone who really deserves you."

"Yeah, yeah, nice guys always finish last," he said bitterly. "I hope you find what you're looking for, Julia." He paused. "If you change your mind, I might still be around. Or I might not. You never know."

Julia blew out a sigh as Michael left the apartment. She felt drained of emotion but also relieved that she'd finally broken it off. She glanced down at the tan line on her third finger and knew she'd done the right thing. That ring had been feeling heavier and heavier the last few days.

"What happened?" Liz asked, returning to the room. "I heard yelling."

"We broke up," Julia said, steeling herself for more criticism from Liz, but for once her younger sister was silent. "Did you know about the house?"

Liz gave a sheepish nod. "Michael wanted it to be a surprise. I've been helping him fix it up. That's what I was sewing—curtains." She picked up the fabric on the floor and set it on the table.

"You should have told me, warned me."

"It wasn't my place. You're always telling me to stay out of your relationship, so I stayed out of it."

"You've been helping him fix up the house. How is that staying out of it?"

"I didn't tell him what to do. I just painted and scraped wallpaper. I knew you were going to be pissed."

"Of course I'm angry. What woman would want her fiancé to buy a house without her input?"

"A woman who saw it as a romantic, loving gesture," Liz suggested. "Didn't it please you at all to know that this man wanted to take care of you, protect you, make your life easier?"

Liz's words made Julia feel foolish and a little guilty. But she had to remind herself that she and Liz were very different women when it came to men and relationships. "It made me feel as if Michael had no regard for my opinion or my feelings," she said. "Maybe to some women it would have been a romantic gesture. That just proves we weren't right for each other."

"You should reconsider, Julia. See the house at least. You might love it. And perhaps if you talk things through, you'll be able to compromise, find a way to work things out. Unless you don't want to work things out? Did you break up with him because of the house—or because of something or someone else?"

Julia knew it would be smarter not to answer Liz's question, but she had the sudden reckless urge to confide in someone, and the words came out before she could stop them. "I kissed Alex last night."

Liz's eyes widened. "So that's it? You dumped an incredible man because you're attracted to a sexy bad-boy photographer? Is Alex really going to be in your life? Doesn't he spend most of the year traveling around the world?"

"I didn't dump Michael for Alex. He was just a small part of it, but a part I couldn't ignore. If I were really in love with Michael, I wouldn't have been so attracted to Alex. How could I marry one man knowing I had feelings for someone else? Michael is an incredible man, but he's not the man for me. And I should have figured that out a long time ago. But everyone loved him so much. I thought I should love him, too."

Liz stared at her for a moment, then shook her head in bewilderment. "You're right about one thing, Julia. Michael is an incredible man. I hope you won't regret this decision."

"I won't," Julia said, praying she was right about that. She glanced around the room, realizing she had other problems to address. "This place is really a mess. I can't believe how many things are broken." She felt sad and angry at the same time. "We have to find out who did this."

"It appears we have a lot to find out. We can't stay here," Liz added. "The lock is broken. My pullout couch is destroyed, and your bed isn't much better. Besides, the police said whoever did this might be back. So what do we do? Go to Dad's place? Aunt Lucia's?"

Julia suddenly realized that she couldn't go to any of those places, not when she might be bringing danger in her wake. "You go," she said. "I don't want to make anyone else a target. It's probably better if I stay away from the family right now."

"You might be right," Liz said with a sigh. "You're going to Alex's, aren't you?"

"He's already involved."

"Yeah, sure. I get it. Call me on my cell if you need me, and Julia... be careful. Not just with this search—with your heart. I may not know as much about life or men as you do, but even I recognize a heartbreaker when I see one, and Alex has that written all over him."

Chapter Thirteen

Alex opened the door to Julia a little before six o'clock on Tuesday evening. He hadn't been sure she'd come to him. She might have gone home with Michael. Her fiancé had certainly made it clear that he wanted to take care of Julia and her sister. But here she was, wearing black pants, a light blue button-down blouse, and a short, trim black jacket. Her blond hair was done up in a ponytail, long hoop earrings dangling from her ears. She was pretty as a picture, he thought, then grimaced, reminded that their relationship had begun with a picture.

"Can I come in?" she asked.

He stepped back and waved her inside. "Where's your fiancé?"

"Probably at his new house—the house he bought for us without asking me," she said, a decided edge to her voice.

Alex let out a low whistle at that piece of information. There was a lot he didn't understand about women, but he did know that making a big purchase without talking to your soon-to-be wife was a huge mistake.

Julia paced around his living room in anger and frustration, but then she'd had a hell of a day—hell of a week, in fact.

"I couldn't believe it, Alex. Michael had our whole life mapped out without any input from me. He simply assumed we wanted the same things."

"Did you ever tell him differently? Most men aren't mind readers."

"You're taking his side?" she asked in surprise and obviously still in a fighting mood.

He put up a hand in defense. "Hey, I don't even know him. I'm just saying that maybe he assumed certain things because you didn't tell him he was wrong."

She put her hands on her hips and sent him an irritated look. "I have a job that I love, and I've told him about it numerous times. But Michael thought I would quit my job, stay home, and have children immediately."

Alex winced. "Ouch."

"And he asked me to quit searching for my past. In fact, he insisted. I said I couldn't. I explained that it's out of my hands now. My God, someone just trashed my apartment. I can't just disappear, even if I wanted to. So I told him that..." She paused, drawing in a long breath.

Damn. Alex had a feeling he didn't want to hear what she was about to say next. As much as he thought Julia needed to break off her engagement, he also liked the fact that there was a tangible barrier between them, a real reason not to get involved. He had a feeling that was about to disappear.

Julia held up her left hand and he saw the naked third finger. "I broke up with him. I told Michael I couldn't marry him. Not because of anything that I just told you, but because I'm not in love with him. I let our relationship drift along, because it was easy, and it was nice. That was wrong. I should have come clean a long time ago. I don't know why I didn't," she added with a shake of her head. "It wasn't fair to Michael. I feel bad about that. I never meant to hurt him, but I did, and that wasn't right."

He appreciated her honesty, her self-critical words.

Julia wasn't a woman to let others take the blame when it wasn't deserved. He liked that about her. He liked a lot about her. Clearing his throat, he said, "What now?"

"Now I have a mystery to solve. That's all I can think about for the moment."

He nodded. "Someone wants something that they think you have."

"Well, that narrows it down," she said with a hint of sarcasm. She took a seat on the couch, kicking up her feet on the coffee table. "We're not getting anywhere fast. By the way, I spoke to that reporter again. She cornered me at the radio station, and get this: She said she found a woman here in the United States who worked in that orphanage and who had seen me there. She said the woman told her they were under threat of death to talk about me. What do you think about that?"

He thought for a moment. "I'm not sure I buy it. Sounds vague and a little too convenient, maybe part of Christine's plan to make you trust her."

"I never thought about that. You think she made up the woman?"

"Did she give you a name?"

"No, that was based on my being willing to work with her. Apparently Christine thinks I'm her ticket to big-time news journalism."

"She might be right. Let's see what else she comes up with. I also did a little digging." He sat down next to her. "I had another conversation with Stan." He paused, still unable to shake the feeling that Stan hadn't been completely honest with him.

"And..." Julia prodded.

"He gave me the name of a woman who worked with the theater group and who was in Moscow with us."

Her eyes sparked with interest. "Really? That's great."

"Not so great. Tanya did remember my father quite clearly and also Sarah, but she had no idea if you were there or not."

"So she couldn't say I wasn't there?"

"No. She said there were a few children with the company. She didn't know who belonged to who."

"It's still possible then that my mother might have taken me to Russia with her."

He nodded, knowing that Julia needed to hang on to that fact, and for the moment they had no proof that it wasn't true. "Tanya also implied that my father was spying for the government," he added, "and I'm starting to believe it."

"It's difficult not to. I have the same question about my mother. Did she really go to Russia just to sew costumes?"

"Doubtful. I called a friend of mine in the State Department. I asked him to check out the key players, Brady, Stan, and your mother."

She flinched at the mention of her mother. "I guess you had to include her."

"Ryan said he'd get back to me as soon as he could." He took a breath, then continued. "I did press Stan on my father's death, on the fact that he didn't do anything to investigate it. He said he received a threat against his family if he didn't mind his own business. Apparently that was enough to make him look the other way." Alex couldn't hide the scorn in his voice. "Hell of a friend he was."

"Don't judge him too harshly. If they threatened his family, he was in a difficult spot."

"Yeah, well, he should have found a way out of the spot. I would have."

Julia gazed at him with her beautiful blue eyes, so full of emotion and concern for him that he had to fight not to put his arms around her. He clasped his hands tightly together and looked away.

She put a hand on his knee, and he stiffened.

"Are you hungry, Alex?"

The question was not the one he'd been expecting. He had to think for a moment. "I guess."

"I haven't eaten since that excuse for a breakfast we had on the plane."

He glanced back at her. "Do you want to go out?"

"Unless you're going to tell me you're a five-star chef?" she asked with a smile.

He laughed at that. "I never learned how to cook more than the basics, and I eat most of my meals on the run."

"Do you have a favorite restaurant you go to when you're in town?"

"No. Why don't you pick?"

She hesitated. "There's a new Moroccan restaurant on Union Street. It's supposed to be good, just like the real thing. Although you've probably eaten in a real restaurant in Morocco, haven't you?"

"Actually, that's one place I haven't been yet."

Her eyes sparkled. "Then it will be an adventure for both of us. Are you game?"

"I'm always game."

"I've been wanting to try it, but it never seemed to be the right time. And Michael isn't an adventurous eater. It will be my treat. It's the least I can do." She smiled as she stood up. "I kind of like this, picking the restaurant, paying for my guest. I think I'll even drive."

"Whoa, slow down. I'm driving."

"You don't think I can drive?"

"I like to be the driver."

"So do I, and I've been the passenger every time we've driven so far. Come on, Alex. You can trust me. I promise not to hurt you."

He sighed. "Fine, you drive. But I warn you, I am definitely a backseat driver, only you'll be hearing my comments from the front seat." As they left the apartment, Alex thought about what Julia had just promised. He didn't believe he was risking his life to ride in the car with her, but he had a distinct feeling that by spending more time together, he was definitely risking his heart. And the funny thing was that until Julia had entered his life, he'd almost forgotten he had a heart.

* * *

Julia entered the restaurant, feeling as if she'd just stepped into another world. The tented ceiling, the thick brocade tapestries on the walls, took them straight to Morocco. They sat down on low, soft cushions, the room lit only by candles. It was a lush, sensual atmosphere, and Julia felt a shiver run down her spine as she glanced over at Alex. He was as comfortable here as he was anywhere. She'd never met a man who could adapt to any environment as easily as Alex did. He made whatever room he was in his own.

A waiter came by to explain the menu and suggest drinks. As soon as he left, a beautiful woman entered and performed a belly dance for them. She seemed especially interested in drawing Alex's attention, and Alex seemed to enjoy every second of her performance. In fact, he looked as if he'd forgotten Julia was even present.

It didn't matter, she told herself. They weren't on a date. They weren't involved. They weren't committed to each other. Alex could flirt with the belly dancer. Heck, he could take her home and sleep with her, and Julia wouldn't have a thing to say about it, except that she really wouldn't like it.

Julia frowned at the turn of her thoughts. She took a sip of wine, relieved when the woman moved away. "She was pretty," she commented, feeling completely insincere.

"Beautiful," he said with a smile. "I'd like to see you in one of those costumes."

"I doubt that will ever happen. I'm far too inhibited." She licked her lips as his gaze roamed her face, as if he were searching for all her personal secrets. There were some things she didn't want to share with him.

"Are you inhibited?" he asked. "Or is that just the way you've been raised to be?"

"It's the same thing."

"It's not. I believe we're influenced by our environment, the people in our lives."

"I suppose that's true. My mother was very big on rules and doing the right thing, telling the truth, never going astray. She and my father made such a big, happy family life for us that it was easy to be content in it. It wasn't until she died that I started to look around and wonder what else I wanted. I must say it's difficult to believe she might have been the biggest liar of all." Every time Julia thought about the lies, her heart hurt.

"She didn't lie about her love for you," Alex said in a tender voice. "She obviously took care of you, protected you, tried to make you happy. That's the important stuff, Julia."

"I'm trying to focus on that, but it's not easy when I'm hit with a new problem every time I turn around."

"You have had a busy week."

"Tell me about it. I can't believe I just walked out and left my apartment in such horrible condition. I should have cleaned it up."

"It will be there when you get back. What's your sister up to?"

"I think she went to my dad's house." Julia sighed. "I don't want to talk about any of it right now. Do you think we could put a moratorium on the subject through dinner?"

"Absolutely," he said with so much relief she had to laugh.

"I'm glad you agree. You know, this is nice."

"It's a cool restaurant."

"I wasn't talking about the restaurant. I was talking about how good it feels to spend time with you—away from all the drama."

"For a few minutes anyway," he said lightly, lifting his wineglass to hers. "To you, Julia, whoever you are."

"Whoever I am," she echoed.

* * *

An hour later they'd stuffed themselves on stewed vegetables, slices of fried eggplant, and a melt-in-your-mouth lamb dish. They'd also shared a lot of conversation about anything and everything, books, politics, religion, and world events. There was no topic that was out of bounds. They argued, debated, and laughed. Julia didn't think she'd ever laughed so much in her life, which made her feel guilty when she stopped to think for a minute. She should be sad that her engagement was over and that she'd probably hurt a very nice guy. Instead, she felt free. That was wrong. Yet it was right, too, and feeling bad wouldn't make Michael feel better. Hopefully time would open his eyes to who she really was and why they never would have been happy together. With that rationalization, she was able to put Michael out of her mind, as well as the rest of the problems in her life. She would have so many things to deal with tomorrow—her apartment, her mother, her past—but for the moment, she wanted to be carefree. And she couldn't have picked a better partner for this outing than Alex.

She loved the way his mind worked. He was sharp, perceptive, interesting—a truly fascinating man. He lived a life that she wanted. Not the photography part, but the traveling part.

"Do you think you'll ever quit?" she asked as they left the restaurant and headed toward the car. "Ever decide to stay in one place and just take pictures at the local mall?" she added with a teasing smile.

"I'd rather shoot myself than work at the mall." He shrugged his shoulders. "I'm used to my life. It works. It's challenging, too. I love being able to get the shot that no one else can get."

"And you really believe that your job is enough for you?"

"It has been so far."

"Even though I just broke off my engagement, I still want to get married—someday."

"Of course you do."

"Why do you say it like that?" she asked.

"I said it before. Most women want to be married."

"And most men—"

"Want to have a lot of sex."

"You can have a lot of sex in a marriage," she pointed out. She saw his teasing smile and had a feeling that no matter how hard she tried, she wasn't going to get a more serious answer out of him.

"I'll keep that in mind," he said. "So, Julia, are we sleeping together tonight?"

At his question, she almost tripped on the uneven sidewalk. "What?"

"You heard me. You need a place to stay, don't you? I'm offering my bed."

"And where are you going to sleep?"

"I'm waiting to hear my options. In the meantime, can I drive home?"

"No," she said, hoping she could bring the same definitive no to the bed question.

She walked around to her side of the car and reached into her purse for her keys. Suddenly a man appeared out of nowhere, tall, burly, and he was heading straight toward her. She didn't have a chance to move, but Alex did. One minute she was standing up; the next she was hitting the ground with her backside and Alex was chasing some guy down the street. Her heart pounded against her chest as she tried to get her bearings. Her handbag was still on her shoulder, although now that she thought about it, she had the distinct feeling that man had been trying to take it from her. If Alex hadn't moved so quickly, she would have lost the doll and her necklace.

She stood up, feeling nervous and abandoned. Alex and the man had disappeared. She was alone in the dark. Suddenly aware of how isolated she was, she searched hastily for the keys. They were at the bottom of her bag. With a shaky hand, she got the key in the lock, opened the door, and slid inside. With the doors closed and locked, she felt a little better. But where the hell was Alex? God, she hoped he was all right.

What if the guy had a gun or a knife? Alex had no way to defend himself. He was on his own. And so was she.

* * *

Alex increased his pace, narrowing the gap between himself and the man who had tried to attack Julia. His heart was beating double time, his breath coming quick and fast as he followed the man around the corner of Union Street, up a short hill and into a small park. It was darker here. No streetlights. Plenty of shadows.

Alex could barely make out the man now. Only the light blue streak of his Windbreaker glittered in the moonlight as he dashed among the trees. Alex couldn't lose him. He had to find out who he was and what he wanted. This was his chance.

But that chance was elusive and fast.

One minute the man was in his sights. The next he was gone. Alex stopped, looked around. The park was empty but edged with a thick line of trees. There was no apparent way out of the park. The man would have to come back in his direction.

Was he hiding?

Alex tried to catch his breath, make his mind work. He had to think.

An eerie feeling of being watched crept down his spine. He turned slowly, sharpening his gaze on each flickering shadow. There were too many trees, too many bushes, all rustling in the whispering breeze. As he listened, the sounds of the night grew louder, the crickets, the faint honk of a distant horn, the rumble of traffic on a nearby road, the sound of laughter from one of the open apartment windows surrounding the park.

"Come out, dammit," he said aloud. "Talk to me. Tell me what you want."

Nothing but silence answered his call. Was the man waiting, watching? Or was he gone? Had he found a way out that wasn't obvious to Alex?

If he had...

Julia was alone in the car. And she was the one they wanted.

What the hell was he doing?

Turning, Alex ran back the way he'd come, desperately hoping Julia was all right.

Chapter Fourteen

Julia flinched at the sound of footsteps coming down the street behind her. She was almost afraid to look. What if it wasn't Alex? What if it was the man who had tried to grab her bag? What if he'd hurt Alex and come back to get her?

She sank down into the seat, hoping he wouldn't see her.

The footsteps drew closer, then paused. Someone whistled. A shadow moved across the front seat, and the door handle on the passenger side was flipped. It was locked. It didn't open. The man stumbled as he tried the door, again.

She couldn't breathe. She didn't know what to do. Should she start the car, try to pull out? What if Alex came back and she wasn't there?

Before she could come up with an answer, the man moved on.

It wasn't the same guy, she realized. This man was older, wearing a bulky coat and pants. His hair was long, and he wore a woolen cap on his head. He had a paper bag in his hand, and as she watched, he raised it to his lips and took a swig. He continued on, trying the door handle on every car parked along the street.

He was probably homeless and looking for somewhere to sleep, she realized. He wasn't after her. She forced herself to breathe again.

Until she heard the sound of someone running.

She'd never been as scared of the night as she was right now.

Please let it be Alex, she prayed. She closed her eyes, afraid to look. Someone tapped on the window. She tensed, then relaxed when she heard his voice.

"Julia, it's okay. Let me in."

She flipped the locks with a wave of relief, and Alex slid into the passenger seat. "Thank God, you're all right," she said, flinging herself into his arms. She hugged him tight, not wanting him to let her go. He didn't. He pressed her face into the curve of his neck, his hand cupping the back of her head. She could feel his pulse jumping beneath his skin, and she could smell the sweat of his desperate chase. But he was safe. So was she. And they were together.

Finally, Alex pushed away, his eyes glittering in the shadows. "I lost him. I was afraid he'd come back here, afraid—" He cut himself off. She could finish the sentence in her head. He'd been scared for her, and fear was a character flaw as far as Alex was concerned. But in her mind, fear was a normal reaction to a terrifying situation.

"I'm all right," she assured him. "I was worried about you. I thought he might have had a knife or some other weapon."

"He ran into a park and disappeared. I didn't even get a good look at him. All I know is that he was fast."

"Was he blond? Did he have a baseball cap on his head? A man came up to me at the radio station earlier today, and he made me really nervous."

Alex's eyes narrowed. "What are you talking about?"

"There was a guy watching me when I was talking to Christine Delaney. He came up to me when she left, and he said something I didn't understand. I think it might have been in Russian. My friends interrupted us, and he took off. Do you think it was the same guy?"

"Could have been. Why didn't you tell me about him before?"

"Didn't I?" she asked in confusion. "I guess I told Michael or Liz. I can't remember now. Did I also mention that Liz said a man with a thick, probably Russian accent called our apartment yesterday?"

"Goddammit, Julia," Alex swore. "What else don't I know?"

"I think that's it. I'm sorry, but everything is happening so fast, and I don't know what goes together and what doesn't." Overwhelmed, she had the terrible feeling she might burst into tears at any moment.

Alex put his hand on her leg. "It's okay. It's fine. We'll deal with it all, Julia. Don't worry."

"The man who came at us just now... He was after my purse, don't you think?" She'd had a few minutes to think, and she distinctly remembered the man trying to rip her bag off her shoulder.

"Yes," Alex said, meeting her gaze. "I'd say it's a safe bet he couldn't find whatever he was looking for at your apartment, so he decided you have it on you."

"Should we call the police?"

"Let's go back to my apartment first and take another look at the doll and the necklace. Maybe we missed something."

She nodded and turned the key in the ignition. She didn't realize she was shaking until she flooded the engine with too much gas.

"Easy, Julia," he murmured.

"I was so scared," she whispered. She gripped the steering wheel so tightly her knuckles turned white and her hands stung, but she didn't care, because it felt good to have something solid to hang on to. "When you disappeared, I didn't know what was going to happen." She looked at him and saw nothing but understanding and support. "I just got back in the car and protected myself. I should have gone after you, but I was a chicken."

"Sh-sh," he said. He leaned forward, putting a finger against her lips. "You did exactly the right thing."

She blinked back a tear. "I was so worried that I was going to lose you, Alex, and I've lost so much lately that—"

Alex cut off her words with a tender kiss. "I'm not that easy to lose," he murmured against her mouth. "I'm fine, Julia. He ran. He wasn't looking for a confrontation."

"Maybe not this time. What about the next time?"

"Don't think about all the things that might happen. It will drive you crazy." He tucked a piece of her hair behind her ear.

"I'm already feeling crazy. Should I stop looking for answers? Should I try to go back to my normal life? How do I even do that?"

"You can't go back to normal, because it doesn't exist anymore."

"If it ever did. What I thought was normal was a fictional story my mother created for me to live in. Nothing about my life was based on anything real."

"That's not true. Your mother may have created a cover story, but she lived her life with you, your sister and your stepfather. I don't think she was spying for the government when she was taking you to Girl Scouts," he added lightly. "In fact, we don't know if she was spying for the government at all. Maybe she simply went on that trip to Moscow because she wanted an adventure, and my father gave her the opportunity."

"I'd sure like to believe that. But if that were the case, why would she have hidden it from me? Why would she have disappeared from her parents' lives? Why would she have changed her name? Lived a lie?"

She wanted Alex to give her the answers, but she knew she was asking for too much. "She might have been spying the whole time I was growing up. How would I have known? Apparently she was very clever."

"I think your mother got out of the spy business, if she was ever in it, after that trip to Moscow, or maybe when she married your stepfather. From what you've told me about your idyllic childhood, I can't believe Sarah was anything but a devoted homemaker."

"I don't know what she was anymore, and that scares me, too," Julia confessed. "We were so close. We shared so many conversations. All the best moments of my life were with my mother. And now I can barely remember those times. My memory is blurred by all the terrible lies that continue to be revealed. Now when I close my eyes, I see Susan Davidson's face crumpled in pain when she realized Sarah had been alive. I hear Brady telling me that Sarah was in Moscow. Even your voice echoes through my head—your words, 'I saw your mother in the square that day.' What's real? What's not real? Why don't I know?"

"Your brain is too full," Alex replied, a smile spreading across his lips. "You've had a lot of shocks tonight. Give yourself a break. You don't have to figure everything out in the next five minutes."

"Maybe I do," she countered. "Who knows what the next five minutes will bring?"

"Nothing bad, I promise. Even the bad guys need to rest."

"How can you joke?"

"Because worrying is a waste of energy. Let's go home." He paused, his eyes suddenly sparkling. "I have an idea. Why don't you let me drive?"

His obvious attempt to regain control of the car made her smile back at him. "No way. I drove us here. I'll drive us back."

His sigh was long and dramatic, and eased the tension of the moment. "If you must."

"I must," she replied, her hands steadier now as she pulled away from the curb.

* * *

"I'll sleep on the couch," Julia said as they climbed the stairs to Alex's apartment a short while later. "I don't want to completely disrupt your life."

"A little late for that sentiment. You're the one who knocked on my door last week and started this ball rolling."

"It's not all my fault. You took the picture. You started this twenty-five years ago."

"Thanks for the reminder." He paused as he took out his key. "You know we slept together last night, and it was just fine."

It hadn't been just fine. She'd spent most of the night fighting an urge to roll into his arms and make love to him. And last night she'd had a barrier, an engagement ring and a fiancé. Now she had neither. But she still had a brain, and right now it was telling her that getting further involved with Alex would not be a good idea. She might not have wanted the steady, suffocating relationship Michael had offered, but she also didn't want to get her heart trounced by a love 'em and leave 'em type, no matter how sexy he was.

"The couch works for me," she said lightly. "Unless you'd rather I go to my dad's apartment and get out of your hair. I just don't want to put him in danger."

"No, you can stay here." Alex opened the door and flipped on the light.

Julia gasped at the sight that greeted them. Whoever had ransacked her apartment had done the same to Alex's, with just as much brutality and violence. Every piece of furniture had been upended, flipped over, ripped, cut, trashed. Even Alex's photographs had been snatched from the walls, the tables, the bookcase. Shattered glass lay on the floor where some of the picture frames had been thrown in ruthless abandon. The fury of the search seemed even worse here, as if the person had grown more frustrated and angry with each passing second.

"Dammit," Alex swore. "I should have seen this coming."

She should have seen it coming, too. Why hadn't she considered the fact that someone might follow her to Alex's apartment?

"I swear, if they broke my camera equipment..." Alex disappeared into the bedroom before Julia could tell him to be careful. She could hear him opening the closet door, slamming a dresser, muttering to himself. She was afraid to move, worried she'd step on something important, do even more damage.

Alex finally returned, looking marginally calmer. "The bedroom isn't as bad as this room," he said. "The cameras are okay. The film was stripped, but nothing was broken as far as I can tell."

"I'm sorry," she said, knowing the words weren't enough to cover the destruction. "They must have followed me here. They must have been watching me. That man outside the restaurant... He probably did this, knowing we were there. When he didn't find what he was looking for here, he came after us. I can't believe how much I'm ruining your life."

"It's okay, Julia. It's just stuff. And you're not the one who's ruining my life."

"Of course I am. If I'd never seen that picture, never come here, never started asking questions—"

"Well, you did, and it's done. We can't start second-guessing now."

"So, what's next? Who's next? Are they going to go to my dad's apartment, to my aunt and uncle's home?" she asked. "They're probably watching me right now. And I hate that I don't even know who I'm fighting. It could be one person or two or three -- who knows?"

"I certainly don't. It's possible there were two, one here, one at the restaurant watching us."

"Should we call the police?"

"In a minute. Let's take another look at the doll and the necklace. They're the only things you have that might have come from Russia."

They set two of the dining room chairs upright and sat down at the table. Julia opened her bag and pulled out the doll and the necklace. Alex immediately began to take the doll apart. "I know we're missing some dolls," he said. "I wonder if that's important." He examined each doll closely, his brows knitting into a frown as he peered particularly closely at the inside of one doll. "I think there's a number scratched here. It looks like a four to me. What do you think?"

She took the doll from his hand and saw the mark he was referring to. It did look like a four. "I think you're right," she said.

He picked up another doll. "And this one is a seven."

Julia took each doll as he discarded it. In the end they had five dolls and five numbers. "What do you think the numbers mean?"

Alex met her questioning gaze with a shrug of his shoulders. "I have no idea. The problem is, I don't think we have all the numbers, because we don't have all the dolls."

"We should go to that shop, Russian Treasures. Maybe that woman can tell us what the numbers mean. They could just be a production code."

"They could be, but there's nothing uniform about the way they look. It's as if someone scratched the numbers with a sharp knife."

His words sent a chill through her, and something stirred in her mind. A distant memory? She struggled to bring it into focus, but her brain wouldn't cooperate.

Alex sat back in his chair, a frown on his face now. "What's wrong?"

"I thought I was remembering something, but it wouldn't come back."

"Something about the doll?"

"I don't know," she said in frustration.

"Julia, don't force it. The memories will come back when they're supposed to."

"How can you be so patient?" she asked. "I thought you were a man of action."

"When it's called for. But I also know how to wait for the perfect light, the right angle, and the clearest view. Your mind takes photographs of everything you see just the way a camera does. Eventually it will develop those early pictures for you."

"Hopefully before I'm dead," she said, her words a mix of sarcasm and real fear.

"Hopefully," he agreed with a small smile. "We'll check out that Russian store tomorrow. Now, are you sure there isn't anything else your mother might have had that could link you to the doll or that trip to Russia?"

"I went through everything in the storage locker, but my father did say that their business and personal papers are at his apartment. I haven't had a chance to look through them yet." She glanced down at her watch and saw it was after ten. "It's too late to go there tonight. I'm a little afraid to go at all. What if they follow me there, too?" She sat up straight, a terrible idea crossing her mind. "Or perhaps they've already been to my dad's apartment. It wouldn't be difficult to find his address. He's listed in the phone book. I have to call him, make sure he's all right." She rifled through her handbag for her cell phone. "At least he lives in a security building. That's something."

"So far they've struck when no one has been home," Alex said reassuringly. "There's no reason to think that will change."

"There's no reason to think it won't, either. We don't know who we're dealing with. I'm calling my dad."

"And I'll call the police. I think it's time we brought them in on the whole story."

* * *

It was almost eleven o'clock at night when Alex ushered two detectives from the San Francisco Police Department out of his apartment. Julia remained in the living room, her heart still racing. The last hour of questions had done nothing to reassure her that she was safe. After telling the police the story of the orphan girl photograph and Julia's recent picture in the Tribune, it had become clear to all of them that the latter event had triggered the break-ins.

Someone had seen Julia's picture, believed her to be that girl, and come looking for something. The detectives had examined the necklace and the matryoshka doll but had been unable to find a reason why the two tourist-type souvenirs would be important. Even if the doll was worth a couple thousand dollars, it wouldn't be enough to trigger the kind of vandalism and burglary that had taken place here tonight or at her apartment earlier that day. There had to be something else.

In the meantime, Julia had called her father and discovered

that he was fine. She told him to be careful and alert to anyone lurking around his apartment building or near the restaurant. She'd left a message for Liz on her cell phone, wishing that her sister had picked up, so that Julia could know she was all right. It had occurred to her that Liz might have gone to Michael's house, so she'd even forced herself to call his apartment, but he hadn't answered, either, and she'd gotten the same voice mail on his cell phone. She had to trust they'd be okay as long as they weren't with her. She was the target, not them.

Alex shut the front door and headed for the kitchen. "How about a drink?" he suggested.

"Anything cold would be great."

"You got it." He returned a moment later with two bottles of mineral water.

Julia took a long draught, feeling a renewed sense of energy as the carbonation tickled her throat. Then she looked around the room, and her energy faded as quickly as it had come. They both had a lot of cleaning to do, not to mention major repairs. A lot of the furniture would have to be replaced or fixed before their apartments would really be livable again.

"I wish I'd never gone to the Legion of Honor," she murmured. "Look at the trouble I've brought myself, you, my family."

Alex shrugged, kicking off his shoes. "Never look back," he advised. "It doesn't do any good."

"Do you think the police will be able to find who did this?"

"Doubtful."

"You can't even try to be optimistic?"

"Sorry, but I think whoever broke in here knew what they were doing. It has a feel of professionalism about it. I don't think they left one fingerprint behind."

Julia traced her finger along a particularly ugly gash in the sofa cushion. "This is nasty. And I don't get it. What would I be hiding in a sofa cushion?"

"Something small," he replied, a thoughtful look on his face. "Which would rule out the matryoshka doll, don't you think? It's almost a foot long."

"Exactly. The necklace?"

"It sure doesn't look like anything special. I don't get it." .

"Then there's something else at stake, something else they

think I have, but I don't. Or I have it, and I don't know it."

He smiled. "That narrows it down."

She blew out a sigh, which turned into a yawn. It had certainly been a long day. She could hardly believe they'd flown back from New York earlier that morning. "We should talk to Mr. Brady again," she said. "Tell him about the break-ins. Maybe he can get someone in his intelligence agency to figure out what's happening."

"I'll call Stan first thing in the morning," he promised. Finishing his bottle of water, he set it down on the table.

For a moment there was silence between them. Julia's mind drifted from the problems of the day to Alex. He was sitting so close, their thighs were practically touching. She could hear him breathing, and the scent of his aftershave washed over her like a warm, inviting breeze—like a call to move closer, to run her lips across his jaw, the corner of his mouth...

Her nerves began to tingle in anticipation. She licked her lips as her pulse quickened.

Should she do it? Should she cross the few inches that separated them, run her hand through his hair, trap his handsome face with her suddenly impatient hands?

Alex cleared his throat. He shot her a hard look, then said, "You should go to bed. I'll take the couch."

Disappointment hit her like a cold shower. He obviously wasn't feeling what she was feeling. "I don't want to put you out of your bed. Besides, this sofa is pretty short, and you're a lot taller than I am." Taller, stronger, sexier... God, why was she so charged up? It must be the extra adrenaline in her body that was making her feel like she wanted to jump on him and not let him up for a long, long time.

"Just take the bed and don't argue. I can sleep anywhere." He quickly got to his feet.

She stared at him, surprised by the harsh tone of his voice. "What's wrong?"

"Nothing. It's been a hell of a day."

"That's it?"

"That's it. Let's call it a night. I'll get the bed made up."

"You don't have to do it. I'll take care of it."

"It's my bed. I'll do it," he snapped.

"Okay." She followed him into the bedroom, watching his sharp, impatient movements as he stripped the tumbled covers and began to remake the bed. "I'll help," she said. "Toss me a corner of the sheet."

"I can do it."

"It will go faster if I help you," she repeated as she moved to the other side of the bed.

"And I said I'd do it."

"Don't be ridiculous." She didn't know why he was being so stubborn. Leaning over, she grabbed the sheet. Alex yanked his end back so quickly that she fell halfway across the bed. Pushing her hair out of her face and feeling extremely irritated now, she tugged on her end of the sheet.

Alex had more strength, but she had a lot of determination. She pulled again, refusing to give up until she'd taken the sheet completely out of his hands. He dove for it. She tried to scramble out of the way, but he landed on top of her, pinning her hands over her head.

She pushed against his chest. He didn't budge. Nor did he appear to have any intention of moving. In fact, his dark eyes glittered with desire as he gazed down on her, and her breath caught in her chest. She was completely at his mercy.

"What is your problem?" she demanded, trying to focus on anger and not desire.

"You. You're my problem. I don't want you in my bed."

"You just said you did. In fact, you insisted."

"I don't want you alone in my bed," he corrected. "You're driving me crazy."

"I am?" she asked, somewhat bemused by that fact.

"I want to make love to you, Julia."

Hearing his intention stated so firmly and clearly made her tremble with anticipation. When he reached out and stroked her cheek with his hand, her whole body tingled. She swallowed hard, trying to think. She'd just broken up with Michael. She couldn't do this.

"You're an amazing woman," Alex murmured, his fingers now tracing her mouth. "So soft, yet so strong when you need to be." She held her breath as he leaned over and replaced his fingers with the tip of his tongue, which he ran lightly across her lips. "Hmm, I want more," he murmured.

So did she, but she couldn't ask, couldn't speak. She could only wait for his mouth to cover hers completely. Despite his words, he didn't immediately deepen the kiss. His mouth hovered just an inch above hers, teasing, taunting, until her nerves began to scream.

Finally, he moved. Or maybe she did.

Their mouths met in a deep, passionate kiss that went on and on. He released her hands, and she immediately flung them around his neck, pulling him closer, running her hands through his hair, enjoying the textures of his mouth, his skin, his hair. His palms skimmed up her sides until his hand covered one breast, his thumb playing the nipple into a tight point. She felt as if she were on fire, losing control with each passing second.

This wasn't her, was it?

She didn't have casual sex, did she?

Not that kissing Alex felt even close to casual.

"Stop thinking," he muttered against her mouth. "I can hear the wheels turning in your brain." He lifted his head to look at her.

"I'm not sure," she whispered. "I just got out of a relationship. I'm not certain I want to dive right into another one." She saw something flicker in his eyes and realized that he didn't want a relationship; he just wanted sex. She felt incredibly disappointed. "Oh," she said. "You're not looking for anything more than tonight or maybe just the next fifteen minutes."

"I think I can do better than fifteen minutes," he said lightly as he sat back. "It doesn't always have to mean something, Julia."

"I think it does—to me." She paused. "I know that sounds like a real girl thing to say, but that's what I am. If we make love tonight, Alex, I'm afraid I might fall in love with you. I don't think you want that."

She wanted him to refute her statement, tell her that's exactly what he wanted, because in truth she was already halfway in love with him, maybe more.

Alex didn't answer for a long tense moment. Then he said, "I'll leave you to make up the bed."

"You're not going to say anything else?"

"I don't make promises I can't keep." He got up and walked to the doorway, then turned back to her. "I don't know what real love is supposed to look like or feel like, Julia. And since you thought you were in love with someone else about eight hours ago, I'm not sure you do, either." On that note he left, closing the door quietly behind him.

She flopped back onto the bed, wondering if she'd made a huge mistake. As she stared up at the ceiling, she considered what he'd just said. He was wrong about one thing: She hadn't been in love with Michael eight hours ago. In fact, she'd probably never been in love with him, not the way she should have been. His kisses had never made her feel so dizzy, so off balance. Michael had been nice, comfortable, caring. Alex was hot, reckless, passionate.

She knew she wanted more in her life than what she'd had with Michael, but Alex was like a stick of dynamite. When it came right down to it, did she really have the courage to go after everything she wanted? She could stay here and play it safe, or she could march out into the living room and take the biggest risk of her life.

Her brain battled her body. Finally logic and caution won out. She couldn't make love with Alex tonight. It was too soon. She was too confused. It wouldn't be right.

But tomorrow was another day.

Chapter Fifteen

Liz sat in her father's kitchen early Wednesday morning, watching him pour two glasses of orange juice. He topped off his drink with a discreet shot of vodka. She knew she should say something, but she wasn't in the mood to argue with him. She hadn't slept well on his couch, and her nerves were strung tight after the break-in at her apartment. She still had to face going back there and trying to put her belongings back together.

Everything was changing, she thought with a small sigh. Her life felt wrong in every way. Just seeing her father padding around the kitchen in mismatched pajamas with his hair standing on end and an air of fragility about him reminded her how different everything was. Breakfast in her family had always been a big, happy affair. Her mother had loved cooking up plates of eggs, bacon, and potatoes, topped off with fruit, pastries and juice. She'd insisted they all come dressed to the table, their hair brushed, their faces washed, ready to face the day

The man in front of her wasn't the father she remembered from those days. He hadn't bothered to wash his face or brush his hair. She wasn't even sure when he'd last taken a shower or gone in to work. She certainly hadn't seen him at the cafe in days. What on earth was he doing with his time? As she watched him drink his orange juice, she knew she had her answer.

Clearing her throat, she said, "Why don't I make us some breakfast? Would you like scrambled eggs, an omelette, maybe some pancakes?"

He leaned against the counter and gave her a bleary smile.

"Your mother used to make pancakes, blueberry pancakes. Those were her favorite."

"I know," she said gently.

He sipped his juice halfway down the glass, licking his lips at the end. She should say something, but the words didn't want to come. Instead, she said, "I could try to make blueberry pancakes. I might have to run down to the store and get some berries, though." She got up from her chair and looked through his cabinets. She was shocked to see how empty they were. "Dad, you don't have any food in the house. What have you been eating?"

"Your aunts take care of me," he said with a shrug. "I don't feel like cooking anymore."

Which meant a lot coming from a man who made his living running a restaurant and prided himself on turning out good, quality food. "Is that why you haven't been down at the restaurant lately?"

"I'm tired of working," he said heavily. "Tired of so many things." He walked over to the table and sat down.

"Is there anything I can do to help?"

He shook his head. "I'll be all right. I'm worried about you and Julia. I think she should stay here, too, although I'm sure Michael wants to take care of her."

Liz saw the question in his eyes and damned Julia for once again not being here to do her own dirty work. She returned to her chair, trying to think of what to say. In the end, she just gave it to him straight. "Michael and Julia broke up last night."

Her father appeared truly shocked by the news. "What?" he stuttered. "How? Why?"

She didn't know which question to answer first. "I'm not sure why, but certainly Julia's push to find the missing pieces of her past didn't help. After Michael saw our apartment last night, he begged her to give up the search. She said she couldn't. She's obsessed, Dad, determined to find the truth. The past twenty-something years don't matter to her as much as the first three or four years of her life that she can't remember. And she seems to have forgotten how good Michael was to her through Mom's illness and how perfect Mom thought Michael was for her." Liz blew out a breath of frustration. "I don't get it. I can't understand why she'd let him go. Maybe he was rushing her a bit, but good grief, they've been together over a year. It's not exactly lightning speed."

"Your mother would be disappointed," Gino said. "And not just in Julia, but in me. I've let my daughter down."

"How do you figure that?"

"I should have paid more attention to what Julia was doing. I should have guided her more."

"It's not your fault. It's Julia's. She's the one making these foolish decisions. She really hurt Michael. I went to his house last night. He was drinking himself into oblivion." As she said the words Liz wondered if her father would see the parallel between Michael and himself. They were both choosing to dull their pain with alcohol. The problem was that once the alcohol wore off, the pain came back.

Gino didn't appear to make the connection. He finished his juice and got up to make another drink. She should say something, she told herself again. But right now her dad was the only one she had to talk to, and that would end if she attacked his drinking.

"Julia is changing right before my eyes," Liz continued. "Can't you make her stop, Dad? I think she'd listen to you."

He put up a hand. "I can't make her stop. I don't know who her biological father is, but if she is determined to find him, then she should be allowed to do so."

"It's disrespectful to you. You raised her. You treated her like your own daughter."

"And that's, the way I think of her. She's my daughter, and I want her to be happy. I'm sorry about Michael, though. He's a good man."

"It's not just her biological father she's interested in," Liz continued. "It's Mom's past as well. Julia is convinced that she's that girl in the picture, which means she had to be in Russia when she was three years old. That means Mom would have had to be there, too. How could that have happened?"

Gino gave a helpless shake of his head. "I can't imagine..."

Liz hesitated to voice her next thought, but she couldn't seem to stop it from coming out. "Do you think Mom could have adopted Julia?"

Gino sent her an angry glare. "No," he said firmly. "Absolutely not. It's impossible. They were close, like two peas in a pod, when I met them. And Sarah would have told me if she'd adopted Julia. She was always honest. She never lied about anything. Don't you remember her telling you over and over that the truth would never get you into trouble—only a lie would do that?"

Liz nodded. She remembered that well. Now she couldn't help wondering if different rules had applied to her mother. "There has to be some reason why Julia looks like that girl."

"It's a coincidence," he said, pouring more orange juice. "Julia was four and a half years old when I met her. I would have noticed if she was speaking Russian."

"That's true," Liz said, relieved. "If she was a Russian orphan, she would have been speaking Russian.

"Of course. Why didn't I think of that? I feel so much better now."

"Julia did have her own little odd way of talking, though," he said with a fond smile. "And she had an imaginary friend she was always whispering to."

Liz's good mood dimmed. "What do you mean, her own way of talking?"

"She'd jumble up words so sometimes they didn't make sense. It was just a phase she went through. It passed. I'm sure you did the same thing. You know how kids talk."

"Yeah, you're probably right." She stiffened as the buzzer rang in the apartment. "I'll get it." She walked over to the intercom. "Yes?"

"It's Julia. Can you let me up?"

Liz pushed the button and glanced over at her father in time to see him pour more vodka into his glass. She drew in a breath and walked out to the living room to answer the door. She wasn't surprised to see Alex standing behind Julia. The two seemed to be joined at the hip these days.

"Hi," Julia said, offering her a tentative smile. "How are you, Lizzie? I called you a couple of times last night, but you never answered your phone."

"I was busy. I do have a life, too, you know."

"How's Dad?" Julia asked, as she and Alex entered the apartment. "I want to talk to him."

"You better talk to him soon. He's in the kitchen sipping vodka and orange juice."

"It's nine o'clock in the morning."

Liz shrugged. "He's a little bothered by all the turmoil. You know, break-ins, pictures in the newspaper, his oldest daughter searching for her past in Russia, of all places."

Julia's mouth tightened. "You don't have to be sarcastic, Liz. I know this is very upsetting for everyone, especially you and Dad."

"And Michael. He was also drinking last night." Liz sent Alex a sharp look. "You better watch yourself. Julia has a way of driving all the men in her life to drink."

"Liz!"

"I'm sorry, but it's true." Liz felt a twinge of remorse for her harsh words, but she didn't intend to apologize to Julia. Her sister was the one who had stirred up their perfectly happy lives. "What are you doing here, anyway? I thought you didn't want to bring trouble to Dad."

"I don't, but I need to look through Mom's papers."

"Julia, is that you?" Gino asked, as he stumbled into the living room. "Are you all right? I've been so worried."

"I'm fine, Dad." Julia gave him a kiss on the cheek. "Is everything all right here?"

"Life goes on," he said with a fatalistic shrug of his shoulders. His eyes narrowed in on Alex. "Who's your friend?"

"I'm sorry, this is Alex Manning," Julia replied. "His father took the photo of the orphan girl. He's helping me find the truth."

Gino stuck out his hand, and Alex shook it. Liz couldn't believe her father was acting so welcoming. She didn't feel nearly as charitable. As far as she was concerned, Alex Manning was egging Julia on. Maybe if he hadn't been in the picture, Julia would have backed off a lot sooner.

"Do you mind if I take a look through Mom's papers?" Julia asked her father. "It's a long shot, but maybe there's something in there."

"Of course," he said. "I have nothing to hide. I don't think your mother did, either. She adored you. You were her baby."

Liz was relieved to hear her father tell Julia that. Someone needed to shake up her sister, remind her of the way life used to be.

"I know she loved me," Julia said, a troubled expression in her eyes. "But some things don't add up. I just want to make them add up."

"I don't want your curiosity to lead you into more danger," Gino said. "You should stay here. I thought Michael was protecting you, but Liz tells me that you've split up."

"Yes. It just wasn't working out. I know you liked him very much. But I feel sure it was the right decision for both of us."

Gino nodded. "It's your life to live, Julia, but Michael is a good man. Your mother loved him."

"I know she did, but I... I didn't. Not enough to marry him. That wouldn't have been fair."

Gino sent Alex a speculative look. Her father was probably wondering the same thing she was, Liz thought, if Julia's feelings about Michael had changed with the introduction of Alex into her life.

"I don't want to stay here," Julia added. "I don't want to put you in danger."

"But you don't mind putting this man in danger? It's not appropriate that you're staying with him." His voice took on a sharp edge. For all his kindness, their father was traditional in his views toward men and women sleeping together before marriage.

"Alex's apartment was broken into yesterday, too," Julia said.

"Are you serious?" Liz asked, stunned.

Julia nodded. "Yes, I think I was followed there."

Liz gazed into her sister's eyes and saw regret, but Julia obviously wasn't sorry enough. "So they could be outside right now," she said, "waiting to do the same thing to this apartment. How could you come here and put Dad in danger?"

"We weren't followed," Alex interrupted. "I'm sure of it. We took separate cars. We changed over to a friend's car in a crowded parking lot before we came here."

Liz sniffed, determined not to let on that she was at all impressed by their cloak-and-dagger maneuvering.

"I also told the police everything," Julia said. "They're going to be watching this apartment, too, just in case."

"You need to stop asking questions," Liz said. "Then we'll all be safe again."

"We won't be safe until we find what they're looking for." Julia turned back to Gino. "Are the papers in the second bedroom?"

"Yes. The room is in chaos. I'm sorry. I haven't had the energy to clean it up. I'll let you get to it, then." He meandered down the hall to the kitchen, probably to refill his glass, Liz thought. When he was gone, she turned on Julia, her anger and resentment coming to the fore. "Dad is drinking himself to death, Julia. Don't you even care?"

Julia took a step back in defense. "Of course I care, but I'm a little busy at the moment."

"Too busy for your own father? That's great."

"Liz, please."

"Please what? He's been drinking orange juice and vodka since he got up. He hasn't been to work. He hasn't gotten dressed in days. Did you even notice?"

"Well, you're here," Julia retorted. "Why don't you stop him, Liz? As far as I can tell, you're doing nothing. In fact, that's pretty much all you've been doing the last few months."

Liz didn't like the way Julia had turned the tables on her. "What are you talking about?"

"You keep waiting for everyone else to do something. You want me to stop looking for my past. You want Dad to stop drinking. You want me to intervene in that. What about you? What do you want? Ever since Mom got sick, you've been drifting along, whining about how everyone else is disappointing you. Are you going to finish college or just work at the cafe for the rest of your life? Don't you have any dreams of your own?"

"I—I don't know." Liz felt overwhelmed by the hard-hitting questions. A flood of tears pressed against her eyes, and she forced herself to hold them back. She did not want to cry in front of Julia and Alex. But suddenly she couldn't contain her emotions, so she ran.

She didn't stop running until she was halfway down the street. She was furious. She was hurt. Most of all she was stunned to realize that Julia was right. She stopped walking to wipe away the tears that were streaming down her face. God! Julia was right. She'd put her life on hold the second her mother had been diagnosed with cancer. She hadn't been able to see the future— because the future would be without her mother. And that was too painful to consider. In the months that had followed, she'd never taken her life off hold. She had no plan, no purpose, no nothing.

And as she looked around, she also realized she had absolutely nowhere to go.

* * *

"I can't believe I just said that. I should go after her." Julia stared at the door Liz had recently slammed, feeling incredibly guilty that she'd taken out her frustration on her sister.

"It sounded like you needed to say it."

"I hurt her feelings."

"Probably," Alex agreed.

She shot him a dark look. "You're supposed to say, 'No, you didn't. Don't worry about it'."

He shrugged his shoulders. "I don't have a sister or a sibling. I don't know the protocol."

Frustrated, Julia waved a hand in the air. "Liz has been on me so much the past few days. She wants to run my life, and she criticizes every decision I make. I guess I got tired of it. You're lucky you're an only child."

"I agree." He paused. "Are you going after her or are we looking for the papers?"

She debated for a long moment. She seemed to be doing that a lot lately. Making decisions had once been easy for her, probably because she'd never had anything really important to decide. Now, every day there seemed to be new, compelling, distracting choices. She'd spent most of the night before weighing the risks and benefits of inviting Alex back into his own bedroom. In the end, she'd taken the safe route and done nothing. She'd slept alone in the bed, with Alex on the couch in the living room. She was still mad at herself for that.

One of these days she would have to do something bold, something completely out of character. Maybe she'd start with letting Liz stew awhile instead of immediately trying to be the peacemaker, as she usually did.

"We're here. Let's search," she said decisively. "I'll talk to Liz later. Maybe if I find out something, it will be easier to make up with her."

"Don't count on it," he said pessimistically. "I have a feeling we've just hit the tip of the iceberg. This situation is going to get worse before it gets better."

"Thanks for that sunny thought," she said as she led him down the hall to the second bedroom.

"I'm a realist. In my job I have to be. The camera doesn't lie."

"But people do. And that's what we have to figure out now. Who was lying and what were they lying about?" She paused in the doorway, not surprised to see the clutter of boxes, books, and clothes. "This will take some time. At least with two of us, it will go faster."

Alex glanced around the room. "What is all this stuff?"

"I'm not sure. My dad sold our family home right after my mom died, and the market was so hot, the house sold in a day. We put some things in storage, because we weren't up to going through it all. I guess the office stuff and my parents' bedroom things are what's in here. Where should we start?"

"Let's work our way into the room."

She knelt down and opened the first box. "It's weird how in the end our lives boil down to things."

"Some really ugly things." Alex held up a statue of a deformed man. "Don't tell me this was on your coffee table."

She laughed. "My mom made that in a sculpting class. It was the first thing she ever made. We took the class together at the recreation center. I wanted to do something artistic, and she wanted to do something with me." Her smile faded as she thought about how much time they'd spent together with all the lies between them.

"Don't do that," Alex said. "Don't replace all the good memories with doubts."

She gave him a curious look. "How did you know I was doing that?"

"Experience. It's a waste of energy. It won't get you anywhere."

"I guess you're right, but it's hard."

"Look at this," Alex said, holding up a manila file folder. He pulled out a piece of paper. "Your birth certificate."

She took the paper out of his hand. She'd seen it before when she'd gotten her driver's license and on other occasions. But now she read it more closely. There was no father's name listed, just her mother's and hers, and the hospital, St. Claire's, Berkeley, California. "It sure looks like I was born here. It has an official

State of California stamp."

"It looks authentic," Alex agreed, "but papers can be bought and paid for, especially if a governmental agency is involved."

"That's what the reporter told me. I didn't know it was so easy to make up an identity for someone."

"If your mother did that, she had help."

Julia dug into her own box, which consisted mostly of scarves, gloves, and other accessories. Nothing there. She turned to the next one.

A moment later, Alex whistled. "You were a chubby little girl."

She frowned, slipping the photo from his hand. It had been taken at her eleventh birthday party, and she was definitely bulging. "They fed me a lot of Italian food," she complained. "My family thinks the more you eat, the happier you are, and I hadn't lost my baby fat yet."

"You're carrying more than a baby there," he teased. "And look at those railroad tracks on your teeth."

"Oh, shut up. I'm sure you weren't always this attractive."

"So you think I'm attractive?" he said with a charming wink.

"I think you're full of yourself, that's what I think."

"You like me."

"I don't." But she was still smiling when she tossed the photo back into the box. "Concentrate on what you're doing."

Slowly but surely she progressed through the boxes and moved across the room, finally landing on a box of costumes. Now that she knew her mother had traveled to Russia as a seamstress, the costumes took on new meaning. She pulled out the red cape she'd worn when she'd played Little Red Riding Hood in the third grade, then the angel costume she'd sported one Halloween. "We always had homemade costumes," she said. "My mother loved to sew. She never said she'd done it professionally, though."

"Of course she didn't," Alex replied. "She obviously wanted to hide her past in every possible way."

"Which means we probably won't find anything here."

"Keep digging. Sometimes people get careless."

With a sigh, Julia set back to work. The next box held Christmas cards and letters and an address book. The floral-patterned address book had been by her mother's bed the day she died. Her mother had wanted to let people know she was sick and was thinking of them, so she'd spent most of the last month writing brief notes. When she was too tired to hold the pen, Julia and sometimes Liz had written them for her. Unlike most of the other items in the room, which were from happier times, the address book reminded Julia of how bad that last week had been, watching her mother fade away before her very eyes. She was glad that she had been with her, but sometimes she was sad, too, because the image of death occasionally overpowered the other memories. She didn't want to remember her mother sick; she wanted to think of her happy and healthy.

Sitting cross-legged on the floor, she opened the address book and skimmed through the pages. There were three letters stuck in the back of the book, addressed and stamped and ready to go. Liz was supposed to have mailed them the day they were written, but she must have forgotten. The first one was to Pamela Hunt, the mother of a close friend of Julia's. The second was addressed to Grace Barrington, one of the waitresses who had worked at DeMarco's for at least a decade. And the third... Julia held the envelope up to the light, realizing that the writing was definitely her mother's, the letters weak and somewhat messy, making the name almost illegible. It took her a moment to decipher the writing.

"This is odd. It's addressed to Rick Sanders. I've never heard of anyone by that name."

Alex came to her side, squatting down next to her. "Why don't you open it?"

"Do you think I should? It's my mom's personal letter. She meant to mail it the day before she died. I remember watching her struggle to write it, but she said she had something important to say."

"Maybe a confession," Alex suggested. "Go on, open it."

"Why would she confess to someone named Rick Sanders?" At his pointed glance, she slid a finger under the flap and opened the envelope. There was one piece of notepaper inside. Julia took a breath and began to read. *'Dear Rick. I know we agreed not to speak, but I must let you know that I'm very sick. I don't think I'll make it another month..."* Julia's voice faltered as she realized she was reading some of her mother's very last words. "I can't." She held the paper out to Alex.

He took over. *"I'll think of you fondly always. I know you were angry with me for what I did, but it worked out the best for all of us. Julia is a beautiful woman now. And I have another daughter as well. My life turned out to be very happy. I hope that you, too, were able to find some happiness. I know you made the ultimate sacrifice, but I was never surprised by your actions. You were and are the most heroic man I've ever known. Love, Sarah."*

Alex lifted his head, his gaze meeting hers. "Who do you think it is?" she asked. "Who is Rick Sanders?"

"Maybe we should ask your father."

"I don't think so. I don't believe he would want to read a letter like this from my mother to another man, one signed with love."

Alex turned over the envelope. "The address is in St. Helena. That's about an hour and a half from here, isn't it?"

"Just north of Napa. You're not thinking of going there, are you?"

"Why not? You said your mother wrote this letter just before she died, and that it was important. I think we should deliver it personally."

"It's odd how she spoke of me by name, as if the person would know me, but not Liz," Julia mused. "You're right. We need to go there."

"What about work? Do you have a show tonight?"

"That was the call I made earlier. I've already arranged to cover my job for a few days, so I can devote my time to figuring out what's going on." She paused. "We haven't completely finished here."

"It doesn't look like these boxes are going anywhere."

"You're right about that. I'm sure my dad hasn't set foot in this room since he moved in." She hesitated. "I should say good-bye to him. And I should probably talk to him about the drinking he's doing. Liz is right. I have been shirking my responsibilities in that regard."

"That sounds like too long a conversation to have right now. And one you should probably have when your father is one hundred percent sober," he pointed out.

"True. I guess it can wait. I just hope my mother wasn't having an affair with Rick Sanders. My father would be devastated—" She stopped abruptly, clapping a hand to her mouth. "Oh, my God. You don't think Rick Sanders is my real father, do you?"

* * *

Julia had two hours to ponder that question on the drive to St. Helena, a small town in the wine country north of San Francisco. She'd been focusing so much on her mother that she hadn't thought about her biological father, but it made sense that her mother would have written to him just before she died. What didn't make sense was that she'd kept him a secret, never told Julia who he was or where he lived, which wasn't all that far from where she'd grown up.

As Alex turned off the freeway, Julia rolled down the window and let the fresh air blow against her face and through her hair. It really was a beautiful area, she thought as they passed apple orchards and fields of grapevines from which were made some of the best wines in the world. Growing up in an Italian family, she'd certainly tasted her fair share of red wine, but she'd never actually toured the wine country. Her father and uncle had gone a few times, but her mother had never been interested.

Why? Because the wine country was too close to someone of significance in her life?

"You haven't said a word in about an hour," Alex commented. "What's on your mind?"

"I keep wondering if I'm going to see my father in a few minutes. What will I say? What will I do?"

"You don't know that Rick Sanders is your father."

"I know my mom mentioned me specifically and then added that she'd had another daughter. He has to be someone she knew before she married Gino."

"That still doesn't make him your father."

"I need to be ready just in case. I used to think about meeting my dad, especially when I was a teenager. I'd look in the mirror, and I wouldn't see my mother in my features. I kept thinking that there was someone else in the world who looked like me. Of course, I didn't imagine that it was a little girl in a Russian orphanage," she said with a halfhearted smile,

He grinned back at her. "Good. You still have your sense of humor. That's important."

"Why is that important?"

"Laughter can get you through life. I've spent a lot of time in Africa, in villages where half the parents are gone, dead from HIV and other diseases. I couldn't believe these people could find anything to smile about, but every time I took out my camera, that's just what they did. They smiled in the face of unspeakable poverty."

Julia turned in her seat to look at him. His eyes were on the road, but she could tell his thoughts were in the past.

"I gave this one little boy a pen and a piece of paper," Alex continued. "You would have thought I'd just handed him a million dollars. He couldn't stop smiling. He played and drew all day long until there wasn't a centimeter of empty space on that piece of paper."

"Did you ever see him again? Do you ever see anyone again— the people whose pictures you take?"

He shook his head. "Most of the time I don't go back to the same location. Occasionally I do. I did return to that village about a year later."

"Please don't tell me he was dead." She hated to think of such a sad thing.

"I don't know what happened to him. The whole village was gone, wiped out by a flood. They said some people got out, but they had scattered to other villages. No one knew about that particular boy."

"So maybe he's still there playing with your pen and smiling."

He offered her a tender smile. "You have a soft heart, Julia. That could get you into trouble."

"I suspect it already has."

"Is that why you let things drag on with Michael? You didn't want to hurt his feelings?"

"Partly. I do care for him, and he treated me well. I never wanted to hurt him." She paused. "But I wasn't referring to Michael. I was thinking about my mom, how I never had the guts to ask her the questions I'm asking now. I let her put me off, because I didn't want to make her mad or upset her. And look where that got me."

"You said you had a good relationship with her, so your silence bought you that."

"I suppose. We talked all the time, even when I moved out of the house. She always knew what I was up to. She just couldn't stop checking up on me."

"How long was she sick?"

"About two years from start to finish. The last six months were particularly bad. It was difficult to watch. At least we had time to say our good-byes. I thought we had taken care of everything important. But I know now that my mom concentrated on things in the present or the future. She never spoke of the past in all the time she was sick. She only wanted to discuss what we would do later, after she was gone. Up until the very end of her life, she kept her secrets. I wonder if I'll ever know why."

"There's a good possibility you will know why, but you may wish you didn't before this is over."

"At this point, I'd take any truth over the uncertainty."

Alex shot her a speculative look. "Easy to say now. You don't know how bad it could be."

"Are you trying to prepare me for something? Do you have some suspicion you haven't shared?"

"I know what you know," he replied. "But I've seen some crazy shit in this world. You never know what people are capable of doing."

She probably didn't know. She'd led a sheltered life, protected from the harsh side of reality, protected by her mother. She sighed as she glanced out the window. The sign for St. Helena came into view. "Ready or not, here we come," she muttered.

"Are you talking about Rick Sanders or us?"

"Both. I don't have a good feeling about this, Alex."

"I haven't had a good feeling since you knocked on my door last Friday."

For a while they drove along a rural frontage road dotted by farms, horses, a couple of cows, and small homes. Julia breathed in the scent of freshly cut grass. It was a beautiful day, with a royal blue sky and a bright sun, the kind of day that reminded her summer was not far behind them and winter was still a ways off. It was also the kind of day that seemed too bright for anything bad to happen. She hoped that would be the case.

Alex asked her to check the map. She told him to turn right at the next intersection. Gradually the landscape grew more crowded with homes, businesses, gas stations, and strip malls. Rick Sanders lived on a street called Caribbean Court. Julia didn't think the area at all resembled the Caribbean. The address they were seeking matched a modest one-story, ranch-style home. There was a beat-up Chevy, at least twenty years old, in the driveway. The grass in the front yard was sparse, dry, with big areas of dirt. The flowers were wilted, weeds growing between rosebushes planted along the front of the house.

Julia's nervousness intensified as they parked the car and got out.

Was she actually going to meet her father? On this day? At this moment?

Would she know instinctively when she saw him? Or would he seem like a stranger?

She put her hand on Alex's arm as he started down the walk. "Wait. I don't think I'm ready."

"You don't have to say or do anything, Julia. I'll handle it. I'll mention your mother's name. We'll see how he responds. You can just watch, listen."

"What if he says something to me when he sees me? What if he recognizes me? What if I don't want him to be my father?" He smiled at her, and she knew she was flipping out. "Too many questions?"

"One step at a time."

"I like to be prepared for any possibility."

"Sometimes the best things come when you least expect them."

"Or the worst."

"Who's the pessimist now?"

"All right." She drew in a deep breath. "Let's go. I hope he's home."

As soon as Alex rang the bell, they heard the sound of a dog barking and a man's voice, telling the dog to quiet down. A moment later the door opened. Julia blinked. The sun streaming in behind them put the man in shadow. All she could see was his blue shirt and white shorts. His features were completely indistinguishable.

Alex grabbed her arm and squeezed tight.

"Ow," she said, but he didn't appear to hear her. He was

staring at the man with shock and horror.

The man stepped onto the porch, and finally Julia could see him. His hair was dark, his eyes a light green.

"Rick Sanders?" she queried.

Silence met her question. Then the man drew in a deep breath and said, "Not exactly. Do you want to tell her, Alex?"

"You know him?" Julia asked in amazement.

Alex's mouth tightened. "Goddammit, Julia. He's my father."

Chapter Sixteen

Alex couldn't believe what he was seeing. The man in front of him could not possibly be his father. His father was dead!

But the brown hair, the green eyes, the long, thin face looked so familiar.

Alex blinked once, twice, three times. The image in front of him didn't change. He still saw his father's face. He was older, definitely. There were lines around his eyes, some gray in his hair, slack in his skin. But he hadn't changed that much. He was still the man who'd supposedly died twenty-five years ago, the man who had driven his car off the edge of a cliff, the man who Alex believed had been murdered.

How could this be? It was impossible. It was unbelievable.

His father—Charles Manning—was alive.

Alex put a hand on his gut, feeling like he was about to throw up. His breath came fast, his heart pounding against his chest. He couldn't think.

"Alex." Charles held out a tentative hand.

Alex jumped back, knocking his hand away. "What the hell is going on? Who are you?"

"You know who I am. You just said so." Charles stared at him through eyes dark with pain and guilt. "How did you find me?"

The question went through his head twice before it made sense. "I wasn't even looking for you," Alex said finally, feeling a deep and bitter anger rising through his body. "I came here looking for Rick Sanders."

"Why?"

Alex couldn't remember why now. His mind was spinning.

"Because my mother wrote you a letter that she never mailed," Julia interjected. "My mother's name was Sarah. I believe you knew her."

His father drew in a quick, hard breath. "Sarah? She sent you?"

"No. She's dead," Julia said bluntly.

Alex saw the surprise flare in his father's eyes. Whatever else he knew, he hadn't known that.

"When did it happen?" Charles asked.

"Six months ago." Julia handed him the letter. "She wrote you the day before she died. I didn't find the letter until today. I thought I'd personally deliver it. I didn't know that you..." Her voice trailed away.

Charles Manning stared down at the letter in his hand but made no attempt to read it. Then he glanced back at Alex. "Will you come in, so we can talk?" He stepped aside so they could enter the house.

Alex hesitated. Did he want to go in? Did he want to listen to anything this man had to say? He was still reeling. His father had let him believe he was dead for years and years. How could he possibly explain that?

"Let's go inside," Julia said quietly, her hand on his arm.

He'd forgotten she was there. He looked down at her and saw compassion in her eyes. "Looks like you weren't the one who had to worry," he said sharply.

"We need to hear what your father has to say."

"What could he say? How could he possibly explain the fact that he's alive and living under another name?"

She didn't try to answer his question. Neither did his father. They both just stared at him. Alex knew he needed to go inside. He needed to talk to his father. But this was wrong. It was all wrong. They had come here to find Julia's father, unlock the secret of her past. He was supposed to be the observer, not the participant. Dammit.

He wasn't ready for this confrontation. He'd never be ready.

This was his father.

The last time they'd spoken, Alex had been nine years old. And right now he felt about nine, overwhelmed with emotions that normally had no place in his life.

Julia tried to take his hand, but he pulled away. He couldn't stand to touch her. Couldn't stand to feel anything more than he was feeling. He walked into the house, looking around the dingy room. There was a green couch along one wall, a ripped, taped armchair in a corner in front of an old television set. A dog barked from behind a gate in the kitchen.

"Noah, quiet," Charles said sharply.

The dog barked once in reply, then sank to the ground.

Alex stared at the black lab with the white streak down its nose. His father had a dog—the pet he'd never been allowed to have. His mother had always said dogs were too messy, too much work, and his father was always on the road, so that was that. But now his dad had a dog. Unbelievable.

"Alex, let's sit down," Julia suggested.

He shook his head, his gazed fixed on his father's face. "You want to talk—talk."

Charles cleared his throat. "I don't know what to say. I wondered if this day would ever come."

"You did? You wondered?" Alex tasted bile in the back of his throat. "When did you wonder? The day we buried an empty box in the ground, or was it later? Were you at your own funeral? Did you watch us grieving over you? Was it a big joke?"

"No, of course not."

"How could you do that to us? How could you let us believe you were dead?"

Charles stared back at him with apology in his eyes. "I'm sorry, Alex. I'm sorry you had to find out like this."

"No, you're just sorry I found out."

"It's a long, complicated story."

"So start explaining. Not that I have any reason to believe a word you say."

"I deserved that," Charles said.

"I don't know what you deserve. Why don't you start with why you faked your own death to your wife and child?"

"To protect you," Charles answered.

"From what?" Alex's hands clenched into fists. He was so angry he wanted to hit someone or something. It was all he could do not to give in to the impulse.

"From the people who were after me because of the photo you'd taken."

Alex hated being reminded that the photo was his fault. He'd blamed himself for his father's death even before this past week. He'd always felt that somehow he'd been responsible. Then when Stan and later Brady told him his father had been murdered... He shook his head as anger raced through him once again. "I can't believe I blamed myself for your fake death."

"Why would you blame yourself for my accident?" Charles asked sharply.

"Let's see—maybe it was because Daniel Brady told me yesterday that you were killed because of that picture I took."

"Brady told you that? Did he tell you I was alive?"

"No, he didn't mention that little fact." Alex's stomach burned once again as he remembered that Daniel Brady had told them Charles was probably murdered, and he'd said it with a straight face. "That bastard," he murmured. "He knew all along you were alive."

"He helped me set up the crash," Charles admitted. "Brady was never supposed to tell you it was anything but an accident." He paused, his eyes serious. "He must have wanted to scare you off. Why were you talking to him?"

Alex ignored that. "Does Mom know that you're alive?"

Charles shook his head. "No."

That was a small consolation. At least he hadn't been the only one duped.

"After the photo was published, I received a death threat," his father said. "I knew you and your mother were in danger. The only way I could protect you was to die. If I was dead, you would be free."

"You're going to have to give me more than that," Alex said, pacing back and forth across the room, adrenaline rushing through his bloodstream. He couldn't handle the emotions ripping through him—anger, frustration, disappointment, sadness, bewilderment...

"It's too dangerous to tell you more," his father replied. "I've protected you all these years. I won't stop now just because you're grown."

"How dare you tell me that you've protected me! You left me fatherless and alone. You let me grow up thinking you were dead.

Do you have any idea what that was like?" Twenty-five years of grief and rage for all that he'd lost with his dad drove him over the edge. Alex picked up the glass vase on top of the television console and heaved it toward the fireplace. The glass shattered into a million pieces. He felt only marginally better.

"Alex, calm down," Julia said, worry in her eyes.

"Why should I? He broke up my life."

"I know you're upset," Charles began.

"That doesn't even touch what I'm feeling. How the hell can you stand there and talk about protecting me when you walked out on me? I wanted to be just like you. God! I can't believe I ever thought that way." He bit down on his bottom lip so hard he tasted blood. "I'm not doing this," he said. He headed for the door, his only thought to get as far away from his father as possible.

"Wait, don't go," Charles said. "We need to talk this out."

Alex paused in the doorway. "How are we going to talk when you won't tell me anything? I'm done. You can keep your secrets. I don't give a damn anymore. I'm out of here." Alex slammed out of the door, striding down to the sidewalk so fast he barely felt his feet hit the pavement. He was so mad. His head was pounding, and his nerves felt as if they were on fire.

"Hang on, Alex," Julia yelled. She caught up with him at the car. "I'm driving."

"No, you're not."

"Yes, I am. You're in no condition to drive. You'd probably run us off the road."

"You must be mistaking me for my father. He's the one who runs off roads and pretends to be dead." He slammed his fist down on the hood of the car, relishing the pain that shot through his fingers and up his arm. He could handle that pain. He could handle what was real, what made sense.

"Give me the keys," Julia said, blocking his way into the car.

"I am fine."

"You're nowhere close to fine. And you know it."

He didn't want to waste time arguing with her. He tossed her the keys. "Drive fast," he ordered. "I want to get the hell away from here."

* * *

They should have stayed and talked it out, Julia thought as she drove Alex back to San Francisco.

There were questions that should have been asked—about the photograph, about Sarah, about herself. Those questions would have to wait. When Alex had time to think, to recover, maybe he'd be more receptive to another discussion. If not, she'd do it on her own. But she wouldn't leave him now. For the first time since she'd met him, he seemed completely overwhelmed and out of control. Every muscle in his body was clenched. There was a nervous, reckless, angry energy about him as he tapped his fingers on his leg, then the armrest, shifting every few minutes as if he couldn't possibly get comfortable. She doubted he would feel comfortable for a very long time.

His father was alive. She couldn't imagine what Alex must have felt when his father stepped onto that porch. She knew how much Alex had idolized his father and how much he loved him. In fact, up until this moment she might have said that Charles Manning was the only person Alex had ever loved with any kind of depth. He certainly didn't seem to possess the same emotion for his mother or for any other woman in his life.

She shot him a sideways glance, wondering what he would tell his mother. But she wouldn't ask. She couldn't push him right now. He was a spark ready to explode.

"Can't you drive any faster?" Alex asked as they crossed the Bay Bridge to San Francisco. "Why don't you change lanes?"

"Alex, chill. Do you want me to turn on some music?"

"No." Alex tugged on the seat belt restraining him and shifted in his seat once more. He breathed out a heavy sigh, then said, "He's not dead, Julia."

She cast him a quick glance, but he was staring straight ahead. "I know," she said.

"I watched them put an empty casket into the ground. I didn't know it was empty at the time. No one explained that to me when I was nine, but I figured it out later. I don't even have to close my eyes to remember the cemetery staff throwing big chunks of dirt onto the casket after they'd put it in the ground. My mother didn't want me to watch, but I couldn't look away." He turned to her. "Where do you think he was? Hiding behind some tree or statue in the cemetery? Was he watching us cry for him? How could he let us think he was dead? What kind of man does that to his child and his wife?"

"I'm sorry, Alex."

He didn't seem to hear her. He was too lost in his thoughts, his memories. "I went into my parents' bedroom during the reception after the funeral. I didn't understand why people were laughing and talking as if nothing had happened. I wanted to feel closer to my father, so I went into the room my parents shared when they'd been living together. He hadn't been there in months, but I thought I could still smell his aftershave. I went into the closet where he had left some clothes hanging in the back. I stayed in that closet for over an hour."

Her heart broke at the image of the lonely, terrified little boy he described. "Did your mother find you?" she asked softly, hoping that Kate Manning had had enough tenderness at that point to pull a nine-year-old Alex into her arms and hold him.

"No, she didn't come looking for me. Eventually, I came out on my own and put myself to bed. He was gone and I had to accept it. So I did." Alex rubbed his forehead with his fingers as if he had a pounding headache.

"I have some aspirin in my purse," she offered.

"I don't need it. I'm fine."

"Yeah, you already told me that."

A few minutes later she exited the bridge and drove straight to Alex's apartment building, hoping she wouldn't find any more surprises. They'd have to pick up their cars later and return the car they were driving to Alex's friend. But at the moment all she wanted to do was get Alex home.

When they entered the apartment, it was just as they'd left it—complete and total devastation. Maybe it was a good time to clean up. It would give them something else to focus on besides the horrible truth they'd just uncovered.

She followed Alex into the bedroom, surprised when he pulled out an overnight bag from the closet and tossed it onto the bed. "What are you doing?" she asked.

"I'm leaving."

She was shocked. Those were the last words she'd expected him to say. "What do you mean?"

"I'm getting out of here. I don't need this," he said, running his hand through his hair. His eyes were wild, filled with reckless anger. "A good photographer doesn't get involved with his subjects. He stays on the right side of the lens," he added. "I never should have gotten involved with you."

"But you did get involved, and you can't leave. We're not finished. We don't know everything."

"I know more than enough. You can talk to my father on your own. I'm sure he can help you figure out the rest. Maybe he'll tell you more if I'm not there, if he doesn't have to protect me," he said with bitterness.

"I know you're hurt—"

"You don't know anything."

"Yes, I do," she argued. "Your father lied to you. My mother lied to me. I know how it feels to have the rug pulled out from under your feet."

"Your mother didn't pretend she was dead."

"She did to her own parents." She paused, letting that sink in. "Don't you think it's another odd coincidence that both of our parents chose to do that to the people they loved? Doesn't that make you wonder exactly what they were involved in? It had to be big, Alex. These aren't tiny white lies, little secrets. Don't you want to know exactly what happened?"

He hesitated, a flicker of uncertainty flashing through his eyes; then he shook his head, his mouth drawing once again into a taut, resolute line. "I don't care about any of it. My father left my life twenty-five years ago. I've gotten along fine without him and without knowing anything else. I can go another twenty-five years the same way."

"No, you can't."

"Watch me." He zipped up his bag and went to the closet to get his camera case.

Julia wished she could find the right words to stop him from leaving, but he seemed hell-bent on doing just that. "Is there anything I can say to make you change your mind?"

"No. You should stay with your father. Don't hang out on your own," he advised.

"What do you care? You'll be gone." She wanted him to reply, but he just continued packing. She walked out of the bedroom, into the living room, hoping with every step that he'd call her back.

There was nothing but silence.

* * *

Julia took a cab to where she'd left her car, then decided to return home and figure out her next step. She could drive back to St. Helena on her own, but it was late afternoon and the traffic would be bad. Besides, she needed time to process everything they'd learned.

When she entered her apartment, she found Liz, dressed in blue jeans and a skimpy T-shirt, doing her own packing. She had two suitcases on Julia's bed and was quickly filling them up.

"What are you doing?" Julia asked, unable to believe she would have to play out the same scene again—this time with her sister.

"I'm moving out," Liz announced.

"Why?"

Liz paused and stared at her as if she couldn't believe the question. "Why do you think? I don't want to be a part of your search. It's obviously dangerous. Not that you care about risking my life."

"Of course I care, Liz."

"But it's not even about that. It's what you said earlier."

Julia felt a wave of guilt. "I'm sorry if I came down too hard on you. I just can't keep fighting you and everyone else at the same time."

"No, you were right. I've been drifting aimlessly for too long. I moved in here because I didn't know where else to go. And I wanted you to get married to Michael, so I'd have a wedding to plan, even if it wasn't my own. I urged you to talk to Dad about his drinking, so he wouldn't get mad at me. I even wanted Michael to let me help him with his new house, so I'd have something else to do besides work at a place where I ladle soup into bread bowls and wait tables."

Julia couldn't believe what she was hearing, but she didn't intend to argue. Instead she said, "It's understandable that you've been drifting, Liz. Mom just died. It was a long illness. I drifted, too. That's why I let Michael and me go on for so long. In fact, I think that's why I started dating him in the first place. Mom had just gotten sick, and I thought how fast life was going and how I was almost thirty and I wasn't close to getting married. I latched onto Michael like he was a buoy and I was drowning." She walked farther into the room. "Don't move out. Let's just start over."

Liz put up a hand in defense. "No. We can't start over, because you're still involved in searching for your past, and I can't be part of that. I'm afraid of where that search will take you and what our relationship will be when you're done."

"We'll always be sisters."

"You say that now, but your feelings might change."

"They won't. I know they won't."

Liz shrugged. "All right, I'll believe you for the moment, but I'm still moving out. I don't want to live here with some madman running around after you, and I also need to take a step forward for myself. This seems like a good time to do that."

"Where are you going? To Dad's?"

"That would be easy, but no. Mary down at the cafe told me that her sister is in Europe for two weeks. I'm going to stay at her place while I look for something more permanent." Liz paused. "I don't think you should stay here alone. Maybe you should move in with Alex."

Julia shook her head. "I can't do that. Alex is leaving."

Liz's eyes widened in surprise. "Where's he going?"

"Back to work," she said simply, not having the energy to get into a lengthier discussion.

"Just like that he takes off? Nice guy. So what will you do now? I thought you needed his help to figure out your secret past."

"I'll do it on my own. I can handle it." She wasn't nearly as confident as her words.

"Maybe I should stay here after all," Liz said halfheartedly. "I don't want you to be alone."

Julia hesitated. She didn't want to be alone, either, but she also didn't want Liz in danger. And she knew that Liz needed to make this move for herself. "I'll be fine. I'll probably find somewhere else to stay, a friend's house or something. Don't worry about me."

"I can't help it." Liz gave her a disgusted smile. "You're my sister." She walked over to Julia and put her arms around her, giving her a quick hug. "Be careful, okay?"

"I will. I promise."

As Liz left, Julia sat down on her bed and gazed around the

room, which was in the same state she'd left it in yesterday. She might as well start cleaning, throwing away the broken pieces of her life. It would give her something to do while she considered her next move. And tomorrow she would go back to St. Helena and talk to Charles Manning. He was her only link to the past. Maybe Alex was right. Maybe his father would tell her more if she were on her own. She just hoped she was ready to hear it.

It was almost midnight when the knock came at her door. Julia started at the sound. She set down the broom she'd been sweeping with in the kitchen and moved cautiously to the front door. She didn't live in a security building, so anyone could come right up to her door. But she did have the dead bolt on as well as a chain. She peered through the peephole and was shocked to see Alex on the other side. She'd thought he'd be on a plane to some other continent by now.

"You came back," she said as she opened the door. Alex still wore the blue jeans and black polo shirt he'd had on earlier, but there was no sign of the overnight bag he'd been packing when she'd left his apartment. "What are you doing here?"

"Hell if I know," he said cryptically, as he walked into her apartment. "I see you've cleaned up."

"As much as I could. Some of the furniture I'll have to replace."

"Where's your sister?"

"She moved out earlier. She's going to get her own place."

His eyes narrowed. "That was sudden."

"Not really. We haven't been living together all that well the past few months. She only intended to stay here temporarily after my mom died and my dad sold the house. One day just ran into the next." She stopped abruptly. "You didn't come here to talk about Liz. So, why did you come? You couldn't get a flight out tonight?"

He crossed his arms in front of his chest. "I went to the airport. I bought a ticket, stood in the security line, waited at the gate. When they called my seat number, I couldn't make myself get on the plane. My bags are on their way to Peru right now, and I'm probably on some FBI flight watch for bailing at the last minute." He looked into her eyes and sighed. "I kept thinking about you, Julia, and the deal we made to find the truth together. You should have called me on that earlier."

"How could I after what you learned today?"

His expression turned grim. "I don't want to talk about that."

"How can we not? Your father—"

"Don't call him my father. Call him Rick Sanders. That's who he is now." Alex looked away from her, but she could tell he was battling his emotions.

She walked over to him and put a hand on his arm, but he shrugged it off.

"Don't feel sorry for me. I don't want your pity," he said.

"What do you want from me?"

A long silence followed her question. Finally, he gazed back at her. "I don't think you're going to give me what I want." He put his hands on her waist and pulled her up hard against his body. "Are you?"

Her breath caught in her throat at the look of intense desire in his eyes. No man had ever looked at her like that. A shiver ran down her spine as he shifted, grazing her breasts with his hard chest.

"I don't know what's true anymore," he said. "There have been so many lies, secrets, inconsistencies in my life. But I know this: I want you, and I think you want me. Is that enough?"

A week ago Julia would have said it wasn't nearly enough, that she needed romance and candlelight, soft words, proper dating, promises. But none of those things had ever made her feel as alive as she felt right now. Alex was right. She didn't know what was true anymore, either. The only person who wasn't lying to her was Alex.

She answered him the only way she could—with a kiss. He gave her a second to lead, then took over, his mouth moving hungrily over hers, demanding entry so his tongue could take possession. She'd never been feasted upon, but that's exactly the way she felt now. His kiss was demanding, consuming, overwhelming, and she didn't want it to end. She gave a small cry of disappointment when he pulled away to kiss a path across her cheek. Then her stomach clenched again when his tongue swirled around her earlobe and he licked a delicious path down the side of her neck.

Conscious thought deserted her as his hands moved up her sides, his fingers flirting lightly with her breasts. She wanted her clothes off and his hands on her—all over her. Then she wanted to return the favor. In fact, she wanted to start right now. She ran her hands under his shirt, touching his hard, muscle-bound chest. He moved closer to her, pressing his groin into her belly. He was hot and hard, and she was melting fast.

He yanked her shirt up and over her head so quickly that a strand of her hair caught in one of the buttons, and she yelped with pain.

"Sorry, sorry," he muttered, pulling her hair free with impatient hands.

"You'll have to kiss it better."

"I intend to," he said, his gaze burning into hers. "I intend to taste every inch of you."

"Oh." Her chest tightened at the promise in his eyes, in his voice.

He pressed her back against the wall, one hand in her hair, the other playing with the light blue lace trim on her bra. He ran his finger back and forth along the edge, his eyes following the path until she wanted to scream. She caught his hand with hers.

"Wait," she said.

"Second thoughts?"

She didn't answer. She simply flipped open the front clasp on her bra. The edges clung to her breasts. She wondered if she had the nerve to peel them away. He didn't give her the chance as he pushed the bra all the way off. His hands covered her breasts as his mouth returned to hers. She didn't know how they got the rest of their clothes off, but somewhere between the living room and the bedroom, they managed to strip themselves naked. By the time they reached the bed, there was nothing but skin and heat.

Love, lust, sex—whatever it was—had never been so hot, so impatient, so demanding. And not just on Alex's part, but on hers, too. Julia found herself making impulsive, bold moves she'd never made before. There were no rules with this man, no boundaries, nothing to hold her back. Every touch, every taste was a risk, but for once she met the risk head-on. She didn't know where they would be tomorrow, but tonight Alex was in her arms, and she was in his, and when their bodies came together, everything was right with the world.

Chapter Seventeen

Julia woke up to the sun streaming through her bedroom window and Alex shifting restlessly beneath her. She lifted her head from his chest and saw that his eyes were wide open and he was watching her. She self-consciously patted down her hair, sure it must be flying in a hundred different directions. They'd had quite a workout the night before. She felt tired but wonderfully loved.

"Good morning," she said, feeling a little shy now that it was daylight. She pulled the sheet up over her shoulders.

He smiled at her, pushing the sheet back down. "You look beautiful in the morning."

"Oh, please, that can't be true."

"It's your eyes. They're so clear, so blue. They're like a window into your heart. You show all your emotions."

She wondered what emotions she was showing right now and was tempted to look away, but there had been nothing except honesty between them until now, and she didn't want to change that. "Your eyes hide everything. I'm never completely sure what you're thinking."

"I like it that way."

"I'm sure you do." She traced his jaw with her finger and saw his eyes darken and his lips part. They'd made love twice already and it still wasn't enough. "We should get up," she said.

"I'm already there," he replied with a grin.

She laughed. "I can see that. Actually, I can feel that." She pressed her thigh into his groin and his arms came around her back. "What are we going to do about it?"

"I have a few ideas."

"Really? You haven't used them all up?"

"I haven't even come close." He rolled her onto her back, pinning her beneath him. His hands cupped her face, and the smile faded from his lips as his expression turned serious.

She wondered what he was thinking. She was afraid to ask.

"Julia," he said, then stopped.

She waited for him to finish. He didn't.

"What?" she asked.

He shook his head, then kissed her, long, slow, and tender, like he was never going to let her go. She ran her hands up and down his back, loving the weight of him in her arms, the way he moved and touched her, the way he made her feel wanted and loved. Not that they'd spoken of love. Maybe for Alex it was just desire, chemistry, physical attraction, but she liked him. She liked him a lot. Probably too much. He'd never promised to stay or to love her. And one day he would go, and she'd probably find herself with a broken heart.

But he wasn't leaving today, and if today was all she was going to have, she'd take it.

* * *

Hours later, Julia was dressed and back in the car, this time with Alex behind the wheel. She'd thought it would take a huge argument to convince him to go back to St. Helena to see his father, but he'd brought it up himself. He said he knew they had unfinished business.

Despite his resolute determination to get to the bottom of things, she could feel his tension as they drove north on the freeway. The closeness they'd shared the night before evaporated with each passing mile. She knew Alex wasn't thinking about her, but about his father and what he would say next.

"Are you okay?" she asked.

"I'm fine," he said briefly.

"Are we back to fine again?"

"All right. I'm not looking forward to this meeting. In fact, I keep thinking about taking the next exit and making a U-turn."

"If you want to, you can."

He shook his head. "No, I don't run away. I never run away."

She didn't remind him that just yesterday he'd done exactly that.

"Okay, maybe I retreat," he amended, giving her a sideways glance. "Then I go back and do what needs to be done."

"You're not doing it alone."

He patted her thigh. "I know, and I appreciate that fact."

She smiled at him. "I'm really glad you didn't leave, Alex. It means a lot to me that you came back last night." She saw his face stiffen and realized she was treading into dangerous territory regarding their personal relationship. "Don't worry. I'm not asking you for anything," she said quickly.

"Dammit," he swore.

"What? Jeez, don't you think you're overreacting a little?"

"There's someone following us." He tipped his head toward the rearview mirror. "Since we left the city, a black Explorer has been on our tail. I'm going to change lanes. Take a look through the side mirror and tell me what you see."

Julia saw the car immediately and her pulse quickened. "I see two men. I don't recognize them." The Explorer moved behind them, staying three cars back.

"Let's see if they're serious," Alex said.

She didn't like the sound of that, but she didn't have a chance to voice her concern.

Alex waited until the last second to take the next exit, veering across four lanes to do so. The black Explorer attempted to move over but was cut off by a truck and a loud booming horn. Once off the freeway, Alex drove under the overpass, making several twists and turns until they were a few miles from the freeway in some part of Napa that Julia had never seen before. Alex pulled the car into the parking lot of a supermarket, ducking in between a minivan and a truck, then turned off the engine.

They had a good view of the only entrance into the parking lot, and they sat for several minutes without speaking, waiting to see if the Explorer had managed to catch up with them.

"You must have lost them." Julia finally released the breath she'd been holding. "Who do you think they were?"

"I have no idea, but they were definitely following us."

"One of them could have been the guy you chased down Union Street. Although I didn't see a baseball cap on anyone's head. What do we do now?"

Alex thought for a moment, then reached behind him to grab the map. "Let's see if we can find a back way to St. Helena that doesn't take us on the freeway."

After reviewing the map, Alex drove back roads to their destination. It was slower going, but they arrived at Caribbean Court without any sign of the black Explorer.

"I wonder if anyone followed us here yesterday," Julia mused.

"I was just thinking the same thing."

"I hope we didn't put your father in any danger."

Alex pulled up in front of his father's house. He threw the car into park so fast, Julia almost hit the windshield. She put out a hand to brace herself. "What's wrong?"

"Look," he said.

She wasn't sure she wanted to look. Slowly, she turned her head, licking her lips, praying she wasn't going to see the men they'd just tried to outrun, or something even more horrible.

It was a sign that had caught Alex's attention. The for rent sign planted on the front lawn hadn't been there yesterday. Her gaze darted to the driveway. The beat-up Chevy was gone. The garage door was closed; the only sign that a car had ever been there was a puddle of black oil on the driveway. She glanced back at the house. The curtains and windows were closed up as if someone had left and was never coming back.

She swallowed hard. What had happened here after they'd left yesterday? Had someone gone after Charles?

"God, Alex," she murmured. "What if they... ?" She couldn't say it. She didn't even want to think it. She reminded herself that their apartments had been broken into when they weren't home. No one had been hurt—yet.

"Let's go," Alex said decisively.

She shot him a quick look, but he was already moving out of the car. She caught up to him on the front porch. The screen door was slightly ajar and crooked. Had it been like that yesterday? Or was it evidence of violence? She wasn't sure she wanted to go with him, but Alex was already ringing the bell, pounding on the door, shouting his father's name.

No one answered. She could feel Alex's tension, his fear. She grabbed his arm when he reached for the doorknob.

"Wait," she said. "Maybe we don't want to go in there."

"Believe me, I don't want to go in there," he replied, "but we have to try."

It was too easy. The knob turned in his hand.

Alex entered the room first. Julia clung to his back, peering around him as he stopped in the living room. She'd expected to see chaos, destruction. Instead, she saw nothing. Everything was gone. There wasn't one stick of furniture left in the room, no evidence of the vase Alex had broken, no sign of the television or the couch. A fine layer of dust covered the hardwood floor, dust that appeared to be untouched, as if no one had ever been in the house. But Charles Manning had stood in this room only yesterday. His belongings, his life, his dog, for God's sake, had all been real. Hadn't they? She blinked, wondering if she was somehow dreaming.

Alex stepped away from her.

"Where are you going?" she asked quickly, reluctant to be alone.

"To check the bedroom. Wait here." He returned a moment later, his expression grim. "He's gone, not a trace of him left. He disappeared into thin air just like he did before."

"How? How does someone leave that fast? It was yesterday afternoon, barely twenty-four hours ago." She felt incredibly disappointed and also unnerved. There was something about the empty house, the fact that someone had gone to a lot of trouble to wipe Charles Manning off the face of the earth again, that was frightening. She hoped nothing had happened to him.

"My father must have had help. Damn him."

"Do you think he did this?"

"He disappeared once before."

She heard the bitterness in his voice and knew he was hurting again. He'd taken a huge personal risk to come here and face his father, and he'd been deserted again. The sound of a car drew her toward the window. She pulled the curtain aside to see a silver Honda Civic park in front of Alex's car.

"Who do we have here?" Alex muttered, as he peered over her shoulder.

Daniel Brady got out of the car. It wasn't the same car he'd driven to the beach. She idly wondered how many he had. Brady looked around him before making his way up to the front of the house. He wore a navy blue suit today with a white shirt and a conservative tie. He looked like a corporate businessman more than a government agent—or whatever he was. Alex's friend in the State Department had never called back with that information. Julia still wasn't sure exactly what Brady's job entailed. Maybe it was time to find out.

Brady opened the front door without bothering to knock. He didn't appear surprised to see them standing in the living room.

"Where is he?" Alex asked.

"I'm sorry. That's classified," Daniel said smoothly.

"Then why are you here?"

"He thought you'd come back. He wanted you to know he's all right, but that your visit yesterday compromised his safety and yours. He had to leave."

"How did our visit compromise anyone's safety?" Julia asked. "Were we followed?"

"It's possible."

"So nothing specific happened," Alex said. "This was just a preemptive strike."

"Exactly. I told you to drop it, Alex. You don't know who you're dealing with."

"Because you won't tell us," Julia snapped. "If you don't, Alex and I may keep stumbling into trouble. Maybe you should explain what's going on."

Brady withdrew an envelope from his inside jacket pocket. "We're providing you with a background, Miss DeMarco."

"Excuse me?"

"Everything you need is in here. Addresses where you lived with your mother before she married your stepfather. We've also listed a job where your mother worked and character references who can testify to her presence in Berkeley during the time in question. We have photographs of you as a toddler playing in the park in Berkeley, long before that picture in Russia was ever taken."

Julia stared at him in amazement. "How can you do that? How can you have pictures of me when I don't have pictures of me?'

"Technology is amazing."

"So it's all fake, and you expect me to use it? Why would I do that?"

"Because you're in danger. And not just you, but your family, your sister, your stepfather, and everyone attached to you. The break-in at your apartment was only the first step."

"How do you know about the break-in?" she asked.

"We have contacts in the police department."

"Do you know what they were looking for?"

"I assume something that you acquired in Russia."

"What do you mean, the first step?" Alex interrupted. "What do you foresee happening next?"

"A direct confrontation. Julia has something they want."

Brady's voice was so deadly serious, it sent chills down her spine. "But I don't know what that something is. You have to give me more information," she pleaded.

"Believe me, I'd like to help you, but I can't. My hands are tied. I'm sorry."

"You're not sorry," Alex cut in. "If you were, you'd help us."

"This is above my level. And I am sorry, because your father was a good friend of mine."

"Don't you mean is a good friend?" Alex asked.

"The last time we spoke, you neglected to mention that my father was alive. How could you make me think I was responsible for his death?"

Daniel tipped his head in apology. "I wanted you to realize this was serious business. It was a miscalculation."

Julia couldn't believe the coolness of his tone or his words. "A miscalculation? Don't you have any feelings at all?"

"In my business, feelings get you killed."

"Apparently it's not all that difficult to be reborn again," Alex said sarcastically. "My father did it. Sarah did it. Did you set up her death, too? Were you the one who called her parents and told them she'd died in a fire?"

"I had nothing to do with Sarah."

Brady sounded sincere, but Julia wasn't sure she could believe him. He obviously made a living with his lies and his secrets.

"Take the envelope," Brady said, holding it out to Julia. "Take yourself out of the line of fire."

Julia thought about doing exactly what he asked. Wouldn't it be easier to end it now before someone else got hurt, maybe someone she loved? Then again, she'd lived her whole life looking the other way and not asking questions. She didn't want to spend the rest of her days doing the same thing. "I can't," she said.

"You're making a mistake."

"At least it will be mine to make. Everyone else has had their turn."

Brady turned to Alex. "Can't you talk some sense into her?"

"I think she's making perfect sense."

Brady held up his hands in surrender. "All right. But if you change your mind, you'll have this. Take it."

He pushed the envelope into her hand, and she thought about what it contained. She glanced at Alex, having second thoughts. "Do you think I'm putting my family in danger?"

He met her gaze with clear, honest eyes. "You might be, but it's your call."

"I guess I should think about it."

"We've got a long a drive home."

"Where did he go?" Julia asked, suddenly aware that Brady had disappeared from the house.

"I have no idea. He truly is a spook." Alex took one last look around the house. "I wonder how long my dad lived here."

"I hope someday you can ask him."

"I'm not counting on it."

As they left the house, there was no sign of the Explorer or Brady as they got into Alex's car. Alex started the engine, then moved to release the emergency brake between them.

"What's this?" he muttered. He pulled out a folded slip of paper that had been tucked under the brake and opened it. "Meet me at Pirate's Cove Cafe, Marine World, four o'clock," he read aloud.

"Meet who?" Julia asked.

"It doesn't say." Alex's gaze met hers. "It couldn't be Brady. He was just here. I think he said everything he had to say."

"Who else could it be?"

"I'd say it's a fifty-fifty chance it's either the men in the Explorer or my father. I'm not sure who I'd rather see."

* * *

"Why would someone want to meet at Marine World?" Julia asked as they pulled into the parking lot of the amusement park near Napa.

Alex considered her question as he surveyed the parking lot, which was crowded even for a Thursday. "Lots of people, neutral location, good place to blend into a crowd, and even if someone is following us right now, they wouldn't expect we'd be meeting someone here."

Julia appeared impressed by his deductive reasoning. "You sound like you've been involved in clandestine meetings before."

"Believe me, I've never done anything like this," he said dryly. And that included getting personally and emotionally involved with a woman he'd spent the night with. He'd managed to keep sex casual and easy the past decade, but there was nothing casual or easy about his relationship with Julia, and it was getting more complicated by the second. Maybe when they stopped living out of each other's pockets, he'd be able to get his feelings for her back into perspective.

"Do you like roller coasters?" Julia asked as they approached the main entrance. A monster roller coaster with three wild, curving loops was just off to the right, and they could hear the screams coming from the cars hurtling down the first drop.

"I haven't been on one in years. What about you?"

"I love them," she said with a smile, "and I haven't been on one in years, either. We should take a ride while we're here. I could use a good scream right about now. Get out all my frustration." She cast him a quick look. "I really thought your dad would be at the house and he'd tell us everything we wanted to know."

"It's my fault. We shouldn't have left yesterday. I was just so pissed off, I couldn't think straight."

"I know, and I completely understood why you had to get out of there."

Alex bought their admission tickets, and they strolled into the park, stopping at an information sign to check the location of the Pirate's Cove Cafe. When he saw the skull and crossbones next to the name, a funny feeling swept over him, a vague, distant memory teasing the back of his brain. He'd been only five or six, and his dad had taken him to Disneyland for his birthday. They'd ridden on Pirates of the Caribbean, and he'd loved the waterfall drops. He'd made his dad take him on the ride three times in a row. He hadn't wanted that day to end, but it had. And the next day his father had left for another business trip. It was a month before they saw each other again.

It had been hard, he realized, all the times apart, and even more difficult for his mother. She used to cry when his dad left. He'd forgotten that—until now.

"I think it's this way," Julia said, tugging his arm. "Is something wrong?"

He shrugged off the memories. "No, everything is—"

"Fine," she finished with a smile. "Your favorite word and always a lie."

"Hey, a little while ago you said I was the most honest man you knew."

"Not when it comes to yourself. You never let on how you're feeling."

He flashed her a smile. "I think you figured me out pretty well last night and this morning."

A warm blush spread across her cheeks, and it made his smile widen. She was so beautiful and sexy, and yet there was also an appealing innocence about her. It was a potent combination and one he probably should have resisted.

"Let's keep our minds on the present," Julia said.

"That's fine with me."

"Yeah, I know," she said with a laugh. "Pirate's Cove is over there."

Alex let her lead the way, enjoying the view from behind. Julia wore tight blue jeans and a clingy camisole top that left her shoulders bare. Her blond hair danced around her shoulders with each step. He had to stick his hands into his pockets to stop himself from reaching for her. He had the insane desire to hold her hand or put his arm around her, and that kind of casual affection had never been part of his life.

"There it is," she said, pointing to a wooden shack with a skull and crossbones painted across the front and a dozen tables with umbrellas set amidst thick green plants and a dark pool of water that was probably supposed to be the cove part of Pirate's Cove.

Only a few of the tables were taken, and those were occupied by families and small children. Alex glanced down at his watch. It was only three thirty. They had a good half hour to wait. "We're early," he said. "Or else they're watching us from somewhere else."

"That's a creepy thought." She took a step closer to him as she looked around the area. "I don't see anyone suspicious."

"Neither do I." He paused. "I have an idea. While we're waiting, why don't we take one of those scream-inducing rides you love?"

Her eyes sparkled. "Really? Do you think we should?"

"Why not? Why should we sit here and wait? Let 'em wait for us."

"Okay. Which coaster do you want to ride?"

"How about that one?" he said, tipping his head toward a square box that rose about six stories, then dropped at breath-stopping speed to the ground.

"That looks fairly terrifying," she said, adding with a teasing smile, "You won't be scared, will you?"

"Not if you hold my hand," he joked.

She pulled his hand out of his pocket and gave it a squeeze. "I'd be happy to."

Her warm touch gave him chills, and suddenly he wasn't afraid of falling six stories, but of falling in love. There was no way he could let that happen. He didn't know what love was really all about, and he didn't believe he would be good at it. Just like his father, he'd always be leaving, always be saying goodbye. It wouldn't be fair to put any woman or kid through that. But right now they were just taking a ride. He could handle a ride. It had a beginning, a middle, and an end. When it was over, it was over.

They waited in line for fifteen minutes before they were strapped into the elevator car that would rise to the top, then shoot to the ground. Alex felt a tingle of nerves as they rose, the ground getting smaller, the view getting bigger. He glanced over at Julia, who stood next to him, her fingers white as she gripped the poles holding her in. She looked scared but brave, which was pretty much the way he'd seen her every day this week; only this time the fear was simple and specific, not vague and complicated.

The car hit the top with a jarring thud, probably designed to give their hearts a jump start on the thrill ride. A second later they were diving toward the ground. Julia's scream rang through his ears, and he found himself joining in. They landed with a soft, gentle thud that seemed completely out of sync with the breath-stealing pace of the ride.

"Oh, my God," Julia said. "I think my stomach is still up there."

"Mine, too," he admitted with a laugh as they exited the car. "But that was great."

"Did you love it?"

"I did." And before he could analyze his thoughts or his actions, he leaned over and claimed her mouth with his, tasting her excitement.

"What was that for?" she asked, looking a bit dazed when they broke apart.

"No reason. Except you look like a bottle of sparkling champagne right now, and I wanted to take a sip." She licked her lips, and he shook his head. "Don't be doing that or I won't be held responsible for my actions."

"Maybe I don't want you to be responsible."

He raised an eyebrow. "That sounds like an invitation. Too bad we're in the middle of an amusement park."

She tossed her hair with a laugh. "I know. Now you have something to look forward to."

Her words made him think about the coming night, and the next day, and the one after, but he didn't want to plan that far into the future. "Yeah, that's great," he said. "We better go back to the Pirate's Cove."

"What did I say?" She grabbed his arm, stopping him in his tracks.

"Nothing."

"No, I said something that made you freak out a little."

"I have a lot on my mind," he said. "Don't be so sensitive."

"Yeah, I was going to say the same thing to you." She paused, tilting her head as she looked at him. "I get it, you know, Alex. Last night was not the beginning of something for you. It was just a night. Maybe that's all we'll have together, maybe not. I'm not going to tie you down, make you promise to stand by me forever, just because we slept together. But I'm also not going to watch everything I say."

"I am not freaking out. I am calm. I am fine." He heard her sigh at the word. "Well, I am. So let's get on with it."

"Fine," she said, the smile returning to her face. She waved her hand toward the cove. "After you."

Alex's nerves began to tighten as they neared Pirate's Cove. He wondered who would be waiting for them. Would it be his father or someone else?

* * *

A man sat at a far table near a thick line of bushes, sipping a soda. He wore a fishing hat, sunglasses, and a short-sleeve shirt over a pair of shorts. He was in his sixties. And he was Alex's father.

Julia looked at Alex. He was paler now than when they'd exited the thrill ride. She had a feeling it took every last ounce of courage he had to sit down at the table.

"Thank you for coming," Charles said quietly.

"Does Brady know you left us the note?" Alex asked.

Charles shook his head. "I wasn't supposed to have any contact with you. It was part of the deal I made twenty-five years ago. As soon as you left yesterday, a moving truck arrived, as well as a package of papers for a new identity. I had no choice but to leave. However, I had a feeling you'd come back, and I didn't want to disappear on you again. So I watched the house and left the note in your car. I hoped you'd come here after you finished with Brady." He paused. "What did he tell you?"

"That we'd compromised your safety," Alex said.

"Mr. Brady also wants to provide me with a background I can show to the press," Julia added. "I told him I wasn't interested. I can't live a lie." She saw Charles flinch at her words, and she almost wished she could take them back, but she didn't. Maybe he and her mother had been able to live their lives pretending to be someone they weren't, but she couldn't do it.

"You should reconsider," Charles said. "It would make your life easier."

"My life has been nothing but easy," she replied. "My mother made sure of that." She deliberately brought her mother into the conversation. "There are things I want to ask you about her. Did you read her letter?"

Charles slowly nodded, a gleam of understanding in his eyes. "Yes, and I imagine you have a lot of questions."

"Questions my mother should have answered, but she didn't, and you're the only one who seems to know anything about her,"

Julia continued. "I know she was in Moscow working as a costumer with the theater group. What I don't know is what I was doing over there and how I got into that orphanage." She watched Charles closely for a reaction, but he was staring down at the tabletop now. "Please, you have to tell me. I can't go on not knowing."

When he raised his gaze to hers, she saw nothing but trouble in his expression, and she had a feeling she was going to be very sorry she'd asked.

"I don't know how to tell you this," he began.

"Just spit it out," Alex ordered.

"Sarah didn't take you to Russia with her. You were already there," Charles said.

It took a moment for his words to sink in. Then Julia's heart stopped. "Are you saying... ?" She couldn't bring herself to finish the question. "Oh, God!" She put a hand to her mouth, terrified to say more. She couldn't take a breath. She felt as if an elephant had landed on her chest.

Alex put an arm around her shoulders, which was probably the only reason she didn't keel over. "Breathe," he said.

"I'm trying." She took several gulps of much needed air.

"Tell her the rest," Alex said to his father.

"Sarah is the one who took you out of the orphanage and brought you to America," Charles continued. "She was a government agent. It was her job to get you out of Russia."

"No." Julia couldn't believe it. "Then who am I? Who are my parents? Why would she pretend I was her daughter? I don't understand."

"Your parents were Russian."

"Were? You make it sound like they're dead. God, are they dead?" Julia pressed her fingers to her temple, feeling a pain racing through her head.

"Julia, slow down," Alex said.

Charles looked around, obviously concerned about their conversation being overheard.

She lowered her voice, then said, "I want to know everything you know. Are my real parents dead?" It felt odd to even use the term real parents, but what else could she call them?

"Yes, they are. I'm sorry."

"Really dead or just pretend dead like you and my mother—I mean, Sarah?"

"They died in an explosion at their home."

"No," she whispered, grieving for the parents she'd never known and never would know.

"You were supposed to be in the house with them," Charles continued.

It took a minute for his words to make sense. "I was supposed to die, too?"

His gaze didn't waver. "Yes."

She bit down on her bottom lip so hard, she tasted blood. "Why wasn't I there?"

"You had been taken from the house and hidden in the orphanage until we could get you out of the country. No one was supposed to know you were ever there."

"But I took a picture of her," Alex said sharply. "I made sure everyone knew she was there."

Charles looked at his son, his expression one of a deep, aching regret. "I'm sorry you got involved, Alex I never should have taken you to the square that day I shouldn't have brought you to Moscow at all. That was selfish of me."

Alex glanced away. "Let's focus on Julia."

Charles turned back to her. "What else do you want to know?"

"How did I get to the United States?" she asked.

"Sarah brought you out with fake papers. She was supposed to put you in an established home that was set up for you, but she didn't. On the trip over, she fell in love with you, and there were other extenuating circumstances."

"Like what?"

He drew in a breath before continuing. "Sarah always had wanted a child, but she'd had a bad pregnancy, ending in miscarriage, and she thought it was doubtful she'd ever have a baby of her own. That fact ate away at her, making her reckless, making her want to take chances. She thought you might be her only opportunity to have a daughter. And she rationalized that she could raise you as well as any other foster home. So why not her? She knew the agency wouldn't agree. They didn't want her connected to you in any way. It would compromise other activities Sarah and I had been involved in while we were in Moscow."

Julia was beginning to understand. "So my mother—Sarah... I have to stop calling her my mother, don't I?"

Charles shook his head. "She was your mother. She loved you so much. Don't doubt that."

"How can I not? Sarah faked her death, just as you did. She let her parents believe she was gone so that she could take me and disappear. She obviously had no moral boundaries. Her life was a lie. And so was mine."

"She faked her death to protect her parents."

"Did you cook up that reason together?" Alex asked scornfully. "Sounds like you were following the same script. Were you also having an affair? Mom certainly thought you were."

"No. Sarah and I were just friends—always. We met in college at Northwestern. We both had an interest in the world. Sarah wanted to go to Russia because her grandmother was Russian. She actually joined the agency before I did. She was the one who suggested I might be able to help with the cover of my photography. Originally I was just supposed to take pictures, but gradually I felt compelled to do more. I met people over there who wanted to be free, and I wanted to help them," Charles said with passion in his voice. "I know you two can't understand. You've never seen what we saw. Back then, there was no freedom. People disappeared. They died on a whim. No one was held accountable."

"And you were going to make them accountable?" Alex demanded. "Who did you think you were, God?"

"No, I was just one person who wanted to make a difference."

"I thought you liked being a photographer. I thought that was your life, your sole ambition. You told me it meant everything to you. Over and over again, you told me that," Alex said. "I grew up thinking it was the most honorable profession in the world, shedding light on the injustices in the world."

"It was honorable, and it still is. It just wasn't enough for me." Charles took a breath, his eyes offering up an apology. "I never thought my decisions would affect you or your mother. I thought I could keep my second line of work separate. I believed I could leave the danger on the other side of the ocean. I was wrong."

"What I don't understand," Julia said, drawing the men's attention back to her, "is why you and Sarah were in danger after the picture was published. What could be gained by going after either one of you then?"

"The people who killed your parents now knew you were alive. They believed I had seen you because I took the picture. If they could find me, they could find you. Since Sarah had you, they could have gone through her as well, or used her parents as leverage. We had to disappear. Without us, there was no trail back to you."

Julia thought about that. It made sense in a strange way. "All right. Let's say that's true. What about now? Why has someone broken into my apartment as well as Alex's place? Why would they want me dead now? It's been twenty-five years, and I don't even know who I am, much less who they are."

Charles clasped his hands together as he rested his elbows on the table. "Your parents made their plans very carefully. For two years they plotted how to leave Russia. It was rumored that they had something valuable to sell, something priceless that would provide them with enough money to live on once they were granted asylum here."

"What was that something?"

"I wasn't cleared for that kind of classified information, so I don't know."

"How could my parents have had something priceless in communist Russia during the Cold War?" Julia tried to remember what she'd learned in world history in high school. "Who were they?"

"Your mother, Natalia—"

"Natalia? That was her name?" A distant memory flashed in Julia's head, a man calling impatiently for Natalia.

"Yes, Natalia Markov. And your father's name was Sergei." Charles paused. "Natalia was a featured ballerina at the Bolshoi Ballet. She was the third generation ballet dancer in the family. Natalia's grandmother, Tamara Slovinsky, danced for the Imperial Court before the revolution. She was in so much favor that she received many valuable presents, jewels, paintings, antiques. It was believed that Tamara managed to hang on to some of those presents, secreting them away or perhaps getting them out of the country. Tamara's husband was Ivan Slovinsky, a famous composer who fled to France during the revolution."

"Oh, my God! Are you serious?" Julia asked in amazement.

"I've studied Ivan Slovinsky. He wrote an incredible number of operas and ballets at the turn of the century. His music was powerful, awe-inspiring. He was truly gifted, and he was my..." She had to think for a moment to calculate the relationship. "He was my great-grandfather?"

"Yes."

"I can't believe it." She turned to Alex in excitement. "Maybe that's where I got my love of music. I've always wondered why I feel such passion for any kind of melody when no one else in my family cares even a little about it."

Alex smiled at her. "It makes sense now."

"What about my father?" she asked Charles, impatient to hear the rest. "Was he also in music or ballet?"

"No, your father, Sergei Markov, was a high-ranking party member and a loyal communist until he fell in love with Natalia. Then he became disenchanted with the government. He could see that Natalia's career could be so much greater if she went to America. Apparently he had information that he was willing to share with our government if he and Natalia were granted asylum here."

"So the Russians killed them before they could leave," Julia said slowly. "That's what happened, isn't it? Did anyone investigate?"

"The Russian government blamed the explosion on faulty wiring. It was considered a tragic accident. They had the last word."

"This is just mind-boggling. I can't wrap my brain around it all." She thought for a moment, trying to make sense of everything Charles had told her. "My mother was a ballerina. I thought about taking ballet once, but Mom—Sarah—wouldn't let me. She always had a reason why she couldn't sign me up."

"Sarah didn't want you to dance," Charles interjected. "She was afraid you might grow up to be like your mother, that someone would eventually make the connection between you."

"Which is probably why she also discouraged me from pursuing my passion for music," Julia finished.

Sarah certainly had a lot to answer for. Only it was too late for her to give any of those answers.

"You can't tell anyone about any of this," Charles said. "If the people who killed your parents find out you know the truth, it will be even more dangerous for you."

"They think I have this priceless object, is that right?"

"I suspect so."

"This is unbelievable." Her head felt heavy with the amount of information she'd received, and she pressed a hand to her temple, feeling the ache spread across her cheekbones and around her eyes. "I don't know what to think. How am I supposed to feel? I know who my parents are, but they're dead. I can't meet them. I can't talk to them." The finality of that made her feel terribly sad. "I almost wish I'd never seen that picture of myself. I could have gone on believing I was just Julia DeMarco and not the orphan girl at the gates."

"You're not the girl in the picture," Charles said abruptly.

Her gaze flew to his. Her stomach did a somersault. "What do you mean? Of course I am." She silently begged him not to spin her around in another direction.

"Of course she is," Alex echoed in surprise. "I saw her. I took her picture. I was there."

Charles looked from Julia to Alex, then back to Julia again. His silence drew her nerves into a tight, screaming knot.

"Just say it—whatever it is," she begged.

"All right. I've told you this much. I might as well tell you the rest. You aren't the girl in the photograph, Julia."

"Then who is?" she demanded.

Chapter Eighteen

"You have a sister," Charles said, his voice slow and deliberate. "A twin sister. She was the one standing at the gate that day. You were inside the building." Shocked silence met his words. Julia didn't know what to say. It was clear Alex couldn't find words, either. The surprises just kept coming, each one bigger than the last.

"That's impossible," she said, finally finding her voice. "Why wouldn't that have come out before, when the picture was published?"

"No one in the general public ever connected the girl at the gates with the twin girls of Natalia and Sergei Markov, who died in an explosion. In fact, it was printed in the Russian newspaper that everyone in the house was dead, including the servants. No one ever came forward when the picture was printed to state your true identity. So if anyone recognized you, they kept it to themselves."

She could barely comprehend his explanation. She was still thinking about the fact that she had a sister. "I would remember," she said, racking her brain for any hint of a memory, but her mind was blank. She didn't remember a sister or parents or Russia, or anything that happened before she was in the United States. Yet something teased at the back of her mind. Why couldn't she bring it forward, let it out?

"Where is she?" Alex asked. "Where is this sister? Why didn't Sarah keep her and Julia together? Did something happen to her?"

Julia caught her breath at his question, silently pleading that her sister wasn't dead, too.

"It was too dangerous to keep the girls together," Charles explained. "They were taken out of the country separately."

"Who took my sister?" She stumbled over the word sister, realizing it no longer applied just to Liz, but to another woman as well.

"Another agent. Before you ask, I didn't know his name or anything about him. I wasn't supposed to be involved in that aspect of the operation. Stan made it clear that my job was to make the cultural exchange look authentic. Divert suspicion and attention by creating media opportunities for the theater group. The Russians wanted positive press."

"Wait," Alex said, putting up a hand. "Stan? Did you say Stan made it clear? I thought he was just an editor."

Charles smiled at that. "Stan was never just an editor. He was a friend. A crazy, wild friend."

Julia didn't understand the gleam in Charles's eye. Nor had Stan Harding given her the impression of being crazy or wild. Alex appeared confused, too.

"Are you saying Stan was involved in the operation to get the Markovs out of Russia?"

"He was a ballet fanatic. He'd met Natalia a few times when she came to the States. She confided in him. He set up the defection."

"So he lied, too," Alex said bitterly. "Big surprise."

"Let's go back to my sister. I want to know where she went after she left Russia, and why we weren't reunited," Julia said.

"Sarah wanted to get you back together," Charles replied. "But she had to keep you under wraps once the photo came out. Your sister had already been placed in a temporary foster home on the other side of the country. When things died down, Sarah wanted to find your sister, but she couldn't ask anyone for help. She broke all the rules when she took you. She was in hiding from everyone, including the agency. No one knew where she was. She had grown up in New York State and went to school in Chicago. Everyone was looking for her in those places. No one was looking for her here. I didn't even know she had you or where she was for over ten years. Then I saw her one day by accident down on the Wharf. I couldn't believe my eyes."

"So she kept me from my sister, the only blood relative I had left? And she deprived me of my grandparents? What gave her the right to do any of that? I should have known about my heritage. I should have known everything," Julia declared, feeling angry and betrayed and sad all at the same time.

"You were never supposed to know any of it. The people who killed your parents wanted the whole family dead. The only way to protect you was to keep you hidden away. If you knew who you were, Sarah was afraid you'd do what you're doing now: go looking for answers that could get you killed."

"That should have been my choice, especially when I became an adult. I can't believe I sat by her bedside talking to her about our life together, our hopes and dreams, and none of this ever came out."

"Don't judge her too harshly," Charles said. "She loved you very much."

"What kind of love is filled with lies?"

"Sarah gave up her life for you, Julia," Charles said. "She walked away from her parents, her home, her community, her identity just so she could raise you. That wasn't cowardly; that was brave."

His words touched her. How could they not? But Sarah's sacrifices didn't make up for the lies. "I don't think I can forgive her."

"Give yourself some time," Charles advised. "Remember, love isn't always simple."

"People like you and Sarah are the ones who make it complicated." She sat back in her chair, the noise from the roller coasters penetrating her brain. She'd been so caught up in Charles's story, she'd lost track of time. Only now did she realize that the shadows were longer and deeper. It was getting late. They'd been talking for a long time.

She glanced at Alex, wondering if he wanted to take the lead now, ask his father some pointed, personal questions. She was surprised by the speculative look in his eyes as he stared at her. "What are you thinking?" she asked.

"That your sister looks just like you."

"Obviously, if she's my twin." She didn't understand his point.

"If that photo of you in the Tribune got picked up nationally, or if Christine Delaney continues her quest to publicize you, your sister might see your picture in the paper and wonder why she has a twin she never met."

"And whoever is after me might go after her," Julia finished, suddenly realizing where his thoughts were headed. "We have to find her and fast." She turned back to Charles. "Do you think Mr. Brady knows where my sister is now? He knew where I was, right?"

Charles shook his head. "Brady didn't know where you were until Stan called him last week. As I said, Sarah disappeared off the face of the earth. Even when we reconnected, she made me promise to stay silent."

"What about my sister? Does she know who she really is?"

"The original foster family was paid handsomely not to ask questions. It's my understanding that that family broke up and your sister went into the system like any other American orphan."

"What's her name? Wait." Julia squeezed her eyes tight as an image popped into her head. *She was playing with a doll. She was looking in the mirror, and she called the doll...* On second thought, maybe she hadn't been looking in the mirror. Maybe she'd been looking at her sister. Yes, that was it. Her sister held the doll she wanted. Julia asked for it back, and she called her... "Elena," she whispered, her eyes flying open. "Her name was Elena."

"You remember her?" Alex asked.

"Just that. I think I've dreamed about her, but I always thought I was dreaming about me. That's weird, isn't it?"

"You'll probably remember more now," Alex told her. "You suffered a huge trauma, being ripped from your home, your parents, your country. It's no wonder you blocked it out."

She directed her attention back to Charles. "You said Brady doesn't know where Elena is. Do you? Or does Stan know?"

"It could be dangerous for you to find her."

"According to you, I'm already in danger just by virtue of being alive."

He tipped his head in acknowledgement. "True. All right. I know that your sister goes by the name Elaine Harrigan. At one point she was a ballet dancer with a Washington DC ballet company. Maybe that will help you find her."

"How do you know that?"

"Sarah found her about ten years ago. I don't know how or

what she ever intended to do with the information. She only said she was worried because Elaine was in ballet and someone might connect her to her famous mother."

Her sister was a ballet dancer. Another surprise, and yet it seemed right. She studied Charles, wondering why he'd decided to come clean. "Why?" she asked. "Why tell me now?"

"Alex is a grown man. You're a grown woman. It's your turn to make your own decisions." Charles's gaze focused on Alex. "Will you tell your mother about me?"

"I have to," Alex replied. "She deserves to know the truth."

Charles pulled a piece of paper out of his pocket and pushed it across the table. "This is where I'll be if you want to talk to me, or if your mother does."

"I thought you were supposed to disappear again."

"I was. Brady won't be happy that we met, but I couldn't desert you a second time, Alex. I understand that you may never forgive me for what I did. But I know in my heart that I did what I believed was right. And I still believe it. You might have grown up without a father, but you lived, and you have a good life now. I've read a lot about you, everything I could get my hands on. You've made me proud."

"You should have come to me sometime in the last twenty-something years," Alex said harshly. "You should have found a way to tell me you were alive."

"I didn't think I had the right. You'd moved on. If you or your mother want to talk now, that's where I'll be. I'll leave it up to you."

"Mom will probably come after you with a gun," Alex said, but he put the piece of paper in his pocket.

"How is she?" Charles asked.

"She's divorced again, her third. She seems to have developed a fondness for her memories of you. She's been publicizing your photos all over town. In fact, your work is part of an exhibit at the Legion of Honor. But you probably already know that. You've been so close to us all these years."

"I started out across the country, but I eventually made my way back to San Francisco. In the beginning I wanted to watch over you."

"You watched me?" Alex asked, a rough edge to his voice.

"A few times. Enough to know you were all right."

"Yeah, I was fine. Just fine." Alex rose. "I think we're done here. Julia?"

"Just one last question," she said. "Did Sarah ever consider telling me the truth?"

"No." Charles looked her straight in the eye. "Sarah was afraid you would hate her for what she'd done. She told me she'd do everything she could to make sure you were happy and that you never lacked for anything, especially a family. She would make certain you were surrounded by love."

"I was," Julia said quietly. And now she had to wonder if Sarah had ever loved Gino, or if he'd just provided the family she so desperately needed to make the illusion complete.

* * *

An hour later Alex pulled off at the exit just before the Bay Bridge and turned into a hotel parking lot. He didn't stop driving until they had gone to the far side of the building, completely hidden from the freeway.

"What are you doing?" Julia took a quick look over her shoulder. "Is someone following us again?"

"No, but we can't go back to our apartments. They know where we live. I don't want someone trying to grab you or your purse. In fact, I don't want them getting anywhere near you."

His protectiveness touched her. She liked that he cared enough to worry about her. "What do you suggest we do?"

"Get a hotel room, call the airport, book a flight for DC first thing in the morning."

She turned sideways in her seat, amazed that she could still feel surprised after everything she'd learned. "You really think we should hop on a plane to Washington DC with nothing more than a name and a ballet company?"

"It's a good start. We'll have better luck tracking your sister there than here."

"If she's still in DC. Your father said the information was at least ten years old."

"But she was there, and she probably had friends in the ballet company. Someone might know where she is now," he pointed out.

"It's so spontaneous. I'm not the kind of person who jumps on planes every other day. It will be expensive, won't it, this close to departure?"

"I have lots of Frequent Flyer miles. It won't cost us a dime. I think of air travel like car travel. Going to DC is like going to St. Helena, except the trip is a few hours longer."

"So speaks the world traveler," she said with a smile.

"Is that a yes or a no?"

"It's a yes. I want to find my sister. I still can't believe I have a sister." Her smile dimmed. "Oh, no," she muttered.

"What now?" he asked warily.

"Liz. She won't like this at all. How will I tell her I have a twin sister who shares my blood, especially now that I know she doesn't? She won't understand. She was worried that she would lose me to my biological father. How on earth am I going to make her understand it doesn't change things?"

"It does change things. How could it not?"

"I love Liz. She'll always be my sister."

"But she won't be your only sister. That will take some adjustment, especially since Elaine or Elena looks just like you."

"Liz will definitely feel like the odd girl out," she agreed.

"Don't tell her yet. It will be easier to present the whole picture when it makes sense. If you give her this much, it will only be confusing and disturbing."

"Which describes my feelings exactly."

He ran his finger down the side of her face. "It's been a rough day for you. And here I thought it would be all about me and seeing my dad again, listening to his lies."

"Yeah, well, I didn't want you to have all the fun," she said lightly, trying to stay on the surface of her emotions. She was afraid if she didn't, she would have a complete meltdown, and it wasn't the time for that. "How was it, seeing your dad again?"

He shrugged. "I don't know."

"I think you do."

"If I do, I don't want to talk about it."

"Are you going to wait to tell your mother about your dad?"

"Yes," he said, without a hint of doubt in his voice. "I want to know everything first."

"We're getting closer," Julia said. "We finally know who my parents are—and that Sarah isn't my mother." She let out a sigh of weariness. "I don't want to talk about this right now, either. I have a headache."

"You need a break, time to let everything sink in."

"I feel like there's a thick curtain in my brain and I can't see past it. How could I have forgotten my twin sister for even a moment? Shouldn't there have been a connection between us? Shouldn't I have felt as if a part of me was missing?"

Alex's eyes filled with compassion. "Don't be so hard on yourself. You were three years old. You were a baby. Your whole life changed in an instant. I'm sure you missed your sister when you were first separated. But you had to bury that pain to survive. Then your life was filled with other people."

"That's true. My mother—Sarah—did manage to get pregnant, despite what everyone else told us. I was there for that part. I wonder if she regretted taking me then. After all, she had her own child. She could have given me away and still had her own family." Julia thought about all that had transpired, how many lives had been touched by her mother's one reckless decision. And up until today, she'd never thought of her mother as reckless. "My mother feels like a stranger to me now. How could I live with her for twenty-five years and not know her at all?"

"I know you're probably mad as hell at her, Julia, but I have to say, who knows what would have happened to you if Sarah had left you in foster care as she was supposed to? It's highly likely that you ended up having a much better life with her. It wasn't as if she stole you from your parents. They were already gone."

Alex was right. Her parents had been killed before Sarah decided to keep her. "I hadn't thought of it like that."

"That's because you haven't had time to think."

She smiled at him. "Thanks for sticking by me. I appreciate it."

"We made a deal to see this through."

"And I couldn't do it without you. You're a rock."

"A rock, huh? I think you can do better than that," he said, moving his hand down to her knee, where he let his fingers stray up her thigh.

She grinned as she put her hand over his, stopping his exploration. "Are you looking for compliments?"

"I'm looking for something," he said with a laugh.

"Behave yourself."

"I'm tired of behaving. I've been good all day." He leaned forward and stole a quick kiss.

That's all it took to send a wave of heat through her body. She was really in over her head, she thought. Far too involved, far too attracted, far too tempted.

Alex leaned in and pressed his mouth against hers, lingering a little longer this time, making her remember the way he'd kissed a path down her body the night before. She tried to get closer to him, but she ran into the gearshift, reminding her that she was making out in a public parking lot.

She pushed Alex away with an embarrassed laugh. "Not like this," she said.

"Good point. There's a hotel room just a few feet away." There was a question in his eyes as he finished his sentence, a question she could easily answer.

"Let's get a king-size bed," she said.

His eyes darkened. "Now you're talking."

"Actually, I don't feel like talking. That's all we've done today. I don't want to think anymore," she replied.

"Neither do I."

"Aren't you worried that I might be using you?" she teased.

"Use away," he said with a crooked grin. "I'm all yours. Come on."

She laughed as he jumped out of the car. She had to jog to keep up with him. She tried to act nonchalant as Alex asked for a room, not that it mattered. The desk clerk wasn't even remotely interested in who they were or whether or not they had any luggage.

They kissed all the way to their room on the fourth floor, laughing like reckless teenagers when Alex fumbled with the key card and couldn't get the door open. She took it out of his hand and did the honors. Finally, they were inside.

Julia didn't have time to see the room, because Alex pressed her back against the door, his lips on her mouth, his hands on her breasts. He was hot and hard, and she was on fire. All the tension of the day blew up in one explosive kiss. They made short work of their clothes, falling on the bed, naked and eager to get as close as possible.

"We should slow down," Alex said with a groan as his hands

roamed restlessly on her body.

"Next time," she said, pulling him into the cradle of her hips. She wanted him inside of her, on top of her, surrounding her with his body, his heart, and his soul. She needed to hold on to something real, and he was beautifully real. She trusted him more than she trusted herself, so she stopped thinking and directed all of her crazy, mixed-up emotions toward him until they both found a blessed release.

It was a while later before either one of them moved; then Alex rolled off her onto his side. He pulled her into his body, spoon fashion, putting his arm across her waist. She blew out a breath and closed her eyes. Maybe she'd just take a little nap. There would be plenty of time to think and worry and analyze when she woke up.

Alex fell asleep before she did, his deep, contented breathing providing a comforting rhythm. Julia let her mind drift, trying to think of something nice, pretty, uncomplicated—a field of wildflowers or a running stream... Instead, her sister's face floated through her mind.

Elena sat next to her on the couch. They were both too short for their legs to reach the ground, so they were kicking their feet up in the air, sometimes kicking each other by accident. Only she didn't always do it by accident; sometimes she did it on purpose, because she was tired of waiting. But Elena sent her a cross look, so she stopped.

Julia looked around the room. It was dark and a little scary. The furniture was big and really old. The pictures on the wall were of people she didn't recognize. They looked mean. The only pretty things in the room were the vases of flowers that her mother received almost every day from her fans.

Everyone loved her mother. Wherever they went, people came up to kiss her hand, to tell her she was beautiful, magical, like a princess. Julia wanted to be a princess like her mother. But Elena would probably make a better one. Everyone said Elena was just like their mother, so graceful, so sweet, and already learning how to dance. Julia didn't want to dance. She wanted to play one of the big instruments that made lots of noise. She thought that would be more fun.

The door opened and a woman came into the room. She wore

a beautiful red dress, and her hair fell down to her waist in pretty blond waves. She smiled at them both and kneeled in front of them, putting a hand on each of them.

She was talking again about leaving. They would be parted for a short time, she said. Only a few days. They would have to be brave little girls.

Julia felt tears gathering in her eyes and fear knotting her stomach. She didn't want to be brave. She didn't want her mother and father to leave. She wanted them all to be together. Her mother was sad, too. A tear dripped out of her eye and down her cheek. Julia put out her hand and caught the tear with her fingertip. As she stared at it, she felt terribly afraid.

Her mother stood up. She blew them a kiss, telling them to have courage and faith, that love was worth the risk.

Then she was gone. Olga helped them put on their hats and their coats, and whisked them away from the house. Once outside, Julia pressed her fingers against the cold pane of the car window, watching her house fade away. She wanted to go home. She began to cry and pound on the window, but they kept getting farther and farther away... and she couldn't stop screaming.

"Julia, wake up. Wake up," Alex said loudly.

She felt someone shaking her, and Alex's voice finally reached her subconscious. Her eyes flew open. It took her a moment to remember where she was—in a hotel room with Alex. She was an adult now, not that scared little girl, but she was still trembling.

Alex ran his hand up and down her arm. "Are you okay?" he asked with concern.

She realized her cheeks were wet and her throat felt hoarse. Had she been shouting? "I was dreaming," she said, rolling over to face him.

He wiped away her tears with gentle fingers. "Bad dream?"

"Bad and good. I remembered the day my mother sent us away. She told us to be brave. She said love was worth the risk. I didn't know what she meant. I was so scared. I felt like I was choking on the fear. I knew I wasn't going to see her again. I could feel it."

He stroked her hair. "At least the memories are coming back now."

"I don't want them back," she said. "They hurt."

"How about some water?"

She nodded. As Alex got up, she slipped under the blanket, not quite as comfortable with her nudity now that they weren't making love. Alex pulled on his briefs and jeans, then returned to the bed with a bottled water from the minibar. He handed it to her, then picked up the room service menu from the nightstand. "What do you think about some food? It's after seven."

It was such a practical question, she had to smile. "I am hungry."

"They look like they have a pretty good menu. Steak, fish, salad. What's your pleasure?"

"Cheeseburger, french fries, and a chocolate milk shake. Oh, and maybe a salad, too, so I don't feel totally guilty."

He gave her a knowing grin. "That's exactly what I order every time I come home. It always makes me feel like my life is back to normal."

"I have a feeling it will take more than a cheeseburger to make me feel that way, but at least it's a start."

While Alex was ordering, Julia rose from the bed and got dressed.

"I liked you better naked," Alex said as he hung up the phone.

His wicked grin was completely lethal. She almost felt like stripping down for him again—almost. After a day of shocking revelations, her brain was beginning to work again. And she needed to start thinking about her current situation and what she was going to do about it.

"Back to work, huh?" Alex asked, obviously reading her mind.

"Is your laptop still in the car?"

Alex glanced around the room. "It must be. You distracted me so much, I forgot to bring it in."

"We need to make plane reservations for tomorrow, and we should try to find the location of the ballet companies in Washington DC. Maybe we can get a head start on tracking down Elena. We can also look up information on my mother and father."

"Thank God for the Internet," he said. "I'll get the computer out of the car." He slipped on his shirt and buttoned it up. "Don't let anyone in while I'm gone."

"I'm sure no one knows we're here."

"I still want the dead bolt on as soon as I leave. We can't be too careful, Julia. My dad made it clear that whoever killed your parents had connections on this side of the world. And we know firsthand those connections still exist."

"Are you deliberately trying to scare me? I just got my heart back to its normal rhythm."

"I..." His expression turned serious. "I don't want anything to happen to you."

"I already slept with you. You don't have to sweet-talk me," she said lightly.

"I mean it, Julia. Lock the door."

"I will." She followed him to the door, prepared to throw the dead bolt as soon as he left. Alex put his hand around the back of her neck and kissed her as if he were leaving forever, instead of just going to the car. Then he was gone.

Shaken, she slid the dead bolt into place, hoping to God he really was coming back. That would always be the problem with Alex, she realized. She'd never be sure how long he would stay or if he'd return. But how could she complain? If she'd wanted a man who never left, she wouldn't have broken up with Michael.

Chapter Nineteen

Liz waited on the dock as Michael helped the last of his passengers off the fifty-foot yacht he used for charter services. The Annabelle was one of two boats owned by Michael's family. She knew he preferred the sailboat over the yacht, but his older brother had seniority in deciding which boat to run. She waved as he saw her. "Hey," she called.

He looked as if he wished he hadn't seen her and that she'd go away, but she was determined to talk to him. "Can I come up?" Without waiting for a reply, she boarded the yacht.

Michael wore his sailing clothes: jeans, a sweater, and a thick jacket. His face was red from the wind, his light brown hair ruffled and damp.

"What do you want?" he asked, a grumpy note to his voice.

"That's a nice greeting. I came to see how you were."

"I'm working. That's how I am."

"You're done working," she pointed out. "And I think you owe me more than attitude. I did help you with your house, not to mention a few dozen other things over the last year."

"Fine. But if you came here to talk about Julia, I'm not interested."

"I didn't come here to talk about Julia. I came here to talk about me. You probably don't care about any of this, but I want you to know anyway. I quit my job at the cafe. I signed up for some classes at San Francisco State. I'm going to finish my education."

"What brought this on?"

"Julia gave me a kick in the butt. She pointed out to me recently that I've been sitting on the sidelines watching everyone else play. And she was right." Liz paused. "I'm still pissed off at her, but what she said about me was true. I have been drifting aimlessly for over a year now. I kept thinking something great would fall in my lap, but I guess it doesn't happen that way." She watched him closely for his reaction, knowing his opinion was extremely important to her. "What do you think?"

He didn't answer right away, and each passing second made her more anxious.

"I think you're on the right track, Lizzie," he said at last, his scowl replaced by the warm smile she loved so much.

"Really?" She felt so relieved. "That means a lot to me. You're important to me, Michael. Not just because of what you were to Julia. I thought we were friends, too."

"We are friends." He patted her on the shoulder. "Don't ever think we're not."

"I won't. How's the house coming along?"

"It's not. I haven't felt like working on it since—"

"But you have to finish it. It's your house. It's your dream."

"A dream is something you share with someone."

"I don't believe that," she said with a toss of her head. "A dream is personal. That house means something to you. I should know. I saw the way you lovingly caressed the walls."

"I didn't do that."

She grinned. "You were close. Anyway, want some help? I have some free time tonight. I can scrape wallpaper, paint, or do whatever you need."

"That's a nice offer, but—"

She cut him off. "I'd really like to help, and if you're smart, you won't turn me down."

"I don't even know if I'm going to keep the house. It's too big for a single guy. Unless you think Julia will change her mind?"

Liz wished she could give him a different answer, but she couldn't. "I'm sorry, but I don't. I think Julia has a lot of plans that don't include you. She's on a quest to change her life. She's like a bird sprung from a cage, and she wants to fly everywhere, see everything."

"You're right. I've been thinking a lot about the relationship we had. Julia started pulling away from me the day of your mother's funeral. I was just hanging on so tight she couldn't get loose." He dug his hands into his pockets and walked to the side of the boat, staring out at the bay. "If it hadn't been this search of hers, it would have been something else that broke us up. I was just so ready to get married. I couldn't see that she wasn't."

Liz didn't say anything. Michael was lost in his thoughts, and she didn't want to intrude. Getting over Julia would be difficult for him, but she believed now that they would both find a better future on their own.

"I never should have bought that house without talking to her," Michael added. "I told my sister about it, and she said she couldn't believe I'd made such a bonehead move. Apparently it's not romantic to surprise a woman with a house."

"I think it's really romantic. If it had been me, I would have been very happy, but that's just me. I still think you should finish remodeling it. It's a great place, and you love it. Someday you'll find a woman who loves it, too. Then it will be ready."

Michael turned back to her. "Maybe I'll paint the back bedroom today. If you want to help, I won't say no."

"I'm your girl," she said, "as long as you buy me a pizza. I'm starving."

"Okay, but we're getting plain cheese pizza. I hate all that fancy—" Michael stopped. "Do you know that guy?" he asked, tipping his head toward a man on the pier. "He's been staring at you since you got here."

As Liz turned her head, the man pulled his baseball cap down over his eyes and walked away. "I don't know him." She licked her lips, feeling a little nervous. "I hope he's not the man who broke into our apartment. Julia said he was following her around. What if he's following me now?"

"The police haven't found out who ransacked your place?"

"No. I'm scared, Michael."

He stepped closer to her, putting his arm about her shoulders. "Don't worry. I'm here. I'll take care of you."

"Thanks."

"I hope Julia has someone watching her back."

Liz had a feeling that someone's name was Alex.

* * *

"It's me," Alex said as he knocked on the hotel room door, his laptop under his arm.

Julia flung the door open, her beautiful blue eyes worried. "Thank God, you're back."

"Why? Did something happen?" He searched her face for a clue to her distress.

"I just had a little panic attack, imagining that someone was waiting for you by the car or something crazy like that. I'm losing my mind, aren't I?"

"Not even close, but you don't have to worry about me. I can take care of myself."

"I know. I'm still glad you're back." She took the computer from his hands and set it on the table, then wrapped her arms around his waist and gave him a long, loving hug. "You don't mind if we stay like this for a while, do you?"

His hands slipped under her camisole top, caressing her back. "Hey, you left your bra off."

"I didn't think I needed it," she murmured.

"You don't," he said with pleasure. "In fact, we could get rid of this shirt, too."

Before she could answer, a knock came at the door.

"Don't answer it," she said, the fear back in her voice.

"Room service," a voice called out.

"It could be a trick," she warned him.

"Julia, we just ordered food," Alex said calmly. He set her aside, looked through the peephole, then opened the door. As the waiter set up the table, the delicious aroma of burgers and fries filled the room. Alex was reminded of how long it had been since they'd eaten. Julia must have realized the same thing. Her panic gone for the moment, she was already into the fries before he finished tipping the waiter.

"Hmm, this is good," she said when they were alone. "I'm starving. I haven't had a big cheeseburger in a long time. I feel so decadent."

He grinned at that. "I can show you more decadence than a cheeseburger."

"Save it for later," she said with a laugh.

Alex pulled over a chair, and for the next few moments they

ate in companionable silence. He finished first, but Julia was a close second. She sat back with her milk shake in hand and a satisfied sigh.

"I think I inhaled that," she said. "And you still beat me."

"I'm used to eating on the run."

"Sleeping on the run, working on the run, pretty much everything else on the run," she said with a knowing glint in her eyes.

"What? You have me all figured out now?"

"Not even close. You're a man of mystery."

"Good. That's the way I like it."

"That's not the way I like it." A frown drew her brows together. "Tell me something I don't know about you. Like a juicy secret."

"You want to know more secrets? Haven't you had your fill?"

She made a face at him. "A personal secret, Alex, nothing that involves foreign governments or spies."

He grinned. "I don't have any."

"You must."

He thought about it and realized that he truly did not have any secrets from her. She knew more about him and his family than anyone. In fact, he'd let her get closer to him than any other person on earth. How had he let that happen? And how was he going to put an end to it?

He'd tried to walk away once before, but he hadn't been able to leave her, not in the middle of everything. He would go when it was over, when they knew everything there was to know. Then he'd leave, wouldn't he?

Of course he would go. He had jobs waiting for him. One call to the magazine, and he'd be on his way to some distant country on the other side of the globe. Just the way he liked it.

Julia would go on with her life. And he'd go on with his.

She'd be a good memory, one of the best. But that's all she would be. Their affair would end like all of his other relationships. He didn't know how to do long term. He'd never wanted to learn. Until now... He drew in a sharp breath, determined to put that ridiculous thought out of his mind.

"It's okay, Alex," Julia said gently. "You don't have to worry I'll tell your secrets."

"I wasn't worrying about that."

"Then what's making you so uptight? You have your stone face on right now, and that usually means something is bothering you."

"I don't have a stone face."

"Yes, you do. Your skin tightens over your cheekbones, and your jaw gets really set, and even your eyes look cold. They have that 'don't ask me any questions' look in them right now."

"Then maybe you should stop asking me questions," he pointed out.

She stuck out her tongue, breaking the tension, and he felt his face relax. He had been tightening up. He just hadn't realized it until she'd pointed it out.

"You know, we're even on the secrets issue," she told him. "I may know yours, but you also know mine." She paused. "Except maybe one."

He waited for her to elaborate, but she simply set down her milk shake and stood up.

"We should get to work," she said. "We need to make plane reservations for tomorrow, and—"

"What's the one thing?" he asked, extremely curious.

"I'm not going to tell you."

"Why not?"

"Because it's personal, and..." She paused for a long moment. "It would probably scare you to death."

He gazed into her eyes and saw a question there, a question he was terrified to answer. "I guess everyone is entitled to one secret," he said lightly. He got up from his chair and retrieved the laptop. He sat down on the bed with his back against the headboard and opened the computer, hitting the button to boot up.

Julia sat down on the bed next to him. "I'll tell you if you really want to know," she said.

"I don't think I do."

"Okay, but fair warning... before you leave for good, I'm going to tell you."

"I'll keep that in mind. Now, I think we should take the first flight out tomorrow." In fact, if they could get on a flight right now, he would. Because another night with Julia wasn't going to make the leaving any easier.

"Let's see what you can get," Julia said.

His fingers flew across the keyboard. Within five minutes they had reservations on a seven a.m. flight to Dulles. "Now what?" he asked.

"Look up my mother's name, Natalia Markov."

"Here she is," he said a moment later, pulling up a page on Russian ballet dancers. There was a grainy black-and-white photograph of the ballerina. He adjusted the screen so Julia could see it better. He heard her sharp intake of breath and knew that she'd remembered something.

"I know her," she said softly. "That's my mother. She's beautiful."

Natalia was stunning, Alex thought. She looked a bit like Julia, but she had a lighter, more ethereal quality to her face and figure. As he studied her picture, he remembered something his father had said earlier, something that had gotten lost in his head until now. "Stan knew your mother," he said aloud.

"That's right," Julia said. "Your father told us that Stan helped them set up the defection. Why didn't he tell us that? He made it sound like he knew nothing."

"He said he was too scared for his family to look into my father's death. I bet he knew the death was fake all along." He thought back to their meetings. "And you—you must have reminded him of your mother. Yet, he gave nothing away. Hmm."

"What are you thinking?"

"I wonder if Stan hired someone to break into our apartments."

"That's ridiculous."

"Is it?" he queried. "Think about it. We went to Stan first. He knew about you before anyone else would have time to find you."

"He's a dignified, respected, older man. I can't see him breaking and entering."

"What about manipulating? Directing? Calling the shots—like he did when your parents tried to defect?"

"You really believe that's possible? What about the guy in the cap? Or the men who followed us to Napa?"

Alex shrugged. "They could all be working together, or different parties could be coming at us from different directions."

"Great. I feel much better now," she said dryly.

"I'm going to call Stan, confront him, see what he has to say."

Alex set the laptop aside and grabbed his cell phone off the table. He waited impatiently for Stan to answer. A message machine came on instead. "Call me immediately," Alex said. "It's extremely important. Don't let me down." As he hung up, Alex realized Stan had already let him down, just like everyone else in his life.

"He'll call back. He cares about you," Julia said, putting her hand over his. "I saw the way he looked at you, as if you were his son."

"Yeah, well, I'm not his son."

"Don't judge him until you have all the facts."

"Fine." He tipped his head toward the computer screen. "Did you learn anything else?"

"I can't seem to focus on reading the article. I can't look away from my mother." She smiled sadly. "How could I have forgotten her until just this second? How could I have forgotten them all? My sister, my father, my mother?"

He put his arm around her, pulling her close. "You suffered a trauma. Everything you knew was ripped away from you when you were too small to understand what was happening. Sarah gave you love and comforted you. She took care of you and became your entire world."

"And she surrounded me with people. First Gino and all his relatives, then Lizzie."

"Exactly. There were so many good people in your life who loved you that there was no reason for you to search your brain for anything else. It was probably too painful to try to remember, so you didn't."

"You're being too easy on me," she said.

"No, you're being too hard on yourself."

"I feel like I betrayed my mom and dad by forgetting who they were, and my sister, too. What am I going to say when I see Elena? How am I going to tell her that for the past twenty-five years I never gave her one thought?"

"You'll say what's right," he assured her. "I'm curious as to whether or not she ever remembered you or your parents."

"I just hope we can find her. What if she's no longer in DC?"

"Then it will take longer."

Julia kissed him on the cheek. "I like your confidence. You make me believe in the impossible. Thanks."

"No problem." He returned his gaze to the computer, but he wasn't thinking about the information on the screen; he was thinking about Julia. She was making him believe in the impossible, too.

* * *

It was a cool crisp September day in Washington DC. The cab ride from the airport was long and nerve-racking after an equally long and nerve-racking flight. They'd hit lots of turbulence, which had done nothing to calm Julia's upset stomach. But at least they were here, and they had come armed with one address, that of the DC Ballet Company, located near the John F. Kennedy Center of Performing Arts. On the Internet, they'd discovered her sister's name, Elaine Harrigan, listed among the former stars of the company. Unfortunately, there had been no photo. Not that Julia needed to know what her twin sister looked like. All she had to do was gaze in the mirror.

"You're missing all the sights, the White House, the Washington Monument, the Capitol," Alex told her. "What's so fascinating about your hands?"

Julia realized she was still staring down at her tightly clasped fingers. "I was just thinking." She lifted her head. "And worrying about what's coming next."

"Hopefully a reunion with your sister."

"I want that—I think. I'm nervous. What will I say? What will she say? Then I worry that we won't find her at all."

He took her hand and gave it a squeeze. "Stop trying to predict the future."

It was good advice, and she wanted to take it. She looked out the window just as the Kennedy Center came into view. It was a beautiful, magnificent building set on the banks of the Potomac River. Her sister had probably danced there, Julia thought. Just like their mother, she'd taken to the stage, danced her heart out, and probably drawn the applause of thousands.

The cab passed by the center and a few blocks later stopped in front of a two-story building with white columns and a fountain in front of it. A sign over the door read DC BALLET COMPANY. Alex gave the driver money to wait for them. Julia kept her large handbag with her. She had a tight grip on it, knowing that even though they'd flown across the country, someone might still be on their tail.

They entered the building and stopped at the information desk in the lobby.

"Can I help you?" a young woman asked.

"We'd like to speak to whoever is in charge." Alex offered her a charming smile, and the woman responded immediately.

"That would be Mrs. Kay," she said. "Can I tell her what this is regarding?"

"Elaine Harrigan," Alex said. "She danced here several years ago. We're relatives of hers, and we're trying to find her. Do you think Mrs. Kay could give us a few minutes of her time? It's very important."

"I'll see if she's available." The receptionist made a brief call, then put down the phone. "You're in luck. She'll see you. Down the hall, second door on the left."

"Thank you," Alex said.

Julia felt herself growing more tense as they walked down the hall. She paused at the first door, glancing in at a large studio with hardwood floors and wall-to-wall mirrors. A group of six women in black leotards was going through a routine. She could hear music in the background and the sharp voice of an instructor. The dancers were all thin but strong, and their faces showed the same resolute determination, reminding Julia that professional ballet was not for the faint of heart. An old memory came back as she saw one girl unlace her ballet slipper. In her mind, she saw her mother taking off her slipper to reveal a bloody big toe. She'd simply wiped it off, bandaged it up, and put the slipper back on.

"Come on," Alex urged, pulling her away. "Let's find Mrs. Kay."

The door to the next room was half-open. A woman stood with her back to them. She was looking out the window behind her desk and talking on the phone. Alex knocked. She turned around and waved them in with an impatient hand.

With the woman still focused on her phone call, Julia had a chance to study Mrs. Kay. She had to be in her sixties. Her hair, a beautiful, vibrant white, was cut short, just past her ears. She was very thin, showing all of her fine bones. Her body was lanky, her legs long. She was probably a dancer, too, or had been. Finally, she set the phone down.

She smiled and said, "Elaine, I haven't seen you in a while. I thought Judy said some of your relatives were here. She must have gotten confused."

Julia gulped. This woman thought she was Elaine, which meant Mrs. Kay knew her sister.

"Your hair is so short," Mrs. Kay said. "I thought you told me you'd never cut it."

"I'm not Elaine," Julia finally managed to get out. "I'm her sister, Julia."

"What?" Her eyes narrowed in disbelief. "Is this some sort of joke?"

"I'm Elaine's twin sister."

"That's not possible. You don't have any family."

Julia drew in a deep breath. "I'm telling you the truth. I'm Julia DeMarco. I was separated from my twin sister, Elena—Elaine— many years ago. Now I'm trying to find her. And I hope you can help me."

Mrs. Kay came around her desk, her gaze never leaving Julia's face. "Come over here," she said, "and shake my hand."

It seemed like an odd request, but after a moment's hesitation, Julia moved across the room and did as she asked.

"You aren't Elaine," the older woman said, still holding Julia's hand, "but you're the spitting image, except for your hair."

"She's my identical twin sister."

"Well, that explains it." Mrs. Kay cocked her head to one side, a confused expression lingering on her face.

"Do you know my sister well?" Julia asked.

"Of course. She lived with me for several years. I should introduce myself. I'm Victoria Kay. I run this dance company. You said your name was Julia and—" She gazed at Alex inquiringly.

"Alex Manning," he said.

"Nice to meet you."

"Does Elaine still dance for you?" Julia asked.

"No. You even sound like her. It's amazing." Victoria shook her head. "I'm sorry. I'm just so bemused by your appearance. Elaine told me everyone in her family was dead. I know she grew up in foster homes.

I actually became her foster parent when she was fifteen. She was such a gifted dancer, I knew I had to find a way for her to dance. She had a rare talent."

"Why isn't she still dancing? Is it just age? Did she get too old?"

"Heavens, no. She stopped right before the peak of her career. It was five years ago. She was crossing the street, running to meet a date. She was late, and she didn't look where she was going. A car hit her, and she broke both her legs. One was beyond complete repair. She never danced again. In fact, she still walks with a limp." Victoria's eyes filled with regret. "That's how I knew you weren't her—the way you walked. It was so tragic, what happened to her. Elaine was truly special. She didn't just dance to the music. She lived it. And her career was over in the blink of an eye."

Julia felt her heart break at the story. "What happened to her after that?"

"She recovered as best she could. She had to start over, find a new life for herself."

"Do you know where she is now?"

"She runs an antique shop on Carlmont Street in Georgetown. You can probably find her there. I don't think she ever leaves. I'll write down the address for you." Victoria moved toward the desk. "Please tell her I'm thinking about her. You know, she once told me that a piece of her heart was missing. I didn't know what that meant. Now perhaps I do. You're the missing piece."

* * *

Julia was still thinking about Victoria's words when they took a taxi to Georgetown. "If Elena told Victoria that her parents and sister were dead, then she must have remembered us," Julia said, looking to Alex for confirmation. "But why did she think I was dead?"

"Maybe the agents told her that. They didn't want her to look for you."

"That makes sense. It sounds like she grew up alone, though."

"It does," Alex agreed. "I wonder what happened to her foster family."

"Maybe it wasn't a good one. God, I hope she wasn't mistreated or abused. That would be so wrong, so unfair."

"Just remember that whatever happened to Elena, it wasn't

your fault, Julia. You were a child, too. You couldn't choose your surroundings any more than she could pick hers."

"I know you're right, but I still feel guilty that I've had such a happy life. And that accident she had sounds horrible."

"Life can deal out some bad cards," Alex said. "She had to play them out. So did you."

"Now we have the chance to start over, don't you think?" Alex didn't respond to her hopeful smile, his face grim. "What are you thinking?"

"That you could get hurt. Elena may not welcome you with open arms."

"She thinks I'm dead, Alex. When she realizes I'm alive, she'll be happy, won't she?"

"I guess we'll find out," he replied.

Julia looked out the window, taking a moment to appreciate the beauty of the neighborhood, the brownstones, the redbrick streets and buildings, the shops, galleries, and restaurants. At least her sister lived in a wonderful area. She must be reasonably successful. Maybe her life hadn't turned out all bad.

The taxi pulled up in front of a store called River View Antiques. As Julia got out of the cab, she forced herself to breathe deeply. She was about to come face-to-face with her past. She didn't know if she was ready, but it was too late to have second thoughts. Alex put a hand on her back and gave her a gentle push.

As they entered the store, a bell jangled. On first glance all Julia could see was stuff. Large pieces of furniture, bookcases, dressers, tables, and antique desks lined the walls. On every available tabletop were knickknacks from decades past: silver teapots, antique jewelry, old picture frames, and ceramic dishes. The room smelled like dust, incense, potpourri, and history. All of these items had once belonged to someone. They probably had fascinating stories to tell. But she wasn't here to browse. She was here to see her sister. "Hello," she called out.

"Be right there," a woman replied.

The voice sounded familiar, or was Julia imagining it?

A moment later, a woman came through a beaded curtain to greet them. She wore black capri pants and a light blue silk button-down blouse. She walked with a slight limp. Her blond hair was pulled back in a barrette at the base of her neck, but it drifted down to her waist, reminding Julia of her mother's hair.

"Hello—" The woman stopped abruptly as she looked straight at Julia. Her blue eyes grew big and scared. "Oh, my God! It can't be you."

Julia couldn't find her voice. All she could do was stand there and stare.

Elena stared back at her. She blinked once, twice, as if she could make Julia disappear.

They were mirror images of each other, the same height, the same build, the same blue eyes, the same nose, the same chin. Only the length of their hair was different. Julia swallowed hard. Even though she had known what was coming, she still felt shocked by the reality.

"I don't understand," Elena said. "You're supposed to be dead. Everyone is dead, Mama, Papa, and you. I'm the only one left. They told me so, over and over again. This is crazy. I must be dreaming. You can't be real, Yulia."

Hearing the Russian version of her name spoken in Elena's soft voice, which was so similar to her own, made Julia's stomach turn over. This was her sister. Her blood. And she remembered her now in vivid detail.

"I'm alive," Julia said. "And I'm real. This isn't a dream." She hesitated, then opened her arms and held her breath, hoping that Elena wouldn't reject her. She really needed to touch her sister, to know with her heart what she could see with her eyes.

Chapter Twenty

Elena moved slowly, uncertainly, finally putting her arms around Julia and giving her a tentative, brief hug. Julia would have liked to hold on, but Elena was already stepping away. They stared at each other again. It would probably take days for reality to sink in, but as the seconds ticked away, memories that had been buried deep within Julia came rushing to the front of her mind. She'd shared a bedroom with Elena, sometimes a bed when one of them had been too scared to sleep alone. They'd played together, fought together, laughed together, and cried together. How could she have ever forgotten Elena? They weren't just sisters, but twins. They were a part of each other, born together, meant to be together forever. Instead, they'd been torn apart, and twenty-five years was a long time.

"Where—where have you been all these years?" Elena asked finally.

Julia didn't know where to start. It was such a long, complicated story. "San Francisco," she said. "I was taken there after we left Russia."

"That's a long way from here. Why were you taken there, and I was brought here? Did they tell you I was dead?"

How could Julia say she hadn't been told anything and she hadn't remembered anyone? It sounded wrong. But she had to say something. Elena was waiting. "I was raised by a woman named Sarah. She told me I was her daughter, and I guess at some point I bought into the story. I don't know when it happened. Until yesterday, I couldn't think of a time when Sarah and I weren't together. She married a man and had another daughter, and we were a family."

"I don't understand. You didn't remember me?"

Julia felt another wave of guilt. She wanted to lie, if only to save Elena from being hurt by her words, but she couldn't let another falsehood be told. "I didn't remember anything until I heard your name yesterday. Then it all came back. I remembered the day Mama told us we were going to be apart. I remember how scared we were."

Elena stared back at her. "I don't remember that. I don't remember our parents at all. I just have blurry images of people whose faces never become clear enough for me to recognize. But your face was always clear. I never forgot about you. Are our parents really dead? If you're not, then—"

"No, that part is true. They died before we left Russia."

"Are you sure? They told me they died when we got here." Elena stopped, her eyes troubled. "Do you know about them? I asked and asked, but no one would tell me anything, not even their names. I just think of them as Mama and Papa."

"We have a lot to talk about." Julia saw Elena dart a quick look at Alex and realized she'd forgotten he was standing there. "I'm sorry. This is Alex Manning," she said. "He helped me find you. Do you go by Elaine now, instead of Elena?"

"I thought I'd always been Elaine, but now that you mention it..."

"You used to be Elena, and I was Yulia, but now I'm Julia with a *J*. I guess they wanted us to have more American names."

"I guess so," Elena said slowly. "It's nice to meet you, Mr. Manning."

"It's even nicer to meet you," he replied. "Is there anywhere we could talk?"

Before she could answer, the bell behind them jangled, and a curly-haired young man in his early twenties wearing baggy jeans and an extra-large T-shirt walked through the door. "What's up?" he said to Elena, then did a double take when he saw Julia. "What the—"

"This is my sister," Elena said quickly.

"I thought you didn't have any family."

"We've been separated for a long time. I need to take a break.

Can you watch the store, Colin?"

Colin couldn't take his eyes off Julia. "She looks exactly like you, except your hair is longer."

"I know. I'll explain later. And I'll be upstairs if you need me." She turned to Julia. "My apartment is on the second floor. We can talk there."

Julia nodded. As Elena mounted the stairs, her limp became more pronounced, reminding Julia that Elena had suffered more than one loss in her life. They had so much to discover about each other, and Julia wanted to know everything.

Elena's apartment was not as stuffed with items as her shop, but it was still warm and cluttered, with knickknacks and colorful but mismatched furniture.

"I wasn't expecting anyone." Elena grabbed a basket of laundry off the couch. "Just sit down somewhere," she said as she headed toward the bedroom.

Julia glanced at Alex. "Well, what do you think?"

"I would have recognized her anywhere," he said with a smile. "It's hard to believe there really are two of you. Double the fun."

She sighed at that. "Let me know when we start having fun. I feel so unsettled. My stomach is churning. I don't even know how to explain it all to Elena."

"You'll find a way."

Julia hoped he was right.

When Elena returned, they sat down together in the large room that seemed to serve as living room and dining room, with a small kitchenette off to the side. After a moment, Julia said, "Why don't you start first, Elena. Tell me what happened to you when you got to the States."

Elena stared down at her hands, clasped tightly together in her lap. "I went to a foster home, the O'Rourkes." I lived there for three years, I think. Then they got divorced and couldn't be foster parents anymore, so I was sent to another home. That's pretty much the way it went for the rest of my childhood. I was moved every couple of years for one reason or another. It was not a happy time for me. The only place I loved was ballet class. No matter where I lived, I always managed to talk my way into a class by either trading chores for the teacher or begging a lot. When I was fifteen, I got into a bad situation at one home, and I ran away. I hid out at the ballet academy where I had taken some lessons. Mrs. Kay found me. She took me in, became my foster parent, and helped me become a dancer." She paused, a dark shadow crossing her face. "Now I run an antique store. Your turn."

Julia knew Elena had left out a lot of her life, but it was enough for a start. "I was raised as Julia DeMarco. My mother, Sarah, never told me I was adopted, and as I said before, I didn't remember anything but the story she constructed for us. She married an Italian man, Gino DeMarco, when I was five. They had a baby girl named Elizabeth. We grew up together. I never thought I was anything but a member of the family, until I saw a photograph of a famous Russian orphan girl. I thought it was a picture of me. It was taken by Alex. I started researching the photo, and it turns out it wasn't me at all. It was you."

"I was in a famous picture?" Elena asked, her eyes wide and surprised once again.

"It was at an orphanage," Julia explained. "I guess we were put there until we could be smuggled out of the country."

"An orphanage?" Elena echoed.

"Yes. Your hands were on the gates, and—"

"Wait." Elena suddenly straightened. "The day was cold and gray. I wanted to go home. I didn't know where you were. I asked everyone I saw, even a boy who came over and took my picture," she finished. "I remember that now. That was you, Alex?"

He nodded. "You said something to me, but I didn't understand. I just knew there was a look in your eyes I wanted to capture."

"I was scared. I didn't know where I was or what I was doing there." She turned to Julia. "What was I doing there? And where were you?"

"I think I was there, too," Julia replied. "We were both there because our parents were important Russians, and they were planning to defect."

"Who were our parents?"

"Natalia and Sergei Markov."

"Natalia Markov, the ballerina? She was our mother? That can't be right. You must be mistaken."

"I'm not," Julia said. "You really didn't know? No one ever told you that you resembled her in any way?"

Lost in thought, Elena didn't say anything for a long moment. "I can't believe it. Natalia Markov. No one ever put the two of us together. But then, why would they?"

"You must have inherited her talent," Julia suggested. "I don't know if I did. I never had an opportunity to dance, but it never really spoke to me, either. I've always loved music more than dance."

"What happened to her? And to our father? How did they die?" Elena asked.

"In an explosion at the house. Our father worked for the Russian government. Apparently he offered to exchange information for freedom."

"Who took us out of the country if our parents were dead? And why didn't they leave us with our grandparents? Didn't we have grandparents?"

Julia hadn't thought that far back. "I don't know about our grandparents. I know our great-grandparents were tied to ballet and music, but they were probably dead before we were born. I was told that U.S. agents smuggled us out of the country somehow; the details have yet to be explained to me."

"They couldn't leave you there after your parents died," Alex interjected. "You probably would have been killed. In fact, I hate to speed up this reunion, but you both may be in danger. And we need to discuss how we're going to address that possibility."

"What do you mean?" Elena asked. "How could we be in danger?"

"My photo was published in the newspaper in San Francisco, with an article announcing that I was the orphan girl," Julia explained. "Then both my apartment and Alex's were ransacked. Someone tried to mug me, and we've been followed. It's all very disturbing. It appears that someone, whoever killed our parents, thinks I have something of value, some sort of family treasure that was going to support our parents and their new life here."

"What kind of a treasure?" Elena inquired with a bemused shake of her head. "This is such an amazing story."

"No one seems to know exactly what the treasure is. When I found out about you, I knew I had to warn you. Since they know I'm alive, it stands to reason they know or suspect you are, too."

"I certainly don't have a treasure," Elena said. "I don't have much of anything."

"I have two things from our past." Julia reached into her handbag and pulled out the necklace. "We each had one of these, remember? You were wearing yours in the picture."

"Yes, of course," Elena said. "I still have it."

"I also found this matryoshka doll." Julia set the doll on the coffee table. "Some of the pieces are missing. Do you have them?"

A light sparked in Elena's eyes. "I do. I'll get them." She went into her bedroom and returned a moment later with the necklace and the doll. "One of my foster parents tried to take these away from me once. I had to fight to get them back. They were all I had left of my family. I wasn't going to give them up. Sometimes I slept with them under my pillow just in case one of the other kids tried to steal them."

Julia frowned. It didn't sound as if Elena had had a very good life.

Elena opened the largest doll, which belonged to Julia, and said, "I want to put them together so they fit right."

As she did so, Julia flashed back to a similar scene. Her mother had taken the dolls apart on her bed. She'd said she wanted them each to have some dolls to take with them on their trip. So she'd divided them, every other one, then handed each of them a set of the dolls. She'd told them a story... What was that story?

"She told us about these dolls," Julia said slowly. "Do you remember?"

Elena thought for a long moment. "She said the doll had been painted for her grandmother."

"She was a dancer, too," Julia said. "Tamara Slovinsky. You followed in their footsteps, Elena. You lived their legacy." Elena blinked quickly, and Julia realized too late the pain her words had created. "I'm sorry. I forgot."

"No, it's all right. I had an accident. I was careless. It's my fault that I can no longer dance."

"I bet you were great when you did."

"I was all right," she said modestly. "I didn't really care about being great. I just wanted to dance. I loved the way it felt to be on the stage, to be lost in a world of make-believe, where the girls were pretty and the boys were handsome and the music lifted you up as if you were flying."

Julia was touched by her sister's words. She felt the same passion for the music that made the dancer soar. They were truly two halves of the same whole.

"Do you mind if I take a look at the doll?" Alex interrupted. "There were some numbers on Julia's set. I wonder if there are any on yours. Do you have a piece of paper?"

"Sure," Elena said, retrieving a notepad from a nearby table.

Alex took the dolls apart again, one at a time, jotting down a number after each one, until they had a string.

"Ten numbers," he mused.

"Maybe it's a serial number for the doll," Elena suggested.

"The numbers are scratched lightly into the surface of the wood. I think someone put them there after the dolls were made."

"Maybe our mother did," Julia said slowly, remembering the sharp knife by her mother's side the day she'd had the dolls open on the bed. "What could they possibly mean?"

"I don't know," Alex replied. "But we should try to find out. I can't believe I'm going to say this," he added heavily. "I'll call my father. He might know something."

Julia knew what a huge step that was for him, and she nodded gratefully. "Thank you."

Alex started to put the dolls back together, then paused. He shook the smallest one. "This is interesting. I hear a rattle." He shook it again. Julia leaned in, hearing the same small noise. The doll was one that had belonged to Elena's set.

"Did you ever notice that before?" Julia asked her sister.

"I haven't taken that doll apart in probably fifteen years. And the smallest one never opened."

"It looks like it was glued shut. There's a fine line," Alex said. He looked at Elena. "Do you mind if I try to open it, see what's inside? It could be important."

Elena shrugged her shoulders. "It's fine with me. I can't imagine what would be in there. What do you need? A knife? A screwdriver?"

"Either would be great." He pressed on the middle of the doll with his fingers.

"Do you really think there's something in there?" Julia asked.

"We know someone has been looking for something and that it's small." He took a paring knife from Elena's hand and ran the tip around the middle of the doll where there should have been an opening. After a moment, he was able to pull the two pieces apart.

Julia held her breath as he produced a silver key.

"Look at this," Alex murmured.

"Why would a key be in there?" Elena asked.

"I wonder what it goes to." Julia took the key from Alex's hand and twirled it around in her fingers. There's a number on it -- 423."

"I have a safe-deposit box key that looks a lot like that," Alex commented.

She met his eyes. "You think this goes to a safe-deposit box?"

"Perhaps that ten-digit number on the dolls is for a bank account." Alex rose. "I'm going to call my father now. Do you mind if I use the bedroom?"

"Go ahead," Elena said with a wave of her hand. "I don't think I made my bed, though. Neatness isn't one of my strengths."

"Mine, either," Alex said with a smile. "I'll feel right at home."

As he left the room, Julia handed Elena the key. "What do you think? Any other ideas?"

"I feel like I'm two steps behind you and Alex. I don't know what we're looking for."

"We don't know, either. We're just winging it."

An awkward silence fell between them. "This is weird, huh?" Julia said, understating the obvious. "You and me, after all these years."

"Really strange," Elena agreed. "I can't stop looking at you. I'm sorry if I'm staring."

"I feel the same way. I know you, and yet I don't."

"We were babies the last time we saw each other, three years old. It's no wonder it feels uncomfortable now."

"But it feels good, too," Julia said.

"Yes, it does. I've really missed having family," Elena confessed.

Julia wanted to say the same thing, but in all fairness she couldn't. She'd had a good family to grow up in. And another sister as well. She still didn't know how she would tell Liz about Elena. That wasn't a conversation she was looking forward to.

"Is he your boyfriend?" Elena asked, nodding toward the bedroom.

"What? You mean Alex?"

Elena smiled. "Of course I mean Alex. Who else would I mean?"

"Actually, I was engaged to someone else until a few days ago. My fiancé didn't want me to search for my real family. It turned out to be the last straw between us, and I'm glad now. I realized he wasn't the one for me."

"Because of Alex?"

"I didn't break up with him because of Alex," Julia prevaricated. "What about you? Any men in your life?"

"Not recently. I was engaged, too, a couple years ago, before my accident. He was a choreographer, a good one. He couldn't bear the thought that I'd never dance for him again. So he left. It hurt, but life goes on. I learned that lesson a long time ago."

Julia scooted forward on the couch, clasping her hands together. "I'm so sorry that your childhood wasn't happy. I wish we could have been together. It isn't fair that I grew up in a loving home and you didn't. I feel so guilty."

"It wasn't your fault. We should have been kept together, not hidden away from the world."

"For our protection, they say," Julia reminded her. Although she wasn't quite sure if that was the true reason or the convenient one. They'd become baggage, children no one wanted to be associated with. That's why they'd stuck Elena in a foster home. Julia was lucky, very lucky. Sarah had wanted her desperately enough to change her entire life and her past just to be able to take care of her. For the first time, she felt a lessening of her anger toward Sarah. At least she had been loved and taken care of. She needed to remember that and be thankful.

Alex returned to the room. "I reached my father. He'll have Brady trace the number. He thinks it's a bank account. He knew your parents made plans before the defection. Your mother had come to the U.S. a number of times with her ballet company. My father believes that she may have stashed away a great deal of money during those visits."

"So the treasure might be cash," Julia said.

"Might be," Alex agreed. "He'll call me back. I told him where we were. He said to stay put. Apparently your parents were planning to live here in DC, because your father was going to work with our intelligence agencies. That's how Elena ended up here. It was the initial drop point."

"You make me sound like a bottle of milk or a newspaper," Elena said with a touch of annoyance.

"Sorry. Those were his words, not mine."

"It would make sense that they'd come here so our father could work with the government," Julia interjected. "Does your dad think the account might be here in the city?"

"That's his guess. Or possibly New York," Alex replied. "Your mother made several trips there as well."

Julia's cell phone began to ring. She slipped it out of her purse and saw Liz's number. "It's my sister," she said, feeling awkward when she said it. "My other sister." She cleared her throat and answered the phone. "Hello."

"Hey, it's Liz. What's going on? I haven't heard from you in a while. Have you found out anything?"

"A couple of things," Julia said. "I don't want to get into it on the phone, though. I promise to tell you everything as soon as I get back."

"Get back? Where exactly are you, Julia?"

She hesitated, then said, "I'm in Washington DC."

"Why? What's there?"

"It's a long story."

"And you don't want to tell me. I get it. I just wanted to let you know that some guy was watching me on the docks this afternoon."

"What did he look like?" Julia asked, her pulse quickening.

"He was big and stocky, and he wore a baseball cap. He left as soon as he realized I'd seen him. Do you think he's the guy who burglarized our apartment?"

"I think he might be. Don't go back to our place, Liz, especially alone."

"I won't. Believe me, I'm not looking for trouble."

"I'll call you when I get home," Julia said. "In the meantime, be careful, Liz. I don't want anything to happen to you."

"I will. Is Alex still with you?"

"Yes."

Liz sighed. "You're crazy, Julia, but I guess everyone deserves to fall for a bad boy once in her life."

Julia wanted to say it wasn't like that, but how could she? She glanced at Alex, who was talking to Elena with a warm, interested look on his face. She wasn't falling in love with him. She was already there. After saying good-bye, she hung up the phone.

"Everything okay?" Alex asked.

"Liz said some guy was watching her. It sounded like the same man who was watching me at the radio station. I feel bad. I'm here. She's there. I don't want her to get hurt."

"Liz is your... sister?" Elena asked, tripping over the word *sister*.

"Yes. She's younger than me, just twenty-two. I've always taken care of her. She's really angry with me for getting involved in all this."

"Does she know about me?"

"I wanted to make sure I could find you first, so I haven't said anything yet."

Elena nodded, understanding in her eyes. "That will be difficult for you, won't it?"

"Probably."

Elena cleared her throat. "I need to go downstairs and check on Colin. You're welcome to stay here and wait for that call."

"Actually, I was thinking about food," Alex said. "And it will probably be hours before my father calls back."

"I'd love to see more of your shop," Julia put in. She exchanged a look with Alex and knew they were once again on the same page. She needed some time alone with her sister, and he was more than willing to give it to her.

"I'll get some takeout and bring it back," he said. "Any suggestions?"

Elena thought for a moment. "If you're adventurous, there's a great Thai restaurant around the corner."

"Oh, my God. You are my sister, " Julia said with a huge smile. "I love exotic food."

Elena grinned back at her. "So do I."

For the first time since they'd arrived, Julia felt optimistic and back on balance. "This is going to be good," she said, and she wasn't talking about the food.

* * *

It was almost midnight when Julia and Elena finally talked themselves out. While Elena went into the bedroom to undress, Julia helped Alex make up a bed on the couch. "Will you be all right out here?" she asked.

"I'd be better if you were with me." He gave her an intimate smile that reminded her how long it had been since she'd kissed him or touched him. "Come here," he said softly.

She cast a quick look over her shoulder. "Elena might see us."

"One kiss."

"It's never enough," she said with a sigh as she moved into his arms. His hands spanned her waist as he kissed her gently, tenderly, with only a hint of the passion they'd shared the night before. "That was awfully restrained," she complained.

"Believe me, if it wasn't, you'd be on your back right now and we'd give your sister the second shock of her life."

"Promises, promises," she said with a smile. She pressed another kiss on his lips. "Thanks for being so great today."

"I didn't do anything."

"Yes, you did. You supported me, and you didn't try to take over. You did good. I owe you."

"And I will collect," he promised. "I just hope my father calls tomorrow. I'd like to get that number resolved."

"I think he will. He wants to help you."

"To absolve his guilt, maybe. Whatever the reason, I'll take it. The sooner we figure out the ending to this mystery the better."

A twinge of pain ran through her at his words. As soon as the mystery was over, they would be over. To be fair he probably hadn't meant it like that, but it was still true.

"Hey, what's that frown for?" He tipped up her chin with his finger.

"Nothing. I was just thinking about all the secrets, the lies, the constant surprises. I never know what will happen next."

"But that doesn't stop you from fighting on," Alex said, a note of admiration in his voice. "A lot of people would have quit or backed away by now, not wanting to risk losing everything they believed in. You're something else, Julia." He ran his fingers through her hair. "Beautiful, smart, and gutsy. Hell of a combination."

"Are you scared?" she asked, half-teasing, half-serious.

"Terrified," he said lightly. He kissed her again, then released her. "Go to bed, Julia, before I can't let you go."

"I'd stay, but—"

"But you two women need to bond. I get it. And believe me, I've had enough girl talk to last me awhile. I'm going to watch something macho on television and not think about anything else until tomorrow morning.

"Good night." Julia stole one last quick kiss before leaving. When she entered the bedroom, Elena was wearing a long T-shirt and sitting on the side of her queen-size bed. She was brushing out her hair, and Julia was struck once again by the resemblance between them.

"If you want to sleep with Alex, it's fine with me," Elena said, setting down her brush. She gave Julia a curious look. "I still don't understand exactly what your relationship is."

"I'm not sure, either," Julia admitted. "I'm afraid to analyze it too much, especially in the middle of everything else."

"But you like him."

"Oh, yeah, more than a little. But that seems crazy, too, because a few weeks ago I thought I was in love with someone else."

"What happened to the other guy? I know you said he was upset that you were searching for your family, but was that all of it?"

Julia sat down on the bed. "No. I told you that my mother, Sarah, died six months ago. Well, Michael was so great through her illness. For two years he was supportive, kind, caring, everything a woman could want. After my mom died, he wanted to get married, and we'd been engaged for so long, I knew I had to say yes. I owed him. Deep in my heart, I knew that Michael wasn't the one for me. He was just taking up where my mom left off. Sarah raised me in a controlled little bubble. She protected me and hid me away from the world. I guess she was always looking over her shoulder, afraid she would be found out. Michael wanted a wife who would stay in his world, who wouldn't make waves, wouldn't want to travel or have a big job or do anything different. That's fine for him, but I would have suffocated."

"Alex certainly doesn't seem the type to put you in a bubble," Elena observed.

"I'm not sure he wants to put me anywhere. He's an admitted loner. He likes to travel light, and he told me that he's never met a woman who made him want more than a casual affair."

"I hope he didn't say that after you slept together."

"No, before. I'm a fool, huh?"

Elena smiled. "He's a good-looking man, Julia. He's smart, successful, exciting—the last thing I would call you is a fool. Just don't let him break your heart."

"I'm trying to keep that in mind."

Elena tossed her a T-shirt. "You can sleep in this."

"Thanks."

Julia took off her jeans and top and slipped on the T-shirt. She climbed into the bed next to Elena, feeling both awkward and strangely comfortable. A moment later Elena switched off the light.

"Was it hard losing your boyfriend when you had your accident?" Julia asked.

For a long minute, there was silence; then Elena said, "His leaving didn't hurt as much as the fact that I couldn't dance anymore, but it was very painful. I really loved him. I made a huge mistake. He only wanted the successful dancer who could bring his choreography to life. He didn't really want me, all of me. He was an ass."

"And there hasn't been anyone since?"

"I've been busy. I had to restart my life, get a new career going. Victoria, Mrs. Kay, she helped me get the shop. She actually owns this building, and I pay nominal rent. There's no way I could afford this area if I didn't have connections."

"The shop is great. I'm so impressed by how many beautiful pieces you have."

"I love knowing that each piece in my shop has a history. I don't love it as much as dance, I'll admit, but I like seeing things find their rightful home. Probably something subliminal about that, huh?"

Because they'd never been able to go home. "Probably," Julia agreed.

"Well, good night," Elena said.

Julia smiled as a long-ago memory flashed through her head. "Good night," she said. "Sweet dreams."

"You, too."

"Don't let the bedbugs bite."

"Julia."

"Elena," she echoed. "You know I hate to go to sleep first."

Elena's soft laugh floated through the shadowy darkness. "I remember that now. You never wanted me to go to sleep before you. Every time I said good night, you said something else, so you'd always have the last word."

"And so I'd keep you awake." Julia stared at the ceiling, watching the moonbeams play across the room. They had once been best friends, as close as two sisters could be. Twenty-five years had separated them, but the connection between them was already back. "I missed you," Julia whispered into the darkness.

"I missed you, too," Elena said softly.

Julia closed her eyes, content now to let Elena have the last word.

Chapter Twenty-One

Julia crept out of bed just after eight o'clock. Elena was still sleeping, and the apartment was quiet. She walked into the living room and saw Alex sprawled across the narrow couch. He'd kicked off his blanket and wore only a pair of navy blue boxers. Her breath caught at the sight of him. He really was an attractive man, and she felt a stirring of desire at his tousled hair and whisker-laden cheeks, the sweep of his dark lashes against his olive-skinned face. She wanted to touch him, wanted to run her hands down his strong arms and across his sculpted abs. She wanted to wrap herself around him until they were touching in every possible way.

Kneeling next to the couch, she leaned over and traced his lips with her tongue. He responded immediately, his hand catching the back of her head and pulling her in for a deeper, longer, more passionate kiss.

"You were awake," she accused breathlessly when she opened her eyes and saw him watching her. "Why didn't you say something?"

"I wanted to see what you would do," he said with a grin.

He had no idea what she'd wanted to do... or maybe he did.

"Did you sleep well?" she asked.

"Not bad. I had a good dream. Want to know what it was about? You were the star."

"What was I wearing?"

His grin widened. "Nothing."

She couldn't help smiling back. "You are bad."

"In my dream you were bad." He pulled her to him, his hands brushing the sides of her breasts.

She would have liked to strip off her T-shirt and join him on the couch, but she could hear her sister moving around in the bedroom. "Elena will be out here any second," she said, gently pushing him away.

"Killjoy." He sat up on the couch, running a hand through his hair. "How are you two getting along?"

"Good." She sat next to him. "I keep thinking it should be more uncomfortable, that twenty-five years should have made us strangers, but there's still a connection between us. We know each other on a very basic level." She felt a little self-conscious at her words. "Maybe there is some sort of twin thing going on."

A cell phone rang from the vicinity of Alex's pants. Julia tossed him his jeans, and he pulled out the phone. "Hello." He glanced over at Julia and mouthed, Brady. "A bank account number, huh? Where's the bank?" He listened for a few more minutes, then said, "Yes, we found Julia's twin sister, the one you neglected to mention. I know, isn't that amazing? Those two should never have been separated or lost in the system. If you guys hadn't screwed up, they wouldn't have spent the past twenty-five years apart." Alex paused for another moment. "Yes, we do have a key, and I have a feeling it will fit. All right. We'll meet you in an hour, as soon as the bank opens." He grabbed a pen off the coffee table and jotted down an address on the back of a magazine. "Got it. What about protection? Julia and I have been followed more than once." He listened, then said, "Fine, see you then."

"What did he say?" Julia asked as soon as Alex had ended the call.

"The numbers scratched in the dolls are for a bank account here in DC. Brady wants all three of us to meet him at the bank when it opens. He also said there's a safe-deposit box, and I have a feeling the key we found in the doll fits right into that box."

Julia felt a rush of excitement. "Good news for a change. But when did Mr. Brady come to DC?"

"Probably as soon as my father called him and told him where we were. Brady said there's a good deal of money in the account. And who knows what's in that safe-deposit box?"

"I can't believe it's right here in DC. We're finally at the end of the trail," Julia said.

"And at your parents' intended destination. This is where they were coming. It would make sense that whatever they'd stashed away was here. And I believe your mother also performed here."

"At the Kennedy Center, probably." Julia smiled. "And Elena danced there twenty-something years later. That's nice, isn't it?"

"It is nice. Your mother wanted you both to have the life she couldn't have."

"Hopefully, somewhere in the universe she's smiling down on us because we're finally back together."

"Apparently the bank account is in both your names, with your Russian surname. Brady says he can get past the red tape. He has paperwork to prove that you and Elena are the heirs to Natalia and Sergei Markov. That will allow the bank to release the money as well as the contents of the safe-deposit box to you."

"I wonder what's in the box," she mused. "It must be valuable enough to still be of interest to the Russian government. Why else would they have people following us?"

"Only one way to find out."

She stood up. "I'll tell Elena to get dressed."

* * *

Julia felt nervous and edgy as they drove into the three-story parking garage next to the downtown bank where Brady had told them to meet. She couldn't believe they were finally nearing the end of their search. Soon she would know exactly why someone was after her. She glanced over her shoulder as they entered the garage, wondering if anyone had followed them here to the nation's capital. But there was no one behind them.

Alex parked the car, and they took a moment to glance around. The parking garage was shadowy and half-full, probably because it was Saturday. A car pulled in next to them. Julia stiffened, then relaxed when she saw Brady get out of the car.

"You must be Elena," he said as they gathered together.

"Yes," she said tentatively. "And you're?"

"Daniel Brady." He turned to Julia. "Did you bring the key?"

"I have it," Julia said.

"Good. The bank account was set up in your names," Brady added as they walked toward the bank. "Yulia and Elena Markov.

I've already spoken to the bank manager and circumvented some red tape to get into the account."

"How did you do that?" Alex asked sharply.

"Let's just say I have friends in high places. At any rate, there is five hundred and twenty-seven thousand dollars in cash in the account."

Julia's jaw dropped. "How did my parents get that much money?"

Brady shrugged. "I'm sure they had their ways. The bank account has been paying off the rent on the safe-deposit box, which is why it wasn't closed in the past twenty-five years."

"What's in the box?" Elena asked.

"I'm hoping there might be something in there to tell us who killed your parents," Brady replied.

His answer surprised Julia. She hadn't considered that possibility. "Do you think my parents knew who set that bomb in their house?"

Brady's eyes narrowed. "I see Charles gave you the whole story."

"He thought I deserved to know." Julia lifted her chin, looking Brady straight in the eye. "And he was right. So I'll ask you again: Do you think my parents knew who killed them?"

"Your father certainly knew he had enemies in his own party. They were watching him. Love can make a man stupid. They suspected he was softening because of his love for your mother. He had to leave Russia, and we wanted to get him out. But they got there first. With any luck, your father may have left us a clue as to who set that bomb." Brady opened the door to the bank. "After you."

Julia stepped into the cool quiet of the bank. There were only a few people working, two tellers, a loan officer, and the manager, who came out of her office when she saw them.

After preliminary introductions, she said, "I've arranged for a cashier's check as you directed, Mr. Brady. It will be ready momentarily."

"Good. Now we'd like to take a look at the safe-deposit box," Brady said.

The manager took them over to the vault area where the boxes were located. She asked both Elena and Julia to sign in, then escorted them all into the room where Julia inserted the key into the lock. Her anxiety made her fumble, but eventually the lock turned.

The manager pulled out the box and set it on the table. "I'll leave you to it."

Julia looked to Elena for guidance. "Do you want to—"

"Go ahead," Elena said. "You know more about this than I do."

Julia drew in a deep breath and looked into the open box. There was a white business-size envelope with their names, Yulia and Elena, scrawled across the top. She didn't stop to open it, setting it aside for the moment. A large manila envelope came next. It was filled with scraps of paper that were yellowed with age and scribbled upon with blue and black ink. It took Julia a moment to realize that the notations were musical scores. She wondered if they had been composed by her great-grandfather. She wanted to linger, but everyone was waiting.

"Keep going," Alex urged. "You can figure out the music later."

The final object in the box was a Russian icon, a framed picture of St. George about five by seven inches in size. Julia remembered it hanging over the doorway in her parents' bedroom. In fact, they'd had icons all over the house. For good luck, her mother had told her. Some luck the icons had brought them.

"That's it," she said. "A letter, musical scores, and a picture." She felt disappointed. "I don't know what I was expecting, but..." She glanced down at the musical scores again. "Wait. If these scores were written by my great-grandfather before the revolution, they could be worth a fortune."

"Really?" Elena asked. "Who was our great-grandfather?"

"A famous composer, Ivan Slovinsky. He ran to Paris during the revolution. He lived in exile there for the rest of his life," Julia explained. "Our parents must have believed the scores would be worth enough to set them up in a new life." She looked down at the letter. "I guess we should read this."

"Save it for later," Brady suggested. "Let's get your check and get out of here."

Julia picked up the envelopes and the picture, and they left the room. The bank manager asked Brady to sign a form, then handed them a check closing the account.

"Why are we withdrawing the money?" Alex asked, as they made their way toward the front door. "This is a bank. Seems like a good place to keep it."

"I assume the girls will want to split it up," Brady replied. "If they tried to get the money on their own, they'd need a lot of forms and new identification. I thought I'd make it easier for them. It's the least I can do." He paused, turning his gaze on Julia. "I do want to take a look at that letter just in case there's anything in there to lead us to the people who killed your parents. May I suggest that we go to one of our safe houses, so that we can all feel comfortable and secure? It's not far from here."

Julia glanced at Alex, who shrugged in agreement. She turned to Elena. "Is that okay with you?"

"Whatever you think is best," Elena replied. "I'll leave it up to you."

"We'll follow you," Alex said, as they entered the parking lot.

"I think the girls should come with me," Brady said. "So I can protect them."

"I can do that, too." The air between Brady and Alex suddenly sizzled as the two men seemed immensely irritated with each other. "I'll take Elena and Julia. We'll follow you to the safe house," Alex repeated, "and we'll keep the letter and everything else with us."

Brady looked as if he wanted to argue, then forced a tight smile. "All right. We'll play it your way... for now."

Julia didn't like the tone of Brady's voice. Was there something else he hadn't told them? She'd thought it was over. They'd found the safe-deposit box. She had the contents in her bag. Everything that had belonged to her parents was now in her possession. She should be feeling happy, not tense or worried, but she couldn't stop the uneasiness sweeping through her. The tiny hairs at the back of her neck prickled as they walked farther into the dark shadows of the garage, which seemed more menacing now than before.

She wished someone else would come into the garage or a car would drive by. It was too quiet—eerily quiet. The only sounds came from their feet hitting the pavement—four pairs of feet. Or was that five?

Julia took a quick glance behind her. She sensed someone was watching them.

She must have paused, because Brady put his hand under her elbow. "Keep walking," he said in a low voice.

She wanted to pull her arm away from him, but he had a tight grip on her. "Hey," she protested.

"I want to get out of here fast," he muttered. His tension seemed as palpable as her own, and that made her more fearful.

"Alex." She didn't know what she wanted to ask him, but she needed him closer to her. But Alex was on the other side of Brady, a good five feet away.

Suddenly, a man came out from between two cars. It was the same man Julia had seen at the radio station and probably the same man who had tried to grab her purse on Union Street. Up close, he was even bigger than she remembered, with a square, angry face and wild eyes. He began to move forward. She tried to back up, but Brady still had a hold on her arm.

"Get in my car," Brady said to Julia, flipping the locks open on his vehicle, which was closer than Elena's car.

"Don't move," the man said in a thick Russian accent. He reached into his coat pocket.

"He's got a gun!" Brady yelled.

Julia gasped in horror as Alex tackled the man around the knees and toppled him to the ground. "Do something!" she cried.

"Get in the car," Brady repeated, shoving her onto the front seat. He grabbed Elena next and pushed her into the back, then jumped behind the wheel, and gunned the engine. He peeled out of the parking lot, leaving Alex and the Russian fighting for the weapon.

"Stop!" Julia yelled. "We can't leave Alex on his own."

"He's already got the gun," Brady said, looking in the rearview mirror. "Don't worry, Julia. Alex can handle it. I've got to get you out of here." He pulled out his cell phone, punched in a number, and barked into the phone that he needed backup at the Hastings Street Garage.

Julia's stomach churned. She looked back at Elena, whose face was white with fear. God, she hoped Alex was okay. She knew he was tough and fearless, but how could he fight a gun? They shouldn't have run. They should have stayed to help. "We have to go back," she said again. "We need to make sure Alex is all right. Please, turn the car around."

"Alex would want me to get you to safety," Brady said. "He knows help is on the way. He'll be fine. Trust me."

"If help is on the way, then we'll be safe there, too," she argued.

"I don't know how many more men are in the garage."

Julia thought about the two men who'd followed them to St. Helena. Maybe there were more people involved. But who were they? And if there were more of them in the garage, then Alex was definitely in trouble.

"I demand that you turn this car around."

He ignored her.

"Please," Elena muttered from the backseat. "Please, do what she asks."

Brady tossed Julia a look that told her he was going to do exactly what he wanted. "I know what I'm doing. I've been in these situations many times before."

She supposed that was true, but it still didn't make her feel better. Her instincts were screaming in protest, her gut telling her something was terribly wrong.

"We need to look at that letter," Brady continued. "You may have incriminating evidence in your bag. We can't allow it to fall into the wrong hands. It might threaten not only your own security, but that of others in our government as well."

His serious words reminded Julia that this mystery had begun a world away. She wondered if the letter from her parents would finally answer all of her questions.

"We're almost there," Brady said as she began to open her purse. "Hang on." He spun around a corner on two wheels, the tires squealing in protest.

Julia's heart leapt into her throat as Brady dodged in and out of traffic. She hoped Brady wouldn't kill them on the way to saving their lives. Five minutes later they were heading out of the city, across the Potomac and into a residential neighborhood. In fact, the area was almost rural, with lots of space and land, with a house every quarter mile. Julia had no idea where they were. Finally, Brady pulled into the driveway of a modest one-story home that was set apart from its neighbors by tall trees on each side of the property. "Inside," he said, looking around as he escorted them into the house. Julia barely had time to see the living room before Brady pushed them into a back bedroom. "Safest place in the house," he said.

When they were all in the bedroom, Julia finally let herself breathe. They were safe, at least for the moment. That security hadn't registered with Elena, whose blue eyes were dark and worried. Her skin was pale, and beads of sweat lined her forehead. Elena was probably even more confused than Julia. Her sister hadn't spent the past week running from some sinister force the way Julia had.

She turned to Brady, suddenly aware that he had taken the contents of the safe-deposit box out of her bag. The letter he'd expressed interest in had been tossed onto the bed. Brady was now fiddling with the frame on the Icon.

"What are you doing?" she asked.

He didn't answer her. Instead, he produced a small screwdriver and took the frame apart. His eyes lit up as he pulled out a dark red stone that caught the sunlight. A ruby?

Julia had the sudden feeling the surprises weren't over yet. "Oh, my God! Is that real?"

"Oh, yeah," he muttered.

The ruby was followed by another huge stone, then another, until there were six in all: an opal, a diamond, two sapphires, two rubies—a fortune in jewels.

"I knew it," he said in satisfaction. "I knew they were in there."

"What do you mean, you knew they were there? Where did they come from?" Julia demanded.

For a moment it didn't appear that he would answer her; then he shrugged. "I guess it doesn't matter if you know. The jewels belonged to your great-grandmother. She was a favorite with the Imperial Court. She received one perfect stone after each performance and had them sewn into her costumes. Then the revolution swept across Russia. The costumes disappeared. Tamara claimed they'd been stolen, but it was rumored that she'd hidden them away." His smile grew smug as he faced Julia. "Your mother told me about them one night. She said they could be used to buy her family's freedom. How could I resist an offer like that?" He glanced down at the stones. "I've waited twenty-five years to hold these babies," he muttered, closing his fist around the stones. "They're finally mine."

"Yours? They're ours," Julia corrected.

"I don't think so."

Julia looked into his cold, dark eyes and saw the truth. Brady had been in Russia at the time of the defection. He knew about her parents. He knew about the jewels. He'd probably worked both sides. He hadn't wanted to help her parents defect; he'd wanted to get the treasure. She swallowed hard, realizing where her thoughts were taking her. She was probably staring at the man who'd set a trap for her parents. "It was you, wasn't it?" she asked, the words escaping from her lips before she could consider the wisdom of saying them. "You're the one who killed my parents."

"They double-crossed me," he said flatly. "They set me up to think I already had the jewels in my possession. It was their ticket to freedom, but they gave me fakes. They deserved what they got."

"They didn't deserve to die," she protested, pain and anger filling her soul at his callous disregard for their lives.

He shrugged. "It had to be done. I couldn't let them leave the country with the jewels."

His coldness, his complete lack of conscience, was now starkly evident. How could Julia have missed it before? How could she and Alex have been taken in by his offers to help? That answer was obvious now, too. They'd trusted Brady because Charles and Stan trusted him. Did the other two know of his duplicity, or had they been conned as well?

"Did anyone ever suspect you?" she asked.

"Of course not," he said in a cocky tone. "I was too clever. The Russians thought the Americans had done it. The Americans believed the Russians had done it. No one ever knew it was me. And no one ever will." He pulled a gun out of his jacket and pointed it at her.

Elena gasped. "No!"

Julia began to shake. She'd never been this close to a real gun before. It was terrifying, but if she was going to die, she had to know the rest. "Why?" she asked. "Why did you kill them? Why didn't you just steal the jewels and disappear?"

"I couldn't take the chance that I would be discovered," he said smoothly. "I told them it was the perfect plan. They give me the jewels. I get them out of the country. Only the real plan was they give me the jewels; then they die." His expression turned ugly, his mouth curving with anger and disgust. "But they tricked me. They gave me fakes. I didn't find out until after they were dead. I thought you were all dead. I thought the game was over. Then a little photograph appeared in a magazine, and I knew there was still a chance the jewels had gotten out with you and your sister. It just took until now to find them, but they're mine now. And it's over. It's all over."

"Why didn't you come after us before?" Julia asked. "Why wait until now?"

"You were hidden away by the time I got to the States. I found Elena." He tipped his head toward her sister, who was shivering so hard Julia could hear her teeth rattling. "I went through her stuff. I saw the dolls, the necklace, but she had nothing else. I thought that you must have it all—that Sarah had taken the treasure, that she was the one who'd outsmarted me. But she'd covered her tracks so well, I couldn't find her."

So her mother had saved her life.

"Sarah didn't know what she had, did she?" he asked.

"I have no idea what she knew," Julia retorted. "But she had me. That's all she wanted."

"She always did think small."

"Don't say that," Julia told him angrily. "You don't know anything about her."

"And I don't care," Brady replied. "This conversation is done. I'm going to finish what I started. Give me your purses. You won't be calling anyone for help. Put them on the ground and push 'em over here."

Julia didn't want to obey, but he had a gun, and she couldn't think what else to do. She put her handbag on the ground and kicked it toward him, wondering how on earth they could get out of this situation alive. She tried to reassure Elena with her eyes, but Elena wasn't stupid. She knew they were in big trouble. Now Julia was glad that Alex wasn't with them. Maybe he'd survive if she didn't. The thought was terrifying. She didn't want to die, not now, not when she finally knew who she was and what she wanted.

Brady tossed their purses through the open door, his eyes

focused on the two women as he backed away. "Think of it like this—at least you'll go together, and it will be quick. Over in a flash," he said with a cruel smile.

Julia's heart began to beat double time. Her parents had been killed by a bomb going off in their house. Was that what Brady had planned for them? Was he going to blow up this house with them in it?

* * *

"You must listen," the man pleaded.

Alex didn't want to listen, but since he had the Russian pinned up against the garage wall, one arm against the man's windpipe and no backup in sight, he could either knock him out or give him a chance to say his piece. "Talk then."

"Brady. He's the one who killed Natalia and Sergei."

There was a spark of truth in his blue eyes, eyes that looked remarkably similar to Julia's, Alex thought. Not that he trusted this guy, but it suddenly occurred to him that Brady was gone, as were Julia and Elena. "How do you know?"

"I'm Roland Markov. Sergei's half brother," he said breathlessly. "I have a driver's license. In my pocket," he added. "I was going to show it to you."

Alex sent him a skeptical look, but he had to admit that despite the fact that Brady had yelled, "Gun," there was no actual evidence of a weapon. "Where is it?"

"In my inside jacket pocket."

"Don't move," Alex ordered, holding the man with one hand as he reached into the pocket. He pulled out a brown billfold and flipped it open. The driver's license photo was accurate. So was the name. The address was in Los Angeles. "You're a long way from home," he said. "And you were in San Francisco. Julia saw you several times. You broke into her apartment and mine."

Roland shook his head. "No, that wasn't me. I saw Julia at the radio station, yes. I spoke to her in Russian. I wanted to see if she understood. She got scared and ran. But I didn't break into her apartment. That was Brady. I saw him and another man enter her building one day. I wasn't sure if it was him. It had been many years since I'd seen him."

Alex didn't know what to believe. "I chased you through the

park. You tried to grab Julia's bag."

"No, that wasn't me. I don't run fast. If you chased me, you would have caught me."

Alex had to admit the man was big and a little slow, which was why he'd been able to pin him against the wall.

"I saw the photograph of Elena in the LA newspaper," Roland continued. "I read the story, and my wife said I must go to San Francisco and see if it is really her."

The fact that Roland correctly identified the girl in the photo as Elena made Alex believe he was telling the truth. He slowly released him, but stayed close.

"So why didn't you just introduce yourself?"

Roland's tongue darted out, sweeping his bottom lip in nervousness. "I realized the girl in San Francisco is Yulia. When I saw others watching her, I became afraid. I didn't know who killed Sergei for sure. Could be secret police, could be friend, could be anyone. I think they come back now to kill Yulia. Or to get what they hadn't gotten before. I decide it is best to wait and watch."

Alex stared at Roland. "Get what?"

"Natalia had several precious stones from a century ago. She and Sergei told me they would use them to start a new life. And they would send for me when they could. When they died, I didn't know what happened to the jewels, until I saw the picture of Elena. If she was alive, perhaps she had the jewels, too."

The treasure, Alex thought. He finally knew what it was. "Wait. Why do you think Brady killed Sergei and Natalia? How could he get the treasure if they were dead?"

"Sergei was worried about betrayal," Roland said heavily. "He told me he had made elaborate plans for the defection to work. Brady must have thought he had the jewels or that he could get them once Natalia and Sergei were dead." He paused, his eyes sad. "They were so careful, but they still trusted the wrong man."

"And Brady let everyone think that the Russians had done in their own people," Alex said slowly, as the pieces of the puzzle came together. "Very clever. So where are the jewels?"

"I believe they were hidden in the frame of a picture."

Alex's heart sped up. The Russian icon. "Dammit. We have to find Brady."

"I've been following him since yesterday," Roland said. "He

went to a house this morning. It's not far from here."

"Let's go." Alex ran for Elena's car. Fortunately, he still had the keys in his pocket.

"We should hurry," Roland said. "Once Brady has the stones, he'll have no reason to keep Elena or Yulia alive."

Alex's heart jumped into overdrive. He gunned the motor and tore out of the parking lot, following Roland's directions to the highway and praying he wouldn't be too late. "Maybe Brady doesn't know the jewels are in the icon," he said hopefully.

Roland didn't answer him. Alex shot him a questioning look.

Roland met his gaze, then shrugged. "He knows."

There was something in that fatalistic shrug that disturbed Alex. "Tell me something, Roland. Did you come here to save the girls or to get the jewels?"

"Perhaps the girls give me small token of gratitude."

Alex was disappointed, but also relieved to get an honest answer for a change. "I won't let you hurt Julia or Elena," he warned.

"I don't want to hurt them. They are family."

"Rich family now," Alex commented. He didn't know if he trusted Roland or not, but he'd deal with him later. First he had to find Julia before Brady found those stones.

* * *

Julia saw Brady backing toward the door and knew they had only one chance to escape, and it was now. No time to plan, think, or analyze. She drew in a big gulp of air, praying she was making the right decision; then she let her instincts and her anger take over. This man had killed her parents without remorse. She would not let him kill her and Elena, too.

She threw her body at the arm that held the gun, hoping to knock it out of his hand. Instead she heard a gunshot, and they both tumbled to the ground. She waited for a searing pain somewhere in her body, but she could feel nothing but an intense desire to stop him from shooting again.

Adrenaline gave her strength and determination as she wrestled for the gun. Brady was bigger than she was, stronger. He knocked her across the face with the back of his hand. Stars exploded behind her eyes. She'd never taken a punch before, and the pain was shocking. But she couldn't let it stop her. He was scrambling to get to his feet. She jumped on him again, knocking him down on the dusty hardwood floor.

He reared back in fury, throwing her against the bed. Her head bounced off the corner of the bedpost, and another shot of pain screamed through her body. She struggled to get her breath, to move. She had to move!

But Brady was getting away.

He stumbled toward the door.

Julia watched in horror, unable to do anything but wait for her breath to come back and her muscles to follow her command.

Suddenly Elena moved. She picked up the only other piece of furniture in the room—a simple wooden desk chair. Brady was so intent on reaching the door, he didn't see her coming. Elena whacked him over the head. The sound of the wood cracking against his skull was something Julia would never forget, but her relief when he landed on the ground with a dull thud was even better.

For a split second she and Elena simply stared at him, unable to believe he wasn't moving, wasn't getting up, wasn't waving the gun in their faces.

The gun... Julia finally got her feet back under her. She grabbed the gun near his hand and tossed it across the room.

"We've got to get out of here," Elena cried, grabbing the envelopes off the bed. "Hurry. The house is going to explode."

"Not without the stones," Julia replied. She forced herself to open Brady's clenched fist, terrified that at any moment he would wake up and grab her arm.

"We don't have time. Please," Elena begged. "The bomb could go off at any second."

"Go without me. I'll be right there."

"No, I can't leave you behind."

"And we can't leave the jewels behind. They belonged to our great-grandmother." Julia peeled Brady's fingers apart. Even unconscious he seemed determined to hang on to those stones. Finally, she got his hand open enough to take the jewels. She grabbed their purses on the way out of the bedroom, and they dashed toward the front door, hoping against hope they'd get out in time.

As they hit the porch, the cool air struck Julia like a welcoming hug. They were out. They were free.

A car came screaming down the street. Alex.

Her heart sang again as he jumped out and came running toward them. He was alive. He was all right. Thank God!

"Brady?" Alex asked, meeting her halfway up the walk. "Where is he?"

"Inside." She grabbed his arm as he headed toward the house. "There's a bomb," she yelled. "There's no time." She pulled him back toward the car, shocked to see the Russian get out of the vehicle. "What is he doing here?"

"Long story," Alex shouted. "But he's family."

His words were cut off by an enormous explosion. A roaring, thundering sound was followed by blazing heat and a tornado of flames that threw them to the sidewalk. Alex's body came over Julia's as debris and fiery ash rained down on their heads. After the initial blast, Alex got up, and they scrambled toward the other side of the car, collapsing onto the ground. Julia saw Elena and the Russian hiding there, too, their bodies paralyzed with fear and shock as they gazed back at the inferno that had once been a simple house.

"You're all right?" Alex asked, his worried gaze searching Julia's face while his hands ran up and down her arms. "He didn't hurt you?"

She shook her head, swallowed, tried to speak. Finally, she tipped her head toward the Russian. "Who?"

"Uncle," Alex said. He gave Elena a reassuring nod. "He's your uncle Roland. I don't know what his story is yet, so don't get too close."

Elena was staring at the man as if she'd seen him before. "I remember you. You always gave us chocolate."

Roland smiled. "Yes, that was me. Your mother used to scold me. She said I was spoiling you."

"Why didn't you tell me who you were when you came to the radio station?" Julia asked. "Why did you speak to me in Russian?"

"I wasn't sure it was you. I wanted to know if you could understand me. But you had forgotten everything. Then your friends came. I knew the time wasn't right. But you're safe now. You're both safe."

While Elena and Roland tentatively embraced, Julia moved into Alex's arms. "Thanks for coming to save me," she said.

"I thought I was going to be too late," he said tightly. "But you saved yourself."

"With Elena's help. She knocked Brady out with a chair while I was trying to get the gun."

"You went after Brady?" he asked in amazement.

"It was our only chance. It was probably stupid."

"Probably," Alex agreed. "And amazingly brave."

"You were brave, too. You went after Roland before you knew he was a friend. When Brady left the two of you fighting, I was so afraid you were going to be hurt or killed. I begged him to turn back, but he wouldn't. He said he called for backup, but that must have been a lie, part of his plan. He needed us to get the jewels and the money. That's all he wanted." She paused, seeing the truth in his eyes, but still she had to say it. "Brady told us that he killed our parents. He thought he already had the stones. They set him up. I guess in the end they didn't trust him as much as we did."

"Maybe they knew him better. Don't beat yourself up, Julia. Hindsight is always crystal clear."

"I know." She touched the swelling around his right eye. "I think you're going to have another black eye."

"It was worth it." He paused, his lips tightening. "God, Julia. I thought I might lose you today."

She blinked back a tear at the raw emotion in his voice. She didn't know if she could call it love, but it was something. She pressed her mouth to his, kissing him with everything she had. It ended all too soon as the sound of sirens intruded and grew louder and louder.

"I think we have company," Alex said. Fire engines and police converged on the block.

"We're going to have a lot to explain." She opened her hand and showed him the stones. "These were hidden in the icon."

"That's what Roland thought. Put them away for now," Alex advised. He reached for his cell phone. "This time I'm going to call for backup."

"Who?"

"My father. I think it's time he came all the way out of hiding."

"Brady fooled him, too. He played everyone. He was very

clever." She looked at the burning house and said with a degree of vengeful satisfaction, "And now he's dead."

Chapter Twenty-Two

It was after midnight before Julia, Elena, Alex, and Roland returned to Elena's apartment to regroup. They'd spent the entire day and evening being questioned by local police and numerous government agencies. The entire story had finally become clear. What had once been thought to be a politically motivated murder had in fact been precipitated by simple, old-fashioned greed, a greed that had nothing to do with nationality.

Once Brady had learned of the existence of the jewels, he had become obsessed with having them for himself. In talking to various government agents, Julia and Alex had learned more about Brady's background. He'd grown up poor and found his ticket out of a Detroit slum at an army recruitment office. While in the army he'd become an expert with explosives. He'd later worked his way up to Intelligence and eventually a career as a spy.

For Brady it had never been about ideals or political freedom or national security; it had been about adventure, excitement, and fortune. On more than one occasion various valuable objects had disappeared under Brady's watch, but no one had ever suspected the career spy of working more than one side, until they raided his apartment in New York City and found a stash of priceless art, jewelry, and cash. Brady had apparently lived well away from the spotlight, and he'd covered his tracks until now. His obsession with the jewels that had once eluded him had made him reckless and careless. Today Brady had been caught in a trap of his own making. Julia supposed there was some justice in that.

"I must say you brought a great deal of excitement with you,"

Elena said to Julia as she slipped off her shoes and stretched out her legs. "I've never had a day like this one."

"I hope you're not sorry I found you." Julia sat down across from her. Alex was outside talking to Roland, and for the first time since they'd been trapped in the house with Brady, she and Elena were alone.

"Of course not," Elena said with a definitive shake of her head.

Julia was relieved to see the color back in her sister's face and the sparkle in her eyes. "You know, I wouldn't have made it out of there alive if it hadn't been for you."

"Likewise. If you hadn't jumped on Brady, he would have locked us in that room. Are you always that impulsive?"

"I'm afraid so," Julia replied with a sheepish grin. "One of my many bad habits. But you were pretty impulsive yourself, grabbing that chair and knocking him out. I was impressed."

"Desperation breeds courage and creative ideas." Elena gave Julia a thoughtful look. "What's next, Julia?"

"I haven't had time to think about the future. I've been a little busy."

"You have a life to get back to, family who love you, friends who are probably worried about you, a job..." Her voice trailed away as she picked at an errant thread on the sofa cushion. "And I have my life to continue here. I guess there's always the phone and e-mail."

"Oh, Elena, please come to San Francisco with me," Julia said. "I want you to meet my family. They'll be your family, too."

"You really are impulsive," Elena said with a small smile. "You should think about that some more, Julia. Your family is not my family. They would surely consider me an outsider, probably even a threat to their relationship with you, especially your sister, Liz. I've been the outsider before, the one people had to tolerate. I'm done with that."

The sadness in her voice broke Julia's heart. She frowned, wishing once again that Elena hadn't had to suffer so much. "You're wrong, Elena. My father, Gino, is wonderful and kind and generous. All the DeMarcos are like that. They adopted me, and they always made me feel welcome. I know that once they understand the story, they'll do the same for you." She paused.

"And I really need another blonde in the family. Everyone else has dark hair, and I've always stood out. Please just don't say no," she added hastily when Elena began to interrupt. "Think about it. If you want, I'll go home first and fill everyone in; then you can come and visit, at least."

"I have the shop to run. And—"

"And you can still take a few days off. I'm sure of that."

"You don't know how busy I am, and I only have a handful of part-time employees."

"You can do it if you want to," Julia said firmly. "And you should want to, because we're sisters. And this is important to me."

Elena rolled her eyes. "You're trying to make me feel guilty."

"Is it working?" Julia asked with a grin. "I really want you to meet Liz. She might be restrained at first, but she will love having another sister."

"Impulsive and optimistic," Elena said. "I will think about it, but not tonight. My mind is too tired." She paused, her gaze moving to Julia's handbag. "You know, we never read that letter."

"You're right. I'll get it." Julia jumped to her feet. They'd retained the letter, but the music scores and the jewels, as well as the check, had been placed in another safe-deposit box at a different bank, just in case Brady had any other associates looking for a shot at the treasure. "I know one of the government agents read it," Julia said as she took the letter out of her purse. "He told me it was personal, with no evidence against Brady." She stared down at it, hesitating. "I'm a little scared. I think we know everything now, but maybe there's more."

"Let's hope the worst is over," Elena said. "If it isn't, at least we're together."

Julia smiled at her sister, then pulled the single piece of paper out of the envelope. Her heart skipped a beat when she realized the letter was written in Russian. "I can't read it," she said with extreme disappointment. "We'll have to get it translated."

"I can read it," Elena replied.

Julia raised an eyebrow. "You remember Russian?"

"No. I took some classes a while ago. It made me feel closer to the family I'd lost." She took the paper from Julia's hand. After a moment, she began to read:

"My dearest girls, if you are reading this letter, then your

*father and I are probably gone. Perhaps we are wrong to risk
everything for freedom, but it is love that drives us—our love for
you, and our love for each other. We are counting on our friends to
deliver us safely to America. If that doesn't happen, we pray that
you both will grow up in a world that allows you to express
yourselves and be who you will be, without restriction. Please
don't be sad. Don't grieve for us. Be happy. Find love and joy in
your lives. That is everything we wish for you. You will forever be
in our hearts. Love, Mama and Papa."*

Julia blinked back tears and saw that Elena's cheeks were wet
as well. "Our parents were willing to risk their lives for freedom
and love, and Brady betrayed them for a fortune," she said.

"I wonder if there was any one moment when they knew the
truth," Elena murmured.

"It probably happened too fast. At least Brady died the same
way. There's some justice in that. That sounds cold, doesn't it? But
I'm not sorry he's dead."

"I'm not, either."

Julia leaned back in her chair, thinking about the note and her
parents. Her mother's face was beginning to come into her mind
more and more. She could even hear her voice. The memories
were finally returning. "Mama was beautiful," she said, looking
over at Elena. "And so brave. I've never had that much courage."

"You did today."

"Because I had to be brave. I was backed into a corner."

"So were our parents."

"I think Mama would have been happy to know that you
became a dancer and followed in her footsteps."

"For a while, anyway."

"Both of your careers were cut too short."

Elena nodded. "Life is never fair or easy."

They both turned as the front door opened and Alex came in.
His right eye was purple and swollen, his clothes wrinkled and
smelling of smoke. "I'm going to take off," he said, surprising Julia
with his words.

She got to her feet. "What do you mean? Where are you
going?"

"To find a hotel room and get some sleep. Roland will give me
a ride. He has a rental car."

"You can stay here," Julia said quickly, not wanting him to leave. She hadn't had two minutes alone with him all day...

He offered her a weary smile. "I'll pass on another night on the couch. I'll come by in the morning and we'll go to the airport together—unless you're going to stay here for a few days?"

"No, I need to get home and tell everyone what I've learned."

"Then we'll leave tomorrow. There's a flight at noon. Will that be all right?"

"Sure." She followed him to the door and out into the hall, put off by his cool tone. "Alex, do you want me to come with you tonight?" She held her breath, waiting for his answer. Because she would go with him in a second. She just couldn't read him right now. She didn't know what he wanted from her. Was he pulling away because he wanted to give her more time with her sister... or was he just pulling away?

"No, you should stay with Elena," he said briskly. "We'll catch up tomorrow."

"Are you all right?"

"I'm fine."

She frowned, wondering if he'd ever give her a different answer than that. She had no choice but to accept it. "Okay." She leaned forward and tried to kiss him on the mouth, but he moved, and she caught the side of his cheek. Then he was gone.

Was he just tired and looking for a good night's sleep? Was that the reason for his distance? Or was this the beginning of the end?

* * *

Alex pretended to sleep on the flight back to San Francisco. He knew Julia wanted to talk, but he didn't. There was too much to say, and yet there was nothing to say. It was over. She finally had her answers, and he had his. There was no more left to do. He could return to work, and he was looking forward to that.

He hadn't picked up his camera since Julia had come knocking on his door a week ago. So much had happened in the past nine days. His entire life story had changed, and so had hers. They were both different people now.

The flight attendant came on with the announcement that they were preparing to land in San Francisco. Julia put her seat back up and gave him a speculative, serious look. "Where are you going when we leave the airport?"

"Home, then to my mother's house. After that I'm going to find Stan." He'd been thinking about his father's friend all way the home. It had occurred to him that nowhere in their discussions the day before had Stan's name come up. Why was that? Why hadn't any of the government agents they'd spoken to known of Stan's role in the defection?

"I'd forgotten about Stan," Julia murmured, her gaze catching his. "Your father said he set the defection plans in motion, yet no one mentioned him yesterday."

It scared Alex that he and Julia had begun to think exactly the same. They'd gotten so close. He almost didn't know where he left off and she began.

"Do you think Stan knew about Brady's double cross?" she continued. "I mean, he was the one who contacted Brady about us. He could have been working with him, setting us up to lead them to the jewels." She blew out a sigh. "I thought this was over, but maybe it's not. Maybe I'll always be looking over my shoulder, wondering who's going to come after me next."

"It won't be Stan. I'll make sure of that. If he's guilty of anything, I will see that he pays for what he did. I can promise you that."

"That's a lot of I's.' What happened to 'we'?"

He shrugged. "You have your life, your twin sister, your other sister, your gazillion relatives, your music. I'm sure you'll be busy. I can take care of Stan on my own."

"Where are you going next?"

"Wherever my next assignment is," he said flatly, trying to ignore the hurt look in her eyes.

"We're not going to talk about us, are we?" she asked.

He didn't answer. What could he say? They were sitting in the middle of a crowded airplane, people all around them. It was hardly the moment for that kind of talk. Not that he intended to find that moment. "I don't do good-byes."

"So I wasn't going to get one?"

"Julia, this isn't the time or the place."

"I don't know about that. You're trapped in your seat. You can't escape. It seems to me the best chance I have for getting a straight answer."

He was glad to hear the lighter note in her voice, even if it was forced. He liked emotional scenes even less than good-byes. "I think your life will be very full when Elena comes out to visit you and your family."

"She's coming only for a few days. Then she'll go back to her life in Washington DC."

"And you'll return to your life. You can pursue your music passion with that extra bit of cash you inherited. And I'm sure the jewels and the musical scores are quite valuable."

"I won't sell them. I'll keep them in the family. That's where they belong, although I might see if I can get an orchestra to play my great-grandfather's music. It should be heard." She paused. "What about your dad?"

Alex shrugged. "I'm sure he'll go on doing whatever he was doing." It occurred to Alex that he didn't even know what that was. Maybe someday he'd take the time to find out, but not any day soon. Julia gave him a long stare that told him she wasn't happy with his answer. "Hey, he chose to be separate. Don't try to make me feel guilty."

"He did that to protect you."

"Does that mean you've forgiven Sarah for doing the same thing to you? For lying about everything in your past?"

She nodded slowly. "I'm going to try. Sarah gave me a wonderful life. And my parents were already gone. Who knows what would have happened to me without her? I think Sarah hurt her parents more than she hurt me. Like you, they had to believe someone they loved was dead. Which reminds me. Susan isn't my biological grandmother. I hate to take that away from her, too."

"At least she has Liz."

"That's my next goal—to persuade Liz to see her. I'm going to blend these families together if it's the last thing I do."

He smiled at her determination. "I don't have any doubts that you'll succeed. You're a strong woman, Julia."

"Stronger now, I think. You helped, you know. I couldn't have survived this past week without you."

The wheels of the plane touched down on the ground, and within minutes they were parked at the gate.

"I'll catch a cab home," Julia said as she released her seat belt.

He was surprised by her words, having been sure he would face the inevitable good-bye at her apartment.

"I can give you a ride," he said halfheartedly. "My car is here. It's no problem."

"That's all right. I can see that you want to be on your way."

She looked at him with her beautiful blue eyes, and it took every ounce of strength he possessed not to weaken. "All right," he said. "If that's the way you want it."

"Thanks again, Alex."

"I don't need your thanks."

Her smile grew sad. "I know. You don't need anything from me. You made that really clear. And it's okay. I don't have any regrets." She got up and joined the crowd of people leaving the plane.

Alex sat in his seat until everyone was gone. She might not have regrets, but he certainly did.

* * *

When Alex pulled up in front of his mother's house an hour later, he was stunned to see a man walking up the steps. Damn him!

Alex jumped out of the car and caught up to his father before he rang the bell. "What are you doing here?"

"I came to tell your mother the truth," Charles said, his words heavy and filled with emotion.

His father had cleaned up a bit and was wearing slacks and a brown sport coat over a white shirt, but Alex knew that his appearance would still scare the life out of his mother. "You can't just show up at her door," he told him. "You might give her a heart attack. Let me prepare her."

"It's my lie, not yours. I thought you were still in Washington."

"I just got back," Alex said. His father had been part of several conference calls the day before, so he was completely up to speed on everything that had gone down. "By the way, have you spoken to Stan?"

"No. I haven't been able to reach him."

"How come no one talked about him yesterday?"

His father appeared taken aback at his question. "I don't know.

I never thought about it."

"Maybe you should. Stan's the one who connected me to Brady in the first place."

"If you think they were working together, you're wrong," Charles said. "Stan would never have gone along with stealing my life and yours and your mother's. Nor would he have ever killed in the first place, not for jewels or money. He's not that kind of person."

"You didn't think Brady was that kind of person, either."

His father's face paled and his jaw tightened. "You're right. He conned me. I just wish he wasn't dead. I would have enjoyed killing him myself."

He'd never thought his father capable of murder, but Alex was beginning to realize that he hadn't known Charles Manning at all, not the real man, not the man who'd gotten involved in a Russian defection plot or the man who had gone underground and lived his whole life in the shadow of the family he'd left behind. The question was—did he want to know him?

"There is something else I've been wondering about," Alex said. "Why did Brady force you to go underground and fake your death? He was the one who killed the Markovs. And he knew you didn't know anything about the girls or about the treasure. I don't get it. How were you a threat to him?"

"It was part of the plot. Brady had to continue to make our government believe that the Russians had killed Natalia and Sergei, that I was in danger. He faked the threats to me to lend credence to the idea that the Russians had long arms. He certainly convinced me that was the case. I honestly believed I was in danger." Charles paused, clearing his throat. "But in retrospect, I think the real reason Brady had me die was to try to flush out Sarah and Julia. He thought Sarah cared for me. He thought if anything would draw her out of hiding, it would be my funeral. She'd come to the service; then he would find out if Julia had the stones."

Alex had never considered that possibility. It made sense. "And later? He never told you anything over the years? What about the other day? Why did Brady make you disappear again?"

"He didn't want me to tell you the story. He tried to convince me I needed to keep silent for your protection, but I knew you wouldn't stop looking. And I couldn't stand the thought of you searching for answers that might risk your life, so I wanted to help you. In the end, I almost got you killed. You found the treasure, and Brady followed you to it."

"So the whole government moving you out of your house again, that was all engineered by Brady? He had a hell of a lot of power."

"Yes," Charles agreed. "Too much. No one ever suspected he was a double agent. Now I believe we may find out other terrible crimes he committed over the years."

"So there was never a time in the last twenty-five years when you didn't think you could come out of hiding?" Alex queried again. "You must have wondered if the danger still existed."

"I know you can't understand, but for at least the first five or six years, I did still believe in the danger. Brady would occasionally catch up to me, relay information that I now know was false. He would question me about Sarah, ask me if I'd heard from her. He kept saying he wanted her to come in, to stop hiding, to be able to live her own life. They were more lies, but I believed him. And then there came a time when I just didn't think I had the right to go back and interrupt your life. Your mother had remarried. You seemed to be doing well."

"And how would you know that?"

"I told you, I watched you sometimes, at school or at one of your games."

It gave Alex the chills to think his father had been that close to him, and he'd never known.

The front door suddenly opened. "Alex, is that you?" his mother asked. "Who are you talking to?"

Fortunately, his father had his back to the front door. Charles was staring straight at Alex, and there was suddenly fear in his eyes. Alex didn't know what to do, how to make this easier for everyone involved. As soon as his father turned around, she'd get the shock of her life.

"Mom," he said tentatively, "I want you to take a deep breath and try to stay calm."

Her eyes narrowed. "What's going on?"

"It's Dad," Alex said. He nodded to Charles. "Turn around."

His father turned so slowly, Alex felt like he was watching a movie. His mother's eyes grew wider and wider until she let out a small cry, putting a hand to her heart.

"No," she said, shaking her head, backing toward the front door.

Alex jogged around his father and up the steps to his mother, putting his arm around her trembling shoulders.

"Who is he?" she whispered.

"It's Dad," Alex said. "He's alive. He's been alive all these years."

His father put up a hand in entreaty. "Kate," he murmured. "I'm sorry."

She put up her own hand as he took a step forward. "This isn't possible. I must be dreaming. This is a nightmare and you're both in it."

"It's real, Mom." Alex's hand tightened on her shoulder. "You always thought his death was suspicious. That's because it never happened."

"I don't understand."

"He's—"

"Let me explain," Charles said firmly. "I need to do this, not you, Alex. Can I come in, Kate? Can I tell you what happened and why?"

Kate turned to look at Alex, her eyes seeking confirmation. "Is it really him?"

"Yes."

For a moment, she looked lost, panicked, completely unlike the mother he'd known. But ever so slowly, she regained her composure. Her back stiffened. Her head went up. Her jaw tightened.

"Then I guess you should come in," she said, a steel edge to her voice now. She led them into the house and took a seat on the white couch in the living room.

Alex and his father took chairs opposite her. Silence surrounded them like a thick, thorny, uncomfortable coat. The only thing breaking the quiet was the ticking of the grandfather clock in the entryway, the same clock Charles had bought for Kate on their fifth wedding anniversary. Alex doubted either of them heard the clock. They were too caught up in staring at each other, although neither gave anything away. He waited for the explosion. He knew one was coming. Maybe his father was right. Maybe he didn't need to be here for this. It wasn't his lie.

But it was his family. And this was the last loose end. He needed to tie it off so he could leave and never look back.

"Well, you said you were going to explain," Kate said briskly. "Do it."

Charles leaned forward, his gaze focused and determined. "I believed that the Russians were after me because of a photograph I took in Moscow. I received death threats toward you and Alex. The government, a man named Brady whom I had worked with for many years, told me that I needed to disappear. I was their only link to the—"

"Orphan girl at the gates," she said. "I get it."

"Exactly. So Brady helped me fake my death. He said you and Alex would be safer if I was gone. The trail would end with my death. In the Soviet Union, I had seen firsthand how brutally people could be killed. I had those images in my mind when I made my decision. It was not an easy one to make." He shot Alex a quick look, probably sensing his disgust, Alex thought. "But I knew it was far more difficult for the two of you to live with that decision than it was for me to make it."

His mother stared at his father for what seemed like hours. Finally she said, "So that's it? You disappeared, and we went on, and you never looked back."

"I looked back every day. I've told Alex that. I'm sure neither of you will believe me when I say this, but I loved both of you very much. And each day that went by I thought of you. I prayed you were well, that I had done the right thing."

"Then why come out now?" she demanded. "Why didn't you just stay dead?"

"I found him," Alex interjected. "Julia and I were looking for her father, but we found him instead."

"Julia," she echoed. "I knew she was that girl in the picture."

"Actually, that's her sister," Alex replied. "An identical twin. Both girls were part of a planned defection that didn't occur because the parents were killed."

"It was my job to help get the girls out of the country through the cover of the theater," Charles added. "It was one of many jobs I had in those years that involved undercover work for the U.S. government. I had gained the trust of certain people in the Russian government. It was easier for me to get around because of that trust."

"So it was your selfishness that left Alex without a father," Kate said pointedly. "Now, that's the first thing you've said today that hasn't surprised me." Trust his mother to turn the story her way, Alex thought. Not that he could blame her. He wasn't too thrilled with his father, either.

"You can go now," she told him with a regal wave of her hand. "I think you've said enough."

"I will go." Charles stood up. "But if you need anything—"

"Why would I need anything? I've made my own way the past twenty-five years. I don't need you for anything."

"I guess you don't. Although you seem to be awfully interested in my pictures these days."

His mother tossed her head. "I had every right to make money off your work and to keep your reputation alive. It was for Alex. He was so proud of you and your accomplishments. I never wanted him to lose that. I was doing it for you and your legacy."

Alex had to admit she had a beautiful way of spinning the truth. It had never been about him, but he didn't intend to get in the middle of this fight. It was between the two of them.

"You're welcome to do what you want with the photos," Charles said. "They served their purpose. They did what I wanted them to do at the time. They showed something important to the world. That's all I ever cared about. That's why you were always angry with me. I wasn't ambitious enough. I didn't want the fame or the celebrity. I wanted to stay in the background."

"Because you were spying on the Russians," she said, "not because you wanted obscurity. And you know, I wasn't stupid. I knew something was going on. And that woman—Sarah—were you sleeping with her?"

"Sarah was always just a friend. She was also working for the government," he added. "We both wanted to do something for the people over there."

"So altruistic," she sneered. "Worry about people you don't even know, but to hell with your family. What kind of heroism is that?"

She had a good point, Alex thought. And his father took the hit hard, his face aging before their eyes.

There were deep, grooved lines around his eyes, across his forehead, and at the corners of his mouth. He'd spent twenty-five years living a lie and feeling guilty. They'd all paid a price, Alex realized.

"I can't defend what I did to you and Alex," Charles said. "I can only tell you that my intentions were to keep you safe, and at least in that effort I succeeded. I'll go now. And I am sorry, Kate, for whatever that's worth. Do what you want with my pictures. I gave up photography the day I died."

Alex was surprised to hear that. "What have you been doing?"

"Working as an auto mechanic. My father was one. He taught me how to work on cars. I never thought I'd want to have that job, but in the end it became my life. I've been able to make enough to survive."

"Did you marry again?" Kate asked sharply. "Not that I care."

"I never remarried," he said quietly. "I never tried to re-create my family. I knew that would be impossible." He drew in a long breath and slowly let it out. "I want you both to be happy. That's all. I'm sorry for everything I've done that hurt you. Not just for faking my death, but for choosing to involve myself in something I knew could bring danger to both of you. That's what I truly regret. I was selfish. I couldn't see past what I thought was so important. I was a shortsighted photographer. I should have turned that camera on myself; then I would have seen the truth." He gave a regretful shake of his head. "Good-bye."

Alex wanted to say something, but he didn't know what.

His mother didn't seem to have the same problem. "You owe me, Charles," she said.

"Whatever you want, Kate."

She hesitated. "I want you to stay dead."

Alex's breath stuck in his chest as he waited for his father's answer.

"I can do that," Charles said. And with that, he walked out of the living room, out of the house, and out of their lives... again.

"I hate him," Kate said a moment later, but there was more pain in her voice now than anger. "You hate him, too, don't you, Alex?" Her eyes pleaded with him to agree.

He wished he could give her what she wanted, but the truth was he didn't know how he felt about his father anymore.

* * *

Julia stared at the house Michael had bought to surprise her. She still couldn't believe he'd made the purchase without asking her first. But she wasn't here about the house or about their relationship; she was here to find Liz. She needed to tell her sister the entire story. Maybe Michael needed to hear it, too. She owed him that much.

She walked up the front steps and saw that the door was ajar. She knocked, then pushed it open, hearing laughter in the kitchen. She walked through the doorway and saw Liz on a short ladder, using a roller on the ceiling, while Michael was on his knees doing the baseboard, complaining that Liz was once again spattering him with paint. He was right. They both wore as much paint as the walls, and they looked surprisingly at ease with each other.

Julia had always known they were good friends, but now she couldn't help wondering if Liz and Michael should have been the couple all along. She cleared her throat, drawing Liz's attention. Her sister almost dropped the roller when she saw her.

"Julia!" Liz squealed.

"Hi," she said. "Michael."

Michael slowly rose. "What are you doing here?"

"I wanted to talk to Liz. My aunt told me she was helping you with the house. It's nice," she added somewhat awkwardly. "This room is really bright."

Liz got off the ladder. "So, tell us—did you find what you were looking for? Did you find your real father?"

Her question made Julia realize how little Liz knew about all the events that had happened in the past few days. "I did. I found out a lot of things about my father... and my mother."

A glint of fear flashed through Liz's eyes. "I don't want to hear this, do I?"

"You have to hear it."

"I'm not your real sister. Mom adopted you, didn't she?"

Julia saw the worry in Liz's eyes and knew she had to put an end to that right now. "You will always be my sister, no matter what, so don't even think about trying to end our relationship. I'm not giving you up."

The tension in Liz's face eased at her words. "But we don't

share the same blood, do we? Come on, Julia, tell me the truth. I can take it."

"We don't share the same blood."

"So you are that Russian girl in the photo?"

"Actually, I'm not. That was my sister."

Liz's jaw dropped. "What?"

"There are two of you?" Michael echoed, shock in his voice.

"Yes, there are two of us. We're identical twins." She paused, letting her words sink in. "Her name is Elena. I think I used to call an imaginary friend Elena, but she wasn't a friend, she was my sister, and I didn't know what had happened to her."

"Dad told me about your imaginary friend and your made-up language," Liz muttered. "That was Russian, wasn't it?"

"I think so." She swallowed hard, trying to figure out the best way to tell the story. "My parents were important Russians. They were trying to defect. We were separated to make it easier to get us out of the country, and they were killed before that could happen. Elena and I were brought to the U.S. by different government agents, and Sarah, who was one of those agents, decided to keep me and raise me as her own."

"No," Liz said in disbelief. "Mom was not an agent. You're not going to tell me that."

"She was. I know it sounds incredible, but it's the truth. Oh, Liz, it's a long story, and I want to tell you everything. But I need to tell Dad, too, and I was hoping maybe we could do it all at once. Will you come with me to see him?"

Liz hesitated, glancing over at Michael. He gave her a small nod of encouragement.

"All right," Liz said, "I'll come with you." She set the roller down in the tray. "Just let me wash my hands." She walked out of the kitchen into the adjacent laundry room and turned on the faucet in the big sink.

Julia stared at Michael, feeling more than a little uncomfortable being alone with him. She didn't know what to say, so she settled for, "I'm sorry about everything."

"So am I," he replied. "But I'm glad you found your past. No more missing pieces."

"It feels good knowing who I am, why I never felt like I quite fit with my parents, why my mom tried to steer me away from things that I loved. She didn't want to lose me. She gave up her whole life to keep me, and she couldn't take a chance that I would ever slip away, so she trapped me with her love. I didn't see it until she was gone."

"And then you thought I was trapping you, too."

"Not exactly—"

He cut her off with a wave of his hand. "No, I think that is exactly what I was doing, although I didn't realize it. I had this image of you that I couldn't let go." He smiled sadly, with enormous regret. "I'm just sorry that I wasted so much of your time."

"You didn't. You were great. It was me. All me. I couldn't commit to you because I knew deep down I wasn't happy with the way my life was going."

"I can't believe I bought this house for you without telling you. Pretty stupid, huh?"

"It's going to be a great family home for you and the right person."

"I hope so."

Liz returned to the room, looking from one to the other. "Are we done here?"

"We're done," Michael said, meeting Julia's gaze. "We're definitely done."

* * *

Two hours and several cups of coffee later, Julia finished telling her story to Liz and Gino as they sat in her father's kitchen. Both had been stunned by the revelations she'd shared, especially in regard to Sarah. She'd tried to soften the blows by emphasizing how much Sarah had sacrificed to build their family, but she knew that Gino and Liz would have to find their own way to acceptance of the woman they'd all loved.

Gino hadn't said anything in almost twenty minutes, Julia realized. And he'd been staring down at his black coffee for at least the last five. "Are you all right, Dad?" she asked, covering his hand with hers.

There was pain in his eyes when he looked at her. "Do you still want to call me Dad?"

"Of course I do. You're the only father I've ever known. I love you. I love Lizzie, too. You're my family."

"But we're not," Liz said.

"Yes, you are. Blood doesn't matter more than love, and we love each other," Julia said.

"If blood didn't matter, why did you need to know your real parents?" Liz asked.

It was a good question. Julia tried to explain. "Because I needed to know myself as much as I needed the history. I've always felt a bit out of step with everyone. I couldn't figure out where I got my love for music or even my looks. I know Mom used to joke that I had her nose and her legs, but I think she just said that to make me feel like I fit in. She did everything to make me happy. I'm angry in some ways, but in other ways I know I've had a good life because of her."

"She should have told me," Gino said heavily. "I should have asked more questions about you and your father."

"She left that life behind. The only truth Sarah lived was with the three of us. The lies ended when she married you, Dad. You have to remember that."

"You think you know a person, but you don't," he said.

"But you did know her. You knew the little things," she said. "You knew the way she liked her coffee, the way she cried at romantic movies. You knew the way she read the newspaper from back to front, and the way she laughed—half giggle, half snort." She smiled at the memory. "We all knew her. We did."

"What about your other sister?" Liz asked. "What are you going to do about her?"

Julia took a breath. "She's flying out here next weekend. I want you all to meet her. I'm hoping..." She paused, waiting for them both to look at her. "I'm hoping that you'll accept her. She's had a tough life. She grew up in foster homes. She has no family, except for me—no father, no sister, no nothing."

"I'm kind of jealous of her," Liz confessed. "She shares your blood. And you're twins. You're going to get closer to her and forget about me, I just know it."

"I have room in my heart for two sisters. What about you?" Julia challenged. "And what about you, Dad? Do the DeMarcos have room for another person at next weekend's Sunday brunch?"

"Yes," he said, a smile crossing his lips for the very first time.

"Of course. We will make room for your sister at our table whenever she comes."

"You are a very generous man," she said, leaning over to kiss him on the cheek, "and I'm lucky to have you. Which reminds me, we need to talk about your drinking, Dad. I know I've been distracted, but not too distracted to notice that you've been drowning your sorrows in alcohol. I don't want to lose you. And I think you should stop. I'll help you, whatever it takes."

He patted her hand. "I feel better when I drink. The pain is not so sharp."

"But Dad—"

"I know," he cut in. "Your sister already talked to me about it."

Julia looked at Liz in surprise. "You did?"

"You told me it was my turn to take action," Liz replied. "Dive in, take charge, stop being a spectator, you said. So I did. Dad and I had a long talk last night."

"I'm glad." Things were going so well, Julia wondered if she should push her luck; then she decided to go for it. "There's one other person I'd like to invite for next weekend's Sunday brunch."

"Alex?" Liz asked with a wry smile on her lips. "I should have figured."

Her heart flip-flopped at the sound of his name, but she shook her head. "No, not Alex. I was thinking about Susan Davidson, Sarah's mother, and your grandmother. I'd like the two of you to meet."

Gino glanced at Liz. "What do you think, honey?"

"I think it's a good idea," Liz said slowly. "If Julia is getting another sister, I might as well get another grandmother, if you don't think Nonna will mind," she said to Gino, referring to his mother.

"She'll be all right with it," Gino replied. "There's always room for one more."

"Good," Julia said with a smile. "You're both being really generous, and I appreciate it more than you know."

"What about Alex?" Liz persisted. "Why don't you invite him, too?"

"Because he's leaving. In fact, he's probably already gone. He couldn't wait to get back to his job." She blinked back a tear. She wasn't going to cry over Alex. She'd had a good time with him.

And he'd been great. She'd known all along that what they had was only temporary.

"You love him, don't you?" Lizzie said quietly, with compassion in her brown eyes.

"I wish I didn't, but I think I do." She paused. "There's something else I need to tell you."

"There's more?" Liz queried. "I thought we knew everything."

"About the past, yes, but I want to talk to you about the future. I'm planning a little trip..."

Chapter Twenty-Three

Two weeks later Julia could barely believe she was traveling by taxi through the streets of Moscow with Elena by her side. She smiled at her sister. "We're here," she said.

"I keep pinching myself to make sure I'm not dreaming. Two weeks ago I didn't know you existed, and here I am in Russia with the sister I thought was dead. Life takes some very mysterious turns just when you least expect it," Elena replied.

"I'm so glad you were willing to come with me. I know it was kind of an impulsive thing to do. And you're more into planning than I am. But I was afraid if we waited too long, we'd never do it."

"Fortunately, the Russian government was willing to extend us visas," Elena replied. "That expedited matters."

"I guess the Russians were happy to discover an American end to an old Russian crime. It certainly released any lingering doubts about who killed our parents."

"It's too bad Mama and Papa told Brady about those jewels. They might have lived otherwise."

"I'm sure they did the best they could with the information they had. They didn't know who to trust, and they took a chance."

"And it got them killed." Elena turned sideways in her seat. "I wasn't sure about this trip, you know. I kept thinking we should let this part of our lives stay in the past, but now that we're here, I'm excited." She paused. "I keep thinking I should remember something, but I don't. Do you?"

"Not at all," Julia said with a sigh. "Maybe when we start walking the streets something will come back. I hope so, anyway."

"Me, too. But whatever happens, I'm glad we came. I'm also glad I met your family. They were really nice to me. I'm grateful for that."

Julia sat back in her seat, watching the sights go by, and thinking about the last ten days. As Elena had said, the DeMarcos had graciously accepted her into their midst, including Liz, who after some initial awkwardness had opened her heart. Liz had also been willing to spend time with her newly discovered grandmother, Susan Davidson, who had finally been filled in on the whole story. It would take some time to blend the families, but Julia was convinced it would happen in the end.

There were still a lot of things they had to figure out, especially about the money, the jewels, and the music scores, but she and Elena had both agreed to do nothing until they'd made this special trip back to the past. They needed to shut that last door before they could completely move on with their lives.

Ten minutes later, the cab pulled up in front of the Hotel Metropole, located across the street from the Bolshoi Theater. Her mother had danced there, so had her great-grandmother, and it was as good a place as any from which to retrace their steps.

Once they were checked in, they proceeded to their room, which was nicely decorated with sketches on the walls, two double beds, a desk, and a chair. While Elena made a stop in the restroom, Julia headed toward the window. The Bolshoi Theater was directly in view. It was a beautiful building, with eight strong columns and the chariot of Apollo sculpture on top. There was so much history to the building, so much history that was important to her family of dancers and musicians.

"What are you staring at?" Elena asked, joining her at the window.

"The Bolshoi."

"It's stunning," Elena said with a sigh. "I dreamed of dancing there one day. But it wasn't meant to be."

Julia put her arm around her sister's shoulders. They had spoken of many things, but not about the accident that had taken away Elena's ability to dance. Someday she hoped Elena would confide in her the rest of her life story.

"I remember watching Mama from the wings," Elena continued. "I thought she was so beautiful, and I wanted to fly like she did."

Julia had brief flashbacks to the inside of the theater as well, but she hadn't enjoyed watching her mother as much as she'd enjoyed hearing the power of the orchestra. "We should go there second," she said.

Elena raised an eyebrow. "Where are we going first?"

"To the orphanage where Alex took your picture. That's how this long journey began. We would never have found each other without that photo. Are you ready?"

"I suppose."

Julia didn't like the sound of hesitancy in her sister's voice. "What's wrong?"

"I'm a little afraid of the memories," she confessed. "Aren't you?"

"No," Julia said, feeling nothing but excitement. "I know it will be sad to see where our parents died and to go their graves, but I feel for the first time in a while that the future is wide open for me. And I'm ready to make peace with the past."

Elena smiled. "Then lead on."

They left the hotel and walked through Red Square, known as Krasnaya Ploschad in Russian. It was a much bigger space than Julia had imagined. At one end was the Kremlin, a medieval walled city on a hill above the Moscow River. At the other end were the colorful domes and spires of St. Basil's Cathedral. The rest of the area was rife with history, according to the guidebook Julia had read on the plane trip. North of the cathedral was Lobnoye Mesto, or "Place of Skulls," a circular raised platform on which public executions were carried out in the days of the tsars. Beyond that, across from the Lenin Mausoleum, was the GUM department store, Russia's version of a shopping mall.

Julia wanted to personally visit each site, but first they were on a mission to find the orphanage. After discussing her goal with several government agents, she'd been given an address, and now they were nearing the place where it had all begun.

In fact, it came out of nowhere, the unpretentious stone building with a fence and steel gates protecting its inhabitants. She had no idea if it was still an orphanage.

Julia stopped abruptly. Elena did the same. She tried to remember ever being in that yard, by that gate, but she came up blank. Maybe she'd never been out there. But Elena had. Julia moved closer to her, until they were shoulder to shoulder.

"I remember standing there," Elena whispered. "I was so scared, so terrified. I knew something had happened to our parents, something beyond bad. I could feel it in my heart. Then a man and a woman came. They took me away. I cried for you, but they covered my mouth, and then we were gone." She put a hand to her stomach. "I feel like I'm going to be sick."

"Maybe you should sit down. There's a bench over there."

"No, I'm going back to the hotel."

"I'll go with you."

Elena put up her hand and took a step away. "I need a little time, Julia. Okay?"

"Are you sure?" Julia didn't want to let her go on her own.

"I'm certain. I'm not as good as you are at sharing feelings. It's going to take me time to feel comfortable with it all."

"I understand. We can leave. We can do something fun."

"Later. I'm tired. I just need a break. Besides, there are some things we need to do on our own." She gave Julia an odd little smile, then walked away.

Julia frowned. She had wanted to do everything together, but she was beginning to understand how much harder it was for Elena to be part of a twosome. She'd grown up alone, forced to keep everything inside. It was the only way she knew how to cope. Maybe with time, that would change.

Julia walked over to the gate and put her hands on the steel. There was no one in the yard. In fact, the building looked vacant. There were no signs, just a sense of bleakness about it, as if nothing happy or good had ever happened there.

"Would you mind if I took your picture?" a man asked.

She whirled around in surprise. "Alex?" She couldn't believe it was him, but there he stood, dressed in jeans, a black shirt, and a black leather jacket. A camera case hung over one shoulder. His brown hair was ruffled by the breeze, his green eyes alight with excitement. He looked impossibly handsome. Her palms began to sweat and her spine tingled. "What are you doing here?" she asked, finally finding her voice.

"I realized I didn't have a picture of you. All that time we spent together, and I never took a photo. What kind of a photographer am I?"

"So you came all the way to Moscow to get one?"

He grinned. "I do what I have to do to get the shot. You know that. I called your apartment a couple of days ago. I spoke to Elena. She told me you were on your way here."

"Is that why she ran off so suddenly?" Julia asked, suddenly making sense of Elena's odd comment that there were some things they needed to do on their own.

He nodded. A moment passed; then he said, "I have something to give you." He set down the camera and pulled an envelope out of his jacket pocket.

For some reason the sight of another envelope made her nervous. "What is it?"

"It's from Stan. I finally tracked him down. He told me everything, how he helped set up the defection, how much he wanted your mother to dance in the United States."

"Did he know about Brady's plan to kill them?"

Alex shook his head. "No, not at all. You see, Julia, Stan had a huge crush on your mother, Natalia. He met her a few times, and he wanted very much to help her. I guess they became friends on a few of her trips to the United States. He was devastated when she was killed. And he told me he was sorry that he hadn't been honest with us. He believed he was protecting me and you. Like my father, Stan thought that the Russians killed your parents. As an apology, he sent you this. Open it."

"I'm afraid. I don't want any more bad surprises."

"This is a good one."

She took the envelope out of his hand and pulled out a photograph. Her heart stopped beating as she realized what she was seeing. It was a black-and-white family picture of Natalia, Sergei, Elena, and herself. She pressed it to her heart as she blinked back a tear. "It's all of us together," she whispered.

He smiled at her. "Stan thought you would like it. He said Natalia gave it to him a long, long time ago."

"I love it. I'll have to thank him when I get back. I'm glad he wasn't involved, Alex. I know you care about him." Julia blew out a breath, seeing a new light sparkle in Alex's eyes. He obviously wasn't finished. "Was there something else?"

"Elena told me that she thinks you're in love with me.

"I can't imagine why she'd say that," Julia replied, her heart racing as he took a step forward.

"Maybe because I told her I was in love with you," he said.

"What?" She couldn't possibly have heard him say the words.

"You heard me." He moved closer until he was just inches away. "I missed you, Julia."

"You did?" she whispered, gazing into his eyes and seeing the love he was talking about.

"Yeah, I missed your smile and your beautiful blue eyes, the way you lick your fingers after you eat something really delicious, the excitement you get when you try something new, the light that shines out of you when you talk about music and changing the world one melody at a time."

"Oh, Alex," she murmured, incredibly touched by his words.

"I tried to forget you. I buried myself in work, thinking it would fill me up the way it used to, but it didn't. There was still a hole in my heart. I didn't actually know I had a heart until I met you. You see, I put it on ice about twenty-five years ago, just a few weeks after I left this very square."

She put her hands on his shoulders. "It must be hard for you, to come back here."

"No, it's easy, because you're here, and because now I know what I want. Which, in case you haven't figured it out yet, is you. I want to be with you, Julia."

"Even if that means a permanent address?"

He nodded. "Wherever you are is where I want to be. I've lived most of my life thinking I was just like my father, that photography was my sole passion, that the world was my backyard, that it was more important to show what was happening in the world than to live my own life. But my father gave it up for love. He gave it up for me." He put his hands on her waist. "And I'm willing to give it up for you."

She bit down on her lip, her eyes tearing. "Really?"

He smiled. "Absolutely. You're an incredible woman, Julia—smart, sexy, brave—and you never quit. You inspire me."

"I feel the same way about you, Alex. Your courage, your sense of adventure, the way you embrace new things constantly amaze me. And you're really good in bed, too," she added with a smile.

"It's about time you mentioned that," he said with a sexy growl. "I think I'm the luckiest man on earth right now." He leaned over and placed a tender, passionate kiss on her lips.

"And I'm the luckiest woman," Julia murmured against his mouth. "Do you know why I came here?" she asked him, pulling away for just a moment.

"Tell me."

"I wanted to connect with my parents. The letter my mother wrote to us made me realize that my parents lived their lives with purpose and passion. They were willing to risk everything for love and family. That's the way I want to live. I don't want to play it safe. I want to follow my heart—wherever it leads. This trip was the first step."

"Where are you going next?"

She moved deeper into his embrace. "Right here. I love you, Alex. I was going to come and find you after this trip." She paused. "I don't want you to stay in one place for me. I want to go with you wherever life takes us. I have some thoughts of my own about spreading music around the world. I could use a partner for that."

"You've got one. And if the last few weeks are any indication, I think you and I are going to have a very exciting life."

She gazed into his eyes and saw a future filled with promise. Now she knew not only where she'd come from... but where she was going.

Book List

About The Author

Barbara Freethy is a #1 New York Times Bestselling Author, who has sold over 2.7 million ebooks since January 2011. Her 31 novels range from contemporary romance to romantic suspense and women's fiction. Twelve titles have appeared on the New York Times and USA Today Bestseller Lists. Her books have won numerous awards. She is a five-time finalist for the RITA for best contemporary romance from Romance Writers of America. She has also received starred reviews from Publishers Weekly and Library Journal.

Known for her emotional and compelling stories of love, family, mystery and romance, Barbara enjoys writing about ordinary people caught up in extraordinary adventures.

Barbara has lived all over the state of California and currently resides in Northern California where she draws much of her inspiration from the beautiful bay area. Barbara loves to hear from readers so please feel free to write her.

For a complete listing of books, as well as excerpts and contests, and to connect with Barbara, visit her website at
www.barbarafreethy.com
You can also visit Barbara on Facebook at
www.facebook.com/barbarafreethybooks and Twitter at
www.twitter.com/barbarafreethy.

CPSIA information can be obtained at www.ICGtesting.com
Printed in the USA
LVOW10s2157010913

350538LV00015B/463/P